HAWKESMOOR 2
BOOK TWO: THE ETHERIC MURDERS

ii

HAWKESMOOR 2

BOOK TWO: THE ETHERIC MURDERS

ANNE MERINO

ISBN: 979-8-218-89646-1

Library of Congress Control Number: 2025927583

Cover artwork by David Cameron. Used by permission.

Printed in the United States of America.

www.sstirrupcupbooks.com

ADVANCE PRAISE *for*
HAWKESMOOR 2: THE ETHERIC MURDERS

Hawkesmoor 2: The Etheric Murders continues the captivating story of Robin Dashwood, Vampyre King of the British Isles and his lovely, ethereally beautiful wife Lady Caroline Dashwood as they, joined by their family, friends and faithful followers combat a series of vicious, deadly attacks upon their fellow countrymen. Written as a sequel to *Hawkesmoor: A Novel of Vampyre and Faerie*, Anne Merino has crafted a world of unusual refinement, elegance, and manners, flitting effortlessly between the drawing rooms of Hawkesmoor Castle to the wind-swept moors of the Orkneys, from the stately mansions of Kensington to the streets of Manhattan, Anne once again draws us under her literary spell, binding us fast with the lure of the unknown, the unbelievable…and the undead. This is a truly wonderful book and a worthy sequel to its predecessor; I recommend it wholeheartedly, and unreservedly.

Sanjay R Singhal, RA

Hawkesmoor 2: The Etheric Murders makes me want to learn more about Welsh and English folklore. The author clearly understands the 'old ways', bringing them to life with a carefully crafted plot that takes the reader on a journey 'across the pond' as the story weaves its magic spell. I don't know any vampires but I would like to meet Robin, definitely and maybe some of his friends. We'd have a lot to talk about.

Jamie Carpenter

Hawkesmoor 2: The Etheric Murders isn't a vampire book or at least, it's not 'Dracula'. It's a story about a group of people, not so different from you and me but in the end, really *very* different from you and me, living in the same world we live in and breathing the same air. They are vampires, but they are also real, emotional, passionate, kind, and caring; they are as unique and different as we ourselves may be, and yet….

This is a strange story. There's a lot in it about Welsh folklore and some really unsettling bits about ancient curses and evilmongers but it really pulls you in. You find yourself caring about these people, and you want to join them for tea. Anne has created a world where family and friendships still mean something, and despite its arcanity remains deeply fascinating.

Victor Robbins

DEDICATION

For old and dear friends, Charles Cameron and Carol
Stanley. They made me a writer.

CONTENTS

ACKNOWLEDGEMENTS

It's not really news that writing is kind of a tough business. Also, enormous fun – so few occupations allow one to create entire universes, populate them with intriguing people and spin them off into adventures. Of course, such universes don't just write themselves and the process can be occasionally frustrating. The novelist toils alone. We make outlines, timelines and lists. We churn out sentences. We then rewrite those sentences. We proofread and feel disgruntled that the word rhythm is always such an easy word to misspell. We churn out better sentences and rewrite those better sentences until, finally, a book emerges. After an all too brief period of celebrating – for me this involves heading off to my favourite Indian restaurant for lunch and a relaxing read – we often try to corral loved ones and busy friends into taking a look, hoping to discover if it's any bloody good. This will be the twin experience of trying to corral critics and readers later. The passage from initial story concept to published novel is long and eccentric.

Here are the people who have made Hawkesmoor 2: The Etheric Murders … well, if not exactly easy, a lot more fun! My husband, Tom. He's a filmmaker and a writer. Also, the most honest and straight forward reader any writer could ever ask to take a look at a first draft. If Tom says it works, it works. If he says the pages need work – it's back to the laptop. Thank you, Tom Merino. Always.

I am the fortunate mother of two fascinating young men who are both exceptional writers in their own right. Emlyn toils in Manhattan as a full-time journalist and makes writing about hugely complex, difficult topics look easy breezy when it very assuredly is not. I remember saying something to him once along the daffy lines of "I don't think I write drivel". Never one to miss a moment especially when it's handed to him on a platter, he patted me on the shoulder and replied, "Mum, let's not kid ourselves." We laughed for about fifteen minutes. David is a screenwriter and filmmaker. He really helped me get through what was a very tough year. After recovering from a major cancer surgery in 2024, I was pretty tired and David decided to take me on a little cruise from San Francisco to Ensenada and back again. We'd never done anything so blatantly fancy before and it was just the most restorative thing being out on the sea with this lovely, gloriously funny young person. We had the best time and it got me energized to be a writer again.

One rarely gets to know a genuine genius. Oxford poet and writer, Charles Cameron was the very definition of the upper-class English eccentric and possessed a large presence in my life for almost forty years. He is very much missed. The world is decidedly less colourful without him.

My dear friend, Sanjay R Singhal. There would be no sequel to Hawkesmoor without his wisdom, exquisite taste and hard work. There will never be enough words to thank him for what he has given.

Carol Stanley – lover of all things literary and fine. She lives and breathes books. Truly a great editor and a dear friend of some four decades.

Steve Hockensmith is the author of the brilliant *Holmes on the Range* mystery series – a series I wish often and devoutly I had written. Elegiac for the Old West, ingeniously plotted, hugely likeable main characters and knitted together with a laugh-out-loud wit – it's everything a mystery reader yearns for and rarely finds. If only Taylor

Sheridan's *Yellowstone* was half as fun! Steve is also a wonderful friend and a deeply appreciated font of wisdom, sympathy and wry publishing industry observations.

Dr. Ardain Isma and CSMS Magazine kept me going over the dread Year of Cancer. A novelist of immense elegance himself, he tirelessly supports other authors with his fascinating podcasts and literary magazine. He kept the flame of Hawkesmoor and my writing burning. Thank you, Dr. Isma.

Some of loveliest people in a writer's world are our beloved friends who allow themselves to be coerced into becoming beta readers. They are kind enough to plough through a first draft and let you know if the thing has any hope. Most of them can spot a typo or a missing period at a hundred yards – of incalculable value! Thank you, Suzanne Elusorr, for all that you have done for my novels. Thank you, Shane English and Joann Goodall, for being there.

To my ballet partner-in-crime, Mark Nash – thank you for always having my back. Mark is the ultimate professional in concert dance and one of the planet's best people. He also has one of the quickest wits in the west. We laugh a lot. Gratified that Mr. Bruce King – former professional ballet dancer and generally, one of the most urbane, sophisticated persons I know – read the first Hawkesmoor and wants to do the same with the sequel. I have arrived!

Beloved Anya Wong keeps me going as a ballet teacher and choreographer. Her kindness is huge and so deeply appreciated.

A big thank you to all my beloved ballet students who make life interesting and infinitely more fun!

Thank you, staff and volunteers of the Lincoln Library! This beautiful retreat for booklovers is one of my regular touchstones.

Readers may recall in the first Hawkesmoor, I wrote of my beloved Hector, retired working dog and my shadow. A professional security "bite dog", he spent his pampered retirement patrolling the local parks and hiking trails seeking out insensate evil. A lot of this novel's plot and concepts were assembled on those long walks and I miss him every day.

AUTHOR'S NOTE

Readers will notice that Chapter One features a conversation between Her Majesty, Queen Elizabeth II and an admiring Robin Dashwood. When I initially wrote the opening to The Etheric Murders, Her Majesty still sat upon the throne and all was well. On September 8th, 2022, the world suddenly changed as this great lady passed from this place to Shakespeare's undiscovered country. After the magnificent state funeral, I dithered for an age about updating the novel to reflect a new reality. Finally sought counsel from my wise and elegant friend, Sanjay. A classically trained architect, he can be counted on for exquisite taste and excruciatingly correct detail. He supported my instincts to leave Chapter One as originally written. So, I have.

I have been fortunate enough to meet His Majesty, King Charles III (then the Prince of Wales) in conjunction with the Kathleen Raine Foundation. His charm and wry sense of humour was utterly disarming and I am forever an admirer. Although The Etheric Murders is set in the present day, I am positive His Majesty will forgive me if within the Hawkesmoor universe, his dear mother remains, by the Grace of God, Queen of the United Kingdom of Great Britain and Northern Ireland, and of Her other Realms and Territories.

Anne Merino
Northern California

Though my soul may sit in darkness, it will rise in perfect light;
I have loved the stars too fondly to be fearful of the night.

Sarah Williams 1837 - 1868

HAWKESMOOR 2
BOOK TWO: THE ETHERIC MURDERS

Chapter One

London, United Kingdom

Her Majesty, the Queen, by the Grace of God of the United Kingdom of Great Britain and Northern Ireland, and of Her other Realms and Territories, Head of the Commonwealth, Defender of the Faith bent forward to give a toast corner to an attentive corgi. She straightened in her chair and returned her attention to Robin DuPlessis. "I must admit," she said in the familiar clipped tones of innumerable Christmas messages and openings of Parliament, "this does take a bit of getting used to. One always imagines vampires as quite bizarre creatures. Pallid with pronounced widow's peaks and opera capes -- that sort of thing."

Robin smiled, struck for a moment by the incongruous coziness of the room. The Queen's Buckingham Palace reception rooms for her official meetings with various government officials, prime ministers and other august persons were extremely formal, suitably burnished with giltwood, ornate period textiles and priceless art. They were settled in what in his day was known as "The Tapestry Room", a smaller space in the northwest corner of the palace that now boasted some excellent Canalettos and a massive Gainsborough portrait of the Duchess of Cumberland whom he had known during his long existence. Despite such gorgeous trappings of princehood, they sat in chairs by a fireplace lit by a modest two-bar electric heater and had tea. Outside a December rain pattered incessantly against the windows.

"Ma'am," he replied, stroking the head of another of her corgis that had found him worthy of notice, "vampires for the most part have fully embraced modern life."

"Understood," The Queen sighed and sipped her tea. "But I always feel as if I must say it every time we meet – this is a most disconcerting development in Britain's history."

"Yes, Ma'am," Robin inclined his head politely – a reverence in miniature.

"Buttercup genuinely likes you. She doesn't take to everyone.' Her Majesty said this as if it carried as much weight as a papal beatification. She set down her teacup and sighed again. "I have finally finished reading your history." Robin's equerry had long ago sent over a detailed dossier of his years since becoming a vampire in 1750. He assumed the Queen's own trusted advisors had then combed through the pages and authenticated every detail.

"Aide de camp to Disraeli. For gallantry during the Gallipoli campaign, Major Robin Dashwood awarded the Victoria Cross," she raised an eyebrow, "posthumously. Lt. Cmdr. Francis Dashwood awarded the D.S.O. for conspicuous bravery in North Africa during World War Two. It seems this country owes you gratitude for several lifetimes of service."

"I will always be at Your Majesty's service, Ma'am."

She smiled at him. "This has been very pleasant. I expect I shall see you again next week?"

Robin stood up to bow. "Yes, Ma'am. I will bear in mind your thoughts about arranging a Commonwealth audience."

"Thank you." The Queen rose from her yellow silk upholstered chair and accepted his politely extended elbow for a walk to the door. The assembled corgis leapt into action as well, pooling around their feet in a happy muddle.

She smiled again, her eyes lighting up with humor. "Your Serene Highness."

"Please -- Robin," he replied with equal good will. "We serve at Your Majesty's pleasure and are proud to do so."

"Imagine after all these years, discovering a shadow monarchy!" The Queen said as if the idea continued to be a rather an exciting one. Several corgis barked cheerfully in response to her slightly elevated tone.

Then after exchanging farewells, His Serene Highness, The Vampire King of All the British Isles, Robin DuPlessis, emerged from his audience. Waiting for him in the Buckingham Palace hallway was his equerry, Cyril Goforth. Cyril was fair, slender and gave the impression of lachrymose patrician frailty. He looked about eighteen but had served as a civil servant in the British vampire court since the Restoration. The third son of a Duke, he had nearly perished in the great London plague of 1666 until a vampire took a fancy to him. Promptly indentured, as was common for a new revenant, he came to court and never left service.

Now, austerely attired in a bespoke suit and Magdalen tie, he opened his ever-present black leather portfolio from Smythson that contained both iPad and paper documents of current interest to the sovereign's working day.

"All well, Your Highness?"

"Yes, amazingly," said Robin, letting out a short breath. "She is a great and remarkable lady. I just worry at rattling her as she adjusts to … well, us."

"I am positive you were exemplary, sir." Cyril studied the page in his portfolio. "You will be pleased to know your diary is now clear for the rest of the day. I took the liberty of placing your equerry box in the car so you could study its contents on the drive to the residence."

And this was why Winnifred had abdicated, Robin reflected as they walked down the long palace hallway. She felt utterly smothered with the administrative aspects of the position and seriously frustrated that her subjects consistently considered her beloved concept of an open society between human and revenant naïve. A revenant from early medieval times, Winnifred Turchil was a stouthearted doer. A former nun, teacher and fully trained nurse, she longed to be out actively doing something immediate for the general betterment of humans and vampires. So, with great relief, she had abdicated, leaving Britain with her partner, Hugh McCandlethorne, to provide desperately needed medical aid to the most downtrodden in the third world.

The crown had fallen to Robin as the last British revenant to bear the royal mark of Morvidous, the oldest known vampire. A natural academic who had thrived both in Victorian politics under Benjamin Disraeli and in the equally ossified administrative rituals of university life; he was the ideal choice for a 21st century vampire king.

Six years past the extraordinary events at Hawkesmoor Castle, in which a deadly clash of vampires amid a potentially disastrous interdimensional bleed had alerted MI5 and MI6 to the possible presence of revenants, a very fragile rapprochement had been constructed between the two races. While the British public continued to sleep unburdened by the knowledge of a hidden kingdom of vampires in their midst, the very highest levels of human government had accepted the concept but with understandable wariness.

It was a dangerous time for vampires. One bloody misstep by a rogue revenant could mean that the human authorities would decide to suppress or even eradicate the perceived vampire threat.

Robin was pondering the issue as he sat in a sleek Rolls Royce Phantom, studying the papers in his equerry box. He was looking at crime statistics and reports that Cyril had put together from every region in the United Kingdom, searching for anything that might indicate just such a rogue attack on a human. What he had told the Queen was, for the most part, true – vampires had embraced the modern world. They utilized blood bank supplies or small infusions from farm animals rather than hunt humans in the old way. New oxygen-carrying blood substitutes were promising to revolutionize the revenant world and, perhaps, one day would allow them to live, as Winnifred hoped, in open society with humans.

Despite the potential for a modern-day inquisition, British revenants were enjoying something of a cultural renaissance. Finally, out from under the shadow of the former vampire king who had been a mercurial Machiavellian sadist, vampires were tentatively and quietly pursuing their talent for the arts, medicine and business in a more public manner. The results of these efforts, Robin believed, would only enrich and benefit human society.

"Your Serene Highness," said Cyril.

Robin refocused on his equerry. A member of the Whig Oligarchy in his human years, he loathed being styled "Serene Highness", but it was an edict that went back to 1007 when the vampire sovereignty of the British Isles was established and any efforts to suggest Cyril might drop the title were politely dismissed.

"You've been staring at the same page for some while, sir," his equerry noted. "Have you discovered something of interest?"

13

"No … no," Robin shook his head. "Nothing seems out of order."

"Sir, if you would just turn your attention to the allocations for the Household Guard. I think you'll find them all in order. Your signature is all that is required."

Robin dutifully found the official form and signed it to Cyril's satisfaction. He closed the blue equerry box with a relieved breath. The Rolls was drawing up to the large detached white house in the heart of Kensington that served as official residence for the British revenant sovereign. Number 7 Audley Square was built in the late 17th century especially for Britain's then vampire king, Southbrook and was a splendid example of early Classical architecture. The house, although smaller than Buckingham Palace, had its own very airy and elegant sets of reception and dining rooms filled with priceless Georgian furniture and art. Under Robin's reign, its ten spare bedrooms served as an ambassadorial hostel for visiting revenants representing other kingdoms and clans. It also featured, since its previous owners had unique needs and tastes, an intriguing underground of secret rooms where prisoners were kept, interrogated and often destroyed. Robin had not yet decided what to do about "the cells" although his Household Guard were campaigning for a pool and work out area.

In the light afternoon rain, Number 7 hardly seemed a vampire palace. His wife, Caroline, had insisted that large Christmas wreaths be installed on the gleaming black door and on the first-floor façade. Lights gleamed softly in upper Georgian windows hinting that the fortunate denizens of such a fine house must be enjoying a cup of tea or curled up with a book. Robin was planning to do both as soon as he escaped to the third-floor private residence and divested himself of his bespoke suit, equerry boxes and well-meaning equerries.

"You are absolutely positive that the diary is clear?" he asked as a member of the Household Guard opened the rear door of the Rolls Phantom.

"Yes, sir. All is well."

A shiver ran down Robin's spine as he exited the car. All is well. Everything was proceeding smoothly. Her Majesty, The Queen liked him. The Prime Minister was far more wary but willing to make an attempt at open mindedness. The future looked towards a bright, peaceful co-existence of her kingdom and his shadow kingdom with considerable mutual benefit. He shivered again. It was just that in Robin's experience the all is well moment was when the Sword of Damocles swung into service and went in for the kill.

Chapter Two

Caroline was also relieved to see Number 7, Audley Square shimmer into view through the late afternoon rain. Christmas shopping amid the harried throngs attacking the fabled halls of Harrod's and Harvey Nichols was always a military sortie fraught with triumph and terror but made vastly more while lugging along two members of Robin's revenant guard. Finally, after checking off everything on her list, she had been happily anticipating an elegant light lunch at Aspley's but allowed the guardsmen to talk her into the new Expendables movie instead.

She drove her Range Rover into Number 7's private garage after Bramwell and Edmund had leapt out to make sure the coast was clear as television detectives termed it.

Of course, it was never fully explained to her why they required so much security but having met the previous vampire king, Garnet Petherbridge, before he was destroyed, Caroline had a pretty shrewd idea of what a revenant coup d'etat attempt might involve.

"No worries,' announced Bramwell who had been an archer for the Royalist forces under Charles I. "And we'll see that your shopping gets in covert-like although it's hard to pull a sham on Ari."

"Have a good evening, Your Highness," added Edmund who had been a member of Detective Superintendent Leonard "Nipper" Read's infamous detective squad most famous for bringing down the Kray brothers in the 1960s.

"Thank you both," she said with genuine gratitude. While their presence made certain aspects of her daily life more difficult, she appreciated deeply that they kept potential danger at bay.

Caroline headed into the ground floor of Number 7 feeling both an uplifting sense of all is right with the world and a vague nausea from eating far too much buttered popcorn in the cinema. She smiled at members of Robin's household staff as they quickly bobbed curtseys or bowed their heads in her direction as they went about their day. The daughter of an Earl, she was accustomed to a certain amount of distinction but the obeisance she now received, as Queen Consort of Robin's shadow monarchy was almost unnerving.

Yet it was just one more baroque level of acclimatizing she had to make since meeting Robin. At first, she believed she had fallen in love with Robin Dashwood, a history professor of some note at NYU. Then she had to make sense of the astonishing notion that vampires and other paranormal beings existed outside the pages of fiction and that the man she deeply loved was one of them. Next, she would learn that Robin was unique among all the revenants for his hybrid DNA of vampire and mysterious interdimensional entities called the Tylwyth Teg. This fusion enabled him to father children and produce a bloodline of his own – something that still mired the revenant world in turmoil as the old ways began to shift and change – and had propelled him to accept the sovereignty of the British vampires.

"Mummy!" called out a young voice as Caroline headed for what had once been exclusively the servant staircase but now served as an egalitarian short cut from using the massive and formal central staircase.

She paused and turned to see her six-year-old daughter, Arianrhod, running to intercept. Following behind at a slower pace was the little girl's nanny, Miss Pratt – a pale blonde, somewhat colorless young-looking revenant who was on loan to them from the vampire biochemist Hugh

Candlethorne's Oxbridge research team. She had wanted to take a gap year from her doctoral work and the reasonably light work of nannying in an exciting city such as London seemed just the thing.

"We're off to take a walk!" the girl announced as she skidded into an enthusiastic hug. "Can you come?"

Caroline hugged her back. "Wish I could, Ari. It's a very busy time of the year."

Arianrhod peered up at her with wise green eyes that belied her youth. "Christmas presents?"

"You might well hope!" Caroline laughed and lifted her head to focus on Miss Pratt who was patiently waiting to collect Arianrhod. "About an hour?"

"Oh yes, Your Serene Highness. Ari has done nicely with her lessons and I'm told Cook has made a special pudding as a reward."

Caroline waved them both off on their walk and headed once again for their private apartments. Along the way she took a few minutes to worry about the future and Arianrhod's education. Ari was an extraordinarily special child. A fusion of human, revenant and Tylwyth Teg, she exhibited traits from both her more supernatural DNA. It was going to be impossible to send her off to traditional schools until she was old enough to know when and where to make use of her abilities. Caroline hoped the quiet, unassuming Felicity Pratt would be able to manage the vibrant six-year-old until they knew better how to proceed.

She found Robin alone in his study. Well, not exactly alone. He was chatting amiably with a large black raven on his desk. He spoke in an odd singsong dialect that sounded rather like Welsh. The raven appeared to be listening intently.

"Oh, hello darling," Robin said, noticing her arrival. "Done with your foray into the shops?"

"Yes." She threw him a puzzled look.

"I was just having a chinwag with Egbert here," he indicated the raven. The bird actually seemed to bob its head at her. "His actual raven name is not pronounceable by any human voice."

"Of course. That makes perfect sense." Caroline smiled at both of them. Sometimes things materialized within her orbit that made her feel as if her mind might explode into little pieces. Talking animals had the potential to be one of them.

Robin grinned back at her then directed a few of the singsong words to Egbert. The bird's black eyes blinked as if winking and it hopped up and down as if very pleased indeed.

"Egbert would be delighted to be introduced properly," he said, lifting his arm and waving a hand gracefully in her direction.

Caroline felt a little gust of energy waft over her like an errant breeze. Then a high-pitched whine started up in her head that quickly morphed into individual notes and then recognizable words.

"Egbert-One-With-The-Apple-Trees," came a cheerful, throaty voice. "Very happy to make the Queen's acquaintance."

She took in a sharp breath and took a step back in surprise.

"Give Caroline a minute, my friend," said Robin. "I promise she adjusts quickly."

"No worries,' sang out the raven.

Caroline reeled in her incredulity. She'd faced more cantilevered neo-realities than a jolly raven. With the can-do spirit that had led her to win major silver cups in show jumping in her youth, she headed towards the first obstacle. "I'm so pleased to meet you, Mr. One-With-The-Apple-Trees," she began tentatively. "Do you … um, live in London?"

The raven tittered with good humor. "Oh, your queen is lovely! Just lovely! I do, Your Highness, indeed I do."

"Egbert descends from a very aristocratic lineage," Robin explained, beaming at Caroline. "He is an invaluable ambassador."

"Speaking of which, I must be on my way." The raven hopped from the desk to the windowsill where an open window to the chilly London twilight beckoned. "Good day to you, Robin. Charmed to have met you, Lady Caroline."

"Goodbye," she murmured in wonder.

Egbert bobbed a little bow in her direction and flew out into the drizzle.

Robin laughed and got up to shut the window. "He thinks you're very pretty. No genius but pretty."

"Ha ha." Caroline heard a dog barking down the street. It translated immediately into Who's been urinating on my gatepost? Who? Who? "Could this possibly be reversed? It's going to drive me round the bend."

"Course, darling. Sorry." Robin waved his hand again. She felt a little painless tug as if a veil was being swept away from her person.

"I didn't know you were our own Dr. Doolittle – a Tylwyth Teg ability?" Caroline breathed deeply and felt herself again. She liked being human with all the inherent limitations and weaknesses of her species, finding it liberating rather than diminishing. It always struck her that the revenants carried a terrible burden along with their flashy abilities. They had all seen too much, done too much

20

and grieved too much throughout long existences alongside generations of humans.

She gazed affectionately at her husband as he returned to his desk chair. None of the history and horrors that he'd seen revealed itself on his flawless face as it would a mere human. Her husband was a tall, slender and innately graceful creature. Like most revenants, Robin possessed a mesmerizing beauty. He had arrestingly angular features dominated by expressive green eyes and his coloring was a striking combination of pale, perfect skin and bright auburn hair that fell past his elegant shoulders. Caroline never tired of looking at him.

"And a very useful and charming trait it is too," Robin said. "Egbert is quite irritated about a new clan of sparrows who have come to live at the Tower. Apparently, they are extremely silly and a bit greedy."

Caroline shook her head at the nonsense of it and nipped around the corner of the desk to jump into his lap.

Laughing, she threw her arms around his neck. "I love you, you very very strange man."

Chapter Three

"Your Serene Highness," came Cyril Goforth's voice of unruffled calm at the bedroom door. "I am most terribly sorry, sir. Sir?"

In the shadow-shrouded room, Robin pulled his mouth away from Caroline's and struggled to return to what he thought of as a human level of coherence. Making love to his wife was always fraught with passion and a kind of reckless madness. He'd had known a love, a sexual thirst for Caroline unlike any other in his long, benighted existence – hungering for her and her achingly beautiful humanity like a drug addict.

He shuddered, trying to shake off the pain. A coherent human might want to know the time – he forced himself to glance at the clock on his night table – almost two o'clock in the morning.

Then forced himself to croak out. "Bit late, Goforth."

"I know, Your Highness, but there's been an … incident."

Caroline reached up, touching his face – an instinctive gesture of reassurance. Robin felt himself shift further towards to what his 18th century father would have called the rational man.

"I love you," he said, his soft voice sounded grief-stricken. The rational man was unable to identify why this would be so. Was his strange, uncanny Tylwyth Teg blood singing to him of change and loss?

"I know," she said, "but it sounds as if you'd better go. I've never heard him so agitated."

Robin managed to laugh in the dark.

A few minutes later he emerged to find his equerry –
despite the late hour -- immaculately turned out as ever and
in possession of his Smythson portfolio.

"I take it all is not well?" asked Robin, raising a quizzical
eyebrow.

"No, sir!"

The Rolls Phantom had swept into a wet night and away
from London to Oxfordshire. It finally came to a halt at
Wynford Park, a 19th century folly house built by some
enterprising textile merchant to resemble a 14th century
Gothic pile hidden away in its own three hundred acres of
farm and park land.

Robin emerged from the car into a cold drizzle. Wynford
Park was lit up as if for a lavish social occasion but the
figures that gathered near its magnificent arched entrance
were far from dazzled guests arriving for a memorable
evening of drinks and dancing. Harshly revealed in the
flashing lights atop a grim assortment of emergency
vehicles, were the sober representatives of human authority
both high and low. He hesitated, scanning the impressive
array of machine and human responders. One didn't have to
be gifted with vampire attributes to know that something
ghastly had taken place at Wynford Park.

"Your Serene Highness," murmured Cyril, "clearly we are
needed inside as soon as possible."

Robin watched warily as members of his household guard
moved with quiet efficiency towards various key locations.
Several of them -- gifted with the coveted ability -- simply
dematerialized, heading for Wynford's rooftops and clear
vantage points. He didn't think their human equivalents
would be pleased with a vampire encroachment.

"The Guard will make every effort to remain invisible," said
Cyril, reading Robin's uneasy expression.

He nodded with a small sigh.

They swept into the central hall of Wynford Park without protest – the busy officers immediately accepting them as important government types who would not appreciate censure from the lower echelons.

Cyril had been given very little real information when the call from the Home Office had come into his mobile. He had been given an address and a secret code word that translated as urgent. Unsure of how to proceed without interfering, they paused in the hall to take in its medieval grey stone and open timbers.

Wynford Park, Robin saw as he looked around, was a handsomely appointed house with a vaguely jarring blend of modern reproductions with a few authentic period pieces scattered here and there. He noted newly created family crests and shields on bright banners hanging from the open timbers and two reproduction suits of armor standing sentry next to a large archway that probably led to some of the more major ground floor rooms. Someone without an ancient family line now owned Wynford Park. A brand-new fortune had acquired the 19th century folly and with middling success had restored it.

He cocked his head, catching the cry of a panicked silver tabby as it streaked up the main staircase to his right. Must hide! Must hide! Must Hide!

A man appeared in between the reproduction knights at the archway. He was late middle age with a blandly handsome face undermined by a slightly receding jaw line. The old bespoke suit and Emmanuel College, Cambridge tie announced him as a civil servant. This particular civil servant was Sir Geoffrey Constable, somewhat peevish aide de camp of the Prime Minister. He was also the only member of the PM's staff with enough security clearance to be briefed on the vampire kingdom. He had not taken to the concept of a blended society of cheerfully co-existing humans and revenants. Sir Geoffrey stalked towards them, wearing a tense, clenched expression as if he were constantly grinding his teeth.

"Kind of you to pop in," he said in his aristocratic drawl that belied a keen and acerbic intelligence. "Thought it might be sooner though."

"Apologies," replied Cyril quietly. "We were held up in some traffic in London."

"You drove … in a motor car?" Sir Geoffrey contrived to look mildly surprised. "Don't you chappies usually flit about in the guise of bats?"

"By Jove," said Robin pleasantly in a perfect impersonation of Constable's pearly Old Boy tones, "not in this beastly weather!"

Sir Geoffrey blinked, unsure if the recently revealed King of The Vampires was taking the mick from the Prime Minister's most trusted attaché.

"There's been an incident," Robin continued, dropping the bluster. "How can we be of assistance?"

The civil servant narrowed his eyes as if remembering something unsettling. "Yes. If you both would be kind enough to follow me?"

"You may remember," he added as they walked towards the open archway, "that the Prime Minister has had concerns about members of your … species … using this – for lack of a better term -- transitional period to attempt some sort of coup?"

"We have been monitoring for such a possibility." Robin threw Cyril a puzzled look. "Nothing has presented itself."

"Ah!" said Sir Geoffrey as if fascinated by this revelation.

They stepped through the arch into a long hallway where Constable had a quiet word with a police officer who immediately made a call on his walkie-talkie asking that a room be completely cleared.

"Wynford Park belongs to Lev Black," said Sir Geoffrey, holding up an arm to indicate they would be heading up the hall to the left.

"The American film star?" Images from a number of hugely popular American blockbusters crisscrossed Robin's mind. Lev Black was not just a star; he was arguably the star of the decade. Equally successful in potboiler action films and quirky dramas, Black had serious acting credentials and tabloid adoration. He glanced at Cyril and caught a shimmer of something unsettled behind the equerry's pleasant but implacable blue eyes. The Sword of Damocles was hanging in a fraying baldrick.

"Yes – that Lev Black. A lucky man, he's married to yet another American star, India Hart." Sir Geoffrey led them to polished walnut double doors with glaring white and blue police tape stretched across the doorjamb. He pulled several pairs of plastic gloves from his coat pocket and handed them out.

Once the gloves were on, Constable grasped the doorknobs and pushed in the heavy doors. "Well, I think we can concur that Lev Black lived something of a charmed life until tonight."

He ducked under the police tape followed quickly by Robin and Cyril. The room had once been one of Wynford Park's more formal drawing rooms but had been converted by Black into a comfortable "family room" as they were called in America. Large, overstuffed furniture had been placed around the long room to take advantage of both the beautiful views of the rear gardens and the gigantic flat screen television. This mammoth screen -- powered up and still repeating the menu options of a science fiction DVD – took pride of place over the marble fireplace. A full-scale cinema popcorn machine and mini kitchen absorbed one corner, custom designed bookshelves featured sterling silver framed family photographs cheerfully fighting for attention among numerous gleaming awards from prestigious acting organizations and humanitarian enterprises. Vintage lobby cards and framed posters for the couple's most famous films dotted the walls of a beloved holiday house. It was managed to be both impressive and unpretentious. The room was a tribute to confidence, undoubted success, and familial happiness.

And almost every bit of it was covered in blood.

Chapter Four

"God," said Robin in a hollow voice.

"To paraphrase an old saw -- God has nothing to do with any of this." Sir Geoffrey crossed his arms and looked pointedly from Cyril to Robin. "Nor, I think, human beings."

Lev Black was sprawled over what had once been a cappuccino-colored sectional sofa. He was propped up against the sofa back as if he had just collapsed there to watch the DVD. By contrast, his equally famous wife, India Hart had been tossed aside like a week-old newspaper. She was hanging face down over the mini-kitchen's small island counter. From the way the actress was positioned with her skirt rucked up around the hips, it seemed possible she had been sexually attacked prior to death.

They had been eaten. Something voracious had devoured the two Americans as if it hadn't fed in centuries. Robin made a cursory examination of Lev Black while Cyril tried to make sense of India Hart's brutalized body. Not an easy task since multiple arterial sprays and spewing body fluids had coated nearly every surface in the family room with a sticky, lucent gore.

The killer had left Black's face alone – that was odd given the appalling damage to rest of the actor. Robin wondered if the attacker had wanted to enjoy the death agonies, wanted the witness. The actor's stomach had been torn open like an eager child's box of chocolates. All of the soft organs and tissue were gone from the ragged cavity as if scooped out and eaten in a frenzy of gluttony. Then Lev Black's skin had been peeled back from the gutted torso and upper extremities. Uneven but relentless bite marks into the underlying muscle and fat showed that the majority of it had been gobbled up as well, leaving the loose skin to pool around what was left of Black's waist like a wet winding sheet.

Robin moved away to take a look at India Hart. The violence done to her was vile but not quite as kinetic as her husband's ordeal. She had been partially consumed and with far less delirium. In a more focused, workmanlike way, her torso had been incised near the spinal cord to gain access to the delicacies of soft tissue. Hart's epidermis had not been ripped back to reveal fat and muscle. Robin had the strong sense that whoever or whatever murdered the Americans had launched at Lev Black first and satisfied its initial hunger. Either that, he thought, or there was more than one killer working in tandem.

"No revenant did this," he said, returning to gaze down at the once dashing Lev Black. The famous face wore an almost dreamy expression – dazed and grey with shock.

Sir Geoffrey produced a dismissive hiss. "Surely you can't be serious."

"His Highness is correct," Cyril interjected as he stood up from his examination of the actor's left hand that still gripped the sofa back. "Vampires drink blood. Vampires don't eat soft tissue. At the rare vampire kill sites of the past, one would have found very little blood."

"Waste not, want not," Robin said, enjoying watching Sir Geoffrey flinch a little.

"You expect me to inform the PM that a human did this?"

Robin shook his head. "Not a human either in my opinion."

"You're suggesting another denizen of the paranormal murdered the Blacks?" The civil servant raised an eyebrow skeptically. "How convenient. Any time your chappies go spare, you can misdirect attention to some sort of mysterious Will O'the Wisp."

"Before you toddle off to the Prime Minister and start pushing for some sort of vampire suppression policy," said Robin. "I suggest you allow us to undertake an investigation. We are uniquely equipped to do so."

He sighed deeply. "I would counsel alacrity. There are those …"

"I have those voices as well," Robin cut in coolly as he and Cyril stepped back from Lev Black's ravaged corpse.

"Neither the PM nor I want to start a pissing contest, Sir Geoffrey."

Constable's eyes widened a little in appreciation of Robin's directness. There was a brief pause as he considered what had been said. Then he nodded.

"I'll have the genuine MI5 investigation file sent to you."

"Not going public?"

"The official report will conclude this was a home invasion gone very badly wrong." Sir Geoffrey led them back to the polished walnut doors. "Certain pertinent – and repulsive -- details missing, of course."

Robin settled back in the Rolls Phantom. It was humming over a windswept M40, heading home to Audley Square. His Household Guard followed closely in its own black Range Rover.

"Something so starved that it tears apart a healthy young man and eats all of his soft juicy bits." Robin shivered.

"Then feeling a little more the old self, rapes the man's wife and makes a dessert out of her organs. Ever hear of anything like that up and operating in Britain?"

Cyril's normally implacable face looked drawn and slightly queasy. "One has heard rumors over the centuries of other things that go bump in the night. Nothing ever definitive or verified."

"Pity," Robin murmured, gazing out the car window at the night sky.

"You know, I was reminded of an ancient American Indian legend. They tell stories about some hideous nature spirit called the Wendigo," his equerry continued thoughtfully. "The Wendigo is propelled by a terrible and insatiable hunger for human flesh. An attempt to make sense of incidences of cannibalism, I believe."

"An English Wendigo." Robin turned his head to give Cyril a baleful look. "Just in time for Christmas."

Chapter Five

New York City, United States

Simon DuPlessis watched as the ballet dancers sailed across the marley floor in the last grand allegro of the class. He was particularly interested in one of the ballerinas – an impossibly lithe dancer gifted with exquisite line and musicality – as she made a tidy glissade into fourth and promptly executed five perfect pirouettes earning her a nod from the company ballet master.

The improbably named Philadelphia Baquero-Florez was a soloist with the prestigious New York Theatre Ballet but rising fast to star status with critics and balletomanes. She was a gorgeous creature with huge hazel eyes, creamy skin and rich dark hair that naturally spun into glossy ringlets. Disciplined, bright and light-hearted, she was simply "Della from Williamsburg" to her friends. Simon DuPlessis – son of the Vampire King of The British Isles – thought he might be falling in love with the exquisite ballerina. He just wasn't positive at all about introducing Della Baquero-Florez into the very very strange, shadowy world of his family and even less sure about trying to explain that he had officially died in 1776. She didn't even know his real name as both he and his father used Dashwood in general human society to avoid any possibility of ancient links to Hawkesmoor Castle being noticed and wondered about.

A few minutes later and applause rang out in the studio as dancers finished their morning technique class. Moments later they streamed out of the double doors – many rushing away to rehearsals in nearby rooms, others pausing in the lobby to exchange news and talk of exciting aspects of the day's schedule.

"Hey," said Della as she came through the double doors, a large black dance bag slung over her right shoulder. She gave Simon a quick kiss.

He smiled at her, catching the bright tones of the citrus-y perfume she always wore. "You positive you have time for lunch? No choreographer is going to scream where the hell is Della in petulant tones?"

The ballerina beamed back. "I absolutely do. Can you believe it? No rehearsals until three. How about you, mi favorito en el mundo?"

Simon was a student in piano performance at Juilliard. He had been keen to experience life outside England, so his father suggested Manhattan where he owned a grand old 19th century apartment building called The Bailey in Greenwich Village. It had been built for the theatre trade and his father had kept it that way, offering remarkably low rents to genuine theatrical artists and often, in the instances of the many ancient retirees who called the Bailey home, no rent at all.

"Today I'm all yours."

"Not just today, I hope," Della kissed him again. "Give me a sec and I'll change into civilian clothes."

Despite the December chill, they walked to the Gramercy Tavern. A light snow had been falling since morning dusting Manhattan in an ethereal white that seemed to guarantee a jolly and profitable holiday season. In response, the New Yorkers and tourists out on the sidewalks seemed energized and light-hearted as they hurried along to work, appointments and shopping.

"Now that's a ring!" said Della spying one in a shop window. She reeled in Simon and pointed at an emerald-cut smoky topaz. The large stone had a lovely cognac color set off by the cooler silver of the band. "Isn't it fabulous?" "How the bloody hell did you spot it? We were -- at the very least -- a couple of yards away." He dutifully peered down at the glimmering topaz in its white velvet showcase. She pretended to smack his shoulder. "Well, okay … I've been looking at it for about three weeks. Isn't it pretty?" "Very," he agreed and then turned to grin at her. "And I must say as Christmas present hints go, this was one of the most unsubtle I've ever received."

"Es un pedazo de trabajo, mi amigo! Imagine me acusa de un crimen como tal!" Della laughed and slid her arms up around his neck. She kissed him with a sweetness that pulled at Simon's heart and conscience. The significance of the ring was not lost on him. But how was he ever to introduce her to his father – the vampire king of Britain? How could he explain that his stepsister was no ordinary six-year but the most powerful human/faerie hybrid since Merlin? Would she feel the same about him if she learned he was reared in the 18th century, viciously murdered and then rescued from an eon of ghostly wandering by his father who was able to time-travel? Surely Della would either run from him in horror of what he and his family were or because she thought he was insane.

Simon pulled her into a hug as a winter breeze swirled down 20th Street, rattling the dormant tree branches of a sidewalk planted White Ash. High-pitched voices rose with the breeze like some sort of Henry Partch wind chime.

He let out a sharp breath and stepped back from Della who looked surprised at his startled retreat. The voices were singing in old Welsh with the volume rising and falling with the intensity of the light, capricious wind. They sang of a fallow deer hunted relentlessly by the legendary hound,

34

Gelert. They sang of stalking and danger. Simon spun around, looking in every direction for any sign – a glimpse of something ominous, something out of place.

All the DuPlessis carried the bloodline of the powerful Welsh faeries, the Tylwyth Teg in varying degrees. Both his father and his stepsister Ari possessed formidable abilities, but he did not. He was far more like his grandfather who had occasionally heard the breezy whisper of the Tylwyth Teg's songs. While his grandfather dismissed the eerie voices as the wind, wishful musing or the effects of a particularly rich dinner, Simon actually had an innate understanding of the ancient Welsh and could sometimes unravel the hidden meanings in their dense, poetic metaphors.

This had been a warning.

"Are you okay?" asked Della, hazel eyes wide with worry. Simon looked sharply to his left; almost positive he'd glimpsed a figure melt into a knot of cheery shoppers heading into an upscale clothing store. Could it be possible that he was being followed?

"Simon?" Della's voice raised a notch.

He let out a breath. Everything now seemed perfectly pleasant – a picture postcard of a snow-dusted Manhattan at Christmas time. If the Tylwyth Teg had been warning him about a potential mugging, the would-be criminal must have decided he and Della weren't a worthwhile target.

"Sorry … I just thought … I saw someone I recognized." Simon scrambled to put together something that would defuse her anxiety. "But I was wrong. Crikey, I'm absolutely starved! Are you hungry?"

Della threw him a suspicious look that quickly morphed into a good-natured grin that lit up her face. "You are so fff-ing weird!" she said moving forward to slide an arm under his. "Okay, I'm jones-ing for their fried eggplant. About two pounds of it."

"And by all that is sacred, you shall have it!" Simon announced in the ringing King Arthur voice of a small, not very enterprising community theatre production of Camelot. The ballerina giggled as they walked up 20th Street towards the distinctive brown awning of the Gramercy Tavern. "You English guys!"

Simon glanced over his shoulder one last time. No shadowy figures darted into hiding. All he saw were Christmas shoppers loaded with glossy bags, holiday banners fluttering from streetlamps and ubiquitous Manhattan traffic. Nothing to warrant a warning from the faerie ethers. He shivered and tightened his grip on Della's slender hand.

Chapter Six

"Not too important, I hope," said Caroline as she joined Robin for a quick lunch between their various engagements.

She had insisted on a kitchen and dining room being made part of their private quarters when Garnet Petherbridge's house was extensively remodeled for the new king. What had once been a small conservatory was now a cheery dining room with a commanding view over the house's locked garden. Robin didn't have the heart to tell her what Petherbridge had enjoyed using the conservatory for back in the days when the former vampire king had potential enemies rounded up.

"Not too important what?" Robin yawned and reached for his cup of coffee. Unlike traditional vampires, his hybrid system allowed him to eat and drink as humans did.

"Not too important a meeting last night, I hope," she asked with an entreating smile.

Robin looked up, catching the wistful note in her voice. He knew the tentative diplomatic alliance between the vampire and human governments was very important to Caroline. Not only did she see it as crucial for both sides if large scale tragedy were to be averted but absolutely central to her understandable desire to live a reasonably normal life with her family.

"Oh," he lied, "nothing earth shattering. The PM's equerry wanted to go over some statistical data."

"In the dead of night?"

"You know they still can't get over the vampire nocturnal thing." Robin poured her a cup of coffee from a silver Queen Anne pot. "Thought it was more convenient for me."

"No worries then." Caroline let out a relieved breath as she sat down at the table opposite him. "What's your day like?"

"Meetings," he replied, thinking about the MI5 murder file he and Cyril were going to pour over in search of clues to the vicious deaths of the American film stars.

"Dad's coming down tomorrow for a couple of days. The annual Sheepfarmers Society meeting – apparently, he's mediating a dust-up between the Blackface and Northern Cheviot breeders."

Caroline's father was the current Earl of Hawkesmoor and since he was a gentleman devoted to rustic pursuits, his visits to London were relatively few.

Robin pretended to sigh deeply as he speared a piece of grilled tomato. "Well, we are a political family."

She let out a laugh. "But might you be free for dinner tomorrow? I was pondering going out. What do you think? I was thinking Simpson's, Wilton's or Rules. You know Dad – standard British fare."

"Our staff here would love the chance to drown your father in Yorkshire pudding and roast beef."

"I know," Caroline picked up her coffee cup and had a sip. She seemed to be pausing to construct her next statement. "But I'd …"

"You'd like to dine out and avoid all the "royal family" feeling around here." He interjected to save her the trouble. She looked relieved. "A little of Audley Square goes a long way with Dad. He's old school."

"Not as old school as I am." Robin grinned at her. "I remember when Rules opened for business in 1798. Georgian steak club in those days. Some monumental drunken brawls in the …"

"Oh, you know what I mean." Caroline made a sour face and picked up an electronic tablet that a staff member had left unobtrusively on the table. She tapped the screen and it switched on with a faint chime. "Can you have Cyril book a table?"

"With pleasure do I serve you, my queen. For no greater mission have I ever been charged," he replied in a Shakespearian voice that ought to have belonged to a third-rate stage actor touring the Northern provinces. It was a joke he had picked up from his son, Simon, who possessed a theatrical bent. "By the Sophie, let the stars align and I shall lay the very Moon itself at your feet ..."

"Oh, my god," Caroline said in surprise. She was gazing down at the lit screen. "That American actor, Lev Black, and his wife have been murdered. Some sort of burglary gone wrong or something."

"Really?" Robin immediately dropped the faux thespian voice. "Any details?'

"Nothing," she said, her eyes scanning the news item, "much. Both stabbed to death. No suspects yet. Those poor people. You'd think they would have had better security."

After lunch, Caroline went off to accompany Ari and Felicity Pratt on their afternoon walk. Robin returned to his study where he found Cyril dutifully waiting for him. "Your Serene Highness," said Cyril, bowing from the waist. It was the long serving equerry's opening gambit at the beginning of every working session.

"So, what have we got?" he asked, relieved to note a silver pot of fresh coffee had been placed on his desk.

Cyril consulted his electronic tablet. "For a start, Sir, the first of the Hong Kong contingent will be arriving shortly."

"Anything yet from MI5?"

His equerry nodded. "A very preliminary report arrived by messenger arrived late this morning, sir."

Robin sat down at his desk and tapped its mahogany surface. "Lay it out, Goforth. I want to see it."

"Sir," Cyril picked up a file from a Georgian sideboard by the study door. He placed it front of Robin. "I believe Sir Geoffrey and the PM would like to take up some of your valuable time. Shall I confirm?"

Robin flipped open the file, looking down at a stack of neatly typed pages and photographs. "Yes, please. Oh, and Caroline's father, the Earl is arriving sometime tomorrow. Alert the staff if you would – please ask them if they'd be good enough again to tone down the bows and curtseys while he's here."

Cyril sighed slightly. A traditionalist, he disliked deviations in the court's operation.

"As with the Earl's Autumnal visitation, shall I secure a table at Rules?"

"Please." Robin didn't look up from the file pages but gestured in the general direction of an empty chair. He took half of the file contents and set it aside for the equerry.

"Gather round, Cyril! I require your astute opinion."

For the next hour, the two vampires silently poured over MI5's meticulous findings, exchanging pages as they absorbed the violent details of the Black murders. Despite the file being classified as preliminary, it was well laid out and thorough. Finally, Robin sat back in his desk chair and stretched his arms over his head. He let out a short, incredulous breath.

"First thought?" he asked Cyril.

The equerry frowned. "Not revenant just as we surmised. The tissue eating isn't our modus operandi."

"But also, not some sort of human stalker or serial killer?"

"No trace of forced entry." Cyril said grimly. "And none of the wounds were inflicted by a weapon. The Blacks were opened up the old-fashioned way – brute force."

Robin nodded. "And despite that, not a fingerprint, not a shred of DNA even though Mrs. Black was sexually penetrated."

"That would seem to suggest a killer more suited to our rather more eerie bailiwick."

"Agreed. But, what? One of your American Wendigos visiting England over the holiday?"

Cyril's aristocratic brow furrowed in thought. "I've never encountered or heard about a predator with this particular style of attack."

"And then there's the other thing." Robin rubbed his right eye wearily. "Did you catch it?"

"Your Highness?"

"No defense wounds. Along with the general lack of forensic evidence from the killer, there was nothing under the victims' fingernails indicating that they fought their attacker. No cuts or bruises either. One might have expected that the Blacks would have tried instinctively and very aggressively to avoid such a hideous ordeal."

A squeamish expression pulled at Cyril's elegant features. "They just submitted to … that … quietly."

"Well, controlling a human is obviously not an unknown idea for us. But the amount of damage the Blacks endured without apparent objection would require tremendous skill at mesmerizing," Robin said as he picked up his coffee cup and had a sip. "Somehow, we have to find this thing first and eliminate it. Otherwise, Sir Geoffrey and his ilk over at Number 10 are going to take a golden opportunity to place the blame squarely upon our shoulders."

Chapter Seven

Simon clattered down the steps of the 66th Street subway entrance, happy to nip away from a sharpish wind that had picked up, flinging drops of drizzle about the mid-afternoon streets near Lincoln Center. The big Atlantic storm the weather forecasters had been predicting all week was beginning to edge into the city. He needed to get back to the Bailey fast. He had the nagging suspicion that he might not have fully closed one of the French doors that led to the outside deck. His father would be highly displeased if the flat's gleaming maple floors warped from a flood of rain or snow.

Other than the possibility of a wet floor, it had been a very good morning. He had gotten to his practice room extremely early as all the pianos were booked solid as students prepared pieces for the mid-term evaluations and Christmas performances. The early hour had turned out to be a small dash of serendipity. He had been deep into the coda of the infamous Chopin G-Minor Ballade when a passing Emanuel Ax had a bit more time than usual to listen to random rehearsals and he had paused, clearly interested, until Simon had struck the final note. The legendary concert pianist had nodded, indicating it was going well -- "Watch your tenths a bit" -- then patted Simon's shoulder collegially.

Simon slung his brown leather satchel over his shoulder as he arrived at the subway platform. Tacit approval from Emanuel Ax helped combat the worry over the potential of destroyed maple. He leaned against a pillar, waiting for the subway train in a large knot of other passengers. With luck, Della would be free for a while before her class. She was dancing Snow Queen and Arabian that evening and he knew she was a little nervous about a particular lift sequence in the Snow pas de deux.

Simon blew out a breath that hung in the chilled air. He really owed his father a lot. His father returned to the 18th century to rescue him from a brutal death. His father also owned the lovely old Bailey – the theatre trade building that had allowed him to meet Della whose grandfather's best friend, a retired flamenco guitarist, resided at the Bailey. They had met at one of the monthly soirees at which elderly Bailey tenants brought their acts out of retirement. He had volunteered to act as bartender and after sitting through two rocky encores of Stormy Weather; Della had rushed the bar for a life-giving glass of Chablis.

He wondered if she'd have enough time for a quick breakfast before she had to get to Lincoln Center.

The station platform was crowded with a cross section of New Yorkers and tourists. Listening to the murmurings and fragments of conversation among the waiting passengers, Simon thought momentarily of the legendary harpsichordist Glen Gould and his experiments recording the accidental concertos of human voice.

Overriding Gould's whimsical notion was the sudden sensation that he was of keen interest to someone. Someone was watching him. Simon turned around sharply, scanning the people behind him. There were other students, executive types and a small clutch of chattering tourists wearing vivid sweatshirts and team jackets from Oklahoma Baptist University. No one staring at him. No one seemed out of place or unusual. Still the feeling of being studied was clear and present.

Simon returned to sort through the crowd in front of him, nearer to the subway tracks. Again, no one out of the ordinary – just more students, businesspeople and tourists with glossy shopping bags.

The train emerged from a tunnel, screeching up to the cement curb with doors hissing open. People spewed from the cars and others began stepping in. Simon followed the pack, nipping into the car and finding a pole to lean against so that ladies could sit on the hard plastic benches. He continued to watch as the other passengers found places to sit or stand. Not a single passenger looked vaguely interested in him. He was just another NYC student.

The subway car lurched as it left the station platform. Simon peered through one of the car windows at rapidly receding expanse of cement and tile. Just a few New Yorkers arriving for the next train. A flicker of something caught his eye – reminding him of the previous time by the jewelry shop window with Della. Possibly a dark figure – a shadow – stepped out from behind a station column and then back again as if verifying the train's departure into the tunnel. The creepy-crawly feeling of being observed had faded away as well.

He was not stupid. If being rescued from a brutal murder plot in the 18th century had taught him anything, it was to be very wary of such odd happenings.

Simon slipped his cell phone out of his coat pocket and tapped his father's icon.

"Esteemed heir," said his father jovially when he picked up, "I have just now read your text -- congratulations on getting a nod from Emanuel Ax."

"Thanks, Dad – do you have a minute?"

His father lost the cheery tone. "Everything all right?"

"All good, really. Well, there is a girl …"

"A girl – you're not planning on spending Christmas with her family, I hope. Ari has big ideas about you and a Christmas party."

"No, no, nothing like that. I'll tell you about her later – she's a ballerina …"

He heard his father give a small sigh. "Oh, I know all about ballet girls."

"New bulletin: it's not 1872 anymore, Dad," said Simon a bit more sharply than he intended. He softened his tone.

"Hey – you wanted me to check in if I thought anything was odd or off in some way."

"I'm listening."

"It's nothing really – just a feeling. Maybe, maybe someone following me. Not obvious or clear – again, just a feeling, Dad. Do you think, maybe, I'm just being jittery?" He hated that he sounded so young and school-boyish.

"New York can sometimes be a bit overwhelming that way. Happy to send guards to keep a weather eye out for you. They could be there in a matter of hours."

Simon took a moment to ponder the idea of a cadre of his father's guardsmen shadowing him – and Della – around the city. He had expressly wished to experience life in New York as a music student without all the trappings of his family's extraordinary life. Once he returned to Britain, the opportunity to just be a lad might never come round again.

"It's nothing – I'm being a plank. Thanks for being there though," he said, hoping he wasn't making a mistake. Homesickness for windswept Yorkshire and his odd but deeply loved family welled up. "I love you, Dad."

"America is dusting you with its pixie dust," his father replied and then seemed to swallow hard. "I love you too, Simon."

Robin put down his cell phone and turned to look at an expectant Cyril Goforth. "Dragos."

Alastair Hope – whose name lent itself naturally to 21st century politics – was a neophyte Tory Prime Minister with fresh dreams and not the least of them was earning a title at the end of a long, wildly lauded tenure. He clearly had not been entirely pleased to discover that an entire sub-species of British subject existed within the realm.

"I had just gotten used to … vampires," Hope said the word vampires as if it caused him considerable discomfort. "Now you suggest that there may be other creatures … species – beings here in England happy to eat prominent visiting Americans who pay substantial property taxes?"

Robin crossed his left leg over the right. The chairs in the PM's Number 10 office were old and venerable but not terribly comfortable. He had a moment to remember a disgruntled Gladstone dropping his heavy frame onto one. He nodded at the PM and Sir Geoffrey who was hovering in the background.

"Prime Minister, we are as dismayed as your good self."

"Oh, I rather doubt that" sniffed Hope. "Surely you are accustomed to atrocity."

"I've seen enough atrocity to satisfy both human and revenant tastes, Prime Minister."

"Yes, yes – no one can deny your heroic war records," Alastair Hope waved a beautifully manicured hand airily. "So – your suggestion on how best to proceed, if you don't mind."

Robin nodded again. "Let us investigate this – without interference."

Sir Geoffrey coughed from behind the Prime Minister's chair.

"You would keep us 'in the loop' as modern PR people like to say?"

Sir Geoffrey coughed again.

This was enough to make Hope flinch a little. "I expect you to be in constant communication with Sir Geoffrey here."

"That is agreeable to us." Robin looked past the Prime Minister. "That's a beastly cold, Sir Geoffrey. Have you tried hot lemon and honey?"

The civil servant looked sour. "No, I have not."

"Your Serene Highness," corrected Cyril quietly from behind Robin's chair.

Sir Geoffrey looked as though he was about to sputter when a sharp knock came at door.

"Tell Winters to naff off." Alastair Hope snapped. "I wasn't to be disturbed."

"Sir," the civil servant moved with surprising brio to the polished wood door. He stepped out into the vestibule beyond and closed the door pointedly behind him.

"I apologize," Hope said as he picked up a pen and toyed with it, revealing a level of anxiety. "Would you care for a drink? Do you drink ordinary things? There might be some biscuits left in the kitchen. I have a very nice whisky although it's bit early ..."

"Very kind but we are quite content," Robin offered him a polite smile, "at the moment."

There was an awkward pause in which the Prime Minister continued to tap his pen against his blotter until Sir Geoffrey abruptly reappeared. He swept in, the very air crackling with electric urgency.

"Well," he announced with a grim glance at Robin, "there's been another murder."

Chapter Eight

Simon reached the Bailey in the first wave of serious rain and sleet from the forecasted big Atlantic storm. He came into the penthouse, reading a text from Della telling him she'd overslept and wouldn't be able to grab breakfast before her class with the company. His disappointment in learning Della had already left for the day was balanced by the happy discovery that his father's maple floor was somewhat damp but completely repairable with the application of a dry towel.

Simon firmly latched the French door he'd carelessly left open, watching wind and rain rush through the leaves of potted plants on the deck. Rain that would turn to snow once the winter temperatures dropped. The thought reminded him to switch on the cheery gas fire his father had installed in the Edwardian fireplace that dominated the main living space.

Not for the first time, Simon marveled at the haven his father had created in the old Bailey Hotel for the theatre trade. Although he had meticulously maintained the Bailey since acquiring it in the Edwardian era, his father had recently done a complete restoration to the entire building so that all its period aspects were refurbished to the highest standards. But he also had all fireplaces, kitchens and bathrooms thoroughly modernized and made sure to include thoughtful details like jetted tubs for his elderly theatre retirees. He even fully restored the original Edwardian dining room on the second floor and staffed it with young culinary graduates anxious for a genuine opportunity to run a restaurant. While an incredible boon to everyone residing in the building, it made sure that the oldest tenants were able to have hot meals every day.

His father's own personal digs – the original owner's offices remodeled with unpretentious elegance and comfort – constituted the perfect Manhattan three bedroom and Simon was grateful every day that he had been permitted to borrow it.

As he settled on one of the two cranberry velvet sofas that framed the fireplace, Simon wondered – not for the first time – what he was going to do after finishing his music study. The original plan was for him to return to England and help run Hawkesmoor Castle – a full-time job for the DeBarry/DuPlessis family. He loved the castle and its attendant rural life, so he had been looking forward to eventually returning to do his part in maintaining the family estate. But now there was Della, and he didn't foresee the brilliant young ballerina happy mucking about in the fields of Northern England.

"What a muddle!" Simon said to the empty room.

Robin and Cyril exited the car in Thurloe Square in South Kensington. An area of very handsome private townhouses, Sir Geoffrey's people had efficiently cordoned off Number 33 in such a way as to not overly excite neighbors or those passing by its entranceway of white columns and a glossy black door.

Sir Geoffrey joined them after he stepped free of his own transport.

"Number 33 belongs to Oliver D'Aubigny," he said.

"The head curator of the V and A's jewelry collection?" Robin had met D'Aubigny in the past when he had outbid the curator at a Sotheby's auction for one of his mother's tiaras. The diamond, pearl and turquoise piece known as the

"Persian Tiara" had been illicitly sold off by a conniving cousin in the late 18th Century to settle a gambling debt. He had waited more than two hundred years for the Persian Tiara to emerge from a private collection and the acquisition of the ornate ornament gave him enormous pleasure when he saw Caroline clamp it on her strawberry blonde head for various formal occasions. One day when her brother, Peter, married and became the recognized Earl, they would give the Persian Tiara to his wife. Then once again, a Countess of Hawkesmoor would wear it.

Sir Geoffrey interrupted his brief flash of family jewelry and history with a short sigh.

"Yes, that Oliver D'Aubigny. Forty-two years old, Cambridge scholar. Shall we discover just how ghastly it is?"

The interior of Number 33 Thurloe Square was more formal than the plush comfort of Liev Black's Wynford Park and furnished with genuine antiques clearly collected over several lifetimes. The D'Aubignys were an old Norman family and although no longer landowners of vast importance, they obviously had managed to hold onto a townhouse in one of the most highly sought areas of London. American actors might have vastly more money but the D'Aubignys had vastly more taste. They were ushered into one of the main reception rooms – a lovely space with French doors overlooking a small urban garden. Robin very much liked the genteel mixture of periods and was quite covetous of a small William Blake watercolor of the goddess Epona that hung over a chimneypiece made from a particularly pleasing creamy yellow stone.

"The study, sir," murmured one of Sir Geoffrey's operatives. For a presumably battle-hardened MI5 type, the young man was a queasy grey. "Down at the end of the hallway, sir."

"Have the room cleared of personnel. We will view it without assistance."

The young man swallowed hard and said that he would do so immediately. Robin exchanged a wary look with Cyril before following Sir Geoffrey from the reception room. They walked down a long hall decorated with two early nineteenth century cabinets by Pierre-Philippe Thomire towards the jarringly modern view of a forensic technician who was waiting for them by a beveled door marked with police tape. The technician wordlessly handed around plastic gloves and shoe covers, then stepped back respectfully to allow Sir Geoffrey to take over.

"Fortunately for the rest of the household, Mr. D'Aubigny was alone in the house." The civil servant reached for the door handle with his plastic-coated hand. "His wife was visiting her sister in Paris – rushing home now, of course. Housekeeper returned after her day off and found him."

"No live-in servants?" asked Cyril, his notebook out.

"Apparently this generation of D'Aubignys doesn't care for full time staff. Think it's old fashioned." Sir Geoffrey looked unconvinced. "More likely the old D'Aubigny money has gotten a bit thin for such expenditures."

He pushed in the door.

At first glance – before glossy pools of congealing blood stole all the attention – Oliver D'Aubigny's private study was a delightful muddle of fine old English furniture, Oriental rugs, books, and pictures including a George Stubbs of the 18th century racehorse Parasol. D'Aubigny had chosen to use a handsome Edwardian refectory table as a desk.

"The irony," said Robin. "Poor man."

Oliver D'Aubigny lay across his makeshift desk. As with the unfortunate Blacks, he had been opened up like a ripe avocado and eaten. Cyril gingerly peered into the gaping chest cavity.

"Heart and lungs appear to have been crudely removed," he said with a wince.

Sir Geoffrey looked a bit green. He had pointedly adopted a safe distance away from the brutalized body and now he moved even further back to the study doorway.

"I'll wait for you outside. I need to instruct my lot about maintaining another official burglary-gone-wrong story," he said as he slipped under the police tape. "If you come up with something, I expect to be immediately informed."

"So, our English Wendigo has struck again," Robin said once the PM's aide de camp had gone. "I don't suppose the D'Aubignys had anything as modern as security cameras."

"Well, you may recall Liev Black had cameras aplenty at Wynford Park," Cyril replied, delicately stepping over a blood pool to look at the body from a different angle. "MI5 report said even those reproduction suits of armor had hidden cameras in the helmets. All the electronics went down – no use-able information."

"Right," sighed Robin. "That brought the private security company for a look-see."

"And then Sir Geoffrey thanked his personal gods that the Blacks' security people held several government contracts so the more appalling details would be tamped down." Goforth continued to study at the left side of D'Aubigny's gutted torso. "I imagine the unlucky housekeeper will get bullied into believing she saw quite a different crime scene as well."

"It does suggest that our Wendigo gobbles up his meals with alacrity." Robin took in the dazed expression on

Oliver's strong, beaky Norman face. He had been an urbane, sophisticated man – a genuine scholar who had written insightful and engaging books on decorative arts. A genuine loss to British culture and society.

Cyril stood up. "Your Highness, may I suggest we await the MI5 file? There is the diplomatic reception for the Hong Kong delegation."

"Can you push that back a bit?"

The equerry frowned and instinctively glanced down at his electronic tablet. Cyril Goforth hated disorder in the day's diary of events.

"Sir?"

"I want to nip over to Wynford Park," said Robin. "I'd like to have a chat with the cat."

Chapter Nine

They arrived at Wynford Park in a mode unique to vampires – molecular transfer. After literally evaporating their corporeal selves in London, they had used the same powerful telepathic abilities to make a shift to Oxfordshire. Once on the grounds of Wynford Park, they reconstituted their outward forms in a shiver of light and shadow. It was a valued trait of stronger, highly skilled vampires. But most used it with great care and caution. Such radical molecular shifts were fraught with potential disaster and vampire legend abounded with tales of unfortunate reappearances into stonework, animals, raging fires and even the bottom of the Marianas Trench.

"Always count my blessings," murmured Cyril as they materialized on the stone steps leading to the house's main entrance.

"I vastly prefer the Rolls." Robin took a step back to take in the country house's gothic façade. "But occasionally, time is of essence."

The cold moonlight in a breezy English December night did not improve Wynford Park's countenance. It was a rather silly, pointless house. Built in the 1860s to appear both formidable and impressively ancient by a newly wealthy maker of men's hats, it boasted several acres of faux medieval turrets, beveled windows and tall chimneys. But for all its faults, Wynford had been a loved house by several owners who had clearly kept it in good nick and enjoyed its conceits. The current tragedy had lent Wynford a kind of genuine poignancy that began to match its overwrought design.

"The last I saw of the Blacks' cat, it was streaking upstairs in a panic," said Robin gazing up at Wynford Park's upper windows.

"Bound to be some security protecting the place from prying press and curious tourists." Cyril joined him in gazing up at the house. "Speaking of which, Your Serene Highness, your own guard will be getting anxious."

Robin scanned the roofline. "Not particularly worried about either of those."

"Maybe the cat was given away?"

"No – I can sense it … hiding in the attics." Robin murmured as he rose off the ground and started the ascent to the roof.

"Sir!" Cyril flew up after his sovereign. Spontaneous decisions never pleased a devoted civil servant.

A scratching sound nudged Simon awake. He'd inadvertently fallen asleep on the couch. The storm had doused most of the winter sunlight, his father's main room now shrouded in grey and shadows, lit only by the gas fire. Snow shuddered past the Bailey's windows.

He sat up, shivering. The room was inexplicably cold. For a moment it seemed possible it was a paranormal kind of cold. Hawkesmoor Castle was home to a number of regularly documented ghosts and when they deigned to be seen, a profound cold seemed to waft in as well.

The scratching sound returned. Simon stood up, alert now, recalling the sensation of being watched in the subway station. With a family as baroque as his, genuine horror could be lurking behind a Queen Anne chair or in the butler's pantry.

Then the scratching became a knock.

"Simon!" came Della's muffled voice at the apartment's front door. "Are you there?"

Shaking off feelings of unease, Simon darted to the door and swung it open to find Della standing in a dim hallway. He could see that her beautiful face was fraught with frustration and annoyance. Also, she was swearing hotly in Spanish.

"The power's out!" she announced, coming past him into the foyer. "And I bought ice cream for you – the good stuff from Dean & Deluca too. It'll be ruined!"

The ballerina tossed her dance bag on a side table along with a paper bag containing the expensive ice cream and turned to look at him through the hard grey light. "Some of the seniors are wandering the halls being dithery. Do you think we should gather the nervous ones into the dining room and give them some coffee or something?"

Simon threw his arms around Della. "You are a darling." She squeezed him back. "We should get out there before one of them falls and breaks a hip."

Robin and Cyril slipped into one of the attics on top of Wynford Park. Dark and frigid, the attic resembled an undisturbed Egyptian tomb being opened by archeologists for the first time. Shrouded shapes hinted at furniture and packed away treasures.

"I don't suppose you have a convenient torch?" asked Robin.

"No, Your Serene Highness," replied Cyril reaching into his breast pocket. "But I do have a mobile phone with a flashlight app."

"Aren't you the clever one?"

"Actually, your phone has one too." The civil servant tapped the screen of his smartphone and a beam of light emanated from the plastic rectangle. He held it up and swept the light slowly over the room, revealing contents far less exciting than King Tut's burial chamber. Plastic crates, cardboard boxes, seasonal decorations and various pieces of unwanted furniture half-heartedly draped with dust cloths. Cyril paused the tour at a life size model of Santa Claus who despite the gloomy surroundings, stood in a corner beaming out Christmas good will to all and sundry "He didn't make the holiday décor this year," Cyril observed.

Robin wasn't listening. "I know you're here," he said to the cold room. "Come out. We're not here to hurt you."

In a moment a small silver tabby cat emerged from behind the beaming Santa. He squeaked a meow and tentatively crept forward to where Robin had crouched down. Robin reached out and stroked the little cat's head.

"He's very hungry," said Robin, continuing to pet the silver tabby. "Mrs. Black was very diligent in hiring exterminators so no convenient mice to eat. He's been too scared to go downstairs."

"I don't blame him." Cyril bent down as well and prepared to take notes on his electronic tablet. "His name?"

Robin smiled as he stroked the cat's ears. "They named him Doodles -- but he prefers Julian."

The Bailey's restored dining room was lit only by the large Edwardian windows that looked out over the Manhattan street and a number of battery-operated lanterns in an old-fashioned carriage lamp design that normally served as pretty table décor. Della – the daughter of a restaurant owner in Williamsburg – had gone into the industrial kitchen to have a word with a harried staff trying their best to organize some sort of lunch despite the lack of power. They readily agreed to allow her to throw together a quick coffee service and some dessert platters for unsettled older residents while they concentrated on rescuing their menu items. Grateful senior residents instinctively gathered near the room's most visible and striking feature – a large mahogany fireplace with an impressive artificial log fire.

"They say the entire block is out," reported Blake Bywaters, a retired soap opera star. He waved his cell phone at Simon. "Something to do with the storm. Con Ed's on it though."

Simon, who was acting as an impromptu waiter, placed a plate of warm apple pie in front of the wheelchair bound Alice Angel, the last living member of the famous Angel Family of aerial circus artists. He gave Blake an appreciative nod and poured coffee into Alice's cup.

"I thought," said Alice in the quaking voice that sometimes plagued the elderly, "we had emergency generators for times like this."

"We do," replied Simon, pouring a coffee for Blake and then former magician's assistant, Maisie Parker. "I don't know why they didn't kick in."

"Well, it was a good excuse to get together," said Maisie gamely.

"I have a cat," announced Ruth – noted jazz singer of the 1950s.

"Wowzers," said Blake. "Getting chilly even with the fire."

"Aye." Simon paused to notice that it really was quite cold. As he did so, the entire room started vibrating as if an energy pulse was moving across through the structure. Simon sidestepped slightly to keep his balance. Coffee cups and spoons rattled on saucers. Surprised residents of the Bailey gasped out loud, uttered various exhortations or inhaled sharply – responses that provoked coughing bouts in those with impaired respiratory systems.

Simon scanned the room. His family bloodline of Faerie had activated a small warning beacon in his neural net. Something was off.

"Julian says the Blacks were very kind to him. Mrs. Black was particularly interested in making sure he had the best organic cat food. He wasn't wild about the self-cleaning litter box in the service pantry but …"

"Sir, anything about the Wendigo?" asked Cyril, tablet at the ready.

Robin held up a hand to stop his equerry from speaking. Then he returned to rubbing Julian's ears and listening to the variety of meows, squeaks and purrs that emanated from the little silver cat.

Simon slowly turned in a circle, gazing up at the ceiling. There was an unsettling sensation of a heavier than usual pressure in the air – as if it had weight like seawater and some massive leviathan swam in it overhead. He half expected to see something materialize out of thin air.

"Julian never saw our English Wendigo," said Robin, picking up the little silver tabby and cradling it in his arms as he straightened to his full height. "Like most cats, he knew to find a bolt hole when the house energy went bad." Cyril sighed and glanced at his wristwatch. "We have a reception to prepare for, Sir."

"But he was in the murder room when the environment started to change." Robin's face was thoughtful. "The Blacks were watching some television. Julian was enjoying an organic catnip toy when the heaviness seemed to sweep across the room. Julian said it felt as if a big hawk or an owl was prowling the air above looking for a hapless kitten to pick up. He got out, hid under a bed in a guest room."

Cyril shook his head in regret. "A pity, Your Highness. I thought we might really learn something."

"I think we have," said Robin. "Thanks to Julian, we now know whatever this thing is, it possesses the ability to travel much as we do. This English Wendigo doesn't just plough through the side door. It's far more sophisticated."

"And dangerous," replied the equerry.

"And dangerous." Robin stroked the silver tabby's head.

"The Hong Kong delegation, Sir?" Cyril opened a screen on his electronic tablet and gazed down at it.

"Yes, of course. One moment though," Robin held the cat away so he could see its small, inquisitive face "Julian – would you like to come to London and live at my house? I have a daughter who would love you to be her companion."

"Sir ..."

Robin rubbed Julian's silver tipped ears as the cat meowed several times. "Then it's all settled. You'll like Audley Square."

He re-directed his attention to his waiting equerry. "Cyril, we shall need the full range of cat supplies – but no self-cleaning litter pan."

"No. Self-cleaning. Litter. Pan," Cyril repeated as he rapidly typed the request into his tablet.

A human sounded in the hallway beyond the attics. There was the tinny tone of hand-held radio of the type often used by security guards.

"I'm hearing voices," said the guard with the self-important urgency of all would-be law enforcement persons. "I'm assuming it's a Code Yellow -- the media."

The door to Julian's attic flew open and the private security guard leapt in, new leather boots and harness squeaking, taser gun extended.

"Aylesbury Security! This is private property ..."

Robin offered him a sympathetic smile.

The guard's anxious young face shifted awkwardly in expression. He had skidded in wearing a shaky veneer of resolute determination. Professionalism careened into sheer panic and then spun away to pure wonder before crashing back at sheer panic as Robin, Cyril and Julian absolutely vanished into the chilled air.

Simon was still scanning shadows in the Edwardian carved ceiling when the power came back online. The dining room lit up, banishing the gloom. Immediately the atmosphere he had sensed looming in the building dissipated. He wondered if he'd simply imagined it all. Perhaps his Faerie bloodline was so polluted by the good old-fashioned human genome that it misfired like a virus riddled laptop.

There came a general cheer from both elderly inhabitants and harried Bailey restaurant staff, punctuated with wheezy coughs from those suffering from congestive heart conditions and emphysema.

"I have a cat!" Ruth announced with undiluted joy.

Della emerged from the kitchen. She was munching on a crisp green apple.

"Got to head to the theatre," she told Simon upon reaching him. "Hope Snow goes well. I got iffy vibes, mi amigo."

"The French guy?" Simon asked, remembering her stories about the new dancer visiting from the Paris Opera who wasn't yet completely adept at the bigger pas de deux lifts.

Della sighed. "The French guy."

Simon slung an arm around her elegant shoulders. "I'll walk you to the subway – kind of a consolation prize."

Chapter Ten

"You look lovely enough to eat with a spoon,"
Robin said as Caroline emerged from her dressing room,
genuinely stunning in a Chinese red gown made of duchess
satin and velvet,
"Just as long as the Hong Kong Delegation doesn't decide
to try a bite," she replied, struggling to close a diamond
bracelet that had once belonged to Robin's mother.
"Darling," Robin reached put to grasp her wrist so he could
affect repairs to the clasp, "they have their own supplies –
it's all very tied up in ritual and some ancient notions of
sacred purity. You would pollute their entire system."
Caroline laughed out loud. "Thanks a lot."
He snapped the clasp shut on the baroque bracelet.
Originally the bracelet had been worn with elegant little
black velvet ribbons. He had the piece reset with a modern
platinum clasp for Lady Caroline – far less dubious security
especially as 21st century women no longer employed a
lady's maid whose main duty was to follow their mistress
about, collecting jewels and jeweled items that fell from that
august person at various formal social events.
The third-floor private apartment, along with the rest of
Audley Square, had been completely renovated by both
Caroline's old school tastes and London high society design
expert, Tarquin Bolt who began his training in the 17th
Century with Inigo Jones.
He and Caroline had restored the ambassadorial sections of
Audley Square with enormous care in the shared
understanding that Audley was a visual representation of the
21st Century British vampire, needing to reflect both a
storied history and promising future. With the strict

exception of cavernous chambers below ground level once used as cells and grisly interrogation rooms that still awaited final decisions from Robin about remodeling, every other historical aspect of the large house had been cleaned, repaired and returned to its early Georgian beauty. The modern world was introduced with high tech electronics, a professional kitchen and discreet elevator.

Caroline and Tarquin decided to cull the very best period pieces from the massive but jumbled collection left behind by former kings. These were used in tandem with a superb collection of pictures and objets d'art, throughout the main rooms to create spectacular spaces for entertaining and running the current affairs of Great Britain's vampire kingdom.

But the third floor was a self-contained home for a modern English family. It featured several sitting rooms, kitchen, a formal dining room and large airy bedrooms for everyone including Caroline's father, The Earl, when he was down in London. Like any other 21st Century family home, it had flat screen televisions scattered throughout the various rooms although Bolt had mostly managed to conceal them with sliding screens and in refurbished armoires when not in use.

Currently their bedroom's flat screen was switched on to the evening news while they readied for an evening with the Hong Kong Delegation. In the background as Robin finished closing the bracelet on Caroline's wrist was the quiet murmur of the news reader as she addressed various stories of local interest.

"Oh, look," said Caroline, reaching for the tv remote on the edge of the bed, "something about those celebrity murders." She pointed the remote at the wide-screen and pushed up the volume.

Robin focused on what had intrigued Caroline who, like all red-blooded English persons, loved a good, vibrant murder. He saw a woman reporter – bottle blonde and dressed in violent pink -- standing on the front steps of Wynford Park. "Apparently the halls and byways of Wynford Park have not been entirely quiet since the tragic murders of American celebrities, Liev Black and India Hart," she intoned with the drawling gravitas all on-camera news people had adopted. "Today – strange sounds echoing in the presumably empty house led to a ghost sighting."

"Good heavens -- the time!" Robin said brightly. "Those Chinese delegates will be wanting to spin us wild stories about Shaolin revenants ..."

"Aylesbury Security guard, Tim Meeks, insists that today while investigating mysterious noises in Wynford's attics, he encountered two full bodied apparitions ... and a cat."

"A cat?" murmured Caroline. Robin knew she was thinking about the kindly little silver tabby he had just brought home as a companion for their daughter.

"They weren't transparent at all!" explained the breathless young security officer who now spoke into the reporter's handheld microphone. "Clear as day! Two men. The one with the cat had longish ginger hair ... dark suits – looked posh ..."

"Talk about desperate," interjected Robin as he moved pointedly towards the door. "Media are just flogging anything they get about the Blacks. Those poor people – should be left to rest in peace. The carrion! Just picking at the bones ..."

"Hold hard, Your Serene Highness," said Caroline flatly, using an equestrian term from her girlhood days in the show ring.

Robin reluctantly pulled to a stop. He composed an expression of polite bafflement to wear on his face before turning to look back at his handsome wife who stood with her arms crossed over the bodice of her Chinese red gown. "Really -- two men and a cat?" she said, raising her eyebrows.

"I haven't the slightest notion ..."

"Ginger hair, toff suits and a striped cat?" Caroline cocked her head to the side like a headmaster questioning a 7th Form student hiding cigarettes behind his back. "So, why, exactly, were you and Cyril in the attics of Wynford Park?

Chapter Eleven

"And I thought vampires were weird enough," said Caroline after Robin had reluctantly brought her up to date with the bizarre murders of the Blacks and Oliver D'Aubigny.

Then she punched him lightly on the upper arm. "Don't hide things from me! I am not a wilting violet."

"Oww!" He protested as if the blow had really hurt. "But you are a bully!"

"Head girl at St. Sophia's," Caroline replied brightly.

Robin rubbed his arm, still pretending it was injured. "I won't keep you in the dark. I promise. Just didn't want to worry you about ravenous spectral beings round Christmas."

"I'm more worried about Sir Geoffrey on the warpath," Caroline said. "Those embedded civil servants can be real pills. Dad could have a word – Sir Geoffrey was his fag at Eton in the 1970s."

He laughed. "I can just imagine him carrying your father's cricket bat and fetching pots of tea. If things go to what the army likes to call "Def-Con 5", I'll call in your father as the nuclear decision."

"So, what's your next move?" She took a last look in a large mirror hanging over the bedroom's fireplace – a white statuary marble mantelpiece overlaid with carvings of bellflowers descending from tied ribbons.

"Don't know yet. Await the MI6 file and see if anything jumps out at me. It's definitely paranormal -- another kind of dimensional entity that I haven't run across before. Once I can deduce how it seeks and finds, maybe I can send it back or destroy it."

"Would the Tylwyth Teg know something about such a creature?" Caroline was moving to switch off the flat screen.

"Even if they did, I cannot contact them," Robin said, referring to an avowal he had made upon being restored to the human plane. "Not for a revenant issue."

He had promised he would not attempt to link with the Tylwyth Teg save for extreme emergency – the proverbial nuclear option. It was not to be cruel or a show of enmity towards the human realm. The Tylwyth Teg – The Fair Ones of Celtic culture had once traveled freely between dimensions. Particularly entranced by the innocence of a new world, they had freely interacted with the inhabitants in mutually beneficial ways and in few rare instances, taken human companions. But sinister beings from darker dimensions had begun to take an interest in the human plane, threatening to devour the little world. The Tylwyth Teg had picked up their literal and metaphorical swords, driving back the diabolical invaders but realizing as they did so that they, too, must leave forever. They returned to their realm -- determined to act as protectors, keeping watch over the dimensional gateways.

Robin, through his faerie bloodline, was the living embodiment of the powerful Lord Pwyll – a Celtic deity of great power. If he were to meld between the human and faerie dimension, it could cause a massive imbalance – an inter-dimensional bleed that, like a brain aneurysm, would flood the worlds. That was the pact, the covenant he had made. If he returned to the human realm, he was essentially on his own.

"Of course." Caroline made a face. "That would be just too simple."

He copied her sour expression. "Wouldn't it just?"

There came a painfully polite tap at the door.

"Coming, Cyril!" Robin called out and offered his elbow to his wife. "Darling, the Hong Kong Delegation awaits."

Simon sat his father's 1907 Steinway "baby" grand. It took up a place of honor in a corner of the living room and was in peerless condition, its mahogany surface hand rubbed to a satin veneer. He ran his long fingers over the keys, playing a smooth rendition of Guess I'll Hang My Tears Up to Dry while the semi-retired jazz chanteuse, Dorothy Knight – Dot to her many friends, rehearsed the melancholy standard. Once a month the veteran performers living at the Bailey put on an intimate variety show for family and friends in what was known as The Lounge. It was a lovely room with a small stage, forty genuine theatre seats, a professional grade grand piano and tech booth. Located on the same floor as the restaurant and the library, The Lounge was something of a legend in the theatre trade and invitations to the monthly performance were highly prized.

"Nice," Simon said as he played the last note.

Dot blew out a breath and laughed nervously. "You really think so? I'm rusty on that one."

He shook his head. "Spot on. Blimey!"

"You are sweet!" She beamed at him and Simon was struck – not for the first time -- by how drop dead beautiful the fifty something singer still was. Dot was known as an "aristocrat" in the jazz clubs – meaning that Dorothy Knight was so elegant and talented that she didn't do "cute" or gimmicky material. Tall and effortlessly chic, Dorothy Knight could simply stand behind a mike, dressed in one of her killer gowns and sing Good Morning, Heartache, or Skylark, absolutely slaying her audiences.

Even today for a casual rehearsal, Dot wore a sleek black cashmere turtleneck, coffee colored wool slacks and Manolo Blahnik loafers. She wore her ebony hair pulled severely back in a low bun that accentuated her high cheekbones. No stodgy "old lady" jewelry for the African American singer. She wore eighteen carat gold Senso cuff bracelets – the ultimate in modern minimalism and at roughly twenty-five thousand dollars a bracelet, a subtle testament to both her great career and wise retirement investment.

"You're pretty proficient, Piano Man, but don't be afraid to loosen it up a little. Jazz hates following the rules." Dot said, coming to look over his shoulder at the thick songbook on the music rest.

"Don't be such a square?" he offered with a grin.

She laughed, nodding. "Don't be such a square. Hey, they want two. What do you think?"

Simon was flattered that she'd ask his opinion. He cleared his throat, cognizant of the honor.

"Strange Fruit", he said.

She looked genuinely surprised. "It's been a long time. That one needs to be good – really, actually good."

"No worries," Simon said simply. "You're the best."

Dorothy's dark eyes looked luminous as if his words had really touched her and she reached out to squeeze his shoulders. "Okay, son. Let's give it a try."

Simon flipped a few pages until he found the melancholy masterpiece. Dot studied the music over his right shoulder for a moment and then she stepped into the curve of the small grand, nodding.

He let the eerie melody drift up from the keys to meet Dorothy's pure and agile voice.

"Southern trees bear strange fruit.

Blood on the leaves and blood at the root ..."

She gasped as if in pain and leaned against the piano, unsteady.

Simon pushed away from the keyboard. "Dot – what's up?"

"I don't know ... "she admitted. "Could be cardiac."

Simon called 911 after getting Dorothy to one of his father's cranberry velvet sofas. She offered him a weak smile as he sat on the coffee table and held her hand.

"This is what you get with us old girls," she said, with a little wheeze.

"Piffle!" Simon replied. "You probably have the flu."

The singer's beautiful face looked haunted. "Simon, can I ask you something? Something weird?"

"Of course." He squeezed her hand tighter.

"You see ..." She winced in pain and paused to take in a short breath. "My family – we all have the sight. You know what I mean?"

Simon thought for a moment. "The sight – you're a sensitive?"

Dorothy nodded, taking in another shaky breath. "You got it too. I can tell."

"Yes," he said. It was not a time to be coy.

"You sense something's changed over the last couple of days? Something bad is here – something in the shadows?"

Dot winced, crying out a little with the pain. "It's been on me for a couple of days. Something's not right. I'm not crazy?"

"You're not crazy. I feel it too."

"Simon ... worried ..." She paused again to breathe. "I'm worried about ... you."

The intercom by the front door buzzed loudly – one of the doormen letting him know the emergency crew was on the way up.

"Hang on, Dot!" He stood, laying her hand gently on her waist. "I've got to let the paramedics in. You're going to be hunky dory."

By the time he reached the front door, the paramedics had rumbled down the hall from the elevator. They swept in, kind, competent but also refreshingly direct and no-nonsense. It appeared possible Dorothy had suffered a cardiac incident. They would transport her immediately to the ER at New York Presbyterian. Simon appreciated the lack of shadowy mystery.

Dorothy was quickly moved to a gurney and given oxygen. Simon walked alongside the rolling stretcher, holding her hand again. She gazed at him anxiously over the rim of the plastic mask.

"I've called Stanford," he told her, referring to her husband who was, in fact, a pediatric cardiologist. "He'll meet you at Pres."

She pulled down the mask. "Watch ... yourself, Simon. I'm worried ..."

The medic on the other side of the gurney replaced the mask. "Ma'am," he said kindly. "You concentrate on getting oxygen. He'll be just fine."

Chapter Twelve

Number 7 Audley Square's ballroom had once been a space in which the former vampire king, Garnet Petherbridge, enjoyed watching his enemies flayed alive while dining on the odd human servant or tradesmen. Robin had restored it to its full Georgian glory as he remembered it before Petherbridge's bloody coup in the Victorian era. Glittering Waterford crystal chandeliers hung from a ceiling of intricately carved plasterwork in a rich Baroque swirl of clamshells and florets. A massive fireplace of creamy Carrera marble dominated pale green walls. Its mantel and sidepieces cunningly chiseled into a scene of the goddess Diana out hunting with her hounds – a subtle commentary on the house's revenant masters.

For the evening's event, the ballroom had been re-envisioned as both intimate recital area for an exchange of cultural performance and 21st century vampire throne room. A large square of polished wood floor in front of the fireplace had been set aside as a temporary stage. To the left of the performance space were two Queen Anne walnut armchairs for Robin and Caroline. To the right were another set of the opulent Georgian chairs for Ai Di – the Chinese revenant Emperor, his three wives – Baozhai, Liqin and Ninghong – and various advisors. Mere invited guests would sit in traditional rows of chairs in front of the recital space where the view of the performers would actually be far superior.

Robin stood to address the room. It was a spectacular gathering. British vampires were turned out in flawless tailcoats and sensational full-length gowns – historic jewels on full display. Emperor Ai Di – who looked twenty-five but was, in fact, one of the oldest revenants to still walk the earth – was attired in dramatic black and red silk robes of the late Han Dynasty from which he had emerged. His wives followed in kind, dressed in rich traditional gowns of red, black and gold. Emperor Ai Di's advisors and aides were also in traditional dress – some with very elaborate black headpieces that denoted their order of service. The Chinese had an ancient and highly formal royal court long before any Western revenant courts had developed.

He lifted his long-fluted champagne glass in the direction of Emperor Ai Di who responded with a small nod. The elegant glass was not filled with sparkling wine but a thick scarlet fluid.

"Your Majesty, noble queens, honorable courtiers, ladies and gentlemen," said Robin. "We salute the brilliance and ingenuity of Chinese science tonight. Lift your glasses and taste the synthetic blood that will free us all from the need to seek human sustenance."

Everyone in the room lifted their champagne flutes including Caroline who had a Bloody Mary in hers – minus the awkward celery stalk.

"Just not natural!" A voice with a pronounced Scottish inflection cried out from the back of the room where the evening's performers were waiting to take the makeshift recital stage. "It's not natural. It's a kind of heresy, I tell you!"

The convivial energy in the ballroom evaporated instantly. Vampires spun in their gorgeous clothes, immediately on guard. Revenant performers not associated with the disrupter jostled to get away from him. They knew vampire kings did not appreciate ugly surprises and after the brutal reign of Garnet Petherbridge, wanted no part of any political statement.

Robin pushed Caroline behind him, spilling her Bloody Mary across the polished floor. His security forces materialized from their covert positions. Bramwell and Edmund flanked Caroline while Emperor Ai Di's aides formed a perimeter around the royals.

Robin's revenants were poised to take down the speaker when he held up a hand for restraint.

"No – let him speak," Robin said, frowning. "Who are you?"

The vampire crowd broke in half, moving instinctively away from the man who walked forward, towards the recital space. To humans like Caroline, the man would appear to be in his early forties. He was well built and handsome in a "out deerstalking in the Highlands" craggy kind of way. Dressed in a kilt, he was one of the sword dancers Robin had asked to perform for the Hong Kong delegation.

"I be Cam Drummond of Caithness," the man replied evenly, hands on his kilted hips. "And I'm not much for this modern science; I can tell you that."

"You've made that quite clear, Mr. Drummond." Robin raised an eyebrow. "Might you have done it in a less dramatic fashion? You have made an exhibition of yourself and worse -- frightened my wife."

"I apologize to Her Serene Highness." Cam offered a rough bow in Caroline's general direction. She let out a short breath and nodded benignly at the craggy Scotsman.

No preternatural abilities just grace and courage to shield her thought Robin with profound admiration although he kept his expression icy.

Drummond had the grace to look a little abashed. He slowly turned around to see the assembled group of vampires – royals, dignitaries, guests, performers and staff -- staring at him in fascinated dismay. It suddenly appeared that the

Scotsman just realized what he had done. He wasn't just sprouting off his opinion down at the pub as he probably often did. When Cam Drummond turned back to face his king, he no longer looked so confident and he swallowed hard.

"Crikey," he said in a suddenly dry voice.

"Shall I end him?" asked Emperor Ai Di who had moved past the ring of his protective aides to join Robin. The black and scarlet silk of his robes fluttered as he held out an arm. One of his revenants ran to place a sword in his outstretched hand.

"I thank you but no," Robin said, tossing Cam Drummond a baleful glance. "At least, not yet."

The Scotsman swallowed again. "I'll just be ... getting back to my group now."

"Oh, I wouldn't dream of allowing that," Robin countered, rounding on the kilted vampire. Emperor Ai Di elegantly shifted his sword to a strike ready position, his flawless silks rustling softly as he did so.

Cam Drummond took an instinctual step back. Caroline's face skittered from worry to aghast and she moved away from her minders to Robin's side.

"Robin, please ..." she murmured.

He held out a hand, indicating that she be silent. Caroline, wounded at his brusque response, crossed her arms over the Chinese red bodice of her gown, looking both furious and unhappy. The vampires in the room drew in a collective breath and each waited, every nerve ending alert. This would be the moment in which the former vampire king, Garnet Petherbridge, would have offered a terrible retribution – one that might have extended to any unsponsored revenant standing nearby.

"Until," Robin continued, his tone softening slightly. "Until you explain your distaste for synthetics."

Tension in the ballroom flipped to surprise. A few revenants even staggered a little as the anxiety rug was yanked out from beneath them. Emperor Ai Di gracefully returned to a neutral stance, his dark eyes watching Robin closely.

"Explain?" Cam echoed hollowly, his face a grey suet pudding of resignation. He had made a terrible mistake. He would soon be dead.

"You said synthetic blood was a kind of heresy."

"Well, aye," the Scotsman shrugged as if stalling for a moment to collect his thoughts. "Haven't we always had the blood of humans? Isn't that what we are?"

Robin cocked his head to the side speaking in Scots Gaelic – one of his Tylwyth Teg strengths was an immediate grasp of all languages. "And who are you in Caithness, Mr. Drummond? What do you do?"

Cam's blue eyes widened in appreciation. When he replied in kind, his words came faster and more easily.

"I am a fisherman like my people have always been – have my own deep-water boat. I love the sea. I love the north of Scotland – have since I was human."

"And when was that?"

"When Caithness saw many a Viking raid, it was." Drummond's voice strengthened, some pride swelling in the burr of his words. "Lived simple and took little. Still the way."

Robin almost smiled and switched back to English, addressing the room. "Mr. Drummond has told me he has existed in the north of Scotland since the Vikings raided there on a regular basis. He has lived quietly as a fisherman, taking only small amounts of human blood. Have I stated this correctly?"

Cam Drummond nodded. "Aye – 'tis."

"Why have you taken so little from the human population of Caithness, Mr. Drummond?"

The Scotsman looked slightly baffled by the question. "It's just The Way. The natural way. I dinna take much. I don't like to scare 'em and we all just continue to be."

"Do you like them – your human neighbors?"

"Aye!" Drummond brightened. "They be a fine, sturdy group. Always have been."

"And that, Mr. Drummond is the power of the synthetic!" Robin held up the champagne flute with the scarlet fluid. "No need to disrupt the lives of humans --especially ones we count as friends or love as equals. We can coexist."

"But canna that drink keep us?" Cam Drummond asked, genuinely perplexed. "It dinna be real."

"Try it," Robin held out his glass. "Humans in need of transfusions will be using this synthetic and others like it more and more as the science progresses. It's not the complete answer but we revenants need to move forward too."

The Scotsman accepted the glass and took a tentative swallow of the synthetic blood. He winced slightly. "Not terrible. It's no bonny lass after a day at the fair but not bad."

There was a rumble of laughter across the crowded ballroom. Robin grinned at Cam Drummond.

"It's a start," he said in Scots Gaelic.

"It's a start," replied Cam and applause broke out, starting with a handful of the assembled guests and then building to a long, relieved ovation.

"It's going to be a long road," Robin said in perfect Mandarin to Emperor Ai Di under the cover of the sustained applause. "There are a lot of Cam Drummonds out there who are really struggling with the idea of coexisting in a new way."

"Then it is good that we revenants have nothing but time," the emperor replied with a serene nod.

"Your Majesty." Robin bowed slightly to the wisdom of the Chinese royal.

"I will return to my chair, Your Serene Highness. My wives feel more secure when I am with them."

"Can I sit with them? My wife looks highly annoyed." Robin glanced at Caroline who was still fuming by her minders.

Emperor Ai Di actually laughed. "You have wit. Most enjoyable." He bowed slightly and moved off to his side of the recital space, his imperial silk robes swirling about him like smoke. His entire entourage rose to their feet in unison and bowed as he approached.

"Your Majesty, noble queens, honorable courtiers and invited guests," Robin said as the applause died away, "let us enjoy an evening of performances from the West and the East."

He walked back to collect Caroline from Bramwell and Edmund who were both trying very hard not to look amused.

"Darling?" he offered her his elbow.

"You've clearly gotten some very uppity ideas from the Hong Kong delegation," Caroline said. She took his arm and gently steered him so they could both see Emperor Ai Di's three beautiful wives surrounding him with obsequious attention. Ai Di accepted their efforts as his due without any noticeable gesture of appreciation.

Robin, in turn, steered her back to where their chairs awaited them next to the recital space.

"I apologize, Caro. It was a stressful interlude."

"Oh, no worries – for one thrilling moment, you reminded me of my father decrying the inadequate treatment of foot rot at the yearly Sheep Breeders conference."

He smiled at Lady Caroline, forever grateful for her ability to demonstrate grace under the most trying circumstances.

"In the modern vernacular -- I owe you one," he said as they sat down on their matching Queen Anne chairs.

"Yes, you do." Caroline agreed with a nod both to him and to the lavishly adored Chinese opera singers who had stepped into the recital area.

"For example," Robin leaning to murmur in her ear, "you might need my valuable assistance in unhooking your dress later."

"I might," she replied, staring straight ahead at the very formal Hong Kong delegation. A smile pulled at the corner of her mouth, threatening to belie her regal gravitas.

One of Emperor Ai Di's courtiers stood and cleared his throat. "From Southern China, The Yue Opera. They sing from the opera Liang Zhu – The Butterfly Lovers."

The assembled dignitaries and invited guests applauded, Cam Drummond's kind of a heresy forgotten as the two doomed lovers from one of China's oldest folk legends began to sing of death's benevolence and the freedom of the grave.

Oh, the irony, thought Robin.

Chapter Thirteen

Simon sat in a third floor waiting room in New York Presbyterian, watching the snow fall outside its bank of windows. It made him think of Della who would now be in her Snow Queen tutu and heavy stage make-up. He sipped at a lukewarm cup of coffee. She'd probably be at a portable barre somewhere backstage, keeping her muscles warm and ready for the spectacular Waltz of The Snowflakes that traditionally brought Act One of The Nutcracker to an end. He hoped the French guy was up to the challenge.

"Simon!" said a deep voice.

He looked away from the snowflakes. Dr. Stanford Culpepper – Dot's husband of some thirty odd years – stood in the doorway.

"Dot?"

"She's going to be okay," Stanford said as he came towards Simon with an outstretched hand. "Thank you for getting help so quickly."

Simon shook Stanford's firm hand. "Didn't do anything really. What happened?"

"Mild heart attack – what we now like to call a cardiac event. She has a family history of cardiac issues, so I'm not totally surprised." He sat down on one of the sage green vinyl chairs and sighed. "We think we do everything right. Exercise and eat sensibly. We have a martini every now and again but we're old school Manhattanites for Pete's sake!"

Simon sat down as well. "Will Dot be in hospital long?"

"A few days for rest, tests and observation. Overnight for most everybody but as a cardiologist on staff here, I get to stamp my foot and demand special privileges." He smiled tiredly. "She's been stressed lately. Agent wants her to join the line up at a jazz festival at Carnegie Hall in February. Record label has been suggesting a new album – apparently Millennial hipsters are rediscovering jazz singers – and a small tour. She's been feeling kind of pushed. Hey – did she say anything to you about ... well, anything?"

"I'm not sure," Simon replied. "What sort of anything?"

Stanford let out another sigh. "I don't know how to put this exactly but ... you got to understand, Dot's originally from the south. Big, tight knit family. Lots of everything – love, laughs, singing, food, church and ..."

"Haunts?" Simon suggested quietly. "Paranormal stuff."

Dot's husband looked relieved, nodding. "She's always been convinced she has certain psychic abilities. They all do, mind – all of her female relatives anyway. They all claim to see things."

"You don't believe in hauntings?"

"I believe in Dot. If she says she sees something, then I think she saw something whether easily debunked by science or not. She's always loved the Bailey. Says all the ghosts there are charming old theatre people bothering nobody. But lately, that's changed."

"She did mention to me that she feels that a kind of dark energy has come to the Bailey," Simon admitted. "Dot's worried about it."

"You know anything about that? Dot told me she thinks you see too."

"I don't think Dot is wrong if that's what you mean," he said, remembering how his father had warned him to keep the family abilities under wraps. Only attract attention with great music was supposed to be his modus operandi while studying in America.

Stanford nodded again. "Well, that's it then. I'm going to have her recoup at a good hotel and then we're long overdue for a vacation. Some place with a beach and palm trees – no shadows!"

He stood up. "Got to get into surgery. Thanks, Simon. Dot and I both owe you one."

"Nonsense," Simon said. "Merry Christmas if I don't see you before."

They shook hands again. Simon watched the long, lanky doctor head out of the waiting room, wondering what sort of dark energy had invaded the Bailey and why.

He felt his cell phone vibrate in his pocket and pulled it out. A text message from Della came up on the glowing screen – Hey – weirdness continues! The other dancer in my dressing room has disappeared! She was here and all ready, but nobody can find her now. I'm going to cover Arabian if she doesn't show up. What a day! Matinee went okay. Love you!

After the performances concluded – featuring some very jaunty and nimble Scottish dancing from Cam Drummond whose profound relief at not having been beheaded was clearly evident in his exuberant footwork – the invited guests and performers mingled for a little longer, enjoying another round of synthetic blood while the royal houses of Britain and Hong Kong retired to smaller rooms adjacent.

Caroline took Emperor Ai Di's wives on a tour of the house's impressive Georgian portrait gallery before settling into the Green Reception room for an elaborate tea service. Although the wives no longer drank it, they still appreciated the formality and breathing in the rich aroma of the hot tea served in exquisite bone china cups. They pushed little cakes about their delicate dessert plates in a fascinating facsimile of eating. One of the Emperor's courtiers, acting as a translator, relayed the wives' gratitude and enjoyment to Caroline who found herself increasingly charmed by the excruciatingly polite Chinese ladies. They had been delighted by the historical portraiture and had asked, through their translator, interesting and intelligent questions about the various personages on display. The Royal ladies had booed softly while gazing up at the huge picture of the former vampire king, Garnet Petherbridge painted in his human days as an aristocratic Cavalier.

Caroline looked longingly at the chocolate and raspberry cakes. She was starving and yearned to gobble up a plateful but had been warned by Cyril that actually eating in front of the Chinese delegation would be seen as showing off and hence very rude. Grateful that she was, at least, allowed some tea, Caroline sipped the fragrant Oolong and smiled at the Royal Wife Number One, Baozhai while Liqin and Ninghong chatted cheerfully in Mandarin to the translator. This courtier bowed and turned to Caroline. "Your Serene Highness," he said, "Their Infinite Majesties are enchanted by the beauty of your Christmas decorations."

"Thank them for the kind words. They must select the pieces they especially like and I shall have them shipped to Hong Kong."

The courtier relayed Caroline's message to the three queens who responded in a torrent of Mandarin, clearly delighted. Then the revenant aide refocused on Caroline.

"Their Infinite Majesties are most grateful for your very great kindness. They would not like to take such perfectly chosen items from – how to phrase it?" He thought for a moment. "From the beautiful overall effect. But they wondered if you might be willing to accompany them to where such things could be acquired. They have heard much about Knightsbridge shopping and something called ... Harrods."

Caroline laughed and nodded. "I would be honored to accompany Their Infinite Majesties. Everyone should see Harrods at Christmas!"

Robin set down his wine glass. "Agreed. Full disclosure to the public at large still lingers on the distant horizon." Emperor Ai Di sipped his synthetic blood thoughtfully. "And that distant horizon you speak of is a Western one, my friend. Many countries, including my own, are much further away in accepting the idea of revenants. There is much danger to my subjects if the Western vampires rush too quickly into this new understanding."

They were sitting in the small reception room known as the "Chinese Room" as it featured a plethora of Asian art collected assiduously by the Marquis of Southbrook throughout the Georgian era. The highlight of which was a massive imperial yellow and blue Han Dynasty vase that stood like an obelisk -- nearly eight feet in height.

Caroline had been wildly impressed with the dynamic and priceless piece, placing it to the right of the fireplace where it could be appreciated from any angle in the room. Robin had decided to avoid telling her that Garnet Petherbridge had used the vase to keep his ever evolving collection of ... severed heads.

"I am absolutely committed to transitioning at a glacier pace," said Robin. "Why not? As you have noted, all we have is time."

"Agreed," replied Ai Di with a nod. It was immediately echoed by all his courtiers who nodded in unison. "And you will speak to this at the Summit in the Spring?"

"Absolutely."

The Emperor extended a hand and Robin reached out to shake it firmly. The gorgeously arrayed courtiers in vibrant silks applauded softly with fans tapping on their open palms.

"This has been a very valuable trip," Ai Di said as the polite tapping of fans continued. "I thank you for your wisdom and hospitality."

"You honor me, Your Infinite Majesty," Robin said in perfect Mandarin.

He had a moment to savor how all was well for British vampires before the Sword of Damocles dropped.

Chapter Fourteen

Simon took the elevator by the Met gift shop and dropped down to the stage door. He was fortunate that Gustavo, one of the Met's security guards, was on duty that evening. Gustavo had a particular admiration for Della who he considered a genuine heroine of the Latin community and that respect had umbrella-ed over Simon. He allowed Simon to slip in despite some excitement backstage concerning the missing ballerina.

"I think she got family troubles," Gustavo confided to him in a hushed voice. "Let me tell you, her mom is full on-stage mom from hell. Always pushing that poor kid. I think Paige just needed a little break – you know, couldn't take all the stress. She'll be back before final curtain."

Backstage at the Metropolitan Opera House at 30 Lincoln Center Plaza was labyrinthine – a rabbit warren of fascinating spaces. Below stage level one could find massive storage spaces, kitchens, a canteen for artists and staff, offices, workshops for all facets of theatrical production, practice rooms for both ballet dancers and musicians as well as break lounges where old school members of the orchestra regularly engaged in poker games. Dressing rooms for principal artists, soloists and corps circled the main stage on various floors. The stage level itself was vast – one of the most cantilevered in the world. The performance space was ninety feet deep and one hundred and three feet wide. Behind the proscenium were "slip stages" that could hold complete sets for each act of a ballet or opera. The patron side offered three thousand, eight hundred places for ticket holders in a gorgeous fan shaped auditorium dressed in gold and burgundy with the twenty-one iconic Met crystal chandeliers overhead. Above stage level, well-heeled patrons were able to dine at The Grand Tier.

Simon was grateful that Della had given him two or three pretty detailed tours, so he had a vague idea of where he was going. Someone going in blind might become hopelessly lost in the maze of halls and odd spaces. He wondered if there were a few moldering skeletons of first day employees or autograph hounds lying undiscovered in the far reaches of the lower levels.

Figuring Della would already be in costume for Snow, he decided to head straight for the wings. It was easier than trying to circumnavigate floors of dressing rooms. Della, as a soloist with the company had a dressing room nearer the main stage than dancers in the corps. Ballet and opera was still steadfastly hierarchal – star performers had the easiest access to the stage, soloists a little less and the corps or opera chorus had the furthest route to the wings.

Stopped by a polite but firm security woman in a red jacket and wielding a walkie-talkie, he was relieved to discover Gustavo had put him on an all-access list. Feeling a kind of brotherly love born of escaping tedious confrontation, he was deciding to get Gustavo a Starbucks gift card for Christmas as he stepped into the wings of the Metropolitan Opera House.

From the shadows, the Met stage blazed with light, music and the energy of concentrated artists focused on their craft. Nutcracker's Party Scene was still underway – the ballet's heroine Clara was performing a series of pique arabesques across the stage marley as she lifted the Nutcracker toy soldier high to show him off to her party guests.

A professional backstage was a quiet, intense place. Genuine performers who had given their lives to the life with all its technical demands and profound sacrifices, saw the theatre as a sacred place – a kind of church – to be treated with devout respect and obeisance. There was a reverence for a standard of excellence that hobbyists who pursued the arts in community theatre settings would never understand. The tradition of leaving a working light on the stage for theatre ghosts after closing had the power to bring a tear to Simon's eye.

Ghosts – his strange blend of human and faerie blood occasionally made them known to him. Usually, they were just a collection of mindless molecules that went through the same set of motions they had performed in their human existences. Rather like an old film replaying to those who had the abilities to make sense of the energy patterns. As he scanned the darkened wings for Della, he saw one – a grey image of a soprano dressed in 1850s costume reminiscent of La Traviata – amid the waiting dancers and stage crew. The phantom paced by the middle wing, occasionally passing directly through a dancer. She looked as if she were going over her stage movements for an upcoming scene. She looked remarkably like the great Renata Tebaldi, one of the finest lyric sopranos ever to grace the stage. Simon quietly offered her a bow of respect and wished her peace wherever her soul had taken flight. Set back from the wings was a large additional space used for quick change areas, to corral large opera choruses and currently pressed into service as a warmup area for the dancers with four metal portable barres lined up for their use.

Simon spotted Della at the barre nearest the back wing. She was resplendent in the white Snow Queen tutu that glittered with artfully designed rhinestones. Her thick, glossy hair was scraped back into a glamorous French twist with an elaborately jeweled headpiece pinned into it. He had a moment to take in her breath-catching beauty as she executed a slow, exquisitely articulated developpe into arabesque. Della was a ballerina gifted with a huge extension. She possessed gorgeous line, innate musicality and had a natural stage presence that made her the one to watch in any group of dancers. Della had become a favorite of choreographers whether they were re-staging classical rep or setting something brand new. She was absolutely going to be a star.

Della rose to full pointe and made an arc into a penchée, pushing her arabesque line into one long fine needle. When she came up, Simon waved at her. Della grinned broadly and came off the barre.

"Novio," she whispered, hugging him. "No problems with Gustavo?"

"Like me, he thinks highly of you," he whispered in return. "Any luck locating the missing Paige?"

She shook her head. "And it's weird! She was already in full costume 'cause Paige always over prepares. She's got …"

"Mother problems," Simon said. "Gustavo mentioned the stage mom."

A warning note sounded in his head. He thought of the power outage at The Bailey and the oppressive feeling he had of a strange probing presence.

"Della, when did you last see Paige?"

"Like I told security, I left her in the dressing room. I went to grab us some coffees and when I got back, she was gone."

Simon studied her worried face bathed in soft shimmers from the diamond rhinestones in her cantilevered tiara. He glanced at the stage – Clara was being led away to bed by her genteel 19th century mother. Tree growing and Battle scene dancers were finding their wing space. Snow Waltz corps girls were warming up at the barres. A tall Gallic looking man in white was bouncing up and down in a series of changements. The infamous French Guy, Simon guessed. Renata Tebaldi had disappeared into the ethers.

"Promise me you will stay here on the stage," he said, squeezing her hands.

Della frowned, puzzled.

"I'm going to have a bit of a look around." Simon cocked his head towards one of the stage access doors. "Don't go back to your dressing room without me."

"I don't get it. What are you …"?

Simon shrugged. "Wish I knew. Just a bad feeling, darling girl."

"Okay," she said in defeat. "But don't be long. I have to change into Arabian fast after the curtain drops."

He kissed her quickly. "Promise!"

"You are pure loco, my friend," Della smiled a little wanly and tapped her temple significantly with her forefinger.

Then she turned away – as ballet dancers always did – to return to the barre.

Chapter Fifteen

Robin knew something was badly amiss when he saw Cyril Goforth entering the Chinese Room at a run. Like most civil servants, Cyril usually shimmered into a room as P.G. Wodehouse used to note of the impeccable valet, Jeeves.

"Your Serene Highness!" he said. "Please forgive the interruption."

Robin rose to his feet as did the Chinese emperor, Ai Di -- immediately followed by both diplomatic delegations.

"What is it?" Robin cut through the formalities.

Cyril let out an anxious breath. "I ... I don't know quite what to ..."

Robin could see that his Aide de Camp was undecided as to whether he ought to speak freely in front of the guests from Hong Kong.

"We're all friends here," Robin said, his impatience sharpening his tone more than he would have liked.

The equerry looked miserable. "There has been a breach, sir."

"Here at Audley Square?" Robin could hear Ai Di's courtiers unsheathing their swords to protect their emperor. The Han Dynasty weaponry might look part of their glorious ceremonial court dress, but each courtier was highly trained in various forms of martial arts.

"Yes, Your Serene Highness," said Cyril.

"And?" asked Robin.

"And we don't know where the intruder is, sir," the civil servant reported. "We lost a security man. Pryce-Atwater."

"My family ..." Robin began.

"Her Serene Highness and the Princess are under protection," Goforth looked to the Chinese emperor. "As are the other royal ladies."

Ai Di nodded curtly and directed his courtiers to join the force protecting Caroline and the Chinese queens. The delegation left the room at a run, their fierce swords no longer decorative symbols of an ancient culture. Then the emperor turned back to Robin.

"I will aid in seeking out and eliminating the intruder," he said. "It seems clear that someone disagrees with the concept of a new vampire reality."

"Someone with considerably more on the game than our Cam Drummond, I fear," Robin said and looked at Cyril Goforth. "So, where are we at with this?"

Cyril glanced down at his ever-present electronic tablet. "Security is fanning out. Presumed entry point below in the lower level where Pryce-Atwater was stationed. He was decapitated – cleanly."

Robin felt sorrow for the loss of an old court retainer. Pryce-Atwater had been in service to the British court since medieval times. But at least, the decapitation suggested a culprit more understandable to vampires than the entity that had devoured the Blacks and the unlucky Oliver D'Aubigny.

Robin held up a hand to indicate the way. "Let's find this intruder."

　　　　Simon arrived at Della's dressing room out of breath. He had run from stage level and taken the steps to her floor assignment. The workmanlike hallway where her dressing room was located had various dancers in costumes from the ballet weaving about the communal space stretching, chatting or headed off on pre-stage errands. He didn't see anything of a security team effort sweeping the area.

The door had a paper reading Baquero-Flores and Dafonseca taped to it. Paige Dafonseca. A girl with Italian bloodlines. Simon thought about that as he opened the door and stepped inside.

With the long and profitable Nutcracker residence at the Met stretching from mid- November to the end of December, the dancers were free to make their temporary digs at the opera house just a little more homey than usual. Both young ballerinas had identical built-in dressing tables on opposite sides of the room with a shared bathroom on the end. Tools of their trade were neatly arrayed on shelves and in make-up cases. Costumes for the next few performances and civilian clothes hung on a rack.

Theatre folk were generally a sentimental and superstitious group. Della and Paige were no exception. Each had personal items taped to the edges of their mirrors and good luck totems such as Della's rosary beads -- hung from a hook by her mirror – were scattered about to remind each dancer to have a successful performance. Simon smiled when he spotted a picture of Della and himself at her parent's 25th wedding anniversary party in Williamsburg. It had been a summer barbecue on a very hot Brooklyn day. They glowed with good humor and sweat.

As much as he would have liked to gaze at Della's collection of family memories, it was Paige Dafonseca he was more interested in for the moment. He pivoted to look at her dressing table chotkes. Paige had an old program taped to her mirror with First solo! scrawled across it with an arrow to her name, a cheerful affirmation card featuring a determined looking toddler with a melting strawberry ice cream cone that read You've got this! and another motivational image featured a rain drenched model leaping a puddle that begged Dance like no one is watching! Simon winced at the appalling grammar and scanned the dressing table for anything useful.

There was a family photograph in a silver frame standing on one of her shelves along with a Teddy Bear and a couple of young adult novels about a dystopian future filled with gothy teens in chic combat wear. The Dafonseca family of four stood in front of a Pirates of The Caribbean entrance at Disneyland. Simon studied them briefly. Genial, round Southern Italian father who looked genuinely proud of his family. Beaming, sturdy teen-aged boy in a Halo t-shirt. Seriously plump non-Italian mother with socially anxious eyes, an artificially wide smile and an overly elaborate dyed blonde bob with clumsy highlights that tried to project a Taking care of myself is a priority! vibe.

And then there was Paige. Standing in the middle of the picture was the Dafonsecas' golden girl. She was a lovely creature who reflected her Southern Italian heritage with a warm, creamy coloring and black hair that shone with blue highlights. Not as tall as Della but lithe and strong with more than a little curve inherited from both parents. Simon guessed Paige – or her infamous stage mom – monitored every bite to ensure she didn't gain too much weight.

She was smiling, he noted, picking up the picture frame to study the holiday photo more closely, but the joy hadn't traveled up to her large brown eyes. Paige's affect was slightly flat – the dutiful daughter playing her role in a family event.

Pop psychology aside, Simon made the connection he had been looking for – Della and Paige had roughly the same coloring. Fully done up in theatrical costume and face paint, a mistake in identity could be made. He didn't know exactly why he imagined that his Della was the genuine target of an unknown perpetrator but his odd faerie enhancement – as frustratingly irregular and inconsistent as it was – warned him that danger was surrounding the girl he loved.

Chapter Sixteen

Simon returned to the run, leaving Della's dressing room and heading back to the stage where he planned to keep the ballerina in plain sight until he could get her away from the opera house.

He careened past giant Mice and Tin Soldiers who were exiting the stage area to return to dressing rooms to ready for the second act. This told him that Della as the Snow Queen had already taken to the stage for the famous Snow pas de deux. He squeezed through the stage access door as the mighty Mouse King and a few of his rodent cohorts chose the same moment to leave the wings.

Through the black velvet wings and the hand painted legs depicting the snowcapped stone pillars of the ballet's mansion exterior, Simon saw Della tossing off five or six supported pirouettes with her French guy partner. The hot stage lights flashed off the rhinestones on their white costumes creating a blur of theatrical snow and ice. As he always did, Simon felt a flare of pride and respect for the profound artistry of ballet dancers.

He moved closer to one of the middle wings, mesmerized by the fusion of dynamic movement and the soaring Tchaikovsky score. Della held her right leg in a rapier sharp extension in seconde, then pivoted effortlessly into a deep penchée arabesque. Simon imagined he could hear members of the audience gasping at her beauty.

As the French guy – who seemed to be a very elegant Gallic type with a beaky nose and long limbs – took Della's penchée into a thrillingly brisk promenade to the left, Simon became aware of a figure standing even closer the wing -- a ballerina in the distinctive costume of the Arabian divertissement in the second act. He wouldn't have been surprised except that NYTB's production of Nutcracker didn't use additional Arabians behind the principal pas de deux. Their version of the pas de deux was dazzlingly athletic and a showstopper on its own.

Della was supposed to take over the role for the missing Paige. Simon frowned. So, who was this Arabian ballerina? Onstage, Della glided down a diagonal line in a series of little bourrées. The mysterious Arabian rose to full pointe, also bourréeing slightly from side to side as if echoing the steps. Simon gasped out loud when three Snowflakes hurried to their wing for an upcoming entrance and ran right through the Arabian girl as if she wasn't there.

A ghost. Simon moved forward to where the phantom ballerina continued to balance delicately en pointe. All around them the Snowflake corps dancers were assembling in the wings. Soon the Snow Queen would be lifted high over her partner's head and he would carry her off into wings in triumphant conclusion to their pas de deux.

"Paige," he said very quietly, coming up to the spectral figure. "Paige, is it you?"

The ballerina shifted suddenly as if startled and turned to look at him with frightened eyes. As with most ghosts, she moved slightly more slowly than the living as if ether had the weight of water.

And it was Paige Dafonseca. His heart dropped – so she was dead.

You can see me? she mouthed, unable to produce sound. Simon nodded. "Where are you?"

The ghost's outward form shuddered, seemingly about to lose the power to hold together.

"Slip stage," Paige said soundlessly and pointed behind the main stage. Then she looked at him with heartbreaking misery. "Scared."

"Paige," Simon pulled out his cell phone so he could pretend his words were directed to someone on the line – just in case some of the Snowflakes thought he was insane, "you mustn't be afraid anymore. You don't have to stay here."

"Where? Where can I go?" She moved closer to him, sheltering in the circle of his arm that held up the cell phone. Simon felt it as a cold breeze gusting in his direction.

"Look about – is there a light? Perhaps it has been following you?" He spoke of something he had known when he had been dead and existed as one of Hawkesmoor Castle's phantoms. But the light had always eluded him. Later he would learn that his faerie bloodline had kept him at the castle just as legend told of Merlin chaining the White Dragon, Saxon, to the land there.

Paige's form flickered again as she slowly scanned the dark wings. She was losing force and direction. He hated to imagine she would become one of the mindless spirits who wandered a spot, repeating a gesture over and over again.

"You will see a light," Simon told her. "It's a kind of stairway. It'll be all right – there will be people to guide you. People you know. People you know who have gone before."

Paige moved away from him, taking two or three steps but then stopped to look back. "Thank you," she said without sound.

Simon lifted a hand in farewell, watching as Paige was encircled by a shimmering veil of light. She smiled joyously as if being embraced by a loved person not seen for a long while – a reunion and a homecoming. Then she was gone. The stage side returned to shadows and a gentle tapping sound of pointe shoes informed him that the first wave of Snowflakes had run onto the stage. He wiped away a tear that had spilled from his eye and said a private word of thanks that the ballerina was safe.

But now that Paige's shade had found its way to the other side of the veil, it was time to locate her earthly remains. Slip stage she had told him. It couldn't be Act One's party scene set, and it obviously wasn't the current Snow scene. That left Act Two's Kingdom of The Sweets.

The security team might be combing the lower levels for her. That would be the logical starting point to look for a girl who either didn't want to be found because she was suicidal or had been the victim of foul play. Perhaps they were not yet finished making phone calls to her family and friends to discover if she had left the opera house or, maybe, nothing much was being done at all yet. The administration might be hoping Paige was in a local wine bar, knocking back a few Merlots after a fight with a boyfriend. They could just be waiting, praying nothing had occurred that would invite Mrs. Dafonseca to seek legal advice.

Simon left the main stage area for the section that held all the set pieces for each act of the ballet. He ignored the Drosselmeyer's grandfather clock and other pieces of pseudo-Victorian furniture belonging to Act One. It was the sparkling turrets of the Sugar Plum Fairy's palace he needed to search.

NYTB's Nutcracker was a production with all the bells and whistles befitting one of America's greatest ballet companies. It's Act Two set was the sumptuous manifestation of a Victorian child's vivid dream. It was a massive Rococo Christmas cake of a palace with candy cane turrets gilded with gold paint and glass that looked like diamonds under stage lights. The Sugar Plum Fairy's court featured two massive, glittering thrones and an elaborately carved sideboard done in the same bright gilt paint. The Rococo side table groaned with golden platters of shimmering sweets and sugared fruit made of wax, plastic and papier mache.

There was also a whimsical gold gilt carriage pulled by a life-sized dapple grey carousel horse in scarlet leather rigging. Clara and her devoted Uncle Drosselmeyer would head for home in it at the ballet's happy conclusion.

And that's where he found her.

"Well, well, well," said Robin, surveying the attic storage room of Number 7, Audley Square, "this is interesting."

Most of the top floor had been converted into very pleasantly updated quarters for staff members who needed a room for overnight duties, but a couple had been left to contain the unwanted remains of Garnet Petherbridge's possessions. These possessions had either been neatly put away in stacked file boxes or covered in dust sheets.

It was clear that Garnet's boxes had been opened and examined. Boxes had been opened, rummaged through and their lids discarded haphazardly across the hardwood floor.

A sheet had been pulled off a large portrait of Lord Scyon. An Alfred Munnings painted in the 1920s, Garnet Petherbridge gazed serenely out at his viewers – the absolute zenith of English aristocracy and masculine beauty. Lord Scyon – a former Cavalier in service to Charles I – was blond, blue-eyed and almost unbearably handsome. He was dressed in his hunting habit, wearing the colors of the Crawley and Horsham. The aquiline face was intelligent and arranged in a pleasing expression. But, despite the slight smile, there was something cruel, atavistic in the blue eyes.

"Someone has broken into a heavily fortified house to poke through Petherbridge's belongings?" Cyril looked utterly perplexed.

"It is odd," replied Robin, "but after our little MI5 field trips, I'm prepared to believe almost anything."

Before Cyril could respond – several urgent cries went up on or near the main staircase. Robin and Emperor Ai Di instantly pivoted, dashing out of the attic towards the harsh sounds.

Revenant royal security had someone cornered on the second-floor landing. Someone who was shouting incoherently as if heavily inebriated or mentally disturbed. Robin dropped down the staircase two steps at a time until he joined his force on the landing.

It was a human – roughly thirty and covered in fresh blood. He was panicked and disoriented.

"My god – where am I?" the invader cried, swinging his blood splattered body wildly one way and then the other so he could see all the vampires cornering him. "Why am I here?"

Emperor Ai Di readied his sword. "Allow me to dispatch this killer of your loyal retainer."

"Kill?" echoed the bloody human with the pronounced slurring of someone who had been drinking. "What do you mean kill? I don't kill people. I work for the Brit … British peo … people."

Robin frowned. Why would a human be engaging a revenant in this particular house and in particular, why would this human penetrate their defenses to murder? He was a slight fellow in what was once a reasonably decent suit.

Ai Di stepped forward – focused and elegant with his blade. The man almost fainted at the intimidating sight but then recovered as if taking instruction from some inner voice. He righted himself and became combative – surging forward.

"Kill the queen!" he shouted as Robin's security team seized him, preventing any further progress.

The Chinese emperor raised his weapon.

"No!" said Robin and Ai Di instantly halted, drawing down his sword. "Something is very wrong here. Cyril?"

"Your Serene Highness?" Goforth was at his side immediately.

"Contact Sir Geoffrey." Robin waved the royal security force back. "I think it's possible this is one of his."

Chapter Seventeen

Paige Dafonseca was slumped upright in the elaborate open carriage as if her farewell to the Kingdom of Sweets was more than a mere dream metaphor. It was a display – meant to showcase her ruined body in the most dramatic way possible. The ballerina had been gutted – slit open from clavicle to right hip. Her intestines had been unfurled from the massive wound and looped around the decorative carriage finials like Christmas garland.

But very little blood, Simon noted as he very quickly and quietly exited the shadowy slip stage – not wanting to be the person who officially discovered the body. That meant a vampire had probably gone after Paige. A vampire who had mistaken her for Della and for some vindictive reason – probably territorial – was trying to get at his father through him.

He had to protect Della. If he alerted anyone to Paige's body, he'd become officially first on the scene and be the focus of the police inquiries.

In the necessary dark of the backstage, Simon was able to extricate himself from the slip stage with nary a glance from anyone. Snow Waltz was reaching its apotheosis. Della would be finishing her series of pirouettes and preparing to be lifted to the shoulder of the French guy for the final tableau. The young dancer from the company school who was portraying Clara would be in her sleigh heading for the wings and a well-deserved twenty-minute intermission. Once the curtain rang down, the stage crew would move in to switch sets.

Simon was reeling with nausea. The gut wrenching of what he had found was taking its toll. He was going to be violently ill.

And then, it all came together in one huge synchronistic explosion. While Simon retched into a large waste bin on one side of the stage, Della and her Snow court exited on the opposite side to thunderous ovations from an enchanted Met audience. The curtain rang down and stage crew dutifully dove into the Act Two slip stage. Panicked shouts of horrified discovery and despair quickly followed.

Sir Geoffrey Constable accepted a cup of tea from Cyril Goforth. "Thank you for not dispatching him."

Robin and Sir Geoffrey watched as the blood-soaked young man was led away by several MI5 operatives. They were slipping him out a side entrance to awaiting van that would ferry the traumatized man into a secure lockdown for observation and eventual interrogation. He was still in some kind of psychiatric state, fitfully crying out that he was to kill the queen – kill her for the good of all.

"I think it's clear he means my queen," said Robin.

"His name is Fletcher Greenwood," replied Sir Geoffrey thoughtfully. "He was one of my men looking into the Oliver D'Aubigny murder. Good, competent man. No history of nervous complaints or breakdowns. Wouldn't be working for me if he had."

Robin turned to look for Cyril Goforth. "The queen and my daughter are completely secure?"

Cyril bowed in the affirmative. "Yes, Your Serene Highness. Emperor Ai Di and his wives as well."

"Dragos," said Robin. "Now."

Cyril bowed again. "At once, sir."

Robin gestured to a nearby chair and Sir Geoffrey took it, setting his teacup on an occasional table.

"Forgive me for sitting in Your Highness' presence," he said dryly.

"Let us not dwell on frippery," replied Robin, tightening his jaw. "Your man broke into this house to murder my wife."

"That would seem apparent," sighed Constable.

"My shadow monarchy is known – as yet – to only a very select few in the British government. Was Greenwood one of them?"

Sir Geoffrey considered Robin's question and then shook his head. "Fletcher was overseeing forensics on the D'Aubigny matter. He had not been included on the need-to-know about vampires list."

Robin sat and looked to one of his guardsmen, Bramwell. "Any chance that a slight, under-exercised forensic tech could have caught Pryce-Atwater off guard and decapitated him neatly?"

Bramwell stepped forward, bowing his head crisply. "No, Your Serene Highness. I do not believe it possible. Prycey was a sharp lad, sir. No mucking about. He'd only go down to someone as tough as himself – and he was tough, sir."

"Understood, Bramwell. Thank you."

As the guardsman stepped back, Robin returned his focus to Sir Geoffrey. "I think we can safely say someone with an excellent understanding of our kind murdered Pryce-Atwater. Your man was just a stalking horse. If he actually succeeded in killing my wife even better."

Sir Geoffrey nodded dolefully. "We should know soon what Fletcher's evening looked like. The techs are running some data – phone, laptop, cctv feeds."

"You're thinking someone, or something retrieved him earlier today?"

The civil servant nodded again. "And went to work on him with god knows what. Whoever did this would like to set your kind against mine."

Robin let out a weary breath. "Connection to the Blacks and/or D'Aubigny?"

"A very different modus operandi. This was obviously one of yours trying to stir the pot."

Robin said nothing, not wishing to alert Sir Geoffrey to the diplomatic event that had taken place earlier as the M.I.5 man would see it as a hotbed of potential revenant political unrest. Perhaps Sir Geoffrey would be right – there had been quite a few British cultural groups present to showcase their arts and crafts – but that was something to investigate once M.I.5 had officially receded from the house.

"Well," said Robin, "let us reconvene at a more civilized hour once your technicians have reconstructed Fletcher Greenwood's day."

Sir Geoffrey set down his teacup and saucer. "Thames House then – my office. Shall we say one o'clock?"

Robin inclined his head in agreement. "Bramwell – see that Sir Geoffrey and his contingent have all that they require."

"Sir!" Bramwell bowed again as Robin swept from the room.

It was time to have a word with Caroline and then …

perhaps the colorful Cam Drummond, the first fly in the evening's proverbial ointment.

Chapter Eighteen

Robin found Caroline sitting by the fire in their private drawing room. Her lovely face seemed bleached of color and she looked tired as she sipped a glass of white wine.

"I am really sorry," Caroline said, "about Pryce-Atwater." Robin nodded as he sat next to her on the little sofa. He slid an arm around Caroline and pulled her close. "A rotten loss. Just now though, I am more worried about you and Ari. How are you, darling?"

She sighed and rested her head against the curve of his shoulder. "Ari's in bed, asleep. I am … well, a bit gobsmacked by our evening. Lurching from potential folk dancing assassin to genuine assassin has been disconcerting."

Robin kissed the top of her head. "You do know you and Ari are safe, don't you? The lads are on top of things."

"Yes – Swinton and Calders are in the kitchen, swigging some of that synthetic stuff and watching the telly which apparently can be used for security surveillance. Who knew?" Caroline sighed again.

"The house is in lockdown. Lads are doing a complete sweep of the house and grounds. Hopefully in the morning, things can return to something closer to normal."

"Good since my father is arriving to mediate the sheep factions tomorrow. I was hoping for some heartwarming Christmas family meals – not mind the severed heads, Dad."

He leaned in and kissed her softly, almost allowing himself to draw Caroline into something far more passionate. He longed to lose himself in her arms but remembering how exhausted she was, reluctantly drew back.

"I do so love you, Caroline DeBarry Duplessis," Robin said, stroking the side of her face with his fingers. "You won't forget, will you?"

She paused for a long moment as if his words had taken her aback. With a fleeting impression of anxiety, her eyes searched his. "That sounds a bit ominous."

"Well, it's not." He gave her a quick kiss on her worried forehead. "Can't a man – or revenant – proclaim simple worship of his wife without any hidden agendas?"

Caroline threw him a quizzical look and then laughed, clearly pushing past any vague sense of unease. She had another sip of her wine. "Oh – there is something else interesting that I wanted to mention. Not really knowing anything about, you know, the Tylwyth Teg."

"Go on," Robin said, suddenly more alert.

"Well, you know how Ari has been able to do odd things like levitate objects and herself."

"I was told," he replied referring to the powerful Celtic deities who claimed his family's ancient bloodline as one of their own, "that her abilities would develop in her own time but never beyond her capacity to control. Rather like a foal learning to walk and run or a bird to fly, I expect."

"How about ceasing all together?" she asked. "Ari told me earlier that she's been trying all day to do her usual party tricks, but nothing happens. She's rather worried about it but I improvised, lamely, and told her it was absolutely normal."

"Expect it is," Robin kissed her forehead again. "I've got to go anyway. I'll pop in and see if she's still up reading surreptitiously on my way out."

"Thank you." Caroline smiled. "She's pretty much figured out I'm no magical being."

"Caroline, you are the most magical creature I know," he said truthfully as he stood up. "I'll be back soon."

Robin had a word in the kitchen with Swinton and Calders, thanking them for their service and then made his way to Ari's rooms. When Petherbridge's house was updated and remodeled, Caroline had wanted a traditional, almost Victorian children's room for Ari with an antechamber for the nanny or governess.

He slipped inside and saw that Miss Pratt's door was closed. A light under the threshold indicated that the young woman was still up reading or watching television quietly.

"Now to see if Ari has got her nose buried in an Enid Blyton," Robin murmured, stepping into the main room that was his daughter's personal space.

It was a very pretty room done up to Caroline's old-fashioned specifications. He wondered if it was a replica of her old nursery at Hawkesmoor Castle. Large and airy with huge windows overlooking Number 7's extensive rear garden, Caroline had chosen a color scheme of comforting cream, primrose pink and Robin's Egg blue. It was cheerfully used in everything from the drapes to the bedclothes. Even the Georgian wingchairs that framed Ari's small fireplace were upholstered in a 18th Century print of cream and blue.

A little disappointed to find that Ari was fast asleep in the mahogany sleigh bed with Famous Five Go to Mystery Moor lying open by her small left hand, he carefully extricated the book and laid it on her bedside table. In the soft light from the table lamp, Ari's pale skin and rich auburn hair glimmered. She was breathing gently, her right hand resting under her cheek – the very picture of contented and happy childhood.

He gazed down at her, his throat tightening as a sudden wave of emotion washed over him. That forces beyond his control could reach out and hurt this lovely little girl filled him with a cold dread. Everything he was trying to accomplish in the so-called vampire renaissance was to keep her future safe. Although he well understood the allure of possessing unusual skills, he almost wished Ari's Tylwyth Teg abilities would never return. He yearned for her to have an uncomplicated life filled with ordinary joys and disappointments. Ari could go to university, maybe marry a nice lad and help the family run Hawkesmoor Castle. She wouldn't ever have to be ready to defend the human plane as her Tylwyth Teg forebears had done.

A soft meow from the direction of the window seat broke into his worries and he turned to see the little silver tabby stretching up to its paws from its perch on the bench cushion.

"Julian," said Robin quietly and crossed to join the cat. "Settling in?"

The cat waited until Robin had found a seat by the window and then climbed into his lap. He rubbed his head against Robin's chest. Through a series of purrs and meows, Julian let him know how much he appreciated the rescue and he adored Ari who was very kind to him. The cat went on to say that he had stayed with Ari throughout the evening's emergency and that she had been very brave.

"Any sense that this was like Wynford Park?"

Julian rose to his hind legs and nuzzled Robin's chin. "No," replied the silver tabby. "No heaviness. Very different."

Robin stroked the cat's back and let out a long breath. He was unsurprised. It tallied with what he sensed about the incident as well. It had been brutal but not potentially paranormal. As Lord Pwyll, a reigning member of the Tylwyth Teg, he had additional powerful traits beyond those granted to him by virtue of his revenant aspect. Although those were considerably muted by his choice to remain on the human plane, he was able to create a kind of energy halo over Number 7 Audley Square that prevented supernatural intrusion by non-human entities. The only way into the British vampire royal house was by stealth hence the crude attack on Pryce-Atwater.

If there was some sort of connection between the evening's intruder and recent flamboyant human kills, it would indicate complex planning and organization. No random murders by some sort of free agent English Wendigo. If it was all intertwined with the ghastly murders of the Blacks and D'Aubigny part of the overarching campaign, then the goal was destruction of his ambitious royal house. The failure of his mandate to modernize British revenant society would mean a retreat to the old ways. Old ways now keenly watched over by humans at the highest levels of government. They would move quickly to protect their interests.

Fair play, Robin conceded. He'd do the same and might be forced to if the tenuous connection between human and revenant was broken.

He patted Julian's head and stood up. It was time to find Cam Drummond. Maybe the Scotsman had observed something in the run up to the performances.

"Julian, you will come and fetch me if you sense any danger to my girl?"

"Absolutely," purred the silver tabby and as if to prove his mettle, leapt from the window seat to Ari's bed. He settled at her feet, contentedly.

Robin smiled, turning away to go. As he did so, he spied a pile of Ari's schoolwork stacked neatly on a little tea table in front of the fireplace. Miss Pratt had evidently left her lesson notebook on top of the schoolbooks and as a former history professor, he immediately picked up the spiral bound notebook, unable to resist taking a look at what Miss Pratt had planned for the week.

Miss Pratt's handwriting was tidy and well organized. The pages were laid out in large weekly calendar blocks and she filled them with typical plans for simple arithmetic and language skills. Although Ari was six, due to her special linage she was intellectually a little more advanced and did schoolwork of a level usually associated with ten-year-olds. He was very pleased to see an age-appropriate amount of British history scattered throughout the school days. Miss Pratt had even drawn in various heraldic devices representing great medieval English families and colored them with pencils.

About to drop the notebook back on the pile, Robin's eye caught an unusual family crest and he paused to study it. A swan above a yellow shield crossed with black bars surrounded by azure marked with the royal fleur de lis. This denoted a French family of considerable power. Not a crest he immediately recognized as belonging to one of the invading Norman families. Surprising as he was former professor of European history at NYU. As he returned the notebook, he pushed away the nagging notion that he had seen the swan crest before and headed out to find Cam Drummond.

Chapter Nineteen

Simon used the ensuing confusion to leave stage side. Security would be just twigging to the notion that they might benefit from restricting people's movements. He figured he had a very short space of time to locate Della and get her out.

The backstage was in uproar. A wave of panic was rolling over the venerable institution unlike anything it had ever experienced despite a long history of behind-the-scenes drama. Dancers staggered back to their dressing rooms. Ashen faced despite the heavy theatrical makeup, they exhibited various aspects of shock – tears, agitation, fear, anger and completely zoned out.

Keenly aware that he didn't truly belong backstage with the crew and artists, Simon moved quickly and quietly. He'd be one of the first to get rounded up by zealous, undertrained security types. Especially the ones hoping to impress bosses and local law enforcement.

Currently, he guessed the house security would be almost entirely focused on the flamboyant crime scene and sealing it off for the NYPD. Very soon they would decide to start quarantining people for questioning by the authorities. Simon wove through agitated dancers, stage crew and orchestra musicians, hooking behind the massive stage on one of outer bands that linked one side to the other. Unlike the gorgeous audience side with its multi-million-dollar lighting system and lush appointments, the backstage hallways were spartan and workmanlike. It could have been any employee only area of a mall or department store except for the colorful costumes of the milling dancers. He successfully crossed to the other side of the stage to where

Della ought to be waiting and slipped into wings no longer shadowed in darkness. Full work lights were on and the hot white light revealed a deserted space. The Snowflakes must have abandoned the wings and scattered into the hallways once security had invaded the area.

As he predicted, theater security was on the stage assessing the terrible murder. They were being briefed by a man who looked as if he might be the head of them all. A huge fellow with an aggressive military style crew cut, he looked both slightly dazed and energized by the genuine emergency. Simon did not want to attract the man's notice, so he very quietly began to retrace his steps out of the wings.

Although the Nutcracker production had gone silent, the theater was alive with sound which covered any noise he might have made escaping. There was deep rumbling and cacophony of clattering bleeding through the heavy curtain from ticketholders milling in the aisles, unsure of how to proceed. Backstage was shrill and panicked. In the distance, a multitude of sirens were going off. Heavy doors were clanging, indicating the arrival of professional law enforcement.

Simon managed to clear the stage area just before a phalanx of NYPD officers literally blew through an outer door and ran to the stage. In a few minutes they would efficiently lock down the working side of the theater and it would become impossible to get Della out, away from whoever or whatever had murdered her dressing room partner.

Maybe Della had returned to that dressing room. He ran towards the elevators where a group of nervous dancers waited, in various states of costume, for the next car to arrive. Della wasn't among them but her best friend in the company, Olivia, was. She was standing in the middle of them, rising from one pointe shoe shod foot to the other.

Still in her Snow corps costume, Olivia was clearly dazed but happy to see him.

"Hi." She offered him a wan smile. "Do you know what's going on? Is it a fire or something? People are saying the craziest things."

"Clueless – like you," he lied. "Where's Della?"

"Oh, she's with that friend of yours," came the unexpected and unwelcome reply. "They left which is weird because you're, like, here."

Simon felt as if he'd had all the wind knocked out of him. "They left?"

Olivia peered at him, clearly surprised. "Yeah. Della changed and they took off. We've all been released to go home."

Until, Simon thought, the NYPD shut the proverbial door in hopes of bottling up the killer or at least, conducting the obligatory interviews of potential witnesses. If he didn't move fast, he was going to get caught in the dragnet and immobilized for hours.

"Of course," he said, forcing a cheerful note into his voice. "Completely forgot that I was supposed to catch up with them."

The ballerina gave him a slightly patronizing smile that informed him that she felt sorry for what might well be a case of a hapless former boyfriend. "Cool – tell Della I have those leg warmers she wanted."

"Yep!" he said before wheeling around and heading off at a run.

The stage area was probably already being isolated and contained. His only hope was to get to the audience side of building and escape in the crowds. The massive wave of ticket holders would presumably be slightly less of a priority to the police than buttoning up the backstage.

116

It seemed clear to him that Paige's murderer realized a mistake had been made and returned to correct it. This vampire had convinced Della to go with him or her. Even a born and bred New Yorker such as Della could be charmed by a vampire on the game. Their innate beauty and magnetism were part of the revenant survival toolbox. Now that Della had been drawn out of the theatre, she was somewhere in New York City and he had no idea how to track her down. As terrifying as that problem seemed, it was not his first priority. His immediate issue was getting shy of the building.

Simon barreled down a long spartan hallway until he reached a second set of elevators. These were used more often for freight such as costume racks, props and beverage/snack supplies for various social spaces. Fortunately, one was free and waiting so he jumped in, riding it up a couple of floors. He emerged into the service area of a level that boasted a public cafe for the theatre patrons. It shouldn't be hard to pass through to the public side. Often the dancers exited in the same way, looking to grab a snack or a coffee on their way home from rehearsal or performance. Della swore by the cafe's hot chocolate. The kitchen had been cleaned and was now deserted so he was able to slip into the cafe without being seen. It was an elegant little spot to have a drink and a nosh before curtain – crisp white linen and shimmering silverware on a collection of small square tables surrounded by handsome leather club chairs. Since the performance had been cancelled, catering staff were closing out the bar and restocking expensive bottles of wine and spirits into a large, wheeled cart to be returned to a locked pantry. None of them seemed to notice him as he slipped through to the patron side. He paused and coughed slightly, gazing at a posted wine list as if choosing his next purchase.

"Sorry, sir," said a young lady neatly dressed in stiff white shirt and black trousers. "We have to close early. There's a number of great places nearby to get a drink."

"What's up?" Simon asked, helping her to form a memory of him as a Nutcracker ticket holder. "This is weird! Bomb threat or something?"

She shrugged and put a bottle of Bombay Blue Sapphire gin in the cart. "They don't tell us anything. Just told us to close out. You should exit too. They want the house cleared."

"You're right. Thanks." He gave her a wry smile and headed for the sweeping staircase that dropped down to the massive, gilded lobby.

The ground floor was swarming with audience members who were trying to make their way out. It was a mixed society of balletomanes. Prosperous New Yorkers for the most part. Sleek upper East Side women with equally glossy children in tow. The little girls wore velvet headbands and Marie Chantal frocks. Their brothers in flawless blue blazers embossed with their school crest. Fathers who were clearly hedge fund managers or neurosurgeons, rode herd in immaculate bespoke suits and hand cobbled shoes. Hipsters were in abundance as well, festooned in quirkier and somewhat less costly grab. Their studied boredom set them apart from the poorer artistic types who seemed actually enthralled by ballet. Middle class outliers from other boroughs, Connecticut and New Jersey who considered a night out in Manhattan the highlight of their holiday season swirled through the mix as well.

All social classes shared the same disappointment at the Nutcracker's cancellation. They were confused and edgy about the orders to exit the building. Complaints and wild speculation filled the air and echoed around the massive lobby. No one knew what had happened backstage. Most seemed to have settled on the specter of terrorist threat. Simon joined the anxious throngs, his line of nervous patrons moving slowly to the bank of exit doors. The famous foyer with its flamboyant modern chandeliers was alive with sound. Strident announcements from ushers asking everyone to continue to the nearest exit, buzzing tones from worried ticketholders and constant blare from police sirens in the streets beyond wove together to create a kind of 21st century symphony of urban anxiety.

There was a ghost too – in the midst of all the chaos. Simon spotted it mingling with the undulating living. A large, bearded man in a wildly improbable full length raccoon coat. The ghost looked bemused and completely unaffected by the stressed environment. Simon watched as the imposing figure swept up the main staircase with the eccentric dash of a deposed Russian grand archduke. A moment later and the ghost's form spun away into the glittering light of the chandeliers, vanishing in the charged atmosphere.

Simon finally made it through one of the doors. He took in a deep breath of the icy air once he emerged onto the Lincoln Center plaza, profoundly grateful to have escaped the police action so he could try and locate Della. He shivered in the cold and pondered what to do next. He hadn't allowed himself the luxury of panic yet but standing on a wet sidewalk, being buffeted by other escaping theatergoers while cars and taxis hurtled past to their various destinations, he felt close to genuine meltdown.

Then the cell phone in his pocket vibrated. He yanked it out. A text: Varekai ASAP.

Chapter Twenty

His Serene Highness appeared, unexpectedly, in what once had been the house's large servant dominion. The rooms were now very comfortably reappointed as offices and common areas for staff. He found several of his guardsmen gathered in the main staff sitting room, enjoying the fireplace with its large gas fire roaring about artificial oak logs.

"Sir!" they said in surprised unison and snapped to attention.

"Stand down, lads." Robin joined them by the warm fire. "It's been a long night."

"Morning now, sir," Culpeper corrected him brightly. He looked as if he were sixteen or seventeen. In reality, Culpeper had been a revenant since Edwardian times when Petherbridge spotted him at Lord's Cricket Grounds playing for Derbyshire.

"Yes – 'tis that," Robin murmured, suppressing a smile. Bramwell was throwing Culpeper an exasperated glare. "What can we do for you, sir?"

"I'd like a word with Cam Drummond – a member of the Scottish dance group. Can one of you rouse him for me?"

"Oh, the provincial rabble rouser?" asked Culpeper, earning him another roll of the eyes from Bramwell.

"That's the one." Robin found a seat on one of the wingback chairs by the fireplace. "Bring him here, won't you?"

"You think he might be part of what happened to Prycey, sir?"

"No, I do not," he replied very precisely.

"Come along, Pep," sighed Bramwell. "His Highness isn't interested in your priceless insights."

Robin watched the two head off and thought back to the days of Garnet Petherbridge. He had kept his household through indenture, intimidation and terror. There were a few such as the invaluable Cyril Goforth who had always served the British king and continued to do so out of pacts of honour and duty.

When he had become king, he had made sweeping changes to the edicts of service. The DuPlessis royal house tore up previous contracts of indenture, offering competitive wages and housing benefits instead. Those who served Garnet Petherbridge and wished to leave royal service – or were clearly sympathetic to his vicious methods –   were given generous pensions and assistance in settling elsewhere in Britain. The majority that remained in service were genuinely interested in supporting the new royal experiment.

After a bit of a lull in which Robin closed his eyes and enjoyed the warmth of the gas flames, Bramwell and Culpeper returned. Neither of them wore expressions common to loyal retainers bearing good news.

"I don't see Cam Drummond," said Robin.

"He's gone, sir," replied Bramwell unhappily.

"Gone?" Robin raised an eyebrow. "Wasn't the idea to lock down the house?"

"Yes, sir, but apparently the Scottish representatives left just after the performance."

Cyril Goforth glided into the staff room. He was immaculate as ever in a bespoke suit that had replaced his earlier white tie. His ever-present electronic tablet was under his arm.

"I sensed a difficulty," he said demonstrating his acute awareness as a long serving civil servant.

"The Scots have hopped it," Robin announced dourly.

"Were they scheduled to leave so early?"

Cyril's pale and ever youthful brow creased in thought. He tapped open his tablet, gazing at a document on its screen.

"They were registered to stay the night in provided rooms," Cyril said finally. "I have a message here that there was an emergency back home and they needed to be on their way immediately. Profuse apologies all round."

"Who was the designated leader?" asked Robin, betting he already knew the answer.

Cyril sighed as he looked at the glowing screen.

"Unsurprisingly, Cam Drummond."

"Damn," said Robin.

"You think he's our killer?" piped up the eager Culpeper in his bright voice.

Robin glanced his way and caught Bramwell knocking the other vampire guard into guilty silence.

Bramwell coughed, removing his elbow from Culpeper's ribs. "What would you have us do, sir?"

"Nothing for now," Robin stood up and held out his hand to indicate the cheery fire. "Get some rest. We may have things to attend to in a few hours."

Robin and Cyril left the staff sitting room, returning to the main part of the grand Georgian house.

"You don't really think Cam Drummond could get one over on Pryce-Atwater, do you?" asked Cyril once they were clear of the staff rooms.

"No," Robin admitted, remembering the Scotsman. Cam Drummond would be about as stealthy as a bagpipe review. "Still, it's hard to ignore that they scarpered just as Pryce-Atwater met his killer. It would also explain how a terrorist type could have gotten past all my external protections and the guard on high alert."

"How would you like to proceed?"

Robin thought for a moment, then he said, "Gabriel Addington."

Varekai, Simon discovered after a frantic search on his phone, was a Gypsy/Roma word for Wherever. It was also two other things – 1.) an elaborate and fanciful Cirque Du Soleil production and 2.) a restaurant/bar open until 4:00 am several blocks east of the Bailey.

Varekai was just the sort of quirky restaurant and bar that thrived in hipster Manhattan. In keeping with its name, the place was done up like the inside of a particularly prosperous Gypsy wagon. Richly colored walls of red, gold and indigo were adorned with gilt framed examples of antique hand woven Eastern European rugs of complex design. Simple, dark wood furniture, copious but muted lighting, Gypsy jazz playing from hidden speakers and huge three-sided gas fireplaces that dominated the bar area and dining space all combined to create an atmosphere both exotic and warmly welcoming. In a corner by the bar was an actual Gypsy caravan restored to its full, vibrant 19th century glory.

At another time, Simon would have been charmed by it all. He scanned Varekai's ornate dining room, anxiously seeking a glimpse of Della. An enticing venue in a city filled with ravenous people with lots of disposable income, Varekai was humming with business. Animated diners jammed the tall ladderback chairs at tables draped in scarlet linen. The adjoining bar to the right of the reception desk was standing room only.

He stood next to the gold gilt reception desk, shivering in inadequate clothing for a pricey Manhattan watering hole. A few diners at a nearby table threw him glances, assessing if he was someone important enough to flaunt the tacit dress code or just a clueless university student. Their disinterested return to their conversations indicated that they duly dismissed him as the clueless student.

A waiter approached. Although the young man possessed the Peregrine Falcon features of a genuine Slav, Simon had a moment to be glad that he was not costumed as if cast in a roadshow production of Esmeralda. The waiter wore the standard NYC wait staff uniform of basic black with a long apron tied at his waist. His name tag pinned on the tidy black Oxford shirt read Andrei.

"Mr. Dashwood?" he asked politely.

Simon raised an eyebrow. "Yes?"

Andrei indicated a direction to Varekai's mid-section. "Your party is by the second fireplace, sir."

Simon darted forward, nipping around other waiters and between the packed tables. He thought his heart would seize up and stop when he spotted Della sitting at a small table next to the roaring artificial fire. She looked unharmed and had a glass of red wine in front of her.

There was a companion at the table – a thin, lithe man in his late 20s. Pale with long thick dark ringlets and a well-maintained goatee, he was dressed like a Russian gangster in black leather and cashmere. Silver rings glimmered on his fingers as he saw Simon and stood up from the table.

"Del – you, all right?" Simon demanded as he came up, ignoring Della's tablemate.

Della smiled at him. "Oh, yes! Alin has been great – thanks for sending him."

"Alin?" Simon frowned. "I didn't ..."

"Dragos," interjected the Eastern European in a rich Carpathian accent. He gave Simon a brilliant smile. "An associate of your noble father."

"My father?"

"Yes," Alin glanced pointedly at Della who was sipping her wine. "I was asked to be of ... assistance if needed."

Della smiled again. "I really appreciated getting out of the theater so fast. I was rushing to change into Arabian, and everything just got crazy. Someone said the tech crew had been shouting, that something terrible was happening and everything was cancelled. Alin appeared and said you asked him to help me. Do you know what happened?"

"No one's texted you?" he asked, wondering how much the New York Theatre Ballet now knew about Paige's murder.

Della shrugged and sipped her wine. "Can't find it. Don't yell at me – I know it's bad to be without a phone in the city, but I'll worry about it tomorrow. Probably in my dance bag somewhere. So, do you know why they cancelled?"

"Oh, just a bomb threat or something," Simon murmured, still staring at Alin Dragos, trying to assess the other young man's veracity. The handsome Eastern European shrugged too and returned Simon's frank stare with an expression of bemusement that informed him that Alin Dragos knew exactly where Della's phone was located.

"Could we speak?" asked Alin, raising an eyebrow.

Simon broke off his gaze and turned to the ballerina. "Dell – I'm going to borrow Alin for a sec, okay?"

"Family business?"

He nodded, grateful that she had offered the perfect excuse. Della gave him a knowing look. "My family's restaurant always has something up too. Go – I'll stay with the cozy fireplace with my wine."

"This way," said Alin, indicating a direction away from the patron side of Varekai.

The tall Eastern European led him to a small room off the main dining room. Completely kitted out as a fortune telling parlor, it was far from the typical psychic shops of spangles, palm reading signs and Walmart religious figurines. Varekai's parlor was flush with heavy 17th century antique furniture, leather bound books and rich, heavy draperies. Simon recognized a genuine Victorian Sarouk Farahan carpet from Persia underfoot.

"What can I say?" shrugged Alin loosely. "My mother still likes to read the cards sometimes. She has the ..."

"How do you know my father?" Simon cut in with a bluntness that was unusual for the former 18th century young man.

"Your father – His Serene Highness of All the British Isles," replied Dragos, raising an eyebrow. "He is well known to us – the King."

"And just who are you?"

"Sit ... sit," said Alin indicating one of the priceless chairs. "I get it. You are worried about the pretty girl and I don't blame you, you should be. Sit – we'll talk."

Simon reluctantly sat and pondered what his next move should be if Dragos proved to be the murderer of Paige Dafonseca. Could he possibly overpower the Romanian and get Della out of the restaurant? What if Dragos had associates scattered throughout the place?

"I am a Gypsy," Alin said, once Simon had perched on a chair. "My family are Gypsies. We have a long history and many secrets – like the revenants. We know them. They know us."

Simon frowned. "Was it a vampire who killed ..."

"Sometimes," the Romanian ignored the question, "sometimes the Gypsy has been of assistance to the vampire. Sometimes as a slave, sometimes if the price has been right but not so much anymore. Times have changed."

"As much as I appreciate the history lesson and you getting Della safely out of the theatre, I really ought to get her home."

Alin shrugged casually as if Simon had made good sense. "Okay – then you die."

Simon stood up abruptly. "Is that a threat?"

"A very long time ago your father did a great kindness for my family," Dragos continued, his grey eyes locking onto Simon's. "We never forget. We will always repay this debt. Your father – may he reign forever – has asked for our assistance."

Simon let out a short breath and sat down again. He felt both validated and dismayed.

"So, there is danger?" he asked finally. "I have been followed. Della was supposed to be mur … umm, the one tonight."

Alin nodded. "Your father does not know who or what yet but there have been … incidents in England. He wishes you to come home immediately. I am here to see that you go."

"I can't just leave Della with a killer after her. I won't do it!"

To Simon's surprise, Alin Dragos seemed to agree. The Gypsy nodded again and leaned forward, resting his elbows on the fortune casting table.

"Your father does not know about the murder or whatever's been skulking about your building in the last day," he said and waved a hand at Simon who was about to ask another question. "Gypsies know things besides I was checking out your place – security recon – when the power blew."

"What ..."

"You shouldn't leave patio doors open, my friend," Alin's grey eyes widened in bemusement. "Don't ask – we Gypsies have our ways."

Simon tried to imagine how Alin Dragos managed to get to a rooftop deck in a 21st century secured building in Manhattan. He gave up and concentrated on what Alin Dragos might have discovered in the Bailey.

"Did you feel that presence too? As if it was overhead searching for a way in?" Simon shivered involuntarily.

"Yes – very heavy stuff. Like nothing I've ever encountered, and I've encountered a lot. I think the protections your noble father put over the building are the only reason it didn't get in. Like a shield, you know."

"Yes, a shield," Simon murmured. He had no idea his father could put supernatural forcefields around things but then, his dad had traveled back to the 18th century to rescue him from brutal murder. Clearly, his father wielded enormous personal powers granted to him by his strange revenant-Tylwyth Teg bloodline.

"I don't think it killed the girl though. That was vampire – old school," Alin said with a shudder of his own. "Like 12th century old school."

Simon frowned. "I found the body. You couldn't have known how Paige was killed."

"We Gypsies ..."

"Have our ways, I know," interjected Simon with some frustration.

"Actually, I have a cousin in the NYPD. He gave me – how you say? – the scoop." Alin made a face. "Sorry, bad choice of words. Poor girl."

Simon let out a short breath, remembering Paige's ghostly figure as she stepped into the golden light. She had known terror and pain, but Paige was now surrounded by love and at peace. His own time haunting the byways of Hawkesmoor Castle had taught him that the universe was a vast, cantilevered and enigmatic thing. Like snowflakes and fractals, there was an order, an intelligence to it that glimmered just beyond human understanding.

"So, I can't leave Della," he repeated. "How do I keep her safe until my father can deal with whatever is going on?"

"The vampire or vampires that killed that girl are fast, fearless and experienced – you know what I'm saying?" Alin said with a sobering seriousness. "Faster than you. You know what I mean?"

"You're saying we can't outrun it, can't reason with it and we can't scare it." replied Simon, his voice going dry with the sudden realization of what he had brought into Della's life.

"I like your brain – very smart," Dragos tapped his temple. "You are good at puzzles. I can tell – it's a Gypsy thing. I've got a plan – kinda simple, kinda complicated but it ought to …"

The fortune telling parlor went black and all electrical hum stopped. Dismayed voices from the adjoining restaurant informed Simon that the power was out all over the building.

"This old one is faster than I thought," Alin hissed in the dark. "We have to move!"

But Simon was already on his feet, heading back to Della who had no idea they were pawns in some internecine blood feud that even his father didn't understand yet.

Chapter Twenty-One

The only light in Varekai came from the gas fireplaces with their large artificial gas flames and distant streetlamps beyond the foyer's glass windows. For a restaurant filled with prosperous New Yorkers, it was strangely bereft of cell phone flashlight apps and screen glow. Simon heard startled voices all around him in the near dark complaining that all the cell phones were down as well as if something had cut off Varekai from the rest of New York.

No one seemed to have remained in their seats. The floor space was jammed with spooked restaurant diners and staff who were speaking all at once in a variety of tempers – some irritated, some on the verge of panic, some stoic and others bossy. It reminded him eerily of the theater after Paige's body had been found and the performance cancelled – a human symphonic crescendo. He didn't want to add to it by calling out Della's name and alerting any apex predators to where she might be found.

He remembered she was sitting near the second fireplace, so his trajectory wasn't too difficult to plot. Darting around the milling people, he was conscious that Alin was on his heels. From near the front of the restaurant, one of the restaurant hosts was asking patrons to stay calm as the power outage was investigated. He promised complimentary wine and soft drinks would be served soon.

Nipping around the glowing fireplace, he dove at the small table where they had left her sipping her wine. The light from the fireplace revealed the table as abandoned. Della was gone.

Momentarily stunned at her absence and what that might mean, Simon almost missed the shimmer of movement in Varekai's foyer. The bar's fireplace threw just enough amber light for him to see two shadowy figures, seemingly dressed in … Simon squinted in the poor light and tried to make sense of it … seemingly dressed in medieval surcoats. There were some eccentric New Yorkers out and about but very few chose medieval military garb to swan down a Manhattan street. One of these must have slaughtered Paige Dafonseca – Alin's 12th century old school vampire. There was something in the ease and confidence of manner that reminded him of a hunting lion. These were apex predators tracking prey and intent on correcting their mistake at the theater.

Varekai patrons – disoriented in the dark and naive to the supernatural – had not yet noticed the restaurant had been invaded by monsters. Then a man stumbled around a chair and inadvertently knocked into one of the invaders.

"Sorry, pal" he said with the slight slur of someone who had downed a couple of martinis. "I can't see …"

The surcoated revenant with a brutal but undeniable grace, seized the New Yorker's head, snapped it almost all the way around and tossed the body aside like an apple core. The cracking sound of the man's neck breaking cut through all the nondescript chatter. There was momentary stunned silence in the front of the restaurant and then the screaming started, alerting the rest of the diners that Varekai had just become a death trap.

Simon became aware that something or someone was yanking insistently on the hem of his trousers. He bent down in curiosity and found Della on the floor as if she had crawled across the floor to find him. She grabbed frantically at his hand and pulled him after her. Elated that she seemed to be all right, he followed her, crouching low to the ground. They scrambled away from the fireplace in the general direction of a what Simon remembered as the restored Gypsy wagon.

The dark had become both claustrophobic and sheltering. Varekai diners were panicked, trying to find an escape route in the blackness and jostling around the restaurant tables like spooked cattle in a railcar. Most of them had no idea why it was so urgent to leave the restaurant. They just knew that they had to get out.

Simon and Della used the chaos to seek out the Gypsy wagon. She had clearly been there before, pulling Simon up the little stairs and into the caravan. Once they were inside, she closed the small painted door and latched it. They fell down onto the carpeted floor and hugged each other fiercely. Too frightened to talk and risk being found out, they got as low as they could on the floor to stay clear of the caravan windows and hunkered down, breathing fast – listening to the anguish as Varekai's patrons struggled to get out.

It didn't take long before the terrified din began to ebb. Simon wasn't sure if that meant most everyone in the restaurant had successfully managed to exit to the street outside or that most everyone in Varekai was dead. He wasn't about to stick his head out and check. When Della inhaled and seemed about to say something, he put his hand against her mouth.

There came a series of disconcerting bangs amid high pitched clatter of shattering glass and falling silverware. Simon guessed the revenants were turning over tables, searching for them. He wondered where Alin Dragos had got to and hoped the lanky Romanian was all right.

"Damnation!" came a hoarse voice in English accent. "This was for naught."

Della jumped at the words and Simon pulled her closer to him. She had no idea that these creatures were specifically looking for her.

"Rare that our senses are victim to misrule," said the other. "I still smell ..."

"Aye – I feel it too."

Simon heard them fan out with heavy footsteps through the rubble. They were continuing to search for their prey. Cabinet doors in the bar area were flung open and bottles swept to the ground with cascading crashes that seemed to buffet the caravan. In another moment they would decide to have a go at the old Gypsy wagon. Della had come to that conclusion too and she was trying desperately to keep tears from developing into outright sobs.

The Gypsy wagon's steps creaked as one of the vampires stepped up and tried the door. It rattled violently on the old latch. Simon put a hand over Della's mouth as she started to give way. He pulled her into a protective embrace so she could bury her face into his chest and pondered his options when the little garish door broke open. He could hurl himself at the vampire and hope the surprise would distract it. Maybe Della would have a chance to escape while they killed him.

The door banged back and forth on the ancient metal latch. Another barrage and it would shatter, revealing their hiding place to the vampires.

Sirens were now wailing in the street, getting closer. One of the fleeing diners must have managed to call for help. For the first time, Simon had the giddy sensation that they might survive the attack.

"Leave it!" barked the first vampire who had spoken. "No more disasters."

"I can handle human intervention. We cannot fail the ..."

"We have already done too much," spat the vampire. "Come!"

The step squeaked again as the revenant jumped off it to follow the command of his superior. They clattered through the debris, towards the kitchens where they could avoid the bright spotlights of the New York police. Varekai now seemed quiet compared to approaching din outside in the street.

"Oh, my god," sputtered Della into Simon's shirt. "Oh, my god – what the hell was that? What the hell?"

Before Simon could frame a reply, the antique latch on the wagon door finally gave way and crashed with a metallic clatter. He and Della jumped at the harsh sound. Simon got ready to launch himself at the intruder.

The door swung open and Alin Dragos appeared in the threshold. He looked grim but unhurt by the vampire invasion.

"Time to go," he said. "My family will talk to New York's finest."

Chapter Twenty-Two

The Chinese delegation from Hong Kong left Number 7 Audley Square with the formality that marked its royal house. They swept from the Georgian porte-cochère to a waiting fleet of gleaming black Rolls Royces and Range Rovers. Dressed in their wonderfully dramatic Han Dynasty robes, they seemed to be sailing away like wondrous Chinese junks.

Robin was enchanted by his daughter, Arianrhod, who stood at attention between Caroline and Miss Pratt. The little girl was transfixed, watching the departing Chinese royalty and their courtiers with wide eyes, barely breathing. She was normally rather a levelheaded girl more interested in horses and books than by her extraordinary life as a modern-day princess. Inured to fancies, she preferred a good mystery story and a trip to the National Portrait Gallery. However, the majestic Ai Di and his beautiful wives had captured her imagination and left her gobsmacked.

He also caught Ai Di's wives gazing at his daughter. Far too polite to stare, they glanced at her with surprising longing. These momentary expressions were swiftly masked as they followed their emperor to the waiting cars. He understood that a vampire king with a biological child was an unknown construct within the world of the revenant. Vampires created "bloodlines" by turning selected humans into more vampires. They were unable to create new life. He saw that Ai Di's wives – creatures of far earlier eras – might long for children of their own. What would have been their traditional role in their human time had been taken from them. They obviously loved and respected Ai Di. It would be a great sadness to them not to be able to offer him a child and heir – a private burden that Ai Di would never be allowed to see.

Ari would seem a miracle, and he had to admit, she was a bloody miracle. She was a beacon lighting a path where revenant kind might travel – child of the Vampire King of All the Britons.

After the Rolls Royces pulled away, Arianrhod ran across the walkway to her father. She was beaming, breathless with excitement.

"Daddy," she asked, "can I have a Han dress too? A yellow dress? Please!"

He laughed and threw an arm around her young shoulders.

"I expect we could ask Father Christmas for one."

"Father Christmas would have to understand that I am a princess," Ari replied reasonably. "I do need a few royal dresses. Do you think he could change my hair to black? I think I will need that too."

"I'm guessing Father Christmas rather likes your carrot top." Robin ruffled her thick, wavy red hair. Ari frowned but didn't look too dismayed. She was a sensible girl.

"Drats," she said.

"If I'm lucky," murmured Robin kneeling down a little so he could look her directly in the eye, "Father Christmas will save me and bring you a Stubben child's saddle. They're hideously expensive."

Ari brightened at his words and was about to reply when Caroline's voice came across the expanse. "Time for your riding lesson!"

"Eerie, isn't it?" Robin said. "He must be listening."

Arianrhod giggled and threw her arms around his neck.

"Major Alanwood says I can ride Rupert today. He's practically a horse!"

136

"You'll be following your mother into the show ring by summer," Robin predicted and stood up as Miss Pratt appeared to take charge of the little girl. The young nanny offered Robin a polite smile and bobbed a curtsey.

Miss Pratt was an unremarkable young woman, he thought, as he acknowledged her obeisance. That in itself was remarkable as vampires were usually magnetic creatures. It aided in developing quick confidences with humans. Miss Pratt must have been off with her nose in a history book when the cup of magnetism was passed around. She was thin and colorless. Dressed simply in a tweed skirt and sweater created in the most unbecoming shade of rust, she was the very image of a governess.

"Come along, dear," Miss Pratt said kindly to Arianrhod who obediently stepped away from Robin. "You have to change into your riding habit."

"Bye, Daddy!" Ari sang out as she turned to go with the nanny.

"Darling?" Robin called after her. The little girl paused and looked back expectantly. "Being good with horses is better than all the magic in the world."

It took a moment but then comprehension crossed her large green eyes. She smiled brightly and nodded before turning to run to her mother. Caroline mouthed Thank you at him before she took Ari off to change into her riding clothes.

Cyril Goforth returned from conferring with some of the guardsmen. He looked thoughtful and officious all at once.

"Your Serene Highness, Gabriel has tracked down an address for Cam Drummond in his archives. Coastal village in northeast Scotland. I've booked tickets on British Airways to Inverness and then on to Wick."

"How many did you reckon?"

"I assumed you wished to travel quietly. Just two of the lads, sir – Tinley and Brown. Steady, very experienced."
Robin nodded. "And Dragos?"
"A bit of bother but Alin Dragos says he has it under control." Cyril replied, checking his tablet. "Simon is perfectly well although Mr. Dragos has taken the precaution of removing him from Manhattan for the time being."
"Simon comes home immediately. Have Dragos put him on the next flight."
"Apparently there is a young lady involved, sir, and your son will not leave her unattended."
"Damn it!" Robin swore, cursing the decision to send Simon off to New York without regular minders. "I'll speak to Dragos now."

Alin Dragos had extricated Simon and Della from Varekai before the NYPD could lock down the scene. It could have been far worse. Other than the poor man who had the misfortune to stumble into the invading vampires, no one else had been hurt or killed. The restaurant itself was a nightmare of broken tables, tableware and abandoned personal belongings. Several members of Alin's family were out on the sidewalk talking to the police, offering a rational story about some kind of opportunistic invasion robbery gone wrong.
He took them out through the back of the restaurant where several of his cousins were patrolling the alleyway for any signs of a vampire. With an all clear, another cousin rolled up in a Mercedes Benz G-Class SUV and whisked them out of Manhattan to Brooklyn.
The Dragos family house was a large, fully detached house in the leafy Brooklyn district of Prospect Park South. Huge by most standards, the seven thousand square foot Victorian

house rambled over one acre with all the eccentric turrets and wrap around porches so beloved of the time. The interior was a tribute to the Beaux Arts craftsmanship of that era with lavish use of mahogany and walnut, whimsical glassworks and ornate plaster. Although Varekai was a richly appointed nod to the European Gypsy legacy of colorful caravans and nomadic life, the Dragos house more resembled the sumptuous fortune telling parlor in the restaurant's rear. It was filled with fantastically rare antiques and textiles beautifully arranged at the apex of taste and discernment. Not at all what Simon expected of a Gypsy household.

Alin noted Simon's impressed expression as they entered the foyer of house with its massive, curving double staircase and Lalique chandelier. He shrugged eloquently.

"We traveled across Europe performing for the crowned heads," he said and then whispered conspiratorially, "and afterwards, stole everything that wasn't nailed down!"

Simon took in a sharp breath and then saw Alin's cousins who had accompanied them on the drive to Brooklyn burst into laughter. One of them slapped Alin on the shoulder and spoke to him in Rom. Alin answered back with a laugh of his own and his jovial cousins strolled off down a hallway.

Della – quiet and trembling all the way from Varekai to Brooklyn – suddenly sagged at the knees and began to fall. Both Simon and Alin leapt to support the ballerina who had fainted.

Alin picked up the slender dancer. "We need to get her warm."

He quickly carried Della into a room off the grand foyer – a drawing room lavishly decorated for Christmas complete with roaring fireplace – and laid her on a couch near the heat. Then shrugged off his black leather coat and draped it over her long frame.

Simon knelt and took her cold hands in his. His voice broke when he spoke, "Della, I'm sorry. This is all my fault … my father, my family ..."

The ballerina opened her eyes, trying to focus on what he was saying. "I'm just so tired, Novio," she murmured.

"Your family couldn't have known. Scary."

"My father is the ..." Simon began.

"She's going to be all right, my friend," interrupted Alin, tapping him on the shoulder. "Let her sleep and you must come with me now."

"I can't just leave Della after what bloody happened."

"We are well protected here. My mother will watch over her." At his words, a very elegant lady drifted into the room. She was tall and serpentine like Alin. Pale as alabaster, Mrs. Dragos was flawlessly dressed in a peacock blue silk dress and ropes of diamonds. Her glossy blue-black hair was coiled ingeniously around her head and accentuated her high, angular cheekbones.

Mrs. Dragos smiled at Simon. It was surprisingly warm. He felt almost intoxicated by her presence and interest as if she were projecting some kind of energy field.

"You are your father's son to be sure," she said in her rich, contralto voice. "We – the Dragos – are always in debt to your father. I will see that your ballerina has tea and some food. Go with Alin."

Simon allowed himself to be led away by Alin, wondering if he too was suffering from the aftereffects of the Varekai vampires. He felt unsteady and exhausted. If only there was a couch by a fire for him. Tea and food sounded good too.

The Dragos house was a Victorian labyrinth of hallways, rooms and anterooms. Normally more alert to his surroundings, Simon felt too weary to keep track and was resigned to following Alin through the Beaux Arts masterpiece.

"We are here, my friend," said Alin with a smile, indicating the library. It was a designed in a dazzling octagonal shape with rows of mahogany bookcases filled with leather bound books embossed with gold gilt. "Big house, no? When my family first came to America in the 1930s, your father offered us rooms at The Bailey."

Simon nodded. "The debt?"

Alin shook his head. "We were grateful for that, of course, but our debt to your noble father is far greater than that." Before Simon could inquire further as to what his father had done for the Dragos Gypsy family, Alin crossed the intricate parquet floor and pressed the spine of one of the books. There came a swooshing sound and one of the bookcases slid open to reveal a secret room. Ultra-modern, this room was a hidden bunker with seemingly CIA level computer banks and optics. More Dragos cousins sat at workstations monitoring complex graphics and algorithms. Some of them spoke quietly into headsets. Simon heard smatterings of French and Russian.

"We do lots of things here," Alin shrugged loosely. He pointed to a wall with a bank of shimmering screens. "Bit coin mining – very very profitable. My cousin Mihai runs that. It's new for us and we start small but growing every day, my friend."

"Alin," said Simon, "why am I here?"

"Oh, yes!" Alin replied as if he'd momentarily forgotten and pointed to a small room made of glass panels. It looked like someone's private office inside with a desk and a sleek computer. "In there, my friend."

Simon let out an annoyed breath, walking over to the glass room. He pulled open the heavy door and stepped inside. The room was completely sound proofed. All noise from the outer area was magicked away, leaving behind an odd stillness – a genuine vacuum. He turned around, wondering what he was supposed to do or what was supposed to happen.

Suddenly one of glass panels came to life. It flared into sharp colors and formed a coherent shape – a picture.

"Dad!" cried Simon, never so glad to see his father.

It was a full-length screen, slightly larger than life. His father stood in front of his Audley Square desk, offering his son a comforting smile.

"Hello, Simon – sorry, it's very late where you are. We've been having some trouble on this end and apparently, it's spilled over to America," said Robin, crossing his arms and leaning back against the desk. "Better if you could come home."

"Is this some kind of bloody territorial fight? Someone wants your job?"

"We don't really know as yet," his father replied with a short sigh. "But it's definitely a serious threat and we're on the game. Can you come home? A ticket will be at the airport waiting for you."

Simon shook his head. "There's … Della. The ballerina. I was hoping to introduce her to you when you came for the recital. She's really lovely, Dad. You'd like her. Anyway, there was a murder – my god, it was awful – at Nutcracker last night and it was obviously meant to be Della. I can't just leave her."

His father looked thoughtful. "Understood."

"And then they tracked her to the Gypsy restaurant! Two weirdos even for vampires and very determined."

Simon saw his father straighten slightly and widen his eyes in interest.

"Weird? How so?"

"Used an old dialect and wore what looked like leather surcoats," Simon said. "I say old as someone who lived in the latter half of the 18th century."

"Point taken." His father looked unhappy. "I wish you would come home. Perhaps she would enjoy a trip to London for Christmas? You both would be safer here."

"Dad," Simon tried to keep the frustration out of his voice, "bring her to Vampire Buckingham Palace for Christmas?"

"Might be preferable to death by vampire in a New York ally," Robin let out a breath as he came to some sort of decision. "All right. Here's what I want you and … Della, is it? – to do."

"Yes – Della."

"The Dragos family are very very good at what they do. There isn't much about our particular universe they don't know about and haven't dealt with." His father's tone softened. "You can trust them implicitly. I want you to listen to Alin and sit tight. He and his family will keep you safe until …"

"Until this is all over?"

His father smiled. It looked a little thin to Simon. He realized that whatever was going on – territorial war or something else – had the revenant King of all the British Isles genuinely worried.

"Yes – until this is all over."

Chapter Twenty-Three

The British Airlines flight for Inverness took off into a cold, clear December sky. It was not a crowded plane, allowing Cyril to book a whole block of seats. This made the trip far easier for the guardsmen, Tinley and Brown, to keep a quiet, competent eye on the other passengers – seemingly a nondescript blend of business commuters and tourists.

"Sir Geoffrey successfully rescheduled?" asked Robin, settling back into his airline seat.

Cyril Goforth nodded. "Apparently, Your Serene Highness, they are still trying to debrief Fletcher Greenwood. Greenwood's wife was able to confirm that he failed to return home after work. She stressed this was unusual as Fletcher Greenwood is a man who rarely changes his habits. He always takes the tube home to Putney Bridge."

"So, plenty of spots where he could have been waylaid." Robin sipped a cup of tea.

"Unfortunately, yes, sir. Very difficult to pinpoint even with all the CCTV cameras in the city."

"No mention of any strange characters in surcoats, I suppose?"

"Regrettably not, sir."

He turned in his seat to look at his equerry. "So, what the bloody hell is going on? Random murders by what appears to be some sort of monster. Fletcher Greenwood turned into a loud but ineffectual assassin – presumably to rattle me. Two antique vampires tracking Simon's friend and committing a flashy murder – presumably to rattle Simon into the open or to draw me to New York, away from my base of power."

"Some sort of territorial coup, sir?" suggested Cyril as he opened the leather cover of his electronic tablet.

"If the monster murders are unrelated – just some paranormal anomaly we have to track down and deal with – then it could be a kingmaker thing." Robin returned to his cup of tea and had another sip. "Any chatter?"

Cyril gazed down at the soft glow of his beloved tablet. There was a page of complex statistics and notes open on the screen. "Obvious threats would be reported to Your Highness immediately," he murmured, studying the page. "Nothing stands out, sir. Ewan McLeod punched a human in the nose in an Edinburgh pub last week over a perceived slur to his clan."

Robin laughed despite the seriousness of their current situation. "I think we can take that old curmudgeon off the list."

"How can we just completely vanish?" asked Simon. "Della has her work and her family is very close-knit – they'll go crazy. I have to tell Julliard something or they'll think I'm a flake."

Simon had managed to steal some sleep after the conversation with his father. The Dragos family had given them a large and airy guest room upstairs. Simon appreciated being able to keep Della near him although the shell-shocked ballerina had been encouraged to drift away with the aid of a mild sedative. Exhausted from the night, Simon hadn't required any help. He had fallen asleep almost immediately, content in the knowledge that his father was actively working to set things right.

Waking only when Alin knocked on the bedroom door and came in with a brunch tray. He'd been happy to wolf down some eggs and listen to Alin's pitch which involved isolating in the Dragos home under their protection until it was safe to emerge. Such an operation would involve no genuine contact with Julliard, the ballet company, Manhattan friends or Della's family.

Alin nodded and leaned forward from where he sat on a Prussian blue chaise. "I understand it's a tough break. We Gypsies understand art and family. But it is time to go radio silent, or to – how do you say? – starve the old vampires of oxygen."

"The two Ivanhoe vampires …"

The Gypsy's Eastern European face broke into a delighted grin. "Ivanhoe vampires – that's pretty good. You're a funny guy for Brit."

"Those old vampires can track us without needing to be private detectives, you know," Simon said with a sigh. "Your house is beautiful, Alin, but I don't see how it can be a fortress against determined revenants."

Alin Dragos made a theatrical sad face that resembled a medieval jester at work. "Your noble father does not underestimate us. He knows what the Dragos can do."

"My god, it's cold," Robin observed as they waited outside the Wick Airport terminal for Tinley and Brown to retrieve the hired Range Rover. Once the British Airways jet had crossed over into Scotland, a grim, iron grey had swallowed them whole. In the far northern end of the country, most of what would have been the quaint local scenery was enveloped in frigid mist and unavailable for inspection.

Cyril glanced at his tablet. "30 degrees Fahrenheit, Your Highness."

"Bloody hell," murmured Robin, pacing back and forth on the pavement.

"They are well protected, sir," said Cyril, guessing that his king was worried about his family. "Your guardsmen are the best in the world. Even Culpeper while occasionally irritating is ..."

"Pryce-Atwater was one of the best too," replied Robin, his breath drifting behind him in the icy air like a streamer.

"Message from Sir Geoffrey," Cyril said, politely ignoring Robin's comment. He read from the tablet. "Good hunting in the Highlands. Fletcher Greenwood has killed himself with a spoon."

"Bloody hell," Robin repeated.

Lady Caroline saw that revenant security was more obvious than usual. Ari's riding lessons were with an old friend, Major Timothy Alanwood of the Blues and Royals at their Hyde Park barracks. She and Timothy had competed against each other in combined training events over the years becoming good friends over many campaigns. He was a brave and intelligent rider with an uncanny knack for getting out of trouble on difficult cross-country courses. And in the end, it was Tim who had gotten a space on the British Olympic team and had won Team Silver.

She watched as Ari trotted Rupert – a large chestnut pony borrowed from a nearby riding academy – around the indoor ring. The little girl was a natural with a lovely leg position and soft hands. Major Alanwood paced the center of the ring, calling out instructions and occasionally glancing out as the vampire guardsmen in their immaculate black suits prowled the spectator areas, clearly scoping the environment for any problems.

"Right then!" called out Major Alanwood, clapping his hands. "Walk him down, Ari. Nicely done today!"

"Okay dokey," sang out Ari and promptly slowed the pretty Rupert to a walk. The pony snorted steam in the cold winter air. She patted his neck. "Good boy. Ten minutes to warm, ten minutes to cool."

Major Alanwood jogged over the ring edge where Caroline stood and gave her one of his lopsided grins. "What's up with all the extra muscle?"

Despite Robin and his vampire renaissance, it was never going to be possible – in Caroline's private opinion – for her to be able to inform her human friends that she was the revenant Queen of All the British Isles. One – in spite of her husband's hopes for a more open society, it was obviously going to be an eon before the average British subject knew about vampires. Two – she wasn't actually a vampire despite being their queen. Her friends and extended family had been told Robin was a historian who now possessed a very important job with the British government. Caroline didn't see that story changing any time soon.

She offered her old friend a sigh. "Some enhanced threat level thing. It's driving me spare."

"You know," he pretended to whisper conspiratorially, "this is a military barracks. It's pretty bloody secure already."

Caroline laughed with a nod. "Complete overkill, I get it."

Timothy Alanwood leaned against the ring rail and crossed his arms. He looked thoughtful and a bit wistful. "She's really exceptional, Caroline. Way ahead of her age group mentally and physically. My Rosie's roughly the same age but terrified of horses. Shrieks every time I put her up in the saddle. God, it's embarrassing."

"Oh, she'll outgrow that," Caroline said, watching as Ari walked Rupert around the ring. "Look at your ten-year-old, Hazel – she's jumping everything in sight."

Alanwood's eyes lit up with pride. "She does all right, that one."

"Why don't you, Tess and the girls come up to Hawkesmoor in the summer with the horses? We'll do the schooling shows and cubbing season."

"You're on," he grinned again. "Remember the time Tess took that orangutan of Josie Falkirk's to the Mainwaring show and Mark had just put in the water element ..."

"Ma'am," coughed Bramwell apologetically as he came up. "What's up?" she asked pleasantly, hoping it wasn't something about supernatural entities invading Hyde Park. "Sorry to disturb you but the Earl of Hawkesmoor has arrived early at the house."

"Gosh, he is early! Must be worried about the Sheepfarmers Society."

Major Alanwood shook his head woefully. "I heard the Blackface and Cheviot breeders are at each other's throats."

"Could be a genuine bloodbath," she agreed, watching as the vampire guardsmen quietly shifted positions, continuing the scan for any sign of the creature or creatures responsible for the recent decapitation of Pryce-Atwater.

Chapter Twenty-Four

"Dad!" cried Caroline.

Her father, the Earl of Hawkesmoor, was seated by the library fire, enjoying a cup of tea and leafing through a leather-bound book on his lap.

"Well, there you are!" he replied, standing up to greet her and Ari who ran forward to hug her grandfather.

"I've missed you," said Ari. "Can you stay for Christmas?" The Earl patted her head. "I believe the plan is for you to come to Hawkesmoor for the big day. Everyone will be there – Peter, Hannah, Simon ..." He looked up at Caroline. "Is that still the plan, Caro?"

"We wouldn't miss it," she grinned at him. "I, for one, am longing for the moors."

"I did bring an early Christmas present," the Earl indicated a cheerfully wrapped package on one of the other library chairs. "Go on, Ari – have a look."

The little girl attacked the present with gusto and tore the gleaming gold paper away to reveal a large modern picture book entitled A Child's Introduction to the Noble Wensleydale. She gasped at the beautiful cover photograph of a regal ewe standing alert and proud in her Yorkshire grazing land.

"Thank you, Grandfather. It's lovely!" Ari promptly sat down on the carpeted floor to look through the glossy pages. "We will need more of these at Hawkesmoor, won't we, Grandfather? Wensleydale wool is so good."

"We will indeed," said the Earl with great affection and then returned his gaze to Caroline. "What a remarkable child."

"Worried about the Sheepfarmers Society?" Caroline asked, noting that the house butler, Potterswood, was hovering, hoping to be of service. The revenant staff adored human visitors as it was an opportunity to showcase their culinary and service skills.

Her father looked haunted. "There must be more support for the Blue faced Leicester. The Cheviots and Blackface cannot be allowed to ride roughshod over everyone. It's a scandal!"

"Potterswood – could we have lunch in the second dining room?" Caroline asked the butler who nodded in affirmation and practically floated out of the room.

Cam Drummond lived outside the small town of Thurso in a fishing village called Machar's Drift. Presumably a picturesque, almost idyllic vision of wild grassland, ancient grey stone buildings and whitewashed cottages in good weather. In winter, Machar's Drift was a harsh, uninviting place. In the fading light of December, the wind-whipped, haphazard collection of buildings huddled like nesting seabirds on a barren patch of land that lay behind a tiny manmade harbor. Occasional snowflakes blew in from the North Sea.

Too eccentrically designed and too old to allow motorized vehicles into the village center, Machar's Drift had a paved car park just outside the village limits that according to a weathered civic sign stood in as a bus stop, mobile library station and fair-weather fish market. Currently there were only three other cars in the entire lot – all belonging to the Caithness County police.

"Three in a village this size, sir?" asked Cyril as they stood next to the Range Rover, gazing down at Machar's Drift's rugged buildings. Flashing lights were down in the village center, strobing off stonework in the twilight.

Robin nodded. "In the modern vernacular, something is up."

"Battle plan, sir?"

"Well, we can't walk down there like this, obviously," replied Robin, indicating his bespoke suit and black cashmere topcoat. "They'll think we're Edinburgh mafia." He raised a hand, sweeping through the air across Cyril, the guardsmen and himself. One of the remnants of his Tylwyth Teg power was an ability to effect simple matter transformations. Not wildly useful most of the time but occasionally the skill came into its own. By the time he lowered his arm, all of them were kitted out in jeans, sweaters, anoraks and wellies.

"You two," he said to Tinley and Brown, "make yourselves scarce. Only come into full sight if absolutely necessary but stay with us."

They nodded and faded away into the icy air. One of the preferred abilities for prospective royal guardsmen was the talent for melting into shade, becoming invisible. All vampires possessed various traits with differing amounts of power. Some vampires had only one or two and were considered weak. Others were gifted with immense personal abilities.

"We're just a couple of antique dealers," said Robin as they walked away from the car park to a footpath down to Machar's Drift, "passing through Caithness and thought we'd stop in at the pub for a beer."

Chapter Twenty-Five

"This can't be a coincidence, sir," murmured Cyril Goforth as they stepped off the footpath and onto a wet strip of old pavement that marked the beginning of Machar's Drift.

Ahead of them was the village center. From where they were, it appeared to possess a handful of tired public buildings, a modest pub, a couple of shops and a tiny expanse in the center with a Victorian obelisk. The ancient, narrow side streets ran in eccentric curves and dips, boasting fishermen's cottages and quarters for harbor business. There was nothing planned or thoughtful about Machar's Drift. It had just erupted in medieval times along with the fishing trade.

Currently, Machar's Drift was crowded with Caithness police. As the December afternoon light fled, the fluttering lights from official vehicles bounced off every available surface.

"Unless Machar's Drift," replied Robin, "is a noted hotbed of fish racketeering, I'm guessing not. Let's pop into the local and see what's up."

They strolled into Machar's Drift with a casual air of tourists inexplicably visiting the most Northern region of Scotland in the dead of winter. There was no accumulation of snow on the rooftops or cobblestones, but it was bitterly cold. The stiff wind off the sea was icy and bit at their faces like invisible fish feeding off dead sailors.

Robin paused as he realized that the sharp wind currents might be difficult for Tinley and Brown. Being a shade could be a very fragile position to be in under certain external conditions. Gravity didn't have quite the same meaning.

"You lads holding up all right?" he asked quietly.

Tinley murmured into his right ear, "Hunky dory just now, sir. Could get dicey if the gusts head up."

"I second that, sir," added Brown softly. "Good for now."

"If you need to reconfigure, do so – but try to stay out of the Caithness constabulary's line of sight. Strangers to this tiny plot are going to stir electric instincts in local detectives if something terrible has happened."

Robin and Cyril Goforth pushed on into the village center. Although there were several idling police vehicles with emergency lights swirling parked around the weathered obelisk, the actual investigation scene appeared to be down one of the narrow side streets that arced up to the right and behind the Twelve Herrings pub. There were more flashing lights up on the street behind the pub. The residents of Machar's Drift had apparently abandoned the village center as no one lurked nearby. Probably tucked away by warm fireplaces or congregating in the street above the pub to watch what the police were doing in their normally placid village.

They crossed to the little triangle of dead grass and the obelisk. The Victorian monument was made of the same grey stone as every other building of consequence in the area. But unlike tall, suitably impressive obelisks in more prominent municipalities that seemed to soar towards heaven with righteous verve, the Machar's Drift offering was only about six foot tall and rather squat – a tribute to underachievement. Robin paused to read the metal memorial plaque – Legend has it, St. Machar banished them to the sea from this very spot in 565 AD. Erected by Machar Drift's Ladies Altar Guild, June 17th, 1901.

"Them, sir?" Cyril sounded baffled. His keen organizational sense deplored vagaries.

"Vikings, presumably," said Robin. "They must have raided this area every time they needed a new bucket."

"The Twelve Herrings does appear to be open, sir," said Cyril with a short sigh. He was gazing across the narrow cobblestone thoroughfare at Machar's Drift's only pub. Like everything else in the village, it was small, very grey, very weathered but clearly serviceable with neon signs glowing in leaded glass windows touting Newcastle and Old Peculiar.

"Tinley, Brown – why don't you two have a little look up where all the action seems to be." Robin lifted a hand to indicate the street above The Twelve Herrings. "Don't be seen but if the weather gets tricky, do what you have to do, lads. Report back in fifteen minutes."

"Yes, sir," murmured Tinley.

"Fifteen minutes, sir," added Brown sounding relieved at the brevity of the assignment.

Robin and Cyril continued across the street and into The Twelve Herrings. Its exterior might be a bit bleak in the winter landscape but inside the pub was surprisingly comfortable and hospitable.

The Twelve Herrings was warmed by two fireplaces roaring with artificial gas flames bent on consuming realistic looking logs – seemingly one of the few concessions to the 21st century – on either side of a lovely mahogany bar with heavy carving and brass fittings. There were sturdy wood tables and chairs arranged on both sides to take full benefit of the warmth. In the amber-ish light from various muted sources, the traditional whitewashed plaster walls were covered in artwork and old photographs in neglected frames that depicted the sea and local fishing life. A few yellowed

Edwardian adverts for beer could be found as well and a nod was made to the holiday season with a brightly lit Christmas Tree by the bar.

For a warm pub on a cold winter's afternoon, it was nearly deserted. One man stood up at the bar talking to the publican. A few others sat at tables, chatting animatedly over pints of bitter. Chatting animatedly until Robin and Cyril had made it past the storm doors and through to the pub's small foyer. At the arrival of strangers, the Machar Drift locals almost gasped in mid-sentences and stared.

"Afternoon, all," said Robin in his most genial voice. "Bloody cold up here, isn't it?"

The Twelve Herrings publican – a hale and hearty type with a red nose that seemed to indicate he might be his own best customer – waved them up to the handsome mahogany bar. "'Tis that," he called to them, "yes. Ye be brave lads traveling this land this time o' year."

Robin and Cyril came up to the bar, grateful to be out of the cutting wind.

"Cognac weather," said Cyril, rubbing his hands together. "Whisky weather, "corrected Robin as all the inhabitants of the Twelve Herrings widened their eyes at the very notion of a French libation. "Two Old Pulteney – neat, please."

The pub owner replaced his horrified expression with one of beatific generosity. "We are always proud tae serve Old Pulteney. What are ye lads doing this side o'Wick in this filthy weather?"

The pub was quiet as everyone awaited the pronouncement. It was clear that Machar's Drift only suffered strangers in the summer when the tourists arrived to take in traditional Scottish sights and fare.

"Driving back from an estate auction in Sunderland," replied Robin pleasantly. "Saw your village on the GPS and thought we'd take a break. I must say this is a very handsome and collectable bar, sir."

The publican laughed as he poured out two stiff whiskies. "Oh, ho ho! Every summer some American offers me the moon for it and I hae to disappoint them. Antiques dealers, are ye then?"

Robin laughed too. The atmosphere in the Twelve Herrings returned to its former state as the locals wrote them off as clueless urbanites who drank French Cognac and were probably gay. He was intrigued that the conversations he heard murmuring across the rooms had switched from English to the North Scots Gaelic favored by the inhabitants of Caithness. One of the locals had announced with the slightly bleary voice of heavy drinker – It be them; I tell ye. They be back and none of us safe nae more!

"Thank you," said Cyril brightly as the pub owner set a whisky down in front of him. "Lots of police lights – what's up?"

The Twelve Herrings publican's jovial red face fell as he placed Robin's whisky on the bar top. "We dinna rightly know. There's been a murder y'see."

Chapter Twenty-Six

"We dinna know much yet," the pub owner continued after Robin and Cyril had made appropriate noises of horror and shallow comfort. He stepped back to retrieve a new pint for a hovering local who had ambled up with an empty glass. "Even our own Constable Murray's gone quiet."

The local, another red-faced fellow who looked as if he could toss a commercial net filled with well-nourished swordfish into a boat all by himself, tossed pound coins on the bar top and spoke up in the region's North Scots Gaelic that presumably he thought was all Greek to outsiders. He couldn't know that one of the young strangers at the bar was infused with the bloodline of the Tylwyth Teg – Celtic elementals of great power – and possessed an innate understanding of all variants of verbal communication – human or animal.

Robin sipped his whisky and pretended to study a dog-eared index card that had all the pub's modest food offerings typed upon it. Fish fried, baked or boiled. Mutton if one was feeling adventurous.

"I tell ye – it not be Cam Drummond," said the local, reaching for his freshened glass. "He set out fer the islands at dawn, he did. Some lady in a bad way needin' hospital."

"Aye," replied the publican in the same Gaelic as he swept up the coins. "No tellin' when he'll put in, poor bastard."

"Sir," came Brown's voice in a whisper at Robin's right ear. "You'll want a bit of a look up there."

Robin made a point of reaching into breast pocket of his coat. He magicked up something that would appear to be a cell phone and pulled it out. "Darling," he said to Cyril whose eyes widened in genuine horror at the endearment, "I'm going to step out and ring Bertie. That Chippendale highboy isn't going to sell itself."

There was some mumbling and quiet laughter among the few locals as displeasure flickered across Cyril's handsome face. The suggestion that they were partners in life as well as in business breached his carefully maintained separation of the Sovereign and the Courtier.

"I'll find a table then and order some food," he replied, clenching his jaw.

"You are the perfect darling!" Robin said, enjoying the sour set to Cyril's normally placid features. "Back in a few."

Once free of the Twelve Herrings, Robin walked a few paces up the street and stopped to lean against a Victorian lamppost.

"I take it there's been a murder," he murmured, pretending to examine the phone.

"And how, sir. Tinley's up there to keep an eye on the plonkers. Not Cam Drummond but it's his cottage."

"Any observations?"

"I floated about, eavesdropping on the locals. They're all in the street, watching just as you'd imagine. Drummond was well liked. Admired for his seagoing skill and altruism. In foul weather, he runs his fishing boat as a sea ambulance. No mean feat up this way, sir."

"The victim?"

"From what I could gather, Drummond's long time lady friend. A librarian with the regional book mobile. Not one of us, sir."

Robin sighed. He was saddened by the loss of an innocent human being who had obviously contributed to the world around her. Sir Geoffrey wasn't going to like it much either and he wondered how long he could keep the Prime Minister's Rottweiler on a chain.

"It's a fairly recent kill, sir," added Brown. "I'd say a few hours ago. Drummond's cleaner popped about an hour ago to check the heater – apparently there's been some problem with it – and found the body."

"Well done, Brown. If you can be careful, nip into the pub and warm up." Robin slid the phone into a pocket and allowed it to evaporate back into air molecules. "I'll be all right with Tinley."

"Thank you, sir," Brown murmured gratefully and was gone.

Robin pushed off the lamppost and walked further along the haphazardly developed walk, passing the post office that doubled as the village shop and then curving up to the street where most of the village and Caithness police force were congregating.

Another narrow byway, it featured five haphazardly planted cottages as if Nordic Frost Giants had thrown them against the hill like seeds and they'd taken root in the stony soil. Grey and squat like everything else in Machar's Drift, there was little to delineate one cottage from another save different sets of colored Christmas lights shuddering in the ever-present sea breeze.

Residents of Machar's Drift had collected in the street, converging around two police cars to watch Caithness' best at work. The slight entrance way to Cam Drummond's cottage was cordoned off with yellow and black barricade tape. Standing outside Cam's cheerful red door were two young policeman who both looked petrified and green in the flashing lights of the emergency vehicles.

Before either the constabulary or locals would take notice of him, Robin faded away to shade and joined the throng. He threaded through Cam's shivering neighbors, picking up bits and pieces of commentary in English and North Gaelic as he went.

"Cam, bless 'im. He will be heartbroken."

"Elsie was such a wee, pretty lass."

"Aye – they did this. They be back and none nae safe."

They again, thought Robin, remembering the other local's exclamation in the Twelve Herrings. He passed by the two young police constables trembling in the cold. He picked up a whiff of vomit and realized one or both of them had recently been ill.

Robin slipped into Cam's modest home – a two up and two down rabbit warren of 16th century design. Before death and the Caithness police had crowded in, it had been a charming and cozy little place to nip in out of the frigid Scottish weather. A gracious fieldstone fireplace held the pride of place with overstuffed chairs on either side upholstered in the distinctive red Drummond tartan. Highland dancing trophies crowded the chimney piece and beribboned medals hung from the Elizabethan open beam work. Books, fishing gear and Highland bric-a-brac competed for space everywhere else. A table tree sat on an end table decorated with Scottish flags and miniature fairy lights.

What was left of Cam Drummond's lady love lay in the kitchen. Robin recognized the English Wendigo's handiwork as soon as he shifted around various police techs and a detective.

Elsie, the book mobile librarian, had been devoured. She had been flung onto a wooden kitchen table, then torn open as if two monstrously power hands had seized her abdomen and ripped it apart like a bag of microwaved popcorn. Her internal organs and muscles had been scooped out in a

161

ravenous frenzy. Greedy, jagged bite marks to her thighs and other soft, fleshy areas attested to a ferocious, wholly unnatural hunger. Arterial spray had glazed every surface, bathing the kitchen in a scarlet shimmer. Blood dripped from the plasterwork on the ceiling and pooled on the floor. As with the unlucky India Hart, it seemed possible from the frantic arrangement of Elsie's blue jeans – open and left hanging down at her ankles – that she had been sexually attacked first.

Robin sent up a short prayer to the universe, lamenting Elsie's loss to humanity and with hopes that she had found her way to Shakespeare's undiscovered country from which no mortal cared to return. He had a moment to wish he possessed his son's most notable Tylwyth Teg attribute. Simon was not a powerful exponent of his unique faerie bloodline in the way that his half-sister Arianrhod had demonstrated before her abilities had abruptly shut down. But his son did possess one fascinating trait. He could perceive the ghost world in a way that Robin imagined might be extremely useful in the current predicament. He'd give a lot to have a short chat with Elsie if she was lingering in Cam Drummond's cottage.

As the Caithness detective gave his team sharp instructions to keep the details of the murder to themselves, Robin took another look at Elsie's forlorn shell, intrigued that her face did not fully reflect the horrors of her last minutes. She had been eaten alive. The pretty Celtic face was pallid with shock but like the other victims, vacant – even uncomprehending.

Having seen enough to be able to alert Sir Geoffrey to another one of the Wendigo murders, Robin extricated himself from both the crime scene and the knot of Machar's Drifters in the street. He ran down the gentle rise to the village center, reconstituting himself as he went and returned to the warmth of The Twelve Herrings.

Chapter Twenty-Seven

Cyril Goforth had booked rooms at the Carberry Hotel in nearby Thurso. The calm gentility of a beautifully restored Regency manor house seemed a world away from the bleak winter face of Machar's Drift.

While the guardsmen lounged nearby, enjoying a warm fire, Robin sat at small table in the crowded dining room and sipped a cup of tea. Because Tylwyth Teg was the dominant side of his odd hybrid state, he was able to do a number of things denied to traditional vampires. He no longer needed to feed the revenant hunger and took in sustenance just as humans did.

The Vampire King of All the British Isles let out a long breath and gazed into the glimmering mahogany of his tea as if seeking a vision from a Welsh cauldron. He felt stymied. Without Cam Drummond and whatever the Scot could tell them, he didn't know what or where his next move lay. It was clear that the Scot knew something. It wasn't a coincidence that their English Wendigo had chosen Drummond's cottage for a visit. Frustrating because it was the first mistake whatever they were dealing with had made – a connection could now be drawn to northern Scotland. They had to find Cam Drummond. Currently Cyril was on watch in Machar's Drift, keeping a weather eye out for the revenant fisherman. By taking shifts, the four of them ought to be able to intercept Drummond if he returned from his mercy errand to the Orkneys. Unfortunately, with marine radio, he'd probably already gotten wind of Elsie's murder and scarpered.

"You look vexed," said a familiar voice to his left.

Robin looked up from his teacup. Gabriel Addington – former medieval monk and now the great revenant librarian who kept their history in a vast underground vault in London – stood next to the table flanked by a concerned looking Tinley.

"Gabriel!" he said, standing up to greet his friend. "Not to worry, Tinley – enjoy the fire while you can."

"Thank you, sir," the guardsman made a small, barely perceptible bob of his head and retreated. They were in a dining room filled with festive holiday guests. It was best they did not suspect that a vampire king had joined them.

"Sit – join me," Robin indicated the chair opposite his. "You know, I quite surprised to see you in Thurso. Not your usual haunt."

Gabriel grinned and did as he was bidden, slipping onto the red upholstered chair. "I'm here in a brief pop up. No mean feat in this weather, I can tell you. Thought I might end up in the loch swimming with bleedin' Nessie."

Although he looked a sunny natured thirty-year-old with thick, unruly sandy colored hair and bright grey eyes, Gabriel was a very old and gifted vampire. He was the master of molecular transfer and rarely used human transport.

"I appreciate the company," said Robin truthfully.

"Speaking of alternative modes of locomotion," the former monk continued as he settled at the table, "you can time travel, my hybrid friend. Why don't you just nip back and put the frighteners on Cam Drummond?"

Robin shook his head. "Time travel is one of the things I gave up upon returning here from the Tylwyth Teg."

"Drats," said Gabriel, looking gloomy. "Goforth's briefed me pretty fully and I don't mind telling you that I'm spooked. These flamboyant murders could ..."

"So, I'm guessing you didn't pop up for Thurso's annual Christmas craft fair?"

The vampire librarian brightened, leaning forward confidentially. "I stumbled across something while I was researching Cam Drummond's past. It's not much but it might be a bolt hole for him in times of trouble."

Robin leaned forward as well. "I'm very interested in bolt holes."

Simon had never really seen Philadelphia Baquero-Florez angry. He had seen her mildly miffed, occasionally frustrated and once, the highly annoyed Della who had spent several hours at the DMV getting her license updated. The current Della in front of him reminded him of a downed electrical line he'd once seen in the wake of a big storm. She paced the Dragos guest room crackling with unpredictable power.

"What do you mean I can't go home?" Della tossed her head and pointed to the bedroom window. "My work, my family are out there just a few miles away. You can't make me stay in this house with your weirdo friends. You can't! I want to go home now!"

"Della," he said, "you saw what happened. Do you want those … people coming to your parents' house?"

She bristled, throwing him a furious glare. "No one – no one would ever protect me more than mi padre, Simon Dashwood. Not you, not this creepy house, nobody! I mean, I get not going back to my place but mi familia? Hey, I got brothers who would …"

"These people would snap your brothers in half in less time than you could land a single pirouette."

The ballerina let out a raw cry of rage, her hands clawing at the air as if she could tear through the veil of space itself and return home to Williamsburg. She refocused on Simon with eyes that flashed with naked fury.

"Just what have you gotten me into?" Della's voice was a near shout -- ragged from the primal outburst. "What have you done, Simon?"

Simon stared at her. "You should know about me – and my family."

"Galetaer Castle," said Gabriel. "Chill Wind coarsely translated. It's a stone's throw from Thurso."

Robin thought for a moment. "You know, I think I've met the current holders of the castle. Sir Ronald Bannatyre and his wife – old friends of Caroline's father. It's hard to imagine Cam Drummond flitting through that social circle."

Gabriel Addington's genial face lit up with the kind of joy peculiar to academics who have discovered something in dusty tomes. "Galetaer Castle was originally the keep of one Sir Neville Ponsonby, baronet. He was given the castle by Henry III as a reward – despite grumbling from the local Scots gentry – for his service as a knight in The Crusades."

"Galetaer Castle is a long, long way from Mother England especially in the 13th century. One might see that as a bit of a rebuke."

Gabriel paused to allow a young Scottish waitress to set down a fresh pot of tea. She was pretty in an unaffected way despite being dressed against type in black trousers, white mess jacket and a black bow tie. The badge on her crisp white lapel read Allie.

"Will you be dining as well, sir?" Allie asked Gabriel, almost blushing as he shifted his grey eyed focus in her direction. "The chef has some lovely salmon or venison – game birds too."

"The salmon, please. I don't need a starter," he smiled up at her. Gabriel's gentle charm – part of what had made him a fine monk – was disarming. Allie clutched her receipt book to her heart and beamed.

"Yes," she murmured, "lovely … lovely salmon."

Robin coughed quietly.

Allie gave a guilty start and fumbled with her pen. "A glass of wine, sir?"

"Tea, thank you ..."

"I … I wasn't eavesdropping, I promise," she interrupted anxiously, nearly dropping her black receipt book. "But did you mention Galetaer Castle?"

Della gasped slightly and stiffened as if stung by a wasp. She fixed Simon with a puzzled stare before starting to give at the knees.

"Simon," she breathed, all her anger seeming to dissolve into the shock of betrayal, "Que me has hecho …"

"Della!" Simon pushed out of his chair and caught her just as her legs gave way. The ballerina collapsed into his arms, unconscious.

Chapter Twenty-Eight

"My brother works there sometimes," breathed their waitress, Allie. "He's a contractor – specializes in stonework. The Bannatyres do their best to keep the old place going but things are always falling off it. Galetaer is proper haunted!"

"Is it really?" said Gabriel, pretending to be fascinated.

"Jack hasn't seen anything himself but one of the housekeepers told him all sorts of stories – disembodied voices, footsteps ..."

"Thank you, Allie," Robin interjected politely. "Would you mind awfully placing that salmon order in with the chef?"

Allie flushed slightly. "Oh, of course. Sorry. I'll bring it straight away."

Robin gave a short sigh as she hurried off to the kitchens.

"Gabriel, Gabriel, Gabriel."

The monk laughed. "That was a nice little drink for me until you gummed up the works. You know she never would have missed a small glass worth's – or remembered anything about it. I'm that good."

"Synthetics, my friend – wave of the future."

Gabriel looked like he just sucked on a lemon and gave a mock shudder.

"So – back to Sir Neville Ponsonby." Robin raised his eyebrows and poured some more tea. "He returned home from the Crusades and got shunted up to godforsaken Scotland."

"It's gets very interesting to a fellow of my research interests here," said the vampire librarian. "You know how I search through history looking for undisclosed revenants. The ones I haven't got in my bloodline registers. Sir Neville fits my bill although I have yet to find absolutely conclusive proof."

"Go on."

"By all accounts an exemplary knight in the Crusades with an unusually loyal band of officers serving under him. He returns home to a grateful monarch who rewards him not with a pretty estate in England but with a Scottish castle as far north in the Highlands as it is possible to get." Gabriel poured himself a cup of tea so he could pretend to drink it. A misdirection that all revenants used almost without thinking when out in public places.

"Sir Neville's inner circle of soldiers go with him into Scottish exile," Gabriel said just as Allie returned with a handsome piece of salmon. He paused again to allow her to place it front of him with more gusto than flourish.

"The cream sauce features chipotle – an American Southwest flavor," Allie announced proudly, mispronouncing it as shy portal. "It's become a big hit here."

"You are a perfect darling," replied the vampire librarian and picked up his fork so he could push the salmon around his plate in a reasonably convincing display of eating.

"Chipotle," Allie repeated, gazing at Gabriel as if he were a magnificent dish of American flavored cream sauce and she hadn't eaten in a week. "So popular here. So very …"

Robin coughed again – a little louder than the first time. The young waitress sucked in a breath sharply. She flashed Robin a guilty look and darted away to another table.

"I wonder what shy portal actually tastes like," murmured Gabriel watching Allie go.

"Sir Neville Ponsonby?"

The former monk nodded, returning his focus to Robin.

"His family's motto is Invicta per ministerium."

Robin raised an eyebrow. "Invincible through service. Workmanlike but not particularly special."

"Once ensconced in Galetaer Castle, Sir Neville devises his own motto – Per omnia saecula saeculorum."

"World without end," said Robin. He sat back in his chair, his face thoughtful.

"I have a blood registry for Cam Drummond only because Lord Scyon had made it law that all revenants had sign in with me if they came to London," continued Gabriel, referring to the former king – Garnet Petherbridge, Lord Scyon. "You know, the ones that didn't fancy being tortured and beheaded if they got caught sneaking into town. Does Lady Caroline know he used to keep the bloody heads in that big yellow vase?"

"No – and don't tell her either. She thinks we're lucky to have it. So, what did Drummond tell you? That he was a vampire knight with Sir Neville Ponsonby?"

The vampire librarian shook his head and pushed his scalloped potatoes around the white plate. "Drummond's a terrible liar – the old medieval soldier types usually are. They're straight forward, honor is everything lads. He said he didn't know who created him. Said he'd been attacked from behind in Mary King's Close in Edinburgh and woke up in a gutter, feeling odd."

"Give you a date?"

"He thought it was sometime in the winter of 1470 but was no longer sure." Gabriel pretended to sip from his teacup. "I knew he was misdirecting but wrote it down anyway. Revenants have their own feelings about being what they are and should only register with me if they want to. Thank you for striking that one down."

"No worries," said Robin. "What makes you think Cam Drummond is one of Sir Neville's?"

Gabriel threw Robin a look of regret. "The Highland dancing and piping competitions. The kilt. He just seemed a little too Scottish. I might be dead wrong, but I made note of it in my private research papers."

Robin thought of Cam Drummond's cottage with its tartan upholstered chairs, clutter of Highland bric-a-brac and jolly Christmas tree festooned with Scottish flags. "Let's say you're right about Cam. You think he might be hiding out at Galetaer Castle? Surely Sir Neville and the rest of his guard are long gone."

"Not a lot about Sir Neville once he came up here. According to the few references I could find, he was much admired for his devout piety to God. His wife had died while he had been away in the Middle East and he took no second wife." Gabriel beamed, at his happiest when pursuing a research topic. "Sir Neville and his guard essentially formed a kind of contemplative religious order at Galetaer Castle, disappearing behind walls and from history itself."

"This is all very interesting to an academic such as myself," said Robin, crossing his arms, "but I still can't see why Cam Drummond would use Galetaer Castle as a bolt hole."

Gabriel set down his teacup. "In a time of extreme danger, Drummond might return to his true home. Surely, he would know the castle better than anyone. Maybe he has even made himself known in the past to the current residents as a construction or field worker."

Before Robin could reply to the librarian's theory, Tinley suddenly left his vantage point and crossed to stand by the table.

"Sir," he said in a low voice, "Mr. Goforth has asked me to inform you that Cam Drummond's fishing boat has been found sailing adrift by Her Majesty's Coast Guard. No sign of him on board and presumed lost at sea."

Robin cocked his aquiline head to the side as he absorbed the update from Machar's Drift. Then he nodded at Gabriel Addington. "Galetaer Castle, it is."

Alin Dragos came fully into the room from the hallway. He wore an apologetic expression on his hawkish face and carried a strange, futuristic handgun with him. It resembled a standard issue service revolver but possessed a slightly longer barrel and a small, glimmering control panel on the body.

"What the bloody hell …" Simon sputtered, clutching Della's limp form protectively. "You shot Della with that thing?"

"She'll be fine – just sleeping, my friend." Alin held up the gun so presumably Simon could admire it. "The Sandman 2000. Tranquilizer gun. My cousin is developing it for the NYPD. Clever, no?"

"You darted my girlfriend like a park ranger?"

Alin almost looked hurt by Simon's horrified tone. "It's almost painless. Hypoallergenic! Far better than tasers or real guns. Everybody wins. She'll be out for an hour if we're lucky. Maybe enough time for us to get a start."

"But why …"

"Some gadjo can handle big trouble, my friend," said Alin, glancing at the drugged Della, "and some can't. A few could even survive knowing about your father's world but most cannot."

Simon thought of his wonderful stepmother and what his father had told him about her level-headedness in the glare of a fantastic new reality. Her love for him had been greater than her fear of the unknown. She was a survivor.

"Then Della can never really know about me, about us," he said, remembering her blinding anger – reaction to the primordial dread of danger and, perhaps, things uncanny such as himself.

"Most of them," Alin made an explosive gesture with his free hand, "minds blown. Not good. Antidepressants, rehab – your noble and wise father was very clear that he didn't want Miss Baquero-Florez's mind blown."

Simon picked up Della and carried her the few steps to the bed. He felt sharp stabs of regret and sadness as he gently settled her under the bed's comforter. What had he been thinking, drawing her into his family's peculiar orbit? Della had a wonderful, worthwhile life filled with family, friends and her art. It wasn't her fault if she could not absorb what and who he was. He had no right to steal her peace, her faith in the world as she knew it.

"Let her sleep, my friend." Alin patted his shoulder. "So – I've been thinking …"

"Uh, oh," said Simon.

The Gypsy laughed. "You are a funny guy for a Brit!"

Rules restaurant in Covent Garden had been a DeBarry family touchstone since Thomas Rule first established it in 1798. Now almost flamboyantly Edwardian in its décor, Rules offered a sanctuary of fine English food and quiet, knowledgeable service in a world that could be coarse despite its technological advances.

Caroline and her father, the Earl of Hawkesmoor, sat at his favorite corner table under one of gilded glass domes of pale green and gold. As always, the restaurant was very busy with an interesting mix of old-line gentry, curious tourists and thoroughly modern business and entertainment people. Wait staff – dressed in impeccable dinner jackets –

attended to every table ensuring that everyone from Mrs. Lebrowski from Cleveland, Ohio to the Earl of Hawkesmoor was well cared for, wonderfully fed and happy.

At the holiday, Rules' curated country house clutter of paintings, marble statuary and object d'art were festooned with boughs of holly and pine lavishly beribboned with fairy lights and glittering ornaments. Even Charles Dickens – who often dined at Rules in his day – would have conceded that the restaurant knew how to keep Christmas.

"Now if the Blue Faced Leicester is to survive in the 21st century ..." The Earl was saying over a glass of his favorite Burgundy – Bonnes Mares Grand Cru.

"I apologize for interrupting, Your Ladyship" came a voice and Caroline glanced away from her father to see a guardsman standing by their table, looking suitably contrite. "Culpeper?" She was surprised. Usually, the guardsmen were very subtle and kept an eye on her without being intrusive. At least he hadn't referred to her as Serene Highness within earshot of unrelated humans. The last time one of them had forgotten and addressed her formally was in front of an unctuous floor manager on Sloane Street. He had been enchanted by concept of visiting royalty and piercingly vocal about it – attracting other eager to please employees, curious customers and a flock of delighted tourists. Completely surrounded at the handbags counter, she pretended that her English was almost non-existent to avoid explaining where her kingdom might be found. Then her guardsmen had staged a polite form of "evac" as they called it.

The young-looking guardsman glanced to each side, assessing the other diners and stepped closer. He leaned forward and said very quietly, "Your … um, husband, ma'am. He's been trying to reach your mobile with no luck." Caroline made a face at the amused Earl of Hawkesmoor. "I turned the wretched thing off. It's the Christmas season, Culpeper. I'm dining with my father."

"Please allow me to offer mine, Your Ladyship," replied the guardsman, holding out his mobile.

Caroline blew out a short breath and accepted the phone. "Hello?"

"Evening, darling," came Robin's mellifluous voice with its pearly tones and slight reedy quality. She never got tired of hearing it. "I need an awfully big favor from you."

"Of course, anything but Dad …"

"Actually, the Earl is a very important part of this favor," he replied. "I can't explain why at the moment, so you'll just have to trust me."

Caroline offered her father an apologetic smile. He saluted her with his wine glass and had a sip.

"I need you and your father to come up to Scotland tonight."

She was genuinely startled. "Tonight?"

"Sir Geoffrey has a private jet waiting for you. You must leave now."

"But Ari …"

"She'll be fine for the weekend with Miss Pratt and the staff. I need your help, Caro." Robin sounded genuinely urgent. "Please."

"Well," said Caroline with a gulp, "yes, of course."

Her father looked at her expectantly as she handed the mobile to Culpeper who politely backed away to await further developments.

"Drink up, Dad," Caroline shook her head at the high strangeness of her married life. "We're headed to Scotland."

"Good lord," said the Earl and downed what was left of his prized Burgundy in a single swallow.

Chapter Twenty-Nine

Caroline and her father had never flown in a private jet before. On loan from the PM's office, the Gulfstream G650ER was sleekly appointed with leather seats, walnut veneers and an attentive pair of flight attendants who served them dessert and coffee. It was also incredibly fast. Within two hours, they were entering the Carberry's lobby where Robin was waiting for them.

A frisson of electric joy shivered through Caroline's nervous system as she saw Robin's aquiline face light up at the sight of her. She was always a bit dazzled that such a fascinating and exquisitely beautiful man had thrown his strange, arcane lot in with hers. In the very back of her mind, there was always a slight apprehension that Robin would tire of her and vampire politics, tossing it all to return to the fantastical realm of the Tylwyth Teg where all of time and space lay at his feet.

"Darling!" Robin said, his extraordinary face beaming at the sight of her. He kissed her cheek quickly and turned to her father.

"Thank you for coming, sir. I could use your help."

"Think nothing of it," the Earl replied, shaking Robin's hand. "I've had Stinker Russell stand in for me at the meeting tomorrow."

"Apologies, Your Lordship. I know you had been eager to weigh in on the Cheviot controversy."

The Earl's handsome face shadowed for a moment and he sighed. "Troubling times for sheep breeders – still family must come first."

Caroline slid her arm under Robin's elbow. "So, what's this all about?"

Robin threw her a grateful smile. "Come – let's go sit by a fire and I'll explain."

With the hour advancing on ten o'clock, the Carberry's lounge had been abandoned by its human guests who were eager to head home or up to a warm bed on a frigid winter's night.

The Hawkesmoor and vampire contingent settled around a large fireplace that had been dutifully festooned with glimmering boughs of holly. The Earl was particularly pleased to see Gabriel Addington. His Lordship had a particular fondness for the former monk that had been forged during the terrifying siege of Hawkesmoor Castle some six years in the past.

Robin, revenant King of All the British Isles, handed his father-in-law a glass of good whisky and then settled next to Caroline on a sofa upholstered in the Black Watch tartan. The lounge – a former reception room in the Regency manor house – had been fully kitted out for Christmas with a tall, lush tree covered in ornate Victorian ornaments that gleamed in the soft glow of twinkling fairy lights. Standing to one side of the cheery gas fireplace, Carberry's classic Tannenbaum was a beacon of peace on Earth and good will to all men … and a well-meaning vampire or two.

"There has been a spot of trouble in our world – the revenant world," Robin began, clearly trying to choose his words carefully. "Something that has ramifications for yours."

Caroline saw her husband exchange a wary glance with Gabriel Addington who sat in a Queen Anne wing chair opposite the Earl. She shivered despite the warmth from the gas fire and wondered if it had anything to do with the awful deaths of Liev Black and his wife.

"You needn't go into detail," said the Earl, sipping his drink. "I had quite enough of vampire warfare at Hawkesmoor."

"Yes … understood. We are looking into it, but I need … I need ..."

Robin paused and then seemed to change tack. "Sir Ronald Bannatyre is a friend?"

The Earl of Hawkesmoor sat back in some surprise.

"Bucky? Yes – he was one of my fags at Eton. Solid sort of fellow generally but one of the rogues currently overbreeding Cheviots."

"Your Lordship," said Robin, leaning forward to make his plea, "I very much need to get into Galetaer Castle for a day or two. Can you arrange to have us stay?"

Caroline's father stared at him. "Can you really be asking me to inveigle an invitation to Galetaer Castle for a group of people during the Christmas season?"

"Robin," Caroline laid a hand on his forearm, "this is very awkward of you."

"I would not ask unless it was vitally important."

"Galetaer just might be the key," added Gabriel, "to everything, Your Lordship."

"Well, if a civil servant such as Sir Geoffrey is arranging flights on ridiculously expensive private aircraft paid for by the overtaxed British people, your difficulty must be of imperative national interest." The Earl of Hawkesmoor took a long swallow of his whisky. "No promises but I'll call Bucky in the morning. Maybe he won't object too strenuously to visitors for the weekend."

"But we don't have anything to wear for the country," pointed out Caroline. "We can't turn up in our evening clothes."

"True," agreed her father. "Bucky and Margaret will think we've lost our minds. They might well anyway."

"I shall have that sorted by morning – not to worry," Robin said. He slid an arm about Caroline's shoulders and pulled her close. "Thank you, sir."

"Well, at least it's not an army of vampires attacking our castle," replied the Earl with a bit of a smile. "Battering rams and boiling oil – what a thing it was!"

The Carberry Hotel was a large manor house with a number of handsomely appointed rooms for their guests scattered over three floors. After bidding the Earl good night, Robin led Caroline to their digs.

"The clothes thing sorted by morning," said Caroline as he unlocked the beveled mahogany door marked 7 with a polished brass plaque. "I take that to mean poor old Cyril has been given the tedious assignment?"

Robin turned his head to grin at her. "But he's such a wizard at sorting things."

"You have a lot to answer for, sir," she sighed, imagining how difficult the morning was going to be, "asking my father to impose on a member of the Cheviot faction."

He pushed open the door and stood back politely so she could cross the threshold. "I repeat – only desperate times could force me to beg your father for this favor."

"Is it really desperate times?" asked Caroline as she passed him. She had a moment to glance around at what was a very pretty room done up in polished mahogany, rose pinks and creams. It managed to resemble comfortable quarters in a fine country house more than an anonymous hotel room. A flash of envy crossed her senses – there were happy humans all over the Carberry Hotel unburdened by vampire reality. There was a metallic click as Robin closed and locked the door. He headed for a sherry decanter that sat on a side table under the window. Beyond the glass, Caroline could see snow, illuminated by the hotel's outdoor lighting, fluttering past.

"Drink?" he asked, ignoring her question.

"No, thanks – I'm thoroughly topped up," Caroline found a seat on a reproduction Duncan Phyfe chair upholstered in a Regency era pink stripe. "How bad is it? I've got our children to worry about – Ari and Simon."

Robin sipped his sherry. "It's only bad," he said finally, setting his glass back on the table, "if I can't discover who or what is behind the Black and D'Aubigny murders, the PM might decide it's vampires after all and instigate some kind of eradication or confinement program. Neither Hope nor Sir Geoffrey is wild about the whole concept of revenants."

She watched as he walked towards her – effortlessly elegant in a bespoke black suit cut in the style of the 1930s. Her husband preferred men's tailoring from the early 20th century and generally either wore his own clothes from the era or had his current tailor at Gieves & Hawkes construct them.

"Darling," Robin knelt in front of her, "I will discover what is happening and I will put an end to it."

Caroline reached out and laid a hand on his cheek. "No doubts."

"I love you, Caroline DeBarry," Robin said, gazing at her in almost a kind of wonderment. "You have blessed my life a millionfold."

Before she could reply, he rose up and kissed her longingly. Caroline felt a deep shiver of pleasure course over her nervous system. That such a fascinating and breathtaking creature could find her – a thoroughly ordinary horse and hound rustic by her reckoning – enticing still took her by surprise.

Robin slid his arms around her waist and drew her up. He reluctantly pulled away from the kiss. "Let's go to bed," he murmured in her ear.

Chapter Thirty

Robin awoke to a light but persistent tapping on Room 7's outer door. Caroline was still asleep in his arms, her head of silky strawberry blonde hair resting in the curve of his shoulder. After dropping a kiss on the top of her head, he cautiously disentangled himself and stepped free of the four poster.

He opened the door to find Cyril Goforth standing in the hallway, looking exhausted and unamused in the artificial light from the hotel's wall sconces. His equerry was also in full possession of his Smythson portfolio so something urgent had blown up.

"It's three o'clock in the morning," Robin pointed out uselessly in a whisper. "Surely fetching a portmanteau of clothes ..."

Cyril's delicate teenager's face rearranged itself into a very sour expression. "No one calls luggage portmanteaus anymore, Your Serene Highness."

"Duly noted, Mr. Goforth."

"Cuthbert Hall, Lincolnshire. We'll have to travel our way." Cyril said with little enthusiasm as he really disliked molecular transfers. "Sir Geoffrey has just arrived by military helicopter."

Robin felt his stomach lurch. "Just give me a minute to get dressed."

Fortunately, Cuthbert Hall and Lincolnshire lay just within the boundaries of possibility for long range molecular transfer. It was a serious risk – especially in the notorious winter weather of northern Britain – but not completely unadvisable.

Robin, Cyril and two guardsmen reassembled themselves a short distance away from Cuthbert Hall – an impressive Elizabethan house currently lit up with the flashing lights of various emergency vehicles. Each vampire breathed out a sigh of relief at their safe arrival. No one wanted to end up impaled on a tree or blown to bits over Ireland in a brutal blast of winter air.

"Culpeper, Brown – to the rooftops. Stay out of sight," said Robin gazing out at Cuthbert Hall.

Even thrashed with harsh emergency lights, Cuthbert Hall was a handsome house – warm and inviting despite its natural formality. A classic Elizabethan E shaped construction, it was built of rose red brick with stone quoins. Large bow windows of leaded glass sparkled in eccentric light patterns that strobed through the cold night air.

"Your Serene Highness?" said Cyril breaking into his reverie. "Sir Geoffrey is waiting."

Robin sighed. He suddenly felt all of his three hundred years in his bones.

"By all means, let us not upset Sir Geoffrey," he said, starting the walk across the lawn towards Cuthbert Hall. Cyril Goforth ran a step or two to catch up. "Too late for that, sir."

They found the aforementioned civil servant in the hall's entry point – traditionally the small horizontal bar of the Elizabethan E-shaped house – waiting for them. Even at a distance, Sir Geoffrey was glowering. His government approved suit and tie seemed to be radiating with displeasure.

"Uh oh," murmured Robin.

The Prime Minister's right-hand man had a word with one of the uniformed officers who left the hall foyer with alacrity. Then he turned the full force of his attention to the approaching revenants.

"The bats have returned to the belfry," Sir Geoffrey said. He didn't sound at all amused by his own attempt at a witticism.

"Sir Geoffrey," Robin replied with a brief nod, "how can we be of service?"

The civil servant gave a harsh laugh. Again, it lacked warmth or genuine humor. Before he spoke, Constable looked around Cuthbert Hall's foyer for any potential eavesdroppers inadvertent or otherwise. Seeing none, he shook his head as if to clear it of competing thoughts and refocused on Robin.

"Cuthbert Hall has belonged to the Tiffin family since Elizabeth I elevated Percy Tiffin for his meritorious service monitoring import weights and measures." Sir Geoffrey held up a hand to indicate the richness of the Tudor inner hall with its black and white checkerboard marble floor, dull red painted walls hung with a number of important gilt framed pictures.

"I knew one of his sons, Miles Tiffin," interjected Cyril brightly in an attempt to derail the history lecture. "He was the Canon of ..."

"Stop!" commanded Sir Geoffrey Constable, his face a study in bitter annoyance. "I don't want to know."

"Go on, Sir Geoffrey." Robin threw Cyril a warning look that advised him to keep any chirpy observations to himself.

"The new Lord Tiffin took over the running of Cuthbert at the death of his father last year," the civil servant continued, leading them deeper into the house. "He and Lady Tiffin are quite young and are well liked by the people in the area. They have two children under the age of ten – Jasper and Lucy."

They turned to the left and entered a long linenfold paneled hallway. At the end of it were bright potable work lights being set up by lab technicians in white coveralls.

Jasper and Lucy – children. Robin felt ill. Nauseated by the thought of more death, more ruined lives because of what Cyril had designated the English Wendigo. He wove on his feet for a moment – dizzy from the sudden onslaught of sick – and almost buckled at the knees.

"Your Highness," gasped Cyril, reaching out to prevent him from falling, "you must sit!"

"No, no." Robin shook his head. "I am perfectly well."

He took in a deep steadying breath and felt the dizziness abate. Looking up, he saw Sir Geoffrey staring at him oddly – almost as if he were having a kind of revelation. A moment more and it was gone, replaced by the civil servant's usual implacable and unruffled expression.

"Lord and Lady Tiffin are away in Australia, overseeing their cattle station there," said Sir Geoffrey, continuing as if nothing untoward had occurred. "They are due back in a week's time."

They walked a few more steps to where the forensic techs were establishing their evidence grid and peered through the doorway into what once had been a secondary sitting room but had been since pressed into service as a very pleasant staff office with well-organized desks and its own kitchenette. Now it more resembled an abattoir. There wasn't a surface from floor to ceiling that wasn't glistening with arterial blood spray and death's sickly-sweet odor was so foul that even hardened crime scene techs were ashen with revulsion. Three of Cuthbert Hall's staff had been eviscerated in what was another frenzy of rending and tearing by a voracious entity. Once it had eaten its fill of their soft internal parts, it had strewn their gutted bodies about the room like discarded candy wrappers.

"The housekeeper, Mrs. Coppin and two security guards who were, it seems, unable to put up any kind of defense." Sir Geoffrey turned away from the appalling vision.

"Discovered by the nanny who had returned home late from a Christmas party in the village. Unsurprisingly, she's gone into shock and is at hospital."

"And the children?" Robin's voice was strained. "Lucy and Jasper?"

The civil servant clenched his jaw. "The children have vanished. Officers are combing the house now for the third time. I very much need you to come up with something. Lord Tiffin is an old schoolmate of the PM's and he is about a breath away from deciding you lot are responsible for everything. Once he goes down that rabbit hole, you can expect a draconian response to you and your kind."

"The Prime Minister," Robin said very quietly, "does realize that my kind will not go gentle into that good night?"

"The PM knows you have chinks in your armor – family connections."

"I do not take well to threats, Sir Geoffrey."

A momentary expression of genuine regret fluttered over Sir Geoffrey's bland features but was immediately shuttered.

"Alastair Hope is not a bad chap, but he is a political animal, the ultimate survivor. Frankly, he doesn't want to take you on – subduing your kingdom would be complex, bloody and dangerous. He'd much rather have a tacit detente. That said, don't make the mistake of underestimating him."

Robin realized that the lifelong civil servant was actually giving him sage advice – counsel that he wasn't obliged to dispense to a revenant king.

"I will keep things tamped down," Sir Geoffrey said, "for as long as I am able but bring me something soon. If possible, let it be those children."

"If the Tiffin children are still alive, I will find them." Robin promised grimly and then looked at Cyril Goforth who was tapping notes into his tablet. "Time to get back and find that wretch, Cam Drummond."

"You've got three – maybe four days before things get really tricky," Sir Geoffrey added in his old boy drawl. "I think I can just manage to keep the proverbial lid tamped down until then."

One of the forensic techs emerged from the blood-soaked room, waving a plastic covered electronic notepad. "Need an authorization, sir, before we can process the bodies." As the civil servant turned away to handle the crime scene details, Robin and Cyril retreated back through Lord Tiffin's impressive family home. They stayed silent since various uniformed officers and techs were also moving along the same route to the central entryway. All of them wore the pinched, ashen faces of first responders on a particularly horrific call. Robin had another moment to wish he had been of more help to Sir Geoffrey and the human contingent.

"Brown wants to show us something," murmured Cyril once they were back outside in the chilled winter air, "up on the roof."

A light snow had dusted everything. If the situation wasn't so dire, Robin would have mightily enjoyed the view of an Elizabethan rose brick house dressed in its winter shroud. As it was, he could only draw in a breath of icy air and suggest to Cyril that they find a quiet spot to spin their molecules up to Cuthbert Hall's roof line.

"What have you found?" Robin asked once he reassembled on the slate roof. Lights thrown from the various emergency vehicles parked near Cuthbert's main entry partially illuminated the roof so they could just make out the craggy geography.

Brown wasn't far – next to a very tall 16th century chimney. The guardsman waved them over with his flashlight, looking grim. The complex roof system was wet with new snow and very slippery, so it took a few minutes for Robin and Cyril to pick their way across the expanse of roof.

"Your Highness," said Brown with a cursory bob of his head.

"What is it?"

"Round this way," he indicated the chimney and handed off the flashlight to Robin. "Had Culpeper do some photographs on his phone. In this weather, it won't last much longer. Not much room so you take a look, sir."

Moving gingerly, Robin stepped around the tall brick structure. He dropped down into a long flat corridor that lay between two roof peaks and allowed modest workspace for repairs. It was a space with just a bit of overhang and protection from the elements. Snow had not yet accumulated within it to the degree of the open rooftop. He aimed the flashlight's beam into the shadowy canyon, looking for whatever had galvanized his guards' attention. Unsurprisingly, the workspace showed both its age and some indifferent Edwardian masonry repair. There were a few abandoned bird nests from the previous summer and what appeared to be the remains of a long-deceased rat. Robin gave a momentary start and took in a short, surprised breath. A child's teddy bear lay on its side as if carelessly dropped, staring back at him dully with its black button eyes.

And there was blood. Lots of blood. There was a clear trail of it running the length of the corridor. Bloody footsteps beginning to lose their integrity in the damp weather. He took a couple of steps forward and then knelt to examine one in the glow of his flashlight.

"You see it, sir?" called out Brown from his makeshift shelter by the chimney. "Or am I losing me bleedin' faculties after all these years?"

"I see it," Robin called back, trying to make sense of what he was looking at – even a vampire could be rattled by dark, strange things.

"Clue me in, please?" came Cyril's anxious voice – a little sharp in the winter breeze.

"Bloody hoof prints," Robin said. He stared down at the set of very large, sticky crimson hooves. Far larger than any domestic farm animal ever seen in the British Isles or indeed, anywhere on earth.

"Come again, sir?" bleated Cyril. "I don't think I heard you properly."

"Cloven hooves. Giant cloven hooves."

Chapter Thirty-one

"You look tired," said Caroline from her place in Room 7's reproduction Regency sleigh bed and watched as her husband carried a breakfast tray towards her. He looked pale even for a vampire king and haunted as if a frightful specter was dogging his heels. "I don't suppose you would like catch me up on all the nocturnal doings? And don't tell me you were just collecting country castle-wear either."

Robin smiled at her and laughed as if the line actually deserved the hearty response. "Country castle-wear. Very funny, darling. One is on fortune's watch fob when one marries a witty woman."

"Robin ..." she began.

"And look here – a piping hot omelet for my lady!" He placed the tray on her lap with great flourish. "English sausage, a croissant ... cup of hot tea, perhaps?"

Misdirection was always Robin's weapon of choice when he didn't want to come clean. Caroline nodded as he held up the silver-plated reproduction Queen Anne teapot.

"Thank you," she said, picking up the warm croissant. "Most kind."

He executed a courtly bow. "I live to serve you, madam."

"Good because once you've done that, you can pull up a chair and tell me all you know."

For once, Robin did not respond to her cheerful rejoinder in kind. Instead, he almost seemed to shudder as if his specter had laid a clammy hand on his shoulder. He sat on the edge of the bed, clearly deciding on a response.

"Is it really that bad?" she asked quietly. "You were gone an awfully long time."

Robin laid a hand on the bedcover – a very feminine pattern of large pink English roses and pale green ribbons – and caressed her knee affectionately.

"Nothing we can't handle," he said finally.

"Another murder?"

Her husband continued to stroke her knee. He didn't look at her. "Something attacked and killed three people. I'd so prefer not to talk about it, Caroline. Please don't ask me to." Caroline understood Robin well enough to know when a subject had gone on the endangered list. Robin was, for the most part, reasonably open about the shadowy realm of the revenants but certain aspects and incidences of it he clearly kept from her. She intuited that he did this to spare her from being forced to comprehend things that no human should carry in their heads and loved him all the more for his consideration.

She speared a section of egg and ate it. "How lovely! The Carberry Hotel certainly makes short work of breakfast." Robin finally looked over at her. The haunted look in his eyes dematerialized as he laughed and stood up. "One of the many, many things I adore about you," he said, "is your hearty appreciation of a good hot meal."

"I do love food," Caroline admitted, glad to see him a bit happier. "One of life's rich pageants."

"That sounds frighteningly like your father."

Caroline turned her attention to the English sausage. "Like father, like daughter."

A polite knock came at Number 7's beveled door. Robin answered it and found a very weary looking Cyril Goforth standing in the hallway. The revenant civil servant closed his Smythson's portfolio and stifled a yawn.

"Good morrow, Your Serene Highness," he murmured with a courtly bow from the neck.

"Cyril. I promise you a holiday after this is all over," said Robin kindly. "A nice cottage by the sea. As our colonial brothers like to say, what's up?"

"His Lordship, the Earl would like you know that Galetaer Castle is a go. Expected for lunch and the weekend to follow."

The morning was spent organizing the foray to Chill Wind Castle. Robin sorted his team – Gabriel, Goforth, Brown, Tinley and Culpeper into watches. Gabriel was charged with making sure the less able Cyril Goforth managed all the molecular transfers. One set would get some rest at Carberry while the other maintained a vigil at Galetaer with strict instructions to pull Caroline and her father out first if anything untoward should present itself. They were to constantly have a weather eye out for Cam Drummond and to stay out of the castle proper unless he called for them or their English Wendigo made an appearance. If it did, all holds barred and they'd do whatever needed to be done.

Robin, at the wheel of one of the hired Range Rovers, made a left onto a gravel road that would, according to the vehicle's GPS, lead them to the Bannatyres and Galetaer Castle. It was a rare sharply clear December day in Scotland which had allowed them to spot the imposing 11th century castle from the main road – a craggy collection of towers and battlements that even from a great distance looked tired under the bright sun and in need of repairs.

"Bucky's very proud of the old heap but I expect arctic temperatures and even colder food," said the Earl from his place in the back. "I hope Goforth packed for the summit of Mt. Everest."

"He even threw a bottle of sherry and some hobnobs in your bag," replied Caroline, turning round in her passenger seat to smile at her father.

"Sir Ronald – tell me a bit more about him if you would," said Robin, pausing the Rover to allow a pair of cheerful farm dogs to trot across the sleety gravel road.

The Earl of Hawkesmoor snorted. "Typical baronet! Sandroyd, Eton, Lifeguard commission and then home to this backwater. Nice enough chap but thoroughly wrongheaded on sheep. Fair warning – if he talks you into hacking out to look at the country, you will never be warm again in this or any other lifetime."

"And Lady Bannatyre?" Robin allowed the Range Rover to move forward again as the dogs loped off into the countryside.

"Lady Margaret in her own right – daughter of the old Duke of Swanbourne. Could have done better for herself but liked Bucky for some unfathomable reason. She occasionally judges the hound group at Crofts." The Earl sighed deeply. "It's a great barn of a place and very little staff. We shall be very uncomfortable and cold."

"Well, we haven't had a full staff at Hawkesmoor since Grandfather handed in his hat," Caroline pointed out.

"Hawkesmoor has proper heating." Her father shook his head. "My god, I hope they have plenty of extra hot water bottles."

Robin arced left, clearing a thick copse of Scots Pine. Galetaer Castle reappeared – one more short stretch and they'd be at the proverbial gates. It was a huge shambling rout of grey stone battlements and hulking turrets. If there hadn't been a Bannatyre flag fluttering on the battlement flagpole, Galetaer would look completely abandoned.

"Remember the story?" he asked as the hired car headed into the castle's interior entrance.

"You are researching a book." Caroline made a face. "We may be human but we're not stupid."

He threw her an affectionate glance. "And what do you do if you spot Cam Drummond, my little porcupine?"

"Do not engage even if he comes bearing hot tea and sandwiches. Alert you as soon as humanly possible."

"Gad," groaned the Earl, "there they are. It's worse than I thought – Buckle is still alive!"

Standing on wide stone steps that led up to the central entry was a small group. A coming together of householder and staff that had been replicated in country houses across the British Isles since Elizabethan times albeit with serviceable changes in costume.

"Buckle?" Robin raised an eyebrow and parked the hired car next to another far more ancient Range Rover and a collection of other vehicles.

"Welcome to Galetaer Castle!" called out a tall and balding gentleman in a tweed hacking jacket. About the same age as His Lordship, the Earl, Sir Ronald Bannatyre was hale and fit from walking his sheepfolds.

"Bucky!" returned the Earl of Hawkesmoor, taking the lead by shaking his former schoolmate's hand warmly.

"Margaret – you are looking well!"

"This good Scottish air," Lady Margaret replied accepting a kiss on the cheek from the Earl. "So glad you could come!" It was clear that in her day, Lady Margaret – a tall and elegant champagne blonde – had been quite a beauty. Despite the chill, she wore a gorgeously cut Chanel suit in pale green and the aforementioned Scottish breeze failed to dislodge a single strand of her immaculately coiffed pageboy.

"It was very very good of you to have us – especially at this time of the year!" The Earl turned to indicate Robin and Caroline who were waiting politely behind him. "You remember Caroline, of course, and this is my son in law, Robin Dashwood."

"Caroline!" Lady Margaret came forward to grasp her hands. "It's been too long. How is Peter? Hannah?"

While Caroline spoke to the lady of Galetaer Castle, Robin stepped forward to shake her husband's large, steady hand. "Sir Ronald," he said with a slight tip of his head to indicate their social caste. He might be the legitimate Earl of Hawkesmoor but in the 21st century human world, he was a former history professor who consulted for the British government.

"A pleasure, Mr. Dashwood." Sir Ronald shook his hand vigorously.

"Robin, please."

"I understand that you're intrigued by old Sir Neville Ponsonby." Sir Ronald released Robin's hand and then clapped him on the shoulder. "We can certainly spin you a few yarns on that score."

"That would be of immense help to my book on 13th century religious fervor," Robin replied warmly – hoping he sounded like an appropriately impassioned scholar. "Very kind of you."

"Think nothing of it!" Sir Ronald held up an arm to indicate both the castle's main entryway and an elderly man in a flawless butler's uniform. "This is our man, Buckle. Don't hesitate to ask him if you should require anything during your stay."

Despite his age, Buckle seemed as hardy as his employers. Possessed of a hawk-like mien and seemingly just as humorless as a raptor, he motioned younger staff to see to the luggage in the Range Rover and then intoned soberly that lunch was waiting in the second dining room.

Once safely through the doors, Galetaer Castle revealed itself as indeed massive and medieval. It gave the initial impression of having had very little done to it since Sir Neville's day despite that being well-nigh impossible. The yawning expanse of the castle just absorbed all the improvements over the centuries until they seemed like bits of flotsam on the surface of the sea.

The Great Hall was cavernous, half-timbered and unapologetically unplastered with all the original stonework visible. A tribute to 13th century life – an enormous stone fireplace held pride of place while rather tired looking Ponsonby and Bannatyre heraldic devices hung from the rafters and an impressive collection of military weaponry lined the walls. Robin glanced about the ancient hall as they were led to wherever lunch was laid out. It was clearly too large for effective daily use and probably ruinously expensive to heat or modernize.

Galetaer, the Earl of Hawkesmoor had warned him during the drive, was a frigid rabbit warren extending over three stories and almost 300 rooms. Most of the castle sat dormant and unused as Sir Ronald and Lady Margaret only utilized one wing for living and entertaining. Unlike Hawkesmoor Castle, it didn't possess elaborate state rooms nor a particularly intriguing history to attract the public. Indeed, as a property in Scotland belonging to an English family since the 13th century, Galetaer wasn't Scottish enough for the Scots and too remote for the English to be much interested so the castle just sat and moldered under centuries of rain, snow and fog.

As he followed the Bannatyres from the Great Hall, Robin could see that even the more modernized wing of Galetaer

Castle was badly in need of restoration and repairs. All of the small staff's work in keeping the place tidy and presentable could not hide cracked plaster and warping floors from foundation issues. Like Poe's House of Usher, Galetaer was sinking in the damp.

Lunch was laid out in what the butler, Buckle, had called the second dining room. A much smaller space dominated by a fireplace with a heavily carved mahogany chimneypiece, it was cheerfully Victorian with deep blue green walls and heavy velvet drapes to keep in the heat. A rectangular dining table of Regency design was situated by the working fireplace. It was nicely laid, Robin noted as he was directed by Lady Margaret to his chair, with Wedgewood's Asiatic Pheasants pattern in the rare teal color. A favourite among Victorians, he had no doubt it was a service that arrived at Galetaer Castle, packed in wooden crates and clean straw, at some point in the mid-1800s.

"Please sit," said Lady Margaret waving a hand at a nondescript local girl in a grey uniform and white apron – the crisp effect a little spoiled by the formidable grey cardigan she wore to combat the damp cold of the castle. "Thank you, Fiona – if you would be kind enough to serve now."

"We thought," said Sir Ronald, pulling out his wife's chair so she could sit, "you might like a ride after lunch – get some fresh air and all that. Then tonight over dinner, we can tell you all we know of old Sir Neville."

"Most kind of you," Robin replied, pushing in Caroline's chair in sync with Sir Ronald – an unconscious social dance. He pretended not to see the Earl's subtle attempt to catch his eye. "I'd welcome the chance to see Galetaer from the back of a horse."

"Wonderful! A storm is coming in so it may be our last chance to hack this weekend." Sir Ronald beamed at the table as he found his own seat.

The Earl of Hawkesmoor coughed politely. "If you don't mind, Bucky, I'm going to beg off and sit by a fire with a good book – Fleece and Folly by Lord Dormer.

"It's hard to go wrong with a classic," sighed Sir Ronald. "I reread it at least once a year."

Robin watched as Caroline suppressed a smile and pretended to find Fiona's placement of a soup bowl in front of her fascinating. He did so love his wife – the ultimate social anodyne.

"I shall stay behind as well," announced Lady Margaret from the head of the table. "Buckle and I will need to see to battening down the hatches. Fiona, Angus and Mrs. Lees will have to evacuate after lunch, I'm afraid, or they'll be trapped by the storm."

Robin saw Fiona who was placing a bowl in front of the Earl, shudder slightly, almost spilling some of the creamed asparagus soup. The local girl moved away to fetch another bowl. It was clear that the Earl was going to be correct about cold food. Not only was the castle too large for its undoubtedly Victorian era boiler system to make a dent in heating it but an indifferently trained local day staff unable to serve from a soup tureen boded ill for hot meals.

"Surely there are plenty of rooms should they need to stay," he prodded, interested in Fiona's reaction. As soon as the words left his mouth, the girl's back stiffened as she retrieved another bowl of soup from the sideboard.

Sir Ronald and Lady Margaret exchanged a quick look. One that seemed to indicate that this was an old point of contention.

"It would be more convenient if they stayed at the castle," Lady Margaret conceded and glanced over at the local girl. "A bit more alacrity, Fiona, please or it'll be teatime before we finish."

Sir Ronald had a sip from his water glass. "Galetaer is a big, ramshackle place and the locals believe it to be haunted. We have excellent groundsmen and cleaners. They just don't like to be here after dark, so we've adapted. Thank god for Buckle! The man is unflappable."

"Is Galetaer Castle haunted?" asked Caroline in genuine interest.

"You know, it might be," he said, winking at his wife. "We've both heard a phantom footstep or two, doors opening and closing. Nothing as exciting as an apparition, I regret to say."

"But don't let such things scare you," interjected Lady Margaret quickly. "Probably all explained away by drafts and the boiler hiccupping. We're very happy to have visitors! The children won't be home until late next week for Christmas, so this is really a treat for us."

"You are very kind," said Caroline with real warmth. "We can't thank you enough for agreeing to let Robin do his research."

"Besides," said the Earl gazing benignly across the table at Robin, "Hawkesmoor has its share of otherworldly things too."

Chapter Thirty-two

Sir Ronald kept several nice horses in what was left of the castle's stables. It was clear from the meticulous condition of the box stalls and barn amenities that as with many rural people, the animals had better care than the humans. He had given Caroline Lady Margaret's grey Cob, Angus, to ride and his son's horse – a 17 hand Draft cross named Pluto – to Robin. They weren't particularly fancy horses but solid, unflappable fox hunters that were a pleasure to hack cross country.

The afternoon was remarkably clear for Scotland and despite a biting breeze, a keen winter sun had cleared away most of the snow. They cantered across one of Galetaer's sheep pastures, popping over a low and ancient stone wall to the exuberant crow-hopping delight of Angus.

"Sorry!' exclaimed Sir Ronald in some dismay, pulling up his big chestnut gelding, Barnaby. "He usually isn't silly." Caroline laughed as she rode out the small bucks with experienced ease and brought Angus to a standstill. The large Cob snorted in the cold air as if to say no one should ever take me for granted. He looked around, clearly proud of himself, while Robin easily cleared the stone wall on his borrowed bay and joined them.

"No worries. He just feels good," she said, dropping the reins to the buckle so Angus could have his head. The Cob shook his head, rattling the Pelham bit with its curb chain. "What a character!"

"Margaret adores Angus." Sir Ronald patted Barnaby's neck. "He's almost old enough to vote in this country but one would never know."

"Beautiful land," said Robin, catching his breath after the long gallop. He gazed out at the low rolling hills dusted with snow and long sweeps of undulating pasture gone deep copper in the dark months of winter. Galetaer Castle loomed in the distance, a grey English gargoyle perching on Scottish land. Behind it the sky had darkened to a slate grey, coils of thick cloud foretelling the impending storm.

"Thank you – not too bad this year." Sir Ronald shifted in the saddle and blew out a long frosty breath. "Hunting's been excellent so no complaints."

Robin pulled his attention away from the December brushed landscape and tossed a glance at Caroline who was absorbed in checking her saddle girth. The Cob was a handsome, hardy breed but their typical conformation featuring broad chests and limited wither meant saddles could slip if the rider wasn't vigilant.

"Sir Ronald," he said, watching as Caroline looked up from the billets in interest, "I have a friend out this way who might have a little connection to Galetaer. I know he admires the place – Cam Drummond?"

It was the proverbial shot in the dark. Time was growing short for British vampires.

The lanky Englishman emitted a cheerful laugh. "Cam – that most Scottish of men. Yes, he pops round quite frequently. Even did a display of Scottish dancing for a Sheep Society do last summer. Caro, you must remember?"

Robin watched as Caroline narrowed her eyes in thought and then slowly nodded. "I remember all the dancing," she said, running her fingertips over the bristles of Angus' traditionally hogged mane, "but not Cam Drummond. There were a lot of them."

"Has he popped round lately?" asked Robin.

Beyond Galetaer Castle came a deep murmur of thunder from the invading black storm. All three horses picked up their heads at the warning note. Sir Ronald gathered up his reins, his gelding Barnaby jigging sideways a step at the clear call to duty.

"We have about ten minutes to get back before it hits," the castle's keeper announced with another laugh, "and we're about twenty minutes out. Should have had more of a weather eye out – follow me!"

With that, he urged Barnaby forward into a canter and in four strides, cleared the three-foot stone wall. Robin saw his opportunity to learn more about Cam Drummond's frequent visits to Galetaer gallop away into the distance and under his breath, cursed the wretched luck. The metaphorical clock was ticking to the moment when the Prime Minister moved to contain what he imagined to be the vampire threat.

"Angus," Caroline said, expertly shortening her double Pelham reins, "time to make your Cob ancestors proud." The grey Cob obligingly broke into a gallop and soared over the ancient stone barrier. Robin had no choice but to follow. Pluto was perfectly amiable but a little hard-mouthed and leaned heavily into the low port kimberwick bit as they headed for the wall. Robin found himself glad of a running martingale as Pluto registered that they were headed back to the stable and his hay and was clearly planning on pulling like a freight train all the way home.

Despite Pluto wanting to change careers to steeplechaser, it was the kind of euphoric hard gallop all confident riders took joy in and despite his heavy worries, Robin's spirits rose with each hoofbeat. For three hundred years, riding horses had made for some of the happiest times of his long existence.

The three horses lit out for the castle stables, covering the rise and fall of the rough Scottish pastureland with a steady assurance born of familiarity with the terrain. Each of the huge grazing pastures were separated by ancient stone walls requiring the riders to jump in and then jump out again as they navigated their way back to Galetaer Castle.

Midway to sanctuary in the castle stable, a harsher wave of Scottish air struck them and with the frigid air came electrified thunder. Robin saw Caroline's horse jump sideways, startled by a streak of crooked lightning that momentarily turned the inky cloud bank above them into a spirit lantern. The grey Cob skittered and slipped on damp gorse, almost coming to grief. Caroline coolly supported Angus with leg pressure and drove him forward. Six strides later and they jumped another stone wall without issue. Another less capable rider might have been left hurt on the ground. Sending up a quick prayer of thanksgiving to the universe, Robin followed on Pluto. He was careful to stay in the rear in case Caroline needed any help with the less agile Cob.

As Pluto cleared the stone wall and hurtled after his stable mate, Angus, the rain began to fall. It quickly shifted from a smattering of heavy drops to a veritable dove grey curtain of water.

Robin knew from three centuries of riding in all kinds of weather that conditions were quickly transforming from an adventure to dangerous. The Scottish gorse in the fields would shortly become waterlogged and very slippery. Visibility was getting poor in the lashings of rain so that neither horse nor rider could be trusted to accurately judge obstacles such as Galetaer's pasture walls. Sir Ronald rode reasonably well but not skillfully enough to get out of real trouble, should Barnaby make a mistake in the pouring rain.

Caroline was mounted on an aging gelding with limited agility – even her brilliance on a horse couldn't make up for a major misfire on the Cob's part.

Robin's throat tightened as he galloped after Caroline. What would he do if anything ever happened to Caroline? The only reason he still walked among humans and vampires was because he could not bear to be without her. He found both passion and peace in Caroline's embrace. If he was able to help vampires fashion a new reality in the 21st century, it would be because Lady Caroline DeBarry was by his side.

He let out a short breath as the 17-hand draft cross lumbered to the right, following an oft-ridden trail through the field and splashing through a pool of rainwater. Robin sent up a request. Not just a thoughtful prayer but a call – one of his few remaining earthly abilities as Lord Pwyll of the Tylwyth Teg. He commanded any Lantern Men in the immediate atmosphere to come to his aid.

Dismissed in the 21st century as ridiculous medieval folklore and patronizingly explained away as an environmental effect such as marsh gas, they were insatiable elemental beings roaming the ethers hunting for energy. Lantern Men hungered for electrical energy be it storm or human. Hapless people still went missing while on an evening stroll, lured away from the footpath by a strange light or two.

As lower Elementals, Lantern Men were bound to serve him, but Robin rarely made use of the edict. Most lower Elementals reminded him of sharks – pitiless, primitive and single-minded.

The downpour slipped up a notch. What was left of the afternoon light was extinguished by both hard rain and menacing storm cloud. The dramatic Scottish landscape, along with Galetaer Castle as visual guidepost, had vanished in the storm. Robin figured they now had about twenty feet of visibility – not nearly enough to get them home in one piece.

Absolutely drenched, he scanned ahead in the murk for any sign of the two other riders. A moment later and he nearly collided with Sir Ronald who had pulled up Barnaby. The cumbersome Pluto braked awkwardly, sliding in mud and half-reared to pivot around Barnaby's prancing hindquarters. Robin rode it out and then, obediently, the Draft cross lumbered to a stop.

"I am sorry," said Sir Ronald, wheeling his chestnut about. "Damned hard to see anything."

"Where's Caroline?" Robin shouted over a rumble of thunder.

"Here!" she cried, emerging from the gloom and joining them. "I'm all right."

"A bit of a tough spot," said their host as the thunder died away for the moment. "I do apologize."

"You're not to blame for the weather," Caroline replied, wiping rainwater from her face. "Is there a way to avoid the walls?"

Sir Ronald nodded. "Longer though. We'll have to negotiate a couple of gates in this."

Robin pushed Pluto into the center. "How many stonewalls left?"

Sir Ronald brightened. "Only one and then it's a pretty short sprint home."

"That's it then," Robin decided, gathering up his reins. He sent up his command to the Elementals: ghost lights only – no human interference and if you cross me, I will crush you into little pieces and let the wind have you.

"How can we possibly jump anything?" Caroline was asking, a note of worry entering her patrician voice. "We'll either crash into the stonewall or each other."

Sir Ronald said something about alacrity and not freezing to death, but it was obliterated by another crash of thunder. Lightning streaked across the sky – electric blue with violent energy. At that moment, lights bobbed against the slate-y cloud ceiling like glowing balloons. A tunnel of visibility opened up, like a thoroughfare lit by old Victorian streetlamps, revealing the path of about two miles over undulating fields.

Only Robin could see the true source of the mysterious illuminations. The Elementals rode the storm wind like the rotting carrion they were, their tattered robes flapping in the sharp winds. Desiccated, vaguely humanoid mummies, they dragged luminous lanterns housed in ornate and unearthly metals through the air.

"Come on!" he shouted, urging Pluto into a gallop and taking the lead. Caroline was quick to dart after him, leaving Sir Ronald to take up the rear.

The Lantern Men prowled the air currents like sharks but did as they were bidden. They held out their mysterious lanterns, providing light for Lord Pwyll of the Tylwyth Teg and did not attempt to misdirect Caroline or Sir Ronald away from the path.

Robin jumped the final stone wall and half-halted Pluto as the horse leaned into the bridle heavily. The big horse was growing anxious, sensing the hungry beings in the air above them and wanted to bolt for the stable. Throwing a glance over his shoulder, Robin saw that both Angus and Barnaby were beginning to panic as they too landed on the other side of the wall – as herd animals, the horse's basic instinct was flight if a predator presented itself. If the less able Sir

Ronald lost control of Barnaby, Caroline could end up getting hurt. He refocused on the way ahead – the final stretch to the stable yard.

Lantern Men, he commanded, rise and be gone. Do not wander the byways of Galetaer Castle again – all who reside here are under my protection.

At his words, the Elementals began to drift upwards, dragging their glowing lanterns to the higher currents by skeletal hands. The lit pathway began to shudder and fade as the Lantern Men gained altitude but just enough of it remained to allow safe passage down the final rise. They clattered into Galetaer's yard just as the last lantern flickered out, lost in the storm.

Chapter Thirty-three

"My god," said Caroline as she yanked off a sodden sweater. "I thought I knew what cold was. Clearly, I have been living in a fool's paradise."

Upon returning to the castle proper from the stable, the ancient Buckle had seen them to their rooms. He no longer moved with the cat-like speed and agility of a younger, fitter butler so, with teeth chattering, they had slowly trailed him up a long set of well-worn stone steps to the family rooms.

Their weekend digs had been recently updated, according to Buckle with just a hint of pride welling up in his dark eyes, and a former sitting room transformed into a bath. Then, with the sober intent of an undertaker with a range of coffins on display, he introduced them to relatively small but handsomely appointed guest quarters. As with much of the livable wing's décor, the emphasis was on quiet country living and it was also abundantly clear that modern day Bannatyres had wisely abandoned the larger spaces to spend their days in Galetaer's smaller, easier to heat accommodations.

Buckle had intoned with deep formality that drinks would be served in the library at seven and departed, presumably to see to the endless details left by the evacuating castle domestic staff. Fortunately for Sir Ronald and Lady Margaret, the stable lads and farm help were made of sterner stuff.

"Yes," said Robin, shivering. "Your father elbowed me in the side and mouthed the words I tried to warn you."

Caroline laughed and peeled off a soaked turtleneck that had been under the sweater. "He's always enjoyed being the

Oracle of Hawkesmoor – that horse has a hole in it somewhere, Bog Goldenrod will take over the north pasture, mark my words – the scourge of scabby mouth will return!"

"Despite my bona fides as a gentleman," Robin threw his wet shirt at her, "I'm getting to the bath first!"

He pivoted and darted for the newly renovated bathroom. It had been done up in gleaming white tile, reproduction Victorian fixtures with both a large ball and claw tub and a separate American style shower. Again, not grandiose as in some glossy magazine's idea of luxury, but handsome and workmanlike. Robin admired the quiet good taste and thought, not for the first time that day, Galetaer Castle had been fortunate in gaining Lady Margaret.

"You are the ultimate Georgian bad boy," said Caroline, following him into the new guest bath. "Going vampire and all that gothic guff."

Robin stepped into the adjoining shower, switched on the water and held out his hand. "Join me? This would have been considered a mild scandal in my day – bathing with the wife."

"How about with the Georgian's well-fixed mistress in town?"

He raised an amused eyebrow. "All bets were off with doxies."

She took his hand and stepped into a stream of hot water blasting from the shower head. "I think I can just barely sense feeling returning to my hands and feet. There was one moment out there when I thought we were all going to get hit with lightning ..."

"You know, in 1750," Robin interrupted, pulling her towards him, "a common vulgarity for a woman's breast was Cupid's Kettledrum."

"Charming," Caroline said.

He ran a hand over her wet skin and traced an arc around a nipple. "You have such lovely kettledrums, Caro."

"Oh, stop – you had me at common vulgarity." Caroline slid her arms up around his neck and kissed him.

Many vampires lost their interest in pure sex, preferring the strange eroticism of feeding to making love to either humans or another revenant. Robin had never joined those ranks. He had a keen sexual appetite and sated it with any number of temporary entanglements over the centuries. As a vampire, he had felt almost human again in the embrace of a passionate lover.

Despite all the women he'd known – many who were extraordinary beauties with extraordinary lives – it was Lady Caroline DeBarry who had enslaved him. Caro's fine Northern features and strawberry blonde coloring were too Edwardian to be considered truly beautiful in the 21st century. She belonged in a Munnings picture, sitting on one of the painter's noble field hunters and such rare beauty captivated him. But what had truly ensnared him was Caroline's innate nobility – her kindness, intelligence and bravery. She was a living link to both his past and future as if everything he had ever loved or admired had distilled itself in one human frame.

He answered her kiss with another – deeper and hungrier. Making love to Caroline always set him alight like a Druid wicker man. As a vampire hybrid, his physical chemistry was complex and unnatural powered by a revenant and Tylwyth Teg interface. Sometimes he discovered so much pleasure and pain in Caroline's arms that his entire nervous system threatened to detonate – shattering his three-dimensional form to molecules.

Caroline leaned back against the wet shower wall, her breath becoming rapid as he moved his ravenous mouth to her neck and down to her left breast. He could feel intense desire threading through her human form, desperate to be allowed to intertwine with his own alien system.

Effortlessly Robin lifted Caroline up and as her legs wrapped around him, he drove deep inside her body. She cried out at the sensuous intrusion and he answered by pressing a brutal kiss to her mouth, cutting off the sound.

"Mustn't frighten Buckle," Robin murmured once he pulled his mouth from hers. He felt his vampire structure weaponize into aggression, the need to dominate, control and absorb – every hot, insatiable nerve ending demanding he devour Caroline sexually.

Too far gone to be subtle and sophisticated, Robin pressed his wife against the wall, moving within her with raw power and urgency. Blistering pleasure, incandescent pain. Blistering pleasure, incandescent pain – an electrified rhythm that threatened to fracture his outer form with its ferocity.

In all their time together, he had never actually broken apart during sex and disintegrated in her arms. Knowing it would frighten Caroline, it was always a battle not to surrender to his strange chemistry.

Pleasure, pain, pleasure, pain … incalculable joy, white hot panic … Caroline threw her head against his shoulder, shivering with human exhilaration as he charged again and again. Pain, panic, pleasure … Robin felt as if he were a Roman candle. No extremities, no limits, no boundaries – only burning, glittering chaos. He'd be lost in another shudder.

"Caroline," Robin grasped at her body, her wet skin, her presence as a lifeline. "Don't let me go."

Panic … panic … pleasure … he gasped and fell against her, complete.

Caroline stroked his back as they breathed together, heart rates beginning to return to normal.

"All right, darling?" she asked softly.

Robin let out a long breath and nodded. Speech seemed beyond him for a time and he wondered if he'd partially dismantled after all. He felt transparent and exhausted as if bits and pieces of him were zinging in the atmosphere, trying to recombine with the main body.

"I love you," Caroline said, kissing his cheek. She made a surprised noise and stepped away from him to examine his face. "Robin, you're bleeding."

Startled, he lifted a hand to his face. "Good god. I am."

"Nosebleed." She looked perplexed.

"It's nothing," Robin tilted his head back, wondering if his assurance was actually right. His vampiric healing system normally made short work of both minor and major trauma to his physical form. Something like a common nosebleed should have been caught up in his neural net and repaired well before it could manifest.

"I'll fetch a towel," said Caroline stepping out of the shower.

Robin turned his face to the warm water and let the shower spray wash away the crimson rivulets. He felt very tired -- as if something was hammering at his aura requiring large energy expenditures to prevent a catastrophic breach. Perhaps that was it. He had placed protections over Number 7 Audley Square, Hawkesmoor and the Bailey in Manhattan. These were esoteric domes of magic designed to repel supernatural interlopers. Perhaps their English Wendigo was testing his defenses. Simon's recent experiences that indicated as much.

"Mind how you go," he murmured, thinking of his son.

"So, I'm basically just bait," said Simon as he and Alin climbed out of the Dragos' black SUV near Central Park.

An autumnal twilight had swept over New York from the sea. Mist rose like urban ghosts from a recent rain, weaving through grey streets and the vast parkland. Although the day had moments of bright skies and sun, it was growing cold. Most New Yorkers seemed eager to duck in somewhere warm to enjoy the holiday season.

"Not just you, my friend," replied Alin Dragos, ever cheerful. His breath hung in the icy air. "Someone else wanted to help too."

Della emerged from a second SUV that had just pulled up to the curve. Her face lit up at the sight of him and she ran across the damp sidewalk to grasp his hands.

"Della," Simon breathed, both dumbfounded and horrified by her appearance, "you should not be here."

Tears flooded her large brown eyes. "I'm sorry for the things I said."

"You had every right to say them. You …"

Della shook her head. "I want to help. Lenka – Alin's wife explained about the syndicate …"

"The syndicate?" Simon squeezed Della's gloved hands and threw a glance at Alin who offered a sheepish grin.

"Lenka told her about the crime organization – the vampires."

"And how your father is a government agent working to bring them down," Della added, sliding her arms around Simon's waist. She rested her head on his chest. "How you're helping to draw them out."

Simon's throat tightened and he wrapped his arms around her, kissing the top of her head. "You shouldn't be here," he repeated, his voice breaking slightly.

"You're not doing this alone, mi amor," Della said. "We are together."

"Oh, love." Simon felt a tear of his own spill over.

Alin Dragos coughed. "We send out a coded message on 4chan and the dark web – baby substitution stuff. We say we are meeting your noble father deep in Central Park. Maybe The Ravine." He referred to a large woodland area in Central Park that allowed urbanites to escape the city and hike in a more remote environment. "Your old vampires will turn up. Like you, they underestimate the Dragos."

"Old vampires don't surf the dark web," Simon pointed out as he disengaged gently from Della who continued to clutch his hand tightly. He thought of Paige Dafonseca and shuddered.

"Old vampires have old friends," Alin said, scanning the area as remaining daylight fled both the wet streets and misty tree-lined pathways of Central Park. "But first, we dine – very fancy at Tavern on the Green – and let them take a good look at you."

"Verification?" Simon shuddered again.

"Exactly – then we become the hunters."

Chapter Thirty-four

The storm that had rolled in from the sea had stalled over the Thurso area. Wind and rain rattled around Galetaer Castle. Its idiosyncratic turrets and rooflines acted as a tuning fork bending the natural elements into an eerie banshee-like wail that echoed through the massive building. They gathered in what Sir Ronald grandly called the library. One of the larger rooms in the livable wing of the castle, it was actually less library – boasting only two 18th century walnut panels, the shelves filled with an indifferent collection of tomes – than truly massive stone fireplace. Worthy of a medieval potentate, the fireplace was large enough for man to stand up and walk about the firebox. A pair of life-sized carved lions sat on either side of the hearth, gazing impassively out at castle denizens. The Bannatyres had seen to it that the huge firebox had been stocked up with hefty logs. The resulting fire was vibrant, crackling with energy and impressive, throwing a radiant heat across the cold castle room.

"We'll lose the power soon," predicted Lady Margaret with an apologetic smile. "It's like clockwork."

"Country life," said the Earl of Hawkesmoor genially as Buckle offered him a whisky from a tray.

They sat on comfortable furniture that circled the showstopper fireplace. Much of the room's lighting came from the burnished flames. The extensive library devoured modern electric light, giving the room an odd effect of being both cozy and disquieting. Webs of shadow draped over every feature, turning ordinary into eerie. Even the stone lions appeared to breathe in the flickering firelight.

Sir Ronald had a puff from his pipe and stood up. Clearly relishing the role of generous host, he moved to center stage in front of the grand fireplace. He sipped his drink and then placed the martini glass up on the chimney piece. A wave of storm wind twisted around one of the nearby castle turrets, sounding ragged and high pitched like the teeth of a comb. "Not much is known of our very distant cousin Sir Neville Ponsonby," Sir Ronald said, "after he returned from the Crusades and took up residence here. He lived very quietly. We don't even really know when he died or where he is buried."

Caroline leaned forward in interest. She sat next to Robin on a dark green velvet couch – a 1960s reproduction of a Regency piece. "That's very unusual," she said.

Sir Ronald smiled down at her. "Isn't it just? Galetaer Castle does possess a pretty good local ghost story about it all though."

"Well, spit it out, Bucky," The Earl said over the rim of his whisky glass. "This sounds like just the sort of tosh Robin has come to Scotland for."

Lady Margaret laughed and threw her husband an affectionate glance. "No worries there, I'm afraid. He lives to tell this tale on rainy nights like this. The local WI still hasn't gotten over it."

"I would love to hear the castle ghost story," Robin said. "His Lordship is entirely correct – right up my alley so to speak."

Galetaer Castle's current owner looked delighted at the request. "Legend has it that on a night much like this one …" He paused for effect -- allowing the wind to shriek down the chimney and push the flames around. "Legend has it that the Devil himself, disguised as a mortal man, sought shelter from the storm at Galetaer Castle. Sir Neville asked the richly dressed stranger in and bade his cousin, Sybil Bannatyre who acted as chatelaine of the castle, to provide a good dinner for the traveler."

"Sybil Bannatyre?" Caroline asked. "Then your family was already on the ground here?"

Sir Ronald took a long puff from his pipe before answering. "Indeed – there's a brief notation in local parish records that she was summoned from her religious order in France to aid Sir Neville in running the castle. Probably thought she'd end up establishing her own order here."

"The best laid plans of mice and men," said Robin with a smile for Caroline. "Perhaps history's most astute motto."

"Especially for Scotland!" Lady Margaret piped up, laughing as Buckle brought her another martini. She sounded giddy – a little anxious as if worried her houseguests would not approve of their stay at the castle. The Earl of Hawkesmoor held up his whisky glass. "Well, here's to both Sybil and the lovely Lady Margaret. They both have done their best for family and Galetaer Castle."

"To Sybil and Lady Margaret!" Their cheery response almost blotted out by a particularly brutal rush of wind. It wailed around the roofline and echoed in the towering chimney. Lady Margaret aimed a beam of gratitude at Caroline's father who saluted her a second time with a small lift of his whisky tumbler.

Sir Ronald replaced his glass on the mantelpiece. "The story goes that the Devil accepted Sir Neville's hospitality and while dining in the Great Hall, noted the lovely, unassuming Sybil as she served him and decided that he wanted the beautiful girl for his own."

"Bad form – the wretch," the Earl observed and glanced pointedly at Robin who mouthed very funny back at him.

"Satan unmasked himself and asked Sir Neville to name his price for a single night with Sybil. Unsurprisingly, Ponsonby was aghast but pulled himself together and ordered the Devil from the castle."

Robin sipped his whisky. "I admire his courage. Most would have left poor Sybil to her fate."

"But did the Devil go as requested?" Caroline asked.

Sir Ronald gave a short laugh and shook his head. "That wouldn't make for much of a local legend. No -- Satan would brook no denial and threatened Sir Neville with the Three Ds."

Caroline's father looked to Lady Margaret. "Speaking of words that begin with D. Looking forward to another one of your good dinners, Meg. Can we possibly hope for venison?"

"You are very kind! Actually, I've had a …"

"The Three Ds," repeated Sir Ronald in a louder, very pointed voice.

Lady Margaret giggled and went silent. She flashed a guilty look at her husband then returned happily to her martini.

"Devastation, Desolation and Damnation!" Sir Ronald went on. "But Sir Neville refused to submit to Satan's foul demand. The Devil flew into a rage but could not take the knight's life as Galetaer Castle was protected by Sir Neville's piety."

"Satan had been bested?" Caroline looked surprised.

"Well, in a way," Galetaer's current owner paused to take a sip from his martini and then spoke again. "Local legend tells us that the Devil hurled Sir Neville into one of the castle rooms and sealed it for eternity. Then he flew up the chimney in the Great Hall, taking poor Sybil with him."

"Do you know which room?" asked Robin cocking his head to the side as he took in Sir Ronald's tale.

Thunder crackled over the castle. It was so violent that the chimney seemed to rattle from the sonic blow. For a moment, the electrical power dimmed, almost cutting out completely before surging back to full power. Galetaer's long serving butler, Buckle seemed to sigh and stepped from the library, either to examine ancient castle wiring for potential issues or to check on dinner's progress.

Lady Margaret looked apologetic as if she were responsible for the wild weather. "According to the BBC, we have several storms stacked up over the sea, waiting to come across. This must be Number 2!"

"Can you show us the room?" Robin persisted, earning a perplexed glance from both Caroline and her father. "I would very much like to see it."

"Sorry," said Sir Ronald. "It's just another one of those legendary lost castle rooms. Almost every castle has one – doesn't Hawkesmoor?"

The Earl gave a short cough. "Mournful Black Monk wandering the byways and a Grey Lady on the stair but no secret rooms."

"Have you looked for the lost room?" asked Robin. "Any idea if it might …"

"You haven't said what happened to them," Caroline laid a restraining hand on Robin's knee, "in reality. What really happened?"

"Unfortunately, Sybil, Sir Neville and his Crusaders disappeared from our history. Little doubt that they did form some sort of contemplative order and retired from the world. The local Scots created a far more exciting version to spin by the fire." Sir Ronald redirected his attention to Lady Margaret. "Any chance that Buckle has dinner in hand?"

"The secret room – really code for a chapter house?" Robin murmured, covering Caroline's hand with his own. He gently squeezed her fingers. "Fascinating."

Chapter Thirty-five

"You know, that wasn't a bad dinner," announced Caroline as she dropped onto a wing chair in their guest room. "Local salmon, decent wines. Cracking job, Lady Margaret. I wonder if Buckle finally gets to put his feet up?"

She frowned, watching as her husband shrugged out of his dinner jacket and pulled open a bureau drawer. He retrieved a black sweater and tossed it on the bed.

"What are you doing?"

Robin returned to the drawer and found a pair of jeans. "Nothing very exciting."

"You're up to no good!" she gasped, recognizing purpose and intent in his movements. "You have a bee in your bonnet about something. Can you let me in on it?"

He started unbuttoning his white shirt. "Darling – let me and …"

"Piffle! I'm just as good as Gabriel and Cyril Goforth. Besides you need me for cover in case you get catched as they say in parts of rural Scotland."

Robin raised an eyebrow. "I won't get catched."

"Buckle looks like he's dealt with several generations of bad hats."

"I could outfox Buckle without any supernatural assistance, thank you."

"News bulletin: you're not leaving me alone." Caroline pushed off the wing chair. "So – what exactly are we doing?"

He stared at her and then smiled. "Dress warmly, darling. We are going on a ghost hunt."

Rain and wind battered the castle windows as Caroline scanned the hallway outside their guest room, looking for any wandering castle denizens. All electrical power had gone out just as Lady Margaret had predicted so no wall sconces or table lamps would be able to provide comforting outposts of light. A bit of a blow to castle spelunkers. Still, it seemed that the Bannatyres and her father had safely retired to their rooms to sleep and ride out the series of storms rolling across northern Scotland.

She ducked back inside and rejoined Robin who was zipping up a puffy green vest over his sturdy sweater.

"All clear?"

"Nary castle cat nor mouse. I don't see how we can possibly do your ghost hunt in that dark. Even with flashlights, it's dangerous." Caroline sat on the edge of the bed and gazed at her husband. "You still haven't told me what this is all about. You don't honestly believe a phantom Sir Neville is wafting about the place rattling his chains?"

"No -- I believe that Sir Neville's private order built a chapter house somewhere in the castle and we're going to find it."

Caroline knew that medieval chapter houses – rooms for business that could be very simple or elaborate in design depending on the wealth of religious body -- had been closed to outsiders and could even be hidden within the cloister in case the order came under attack. Even if Sir Neville had constructed a secret chapter house, it was difficult to imagine that one could have remained hidden from centuries of Bannatyres and their households. Before she could inquire as to why Robin was so determined to find the mythical chapter house, Cyril Goforth and Gabriel suddenly materialized in the middle of the guest room. The pair of them looked soaked and miserable. Cyril's blond locks were plastered to his wet head and water was pooling on the oriental carpet under his sodden shoes. Gabriel sneezed.

Robin waved his hand in their general direction, setting into motion one of his Tylwyth Teg enhanced matter transformations. Rainwater evaporated. Dripping clothes were replaced by dry garments suitable for a night investigation in a frigid Scottish castle. Caroline had a moment to miss when she was actually taken aback by such miraculous doings.

"No sign of Cam Drummond or anything unusual," said Gabriel. "Your lads are the real deal – tough as nails."

"Anything interesting in the equerry box?" Robin turned his attention to the aide de camp who was already checking his ever-present tablet.

"No English Wendigo appearances, Your Serene Highness," replied Cyril in the crisp business-like tone he employed for the vampire king's affairs. "Sir Geoffrey's done an admirable job keeping his proverbial lid tamped down."

"Well, that's something," sighed Robin before launching into a recap of Sir Ronald's tale of Sir Neville Ponsonby and the Devil.

"Chapter houses tended to be located to the east," Gabriel said once Robin had finished. "Any idea where the original castle chapel is located?"

"Through the centuries, the Bannatyres have lacked the capitol to make many major structural changes to Galetaer. Sir Neville had his chapel constructed so that it adjoins the rear of the Great Hall."

"Easy access -- hearty feast days to guilty prayers in a matter of moments," laughed Gabriel, the former monk. "I remember those grand old days."

"How would you like us to proceed, sir?" asked Cyril with a cough.

"We'll make our way down to the chapel and then split into two teams to explore the unused portions of the castle. I see no sign of a chapter house in Sir Ronald's rehabilitated living quarters so we can avoid this wing."

"A drop in the ocean," said Caroline.

Robin flashed her a smile. "We have about eight hours until dawn. Sir Neville's chapter house will take a lot of skill and luck to locate – don't know if there will be any molecular trace of the old order left to follow so old school observation and historical education may have to suffice."

"But I don't understand its importance." She looked perplexed. "How can it help find Cam Drummond?"

Gabriel sat next to her on the edge of the bed. "If Sir Neville was a one of us and if Cam was one of his lads, this chapter house – if it exists – may be able to tell us what happened here."

"A small religious order of revenants is unusual – then and now," added Robin, handing her a flashlight. "I want to know what happened to them and why our English Wendigo took an interest in Cam Drummond."

"Shall we transfer down to the chapel?" asked Gabriel.

Cyril Goforth looked queasy. "No, thank you."

"Oh, stop being such a great nancy."

The equerry drew in a breath sharply at the vampire librarian's jibe – clearly affronted.

"Cyril's right," Robin interjected. "We don't know the Galetaer's interior design and I'd prefer not to become an amusing fresco for Sir Ronald to point out to guests."

Galetaer Castle, without benefit of electrical lighting, seemed to Caroline as black, cold and claustrophobic as diving in the Mariana's Trench. The storm outside the castle walls seemed to accentuate the cavernous sensation – the icy, inky air was alive with sound. Rain struck the windows as if entities were pounding the glass, desperate for attention or issuing urgent warnings. Wind whistled around rooflines, turrets and trees creating odd phantom rattle and hums.

She held Robin's hand as they descended the main staircase. Occasionally an errant flash of lightening strobed through windows, providing brief glimpses of the castle. Family portraits, object de art, heraldic banners and interior fixtures flared up instantly and then returned to blackness.

Caroline had grown up in haunted Hawkesmoor Castle and had often experienced what her family liked to call Ghost Walkabouts, but she found the electric atmosphere in Galetaer unsettling. It was heavy and off balance as if Galetaer Castle belonged to the living Bannatyres only during the day.

"Buckle. Damn," whispered Robin in a barely registerable tone. He doused his flashlight and pulled her down against the thick banister railing. Behind them, Gabriel and Cyril did the same.

A human unburdened with knowledge of vampires, would have wondered how Robin could possibly have realized the butler was on the move long before a flashlight beam announced his presence. Caroline knowing his hearing was far more acute than hers, was unsurprised to see a light on the ground floor. It emanated from the direction of the main entryway. They were on the first-floor landing, above the Great Hall. Pressed against the banister, they watched in the lightning flashes as the ancient butler crossed the flagstones. Presumably Buckle had been performing one last check on the doors and windows in the violent storm before heading to bed.

Caroline thought that whatever Sir Ronald paid him was not enough. Buckle was an old school retainer who had devoted his life to their service. In earlier times, he would have had a proper staff of servants with whom to delegate such jobs as checking the doors.

Like the domestic bloodhound he was, Buckle paused as if smelling the air and sensing something was amiss. He raised his flashlight beam to the main staircase. They hunkered down on the landing carpet, barely breathing as Buckle's relentless light came up the steps. Fortunately, the beam came to rest against the rear wall of the landing where a large and impressive Tudor walnut sideboard held pride of place. It supported an equally impressive pair of silver candlesticks that glowed in the shaft of light. As the sideboard and candlesticks were possibly two of the most valuable decorative items in Galetaer, the old Butler had instinctively checked to see if they were secure.

Thunder rolled over the castle rooftop, apparently satisfying Buckle that his inner butler had been fooled by storm noise and he retracted his flashlight beam back down the staircase. He continued on his way to the Bannatyres' domestic wing and his bed. The light from his torch faded as he stepped through an archway and down a hallway to the staff rooms.

They let out a collective breath and sat up in the dark. A couple of lightning streaks illuminated the Great Hall for a moment and allowed Caroline to see Cyril Goforth letting out a long breath of relief. He shook his head as if doubting the wisdom of his sovereign.

"Give it a minute," murmured Robin. "Give the noble Buckle a chance to close a few doors between him and us." Lightening flickered again through the leaded glass of large chevron shaped windows that had probably been added to the castle's central tower in the Tudor era. While also a time of great danger for incautious castle owners, it was less likely to arrive in the form of an enemy force with deadly archers.

Robin stood up after a short time and offered his hand to Caroline. She grasped it and got to her feet, grateful to be moving again. The cold of the Scottish castle was beginning to seep into her joints.

"Prefer to head back to bed?" he asked.

"You're stuck with me." Caroline shook her head. She couldn't imagine anything less appealing than waiting alone in the guest room.

Gabriel brushed past them. "Onwards to the chapel. I can smell the old incense from here and it brings back so many pleasant memories of Compline."

They switched on their flashlights again and descended Galetaer's main staircase without further disruption from the conscientious Buckle. Heading north from the base of the staircase, the entrance to Sir Neville's center of worship was found adjacent to the Great Hall. The chapel sat behind a suitably massive wooden door that appeared to be ancient and original. The hardware impressed upon the wood was iron blackened by age and of simple design. Two plain iron rings served as handles. A Victorian brass plaque had been affixed as well – But seek first the kingdom of God and his righteousness.

"And all these things will be added to you," sighed Gabriel, reaching out to touch the embossed letters. "Mathew 6:33."

Caroline shivered in front of the chapel doors. Rain was hammering the castle and the sound ricocheted through its vast empty spaces. She wouldn't be surprised to see a silvery monk glide through the old stone and wood.

"The energy in the castle is really amped up," Robin observed, glancing around the shadowy hallway.

"Agreed," said Gabriel. "The storm."

"What does that mean?' Caroline asked with another shiver.

"The electromagnetic energy of storms," explained Cyril as thunder rumbled overhead. "It can provide assistance to extrasensory, paranormal events,"

One of the iron rings suddenly banged on the heavy wooden door as if an invisible hand had grasped it and knocked. The sound hard and hollow as the iron cuff hit the wood. It seemed to reverberate through the castle. Caroline sucked in a sharp breath, genuinely surprised, and jumped closer to her husband who slid an arm about her shoulders. She wondered if Buckle would be running to see if the family silver was still in its rightful place.

"Could be vibration from the thunder," said Gabriel.

"Or something wants our attention," murmured Robin, stepping away from Caroline. He reached out and grasped the noisy ring. "Let's go take a look."

He pulled open the chapel door. Despite its weight, it seemed to move easily over the old flagstone floor. A rush of musty air poured out of the newly created opening attesting to the fact that Sir Ronald and Lady Margaret preferred services at the local village church.

They moved through the old chapel, flashlights strobing in different directions picking up more of the castle's stonework, white plastering and dark, handsome exposed timbers under a Victorian addition ceiling heavily plastered and painted brightly with heraldic devices associated with the Ponsonby and Bannatyre families. The chapel was long and narrow with the altar as its natural focus at one end. Galetaer's chapel nave was lined with well used wooden stalls on either side, set against the walls.

"Really quite lovely,' said Caroline, appreciating the beauty of the chapel's simplicity. The elaborate ceiling aside, it was not ornate in the late Georgian or Victorian sense. Rather it was a masculine, almost severe place of worship for stout-hearted medieval knights. She could well imagine Sir Neville's loyal officers gathered in the facing stalls to worship the God who had sent them crusading to the Middle East.

Cyril rubbed his arms. "Freezing though."

Rain pelleted against the large stained-glass window behind the altar. It was the only window in the chapel and occasionally a lightning streak would illuminate the colored panels, revealing a romantically handsome medieval knight standing on a scroll that read For the Glory of God.

"Presumably Sir Neville," said Robin shining his light on the intricate colored glass. "The Victorian Bannatyres paying tribute."

"Where would a chapter house be hiding itself?" Gabriel walked the nave, examining the stalls with his flashlight. "I hate to be the wet blanket but …"

"Agreed," Robin interjected, moving his attention from the window to the altar which sat in an alcove. A heavy oak table, it had no linens or elaborate silver Communion service, boasting only a cross made of brass. "There's no space here for a secret chapter house and there's nothing that tells us any more about Sir Neville either."

Cyril shivered in the cold. "Our next approach, sir?"

"Two teams – we fan out in the unoccupied areas of the castle. You and Gabriel take the stores below and first floor. Lady Caroline and I will do the second and third."

Lightning lit up Sir Neville's window. In the electric flash, Caroline saw a figure standing in the center of the nave. A young woman in a greenish gown of medieval design. A woman who was staring at them, her eyes stricken with panic. Then the nave returned to shadows taking her with it.

"Robin," Caroline breathed, pointing her flashlight to the prayer stalls, "there's someone … well, there!"

The three vampires spun around, illuminating the area with their flashlights. No figure stood there. The nave was empty.

"But she was here," Caroline said, running the few steps to where the medieval woman had been. "Green dress. Looking at us as if she wanted to say something."

"They always do," sighed Gabriel.

"They?"

"Ghosts, phantoms," said Robin with a sad shake of his head. "They're just bits and pieces of molecular debris. Maybe your Green Lady stood there once and watched her servant drop an illuminated manuscript."

Cyril joined Caroline and looked about, making certain that the Green Lady was gone. "Maybe it was her," he offered, peering into one of the prayer stalls.

"Explain," Robin crossed to Caroline as well and put an arm around her, "her."

"Sybil Bannatyre – the Devil's plaything."

"Well, at least she might know if there's a chapter house," said Robin. "We could use the help."

The chapel door suddenly swung and slammed shut. Its old hardware rattled with the force of the blow and sent a tsunami-like wave of cold castle air rolling across the long, narrow space. It almost had a palpable sound like a sigh.

"Perhaps Sybil has a singular lack of humor," said the vampire librarian, aiming his flashlight at the chapel entry. "That took a lot of energy. Galetaer Castle certainly lives up to the reputation of haunted Scotland."

Caroline felt Robin pull her closer. "You all right then?" he asked quietly. "Not too late – I could see you safely tucked in the warm guest room."

"Absolutely not! If Sybil Bannatyre is clomping around the castle, I don't want to miss it." She smiled up at him. "Talk about adventure!"

He kissed her quickly. "Gentlemen, you heard your Queen. Let us go adventuring."

Chapter Thirty-six

Galetaer's second floor was a rabbit warren of empty rooms. Abandoned since Tudor times, it seemed that any decent bits of furniture or decor had been shifted to the warmer climes of the current Bannatyre wing. Unlike Hawkesmoor Castle which had benefited greatly by having two wealthy aristocratic families keeping it vital over the centuries, Galetaer had the Bannatyres -- good yeoman stock elevated suddenly to castle owners after Sir Neville's religious order disappeared. There had never been enough money to rehabilitate the castle into a genuinely fashionable country estate.

"Sir Neville centered life in the Great Hall and the chapel. These rooms were probably divided among his soldiers and servants," said Robin as they peered into a room off the third floor's surprisingly narrow central hallway.

"Pity," murmured Caroline, shining her flashlight around the large room. It was without decoration – ancient, whitewashed walls dappled with dirt and cobwebs – but featured two leaded glass latticed windows that lent the space an austere handsomeness. "This wouldn't be bad with some work."

"Obviously Sir Neville couldn't be bothered. Guessing he and his soldiers just wanted monastic cells. They were used to sleeping rough on their crusade." Robin walked through the doorway and aimed his light at the one of the interior walls. "The Bannatyres have done their best keeping the castle going, bless 'em."

Caroline was surprised to see her husband come to a standstill and close his eyes as if concentrating intently. He stood in that mode for a long moment, then opened his eyes and sighed a little.

"Not here," Robin said with regret.

Lightning flared in the lattice windows. One of the lower panes glinted sharply as if it had a hairline break. Caroline thought it was unusual that the cracked piece of glass seemed to have a momentary gleam of the unnatural, the artistic. She crossed the room to get a better look. The beam of her flashlight lit up the old glass, revealing the damaged triangular pane.

"Robin," she breathed, "it's an etching!"

Under the direct light, the pane revealed scratched words in its rippled yellowed surface and a rough signature – Sybil.

"I'll be damned," said Robin, frowning. "Sanctum sanctorum, Sybil."

"My Latin is schoolgirl at best. I think I remember that sanctum sanctorum means holy of holies or something."

"Most sacred, sealed place," agreed Robin, running an index finger over the etched words. "A much more interesting interpretation: There are secrets – and then there are secrets."

"The Chapter House?" asked Caroline.

"Logical," He reached out and stroked her cheek. "I am a most fortunate creature to possess such a wife."

Caroline felt a familiar flutter in her nervous system. From the moment she'd first seen Robin Dashwood in a Manhattan art gallery, he had the effect of disarming her completely. He was the most magnetic person she's ever known.

She was about to suggest they take a cell phone picture of the scratched glass for Sir Ronald when three bangs on the door interrupted her train of thought. They were loud, almost angry and in rapid succession, demanding attention.

Robin jumped away from the window and pushed her behind him. He shone his flashlight at the doorway and they both stared at the empty threshold. No one stood there. Neither Gabriel or Cyril -- or even Buckle – stood in the doorway.

"The storm energy thing?" whispered Caroline, remembering what the three revenants told her about electro-magnetic energy.

"Something powerful." Robin took a cautious step forward. Three loud knocks sounded on one of the windows behind them. The sound was higher pitched and sharper. Robin spun, again pushing Caroline behind him. This time the space was not empty. The phantom from the chapel stood by the lattice window, staring at them in something that looked like panic or desperation. Translucent and lit from within like a paper spirit lantern, the young woman's form rippled gently with the impermanence of smoke or cloud. It seemed possible that her medieval dress was a dark green and richly made, featuring a leather girdle embossed with semi-precious gems. Gold rings adorned the slender white hands that she held up towards them in some kind of entreaty. Thunder rumbled over the castle, vibrating through the old window glass and she vanished.

"Well, this beats the St. Sophia's Old Girls dinner I was supposed to attend tonight," said Caroline, slipping an arm through her husband's. "Is it Sybil, do you think?"

Footsteps ran down the hallway beyond. The light footfalls of a lady. The rustle of heavy fabric. Robin made for the door, pulling Caroline after him.

"I don't know but let's follow her anyway."

Chapter Thirty-seven

A frigid and wet December night meant that Central Park would see considerably far fewer of its committed urban athletes and explorers. In fact, the normally well used public space seemed eerily abandoned as they left the SUV near West 102nd and headed onto one of the curated paths that would eventually lead them to The Ravine. Even the birds who found sanctuary in the vast city park seemed to have closed up shop until dawn.

Simon glanced about the wooded areas to the side of the path, keen to listen for any possible messages from the Tylwyth Teg drifting by with an errant winter breeze. Such a thing would suit the area, Simon reflected, remembering something he'd read about the original Ravine designers modeling it after the infamously eerie Catskill Mountains. Washington Irving would feel right at home. Simon half-expected to see the Headless Horseman himself loping towards them in the half-light. But so far, no helpful hints from the Celtic realm of deities.

Alin switched on his flashlight and the city streets seemed to evaporate into the damp mist.

"We head for the Loch and its old bridge," he murmured. "Stay on your toes."

Simon breathed in some of the early evening air. Long used to the brutal Yorkshire cold, he found New York quite bearable. "You do have back up?"

"Again, with the underestimating, my friend. Gadjo always underestimate the Gypsy."

Simon made a sour face. "These are vampires. They are not normal people … criminals."

Della slid her arm around his elbow so she could press close to him as they walked.

"Lenka told me about the two major crime families – vampires and the werewolves."

"Hunky dory," he sighed. "You're thoroughly sound on vampires."

Then he widened his eyes in surprise as Della's words penetrated his auditory senses. He looked sharply at Alin Dragos. "Wait – werewolves?"

Alin held up a hand for them to pause. "The Loch bridge isn't far – hear the falls?"

In the near distance, the sound of cascading water wove through the park trees. It was rhythmical and calming much like the murmur of Manhattan's traffic but there was also another acoustic – something sharper, something silvery and metallic. Simon strained to make sense of it. A familiar echo from his past, fencing lessons in the ballroom at Hawkesmoor. Steel sliding against steel. Swords. Swords being unsheathed in Central Park.

Caroline's feet stung as they struck the cold castle floor as they ran. The medieval phantom now just a few footsteps and a shadow glimpsed occasionally in strobes of flashlight or errant lightning. As fascinated as she was by the appearance of an ancient ghost, Caroline wondered how it possibly could relate to Robin's search for Cam Drummond or a possible chapter house at Galetaer. Her husband was clearly under tremendous pressure to provide answers to both human and revenant fractions. Robin looked tired and drawn despite an otherworldly constitution that had served him well through nearly three centuries. That he would suddenly suffer a nosebleed had to be warning beacon of extreme exhaustion and stress. She was

worried – frightened even – but unsure of how to approach
him without adding to the burden he carried.

They dashed down the hallway. It was narrow – designed to
prevent enemy shields from being deployed effectively –
and frigid without any heating system. Their breath came
out in streams, hanging in the icy air like short-lived cloud.
A tantalizing shimmer of shadow and they arced left at a
fork in the hall.

"We're directly over the chapel," said Robin, slowing to a
stop. The phantom footsteps had fallen away along with the
shadow figure. Thunder rumbled in the distance – further
away as the last of the sea storms passed over the castle.

"Where is she?" Caroline bent over to catch her breath. "I
haven't run like that since my field hockey amazon days."

"I wonder, I wonder," murmured Robin. He walked a few
steps down the hall and back again.

"Robin!" cried Caroline as she straightened up and found
him in her flashlight beam, "you're bleeding again!"

"Good lord," he said, reaching up to touch his face where
blood was streaming from both his nose and ears.

Caroline handed Robin a couple of tissues she had found in
the pocket of her puffy vest – probably left over from some
equestrian event she'd been tramping around. He had sat
down on the floor and was resting his back against the cold,
unplastered wall.

"We should let Cyril and Gabriel finish the search," she
said, using one of the found tissues to daub away blood
from his left ear. "Seems clear to me that there is no chapter
house and no conveniently situated Cam Drummond."

Her husband wiped away blood from his nose. "It's the only
thread I have, Caro. This thing – whatever it is – attacked
his house, murdered his lady. Drummond is a known visitor

239

here and he was present under our roof when Pryce-Atwater was killed."

"But what about Sir Geoffrey's man, Fletcher Green-something?"

"Couldn't have done it," Robin said, his voice tired. "He was just a distraction."

Caroline frowned, not liking how exhausted he looked. He gave the appearance of literally collapsing in front of her – as if he was being crushed by a great weight.

"Well, Cam or not Cam -- you are officially done for tonight. It's back to a heated room …" Her voice trailed off. Robin's head had fallen forward, his chin coming to rest on his chest. He was gone -- unconscious.

Chapter Thirty-eight

Robin opened his eyes. He was standing in Galetaer's abandoned hallway, but it was no longer cold and shrouded in shadows. The narrow byway was lit with a stark bottle blue light revealing the castle's original raw stonework and odd mismatched collection of old handmade doors with heavy iron hinges.

He knew this world. Ghost world where melancholy shades of former humans wandered -- pathetic collections of loosely bound molecules and electromagnetic energy animated by some vague memory. His son had tried to convince him that there was far more to this sad reliquary than he had yet experienced. Simon – lost in the ghost world for so long – surely understood it far better than he.

The sound of a foot scraping across the stone floor caught his attention. He pivoted to see a lady walking down the hall towards him. She was quite young and relatively tall for one in such ancient raiment. The dress was richly made, featuring a girdle embossed with semi-precious stones and suited the girl's pale patrician beauty.

As befitted melancholy White, Grey and Green Ladies found on country estates all over the British Isles, the regal phantom was distraught. Wringing her hands, she staggered awkwardly in her grief and fell to her knees.

"Sybil Bannatyre?" Robin asked.

The unhappy shade lifted her face from her bejeweled fingers. She stared at him and without a word of reply, lifted her left hand. In the blue light, a ring glinted on her finger – a band of gold.

He tried again. "Lady Ponsonby?"

She nodded. Grief-stricken.

"But why do you walk here?" Robin asked, remembering Gabriel's research on the castle. "You never lived at Galetaer Castle."

Lady Ponsonby still stared at him. Her large melancholy eyes widened as if she was beginning to take in his measure. She lifted a damask upholstered arm and pointed to the stone wall.

"Save him," came a whisper – both desperate and very sad. Although Lady Ponsonby ostensibly had spoken, her lips had not moved. Her words seemed to radiate through the air like a radio signal. Robin wished again he understood the ghost world better than he did. It was clear that Simon was right about the complexities.

"I have waited long for one such as you." Lady Ponsonby's whisper floated across to him. She rose to her full height and took two steps to her right, laying a long, pale hand on the stonework. "Send him to me so that I may take him home."

"Sir Neville remains?" asked Robin.

Lady Ponsonby turned away from the wall and came towards him, lifting a hand to his face. When her white fingertips reached his cheek, he shuddered at their chill. It was a painful cold that radiated out from her touch and coursed through his system like a rampaging virus.

Robin buckled at the knees and fell. The ghost world collapsed with him as if it were book cover slamming shut.

For once, Alin Dragos' face lost its laconic good humor. He motioned them to follow him. "Move fast but quietly," he said, switching off the flashlight.

"If it's them, it won't matter." Simon had experienced his father's preternatural hearing.

Alin nodded. "I'll ask you to get Della out if … well, you know, my friend."

"Thank the Lord," he heard Gabriel's voice saying. "Seems to be coming round."

Robin slowly opened his eyes. Three worried faces were peering down at him. Gabriel, Cyril and Caroline who was the nearest as she had her arm firmly about his shoulders. She had a tear coursing down her cheek.

"Your Highness," said Cyril from the other side of him, "do you think you can stand?"

"Fascinating," Robin said.

"He's still out of it," Gabriel pronounced with a shake of his head. "Let's get him up and back to the warm wing of the castle."

"Can you stand, darling?" asked Caroline, wiping at her cheek with her free hand.

He nodded and awkwardly staggered to his feet with Gabriel and Cyril's aid. "I know where it is."

"We'll have you back to rights in no time," said Gabriel, sliding an arm around Robin's waist. He and Cyril started to walk him in the direction of the main staircase.

"The chapter house." Robin shook free of their support. "I know where it is."

Caroline stepped in and gripped his forearms fiercely. "You have to stop, Robin!"

"Don't you understand?" His voice almost broke. Robin felt as if he was coming apart at the seams. The importance of what he had to accomplish was a weight threatening to drag him down to his knees. "If we can't stop this … this thing, they won't just go after vampires. You, Simon … Ari!"

"Your Highness," breathed Cyril, his normally inscrutable expression replaced by surprise and deep concern.

Robin pulled away from Caroline who followed him anxiously as he stumbled towards the side of the castle hallway. He pointed to the stone.

"Here is Sir Neville's chapter house."

"It's just a wall," said Gabriel. "There's no evidence of a …"

"If you are right about Sir Neville and his men, they wouldn't need a human door."

The former monk joined Robin by the wall. "It's possible there's a negative space above the chapel's buttressed ceiling."

"Sanctum Sanctorum," murmured Caroline. "There are secrets and then there are secrets."

Robin flashed her a tired smile. He hoped his wife realized just how much he loved her. How could he not adore a woman so bright and brave?

"I have to go in," he said, also hoping that Caroline would understand the next move he was about to make. If it didn't work, he prayed she wouldn't return to haunt Galetaer Castle as Lady Ponsonby had.

Cyril pushed past Gabriel. "Sir -- if this room doesn't exist, you'll recombine in the stonework!"

"A fair point, my friend," said the vampire librarian leaning against the wall and crossing his arms.

"Give me fifteen minutes. If I'm not back by then, you can assume the worst." Robin turned to Caroline who was beginning to wring her hands rather disconcertingly in the style of Lady Ponsonby. "Darling Caro, you know I wouldn't do this unless it was vital."

She looked miserable. "I do know, yes. Simon and Ari."

Robin took a moment to grasp Caroline's shoulders and pull her to him for a quick kiss. He could sense her fear and how hard she was trying to keep from panicking.

"Fifteen minutes," he whispered in her ear. "I'll be back."

"You'd better or I'll be most annoyed." A tear glittered in her eye and she wiped it away. "Fifteen minutes then."

Robin took in a deep breath, releasing her shoulders and turning to face Galetaer Castle's imposing stone.

"Gentlemen, a weather eye to your timepieces. With luck, we'll learn something useful."

He wished he was in better shape for such a difficult investigation. Pressures applied to his shields both physical and metaphysical were draining him. Somehow, he had to hang on until he had answers for the prime minister and Sir Geoffrey.

Before he could change his mind about retreating to a chair by the fireplace, Robin began to dismantle his outer form.

Chapter Thirty-nine

Robin came back together in complete darkness. His first thought was of Dante's Hell – And to a place I come where nothing shines. He tentatively took a step forward and was grateful to realize that the all-encompassing black did not mean he was encased in the castle stonework.

His eyes adjusted to the dark – a revenant enhanced ability that gave him an apex predator's night vision. It was indeed a room. A rectangular space with rotting wood benches lining the walls. A large unadorned cross was carved into the stone on one side. It was the chapter house of former soldiers who had no need for fancy accoutrements for worship.

As his vision improved, he saw there was something else as well – words scrawled not on the walls but in the air itself as if the writer had imprinted them on molecules with the tip of a finger. They hung in the air, hot red and yellow lines burning with electromagnetic energy. Over and over again – Ibi Cubavit Lamia, Ibi Cubavit Lamia, Ibi Cubavit Lamia. Hundreds, thousands of lines. Big versions, small versions, beautiful, angry and frantic versions floated through the icy black air.

Robin recognized the Latin phrase as having come from Isaiah 34:14 – There shall be the lair of the night monster.

"Sir Neville?" he said quietly. "You must be here."

There was a sound – a thin cry or a howl – that seemed very far away but gaining in volume as it neared like an incoming missile.

"Blood!" The howl took shape and wrapped around Robin. "Blood sings. Pain. Pain. PAIN."

Humans would not be able to hear the subsonic frequencies. They would only sense the unstable energy and refer to it in vague terms such as heavy or haunted.

"Sir Neville," Robin repeated, "can you hear me?"

He realized that the wretched Sir Neville had indeed once been a revenant but was now a disembodied consciousness driven mad by a terrible hunger that could never be assuaged. Somehow Sir Neville had been trapped in the chapter house to starve. His three-dimensional form had disintegrated leaving behind only traces of a mind. Robin felt genuine grief for the medieval soldier. He had once been imprisoned and left to starve by Max Aosta, the vampire king of Manhattan. Only an odd twist of fate had allowed him to escape. Sir Neville had not been so fortunate.

Robin had acquired vast supernatural powers from his Tylwyth Teg bloodline – abilities that dwarfed his revenant traits. As it seemed clear that very little of Sir Neville's sanity remained, he decided to try and create a kind of bell jar. A hermetic dome in which he could return Sir Neville to an earlier version of himself. Such a creation would take a lot of energy to build and sustain yet it needed to be done -- not only for the value of any information he could glean from the medieval soldier but out of respect for Sir Neville. With a bit of luck, he wouldn't collapse under the strain.

He breathed in some of the chapter house's fetid air and organized his energies, directing it to weave a spiderweb. It shimmered away from him like ectoplasm, lighting up the black hidden space of the Sir Neville's pious retreat. Another rush of power and Robin pulled Sir Neville's consciousness towards him while simultaneously reversing the knight's timeline. As Sir Neville neared, he began to take form. An orb pulsating red and black struggled out of the stagnant air and was immediately surrounded by veins, brain tissue and skull. The brain stem dropped down into a skeletal spine that then, in turn, spawned ribs, a pelvic cage and four limbs. Tendons, arteries, muscles and flesh coursed over Sir Neville's skeleton. A moment later, the figure was clothed in suitable medieval raiment and the knight's personal features locked in. Sir Neville Ponsonby had returned.

Robin was impressed. In his imagination, he had thought of Sir Neville as an older, retired soldier. The man standing in front of him was young, powerful and strikingly handsome. Sir Neville was tall, fit and broad shouldered with enviable thick tawny blond hair. His facial features were Byronic lit up by sharp blue eyes that radiated intelligence. Whoever had bested Sir Neville and left him to rot at Galetaer was no mean opponent.

"What sorcery is this?" asked Sir Neville, his battle-hardened hand hovering over the dagger at his waist. He spoke in a variant of Old English that Robin found turgid and difficult to listen to with his more modern ears.

"I am Robin, Lord Merritt of Hawkesmoor Castle," Robin replied in Old English, almost wincing at the heavy sound. "I have come to help you."

Sir Neville's blue eyes sparked with bitterness. "You cannot help the damned, Earl's whelp."

The knight spun in his bootheel as if to stride away but hit the dome's shimmering barrier instead. He turned back to Robin, clearly perplexed. His hand returning to the hilt of his dagger.

"Surely you have seen too much, Sir Neville, to be taken aback at the supernatural."

The sadness that crossed Sir Neville's told Robin that his comment had struck deep. "What do you want of me?" he sighed. "You must know that I am ungodly."

Robin felt a slight tremor cross his nervous system. The strain of maintaining Sir Neville's bell jar was beginning to make itself known. He ignored it and focused on the knight. "I can guess that you and your men went to the Holy Lands where something attacked you – changed you." Robin watched as Sir Neville gave a shudder and nodded. "You did your duty over there. Perhaps too well, yes?"

"We cut down those poor bastards as if they were stalks of wheat. Men, women … babes." Sir Neville's voice had gone hoarse. "Unnatural, not of God …we had become fiends, yet we fought for God. We fought for God!"

"After the campaign," Robin interjected before Sir Neville could unravel any further, "you retreated to Galetaer Castle with your men."

"I returned to England to find my wife had died of blood poisoning. Fitting punishment for one such as I." Sir Neville's jaw tightened." King Henry gave us riches for our service. We decided – as a cohort – to withdraw from the world and form an order. We would spend our days begging God to forgive our trespasses."

Another tremor ran down Robin's frame. He wouldn't be able to hold together the dome in his current weakened state much longer.

"How could we know days meant hundreds of years and that Scotland would be our hell?"

Robin straightened at the knight's words. "Hundreds of years?"

"We took nothing from the people here,' Sir Neville said with a sigh.

"We sustained our community with sheep, deer and prayer – until she came."

"She? You mean Sybil?"

Anger infused Sir Neville's handsome face. "You know of the bitch?"

This was hardly the reaction Robin had expected to the pious, courageous cousin of Sir Ronald's tale. At her name, an agitated Sir Neville began pacing the confines of the softly gleaming bell jar.

"Is she not your cousin?" he asked in some surprise.

"Cousin?" The knight spat at the floor as if warding off a demon. "I share no blood with the likes of that common doxy. She came to us, claiming to share our affliction and begging to join out order."

"You said no, of course," Robin guessed, understanding that even a medieval revenant monastery would not accept women. "What year was this, Sir Neville?"

"1440. We took her in as a servant as long as she abided by our ways."

A tremor caused Robin to rock back on his pins. He would have to make a choice between helping himself or helping the vampire knight. The dome was weakening.

"The bitch bade him come to Galetaer Castle," Sir Neville spat again. "Him with his noble words and temptations. They all fell to him save Asher Grey. We were lost. The pact was broken."

"You wife asked me to bring you to her," said Robin, fighting to hold the bell jar. If it collapsed, Sir Neville would return to the ethers and madness. "It's high time to leave this place."

Sir Neville paused. His blue eyes softened. "Eleanor? But she is with God. She cannot be concerned with the likes of me."

"God has long forgiven you, Sir Neville," Robin said, his throat tightening as he saw a tear fall from the knight's eye.

Caroline stopped pacing the frigid hallway. "Has it been fifteen minutes?"

She saw Gabriel exchange a wary look with Cyril. Panic was beginning to pull at her nerves. The idea that her husband might be entombed in Galetaer Castle's stone structure was unbearable and she pushed down a wave of nausea that threatened to bring up the Bannatyres' festive dinner.

"It's been almost twenty," sighed the vampire librarian. His face gloomy.

"Oh, my god," said Caroline feeling as if her legs might give way. She swayed dangerously and leaned against the wall.

Cyril darted forward to take her arm. "Your Serene Highness!"

Before Caroline could force her swimming mind to focus, a shaft of light illuminated Galetaer's abandoned hallway. Not lightning forking down from the storm and penetrating the castle roofline, the beam seemed to emanate from the stone itself. As the blue-green light widened into a kind of bubble, a figure stood within – a medieval man in simple grey robes, a cross of gold hung around his neck by a strip of leather.

"Bless me," murmured Gabriel. "It must be Sir Neville." Caroline felt hot tears of relief spill out of her eyes. "Thank god, thank god he's all right."

Robin's equerry patted her forearm, understanding that her joy was not about the return of Sir Neville Ponsonby.

The bubble – a genuine spirit lantern – rippled as if the power sustaining it was failing. Sir Neville stared at them, his eyes widening in fascination. He stepped forward as if to say something, but the blue-green energy faltered again and began to ebb. Apprehension crossed Sir Neville's handsome face as he momentarily faded and then regained a full presence.

It was then that another light strobed into the hallway – glimmering a warm gold instead of the icy blue. A lady materialized within the new light. She was tall, elegant and in a green gown of 12th century design. The lady held out her bejeweled hands to Sir Neville. He seemed almost overcome at the sight of her and dropped to one knee as if begging her forgiveness.

The lady came towards him, bringing the soft glittering light into his cold prism. Blue light faded into the gold as she laid a hand on his tousled blond hair. Sir Neville looked up, his noble face drawn with both wonder and a deep euphoria. He stood and embraced his lady, lifting her off the ground in exultation. The shaft of light deepened to a darker gold and began to retract, the two embracing medieval figures fading with it. In another moment, the light completely guttered out and Galetaer Castle's hallway returned to darkness.

"Well done, Robin," said Gabriel, wiping at one of his eyes and taking in a short breath.

Lady Caroline pushed off the wall and shone her flashlight up and down the hallway. "But where is he?" she asked, thoroughly shaken by the night's events. "Shouldn't Robin be back by now?"

"Gabriel?" Cyril held his flashlight up to the portion of the hallway where Robin had indicated the chapter house probably existed. "Her Highness is entirely correct."

The vampire librarian dragged his attention away from the site of Sir Neville's reunion with his loved one and joined them by the wall. "I'm on it," he said and disappeared to find his king.

Chapter Forty

Gabriel reappeared moments later with a bleeding and unconscious Robin draped in his arms. "I found him on the floor in there," he said, breathlessly. "Should I get him to the guest quarters?"

"Yes – go! We'll meet you there," Caroline was already turning to head back. Cyril immediately moved to accompany her.

Galetaer Castle seemed to be even larger and more convoluted as if their worry had stretched its dimensions. They careened through its labyrinth of narrow, empty hallways -- all looking the same in the cold dark. The sea storm had settled into a steady rain without the rattle of thunder or strobing lightning outside ancient leaded windows. Caroline was grateful that Cyril had taken charge of the navigation, leading her down to the main staircase where they had hidden from Buckle and then off to the warmer realm of the Bannatyre wing.

She was breathing hard once they slipped into the functioning area of the castle. Normally quite fit, Caroline felt as if her heart was going to explode. The combination of stress, sudden bursts of energy and paranormal shocks had depleted her reserves. If anything happened to Robin, she wasn't at all positive that she would be able to cope.

"Let's go quietly here, Your Highness," whispered Cyril as they reached the main hallway that led to occupied bedrooms. "Better to avoid waking the human contingent."

Caroline nodded, not trusting herself to speak. Her lungs ached from taking in deep drafts of icy air. All she wanted to do was see to it that her husband was in one piece. Normally he never appeared to tire or suffer from illness –

when needed his revenant healing system made immediate repairs.

They had made it to the guest room when a door opened across the way and Caroline's father peered out. His eyes widened at the sight of both Caroline and Cyril in puffy vests and footwear suitable for cave spelunking --

"Hi, Dad," said Caroline, still breathing heavily. "You see Cyril is here to check in with Robin about … about …"

The Earl held up a hand for her to stop. "You can tell me in the morning after I have successfully digested Margaret's large dinner."

Caroline found a smile for her father. "Thanks, Dad."

"Your Lordship," said Cyril with a polite bow of his head.

The Earl of Hawkesmoor threw the equerry a sour expression. "Stripling youths in the middle of the night fussing about," he muttered before shutting his door.

Cyril sniffed, his face resembling a puppy that had been reprimanded for chewing a slipper. "Your father does know I'm almost five hundred years?"

"He will never admit it," Caroline said as she opened the door to her room and hurried in to discover how it was with her husband.

Robin was sitting up in one of the wing chairs with a blanket over his knees, talking to Gabriel when they came in. He was sipping a hot drink that Gabriel had presumably created with the little electric kettle and selection of teas Lady Margaret had thoughtfully installed in the guest room.

"Hello darling," he said to Caroline who rushed to his side to stare at his face, searching for any signs of damage.

"Sorry for the scare. Retrieving Sir Neville took a lot more energy than I imagined possible."

She dropped down to sit on the floor in front of him, relief coursing over her tired frame. "I would like to beat you about the head and shoulders with that cup," Caroline said finally.

"Her father's daughter,' Robin observed fondly.

"But did you find out anything about Cam Drummond?" Cyril came to sit on the edge of the guest bed next to Gabriel.

Robin sighed and shook his head. "Not enough time. I did discover three intriguing things and two powerful suppositions."

If Caroline wasn't so weary and so worried, she might have laughed. Robin had spent much of his more modern existence as a university professor and occasionally the patter of the lecture hall entered his speech.

"I'll let Gabriel give you the goods." Robin closed his green eyes. "I'm just going to drink my tea for a few minutes."

The vampire librarian brightened. "Intriguing fact one – Sir Neville and his men were indeed revenants. One of us got to them in the Middle East. They decided as a group to retreat to Galetaer and form a lay religious body in hopes of doing penance for their sins in the Crusades."

"Surely the locals would have noticed that a phalanx of vampires had moved into the neighborhood?" Cyril asked, politely masking a yawn. "Pitchforks and torches. Burn the witch! And so forth."

Gabriel grinned. "The good old days. The reason the local Scots didn't take umbrage -- like our dear Winnifred who remained in her convent by taking sustenance from farm animals -- Sir Neville and his men foreswore human blood. They performed good works for community and spent their time in prayer. The local Scots probably thought of them as naïve push-overs."

"When did Sybil arrive to look after Sir Neville?" Caroline slowly got to her feet and headed for the electric kettle. She longed for a cup of hot tea herself. "Sybil's a big part of the Devil Came to Galetaer legend."

"Interesting fact number two – Sybil didn't arrive at the castle until the 15th century."

Caroline switched on the kettle and then turned to look back at Gabriel. "How is that possible? Sybil was the beloved cousin, summoned from her convent in France to help Sir Neville run the castle."

"Apparently Sir Neville told Robin that she was a vampire who came to the castle begging to join the order. They allowed her shelter and housekeeping duties instead," said Gabriel with a short laugh. "As a former monk, I can attest to the sexism of the era."

"And the Devil who took her up the chimney?"

"Interesting fact number three – Sybil brought a man or masculine humanoid to Galetaer. Whoever or whatever this creature was managed, somehow, to break up the brotherhood."

Caroline pondered Gabriel's words as she tore open a teabag packet. "Supposition number one – this man is the legendary Devil of the old story who sealed Sir Neville up in a room forever."

Robin opened his eyes. "Clever Caro," he said. "Sir Neville was bitterly disappointed in his knights who were lured into temptation by this particular devil's fancy words. All except one – Asher Grey."

"Supposition number two," gasped Cyril.

Caroline forgot all about the kettle which had begun to whistle. "Asher Grey is Cam Drummond!"

Chapter Forty-one

The hour was very late. Gabriel and Cyril returned to the Carberry Hotel to regroup. Caroline got into bed next to her husband. He slid an arm around her shoulders and kissed her forehead. She laid her head on his chest, enjoying both the quiet and the warmth.

"I know you want to ask what's going wrong with … me," he said, stroking her strawberry blonde hair. "Whatever, whoever we're looking for is – for lack of a better word -- leaning on my etheric energies, looking for a chink."

Caroline shivered, remembering the shadow beings who had tried to force their way into their world at Hawkesmoor some years before. She didn't understand the cantilevered realms that Robin inhabited. He seemed to exist on several different levels simultaneously. A Dylan Thomas poem that she had read in university came to her, unbidden:

> *I, in my intricate image, stride on two levels,*
> *Forged in man's minerals, the brassy orator*
> *Laying my ghost in metal,*
> *The scales of this twin world tread on the double,*
> *My half ghost in armour hold hard in death's*
corridor,
> *To my man-iron sidle.*

Robin pulled her closer. "I will never allow any harm to come to you or the children."

"I know," she murmured and was surprised when Robin turned to kiss her. He shifted his weight over hers and deepened the kiss, drawing her into an intense embrace. Despite the passion, Caroline sensed something bittersweet, something profoundly sad in his embrace as if he was a desperate man escaping physical pain or a deep, painful truth.

The Loch – a narrow watercourse that flowed through Central Park's North Woods, boasted three waterfalls with one of them possessing an old bridge over the descending water. Simon had walked the bridge on various hikes through the North Woods and usually it was a peaceful, contented place with New Yorkers and tourists alike enjoying nature, amateur birdwatching and grabbing selfies from the bridge center.

Currently, it was the scene of a tense stand-off.

At the apex of the bridge stood the two vampires who had laid siege to the Dragos restaurant. Not diffident modern vampires – no hint of the serpentine elegance that seemed to define 21st century urban revenants – the two on the bridge were the personification of medieval power and yet, they had voluntarily thrown their swords aside. Garbed in their leather surcoats and crossed with chainmail, they held up their hands in surrender and warily eyed the Gypsies who surrounded them with modern assault rifles. Although the proverbial fish out of modern water, it was clear that they understood the significance of red tracer dots on their foreheads. One poorly conceived movement and the Dragos would blow their heads to bits – the one way to eradicate a vampire's three-dimensional form.

Still, thought Simon as he and a trembling Della followed Alin out of the tree-lined path into the open, something wasn't right. Were medieval revenants less skillful – unable to reduce their outer forms in an instant to escape human interference? Or was this some kind of dangerous feint? He knew that Alin was very uneasy too. The plan had been to lure the Ivanhoe vampires into revealing themselves at a sham meeting with his father and taking them out quickly in seconds not minutes. Threat terminated. Simple. With the side benefit of allowing Della to know with absolute certainty that she was safe.

But not only had the medieval vampires understood the meeting to be a complete fake, they had arrived without stealth and immediately divested themselves of any superficial advantage.

"Two dead," Alin announced, walking into a puddle of light cast by his people's tactical gear. A steady rain gusted in the artificial light, glittering from time to time like shards of glass. "Lots of trouble. Lots of attention."

The taller of the two vampires, a massive specimen with a rough tangle of brown beard and long hair surrounding a harsh face, spat at the ground. "Gypsies," he said with revulsion.

Red dots on the vampires' foreheads shifted erratically as the armed Dragos cousins worked to contain their annoyance. The second vampire threw an assessing glance at Simon and Della who let out a long breath, tightening her hold on Simon's arm. He pointed at them.

"Parley."

Alin shook his head. "Parley? What the f …"

"A temporary truce," said Simon. "They want to negotiate."

Chapter Forty-two

Robin had the last sip of his breakfast coffee and sat back in his chair. He felt as if the night's sleep and his revenant repair system had banished the exhaustion. Grateful for the reprieve, he gave Lady Margaret who was seated to his right, a warm smile.

"Thank you for your very great generosity," he said. "It was extremely kind of you to allow us to impose on your household during the Christmas season."

Lady Margaret beamed at him. "Nonsense! It has been a joy – and good practice for Buckle as our children will be popping up soon for the holiday."

Robin thought that the noble Buckle could probably had done with less rehearsal for a busy couple of weeks featuring fancy meals. He gave his hostess another smile and tilted his head at the sideboard with its line of silver salvers loaded with breakfast offerings.

"Could I fetch you anything more?"

"Oh, no – thank you! Did you find what you were looking for here, Robin?" asked Lady Margaret in genuine interest. "Ronald does love to pull out all the stops with his Sir Neville and the Devil story."

"I got just what I needed," he said truthfully.

"Bucky," Caroline's father poured some orange juice from a crystal pitcher of Victorian vintage, "I feel I must meet the wind head on. The rise of Cheviot ..."

"Dad – no politics at the table," warned his daughter. "Sir Ronald has every right to champion a hardy, practical sheep up here."

The Earl pretended to glower at his eldest child. "Betrayed by my own daughter -- someone I believed sound on animal husbandry."

"Oh, Dad!" Caroline shook her head with a grin.

Sir Ronald laughed out loud. "No need for family discord. I am happy to discuss bringing the Blue Leicester to Galetaer."

"Ha! Well, now my Christmas is complete." Caroline's father saluted the table with his orange juice. "I thank you all for a delightful and very useful weekend."

"You know," said Sir Ronald turning his attention to Robin, "I was telling Margaret that the power outage last night prevented me from showing you our portrait of Sybil Bannatyre."

Robin sat forward; his curiosity piqued. "A portrait of the Sybil?"

"Someone named Asher Grey did a portrait of her in the 1880s," interjected Lady Margaret with a small laugh. "Naturally, it can only be a complete fantasy but it's quite striking."

Robin caught Caroline jumping slightly at the artist's name. She pretended to brush something off her lap. "Very much like to see it," he said, pushing his chair back and standing up.

"I would too!" Caroline popped up like a dolphin leaping for a trainer's sardine. The table rattled at her urgency. "Please."

"Meg – would you mind?" asked Sir Ronald. "I'm going to negotiate Blue Leicesters while I can."

Lady Margaret obligingly returned her coffee cup to its saucer and rose with considerably more decorum than her guests. "We keep her cooped up in the second reception room – this way."

"We do not parley with Gypsies," said the second vampire, ignoring Alin and casting his gaze upon Simon. "We will speak with the son of Robin DuPlessis."

Alin turned away from the vampires. "You do not have to talk to these vampires, my friend. Your father would want the Dragos to destroy them."

"I am the son of Robin DuPlessis," Simon said, slipping from Della's grip. He stepped forward to confront the vampires who had brutally murdered two humans to get his attention.

They exchanged a knowing glance at his approach. Simon sensed a kind of sly humor behind the look, triumphant grins tamped down and concealed. There was something very foreboding about it as if a certain outcome was never in any doubt – that they had puppeteered him exactly where they wanted him.

Galetaer's second reception room was a pleasant room that shared many qualities with other Bannatyre living quarters in the castle. It was relatively small and therefore easier to heat, oriented on a fireplace with a pretty carved chimney piece in the Regency style of Robert Adams. The room's comfortable but not priceless furnishings were a friendly mixture of antique and reproduction. Its walls – gifted with some crafty 19th century plaster molding -- were painted in a soft, relaxing yellow with subtle color matches in upholstery and drapes.

"We use this room more than some of the others," said Lady Margaret as she led them inside. She laughed and pointed at a large reproduction Charles II cabinet that stood next to the fireplace. "There's a television secreted away in there."

"Very comfortable," agreed Caroline.

Lady Margaret looked pleased and pointed again to the rear of the room where a genuine Regency console table held pride of place. "She's over there. It's very Victorian Medievalism, I'm afraid."

Robin strode across the room towards the mahogany console table. The picture hanging above it was in a heavy gold gilt frame. He noted it was standard Victorian portrait size, roughly 24 by 20 and featured a woman in brown. Drawing closer, the brown color represented the rough wool of a very austere medieval dress. Indeed, the dress wasn't the idealized religious order costume the Bannatyres probably assumed it was. No symbolic cross had been painted -- it was the coarse dress of a household servant. Coming into range, Sybil Bannatyre herself began to take shape. Cam Drummond/Asher Grey was not an exemplary artist, but he was serviceable. He had painted from memory, a drab sparrow of a girl. Sybil was in her early twenties, completely ordinary with a small round face surrounded by mousey brown hair that looked vaguely unkempt and as if it would smell of sweat and oil. She stared out at the viewer with a sulky expression belied by shrewd, acquisitive eyes – her right hand pressed against her bodice as if she were pledging allegiance to something. The only real flash of color in the portrait was in the ring she wore.

Robin actually gasped and stepped back. A chevron shaped ring -- A swan above a yellow shield crossed with black bars surrounded by azure marked with the royal fleur de lis.

Chapter Forty-three

As soon as he recognized the shield on Sybil's finger, Asher Grey's amateur likeness of Sybil Bannatyre aligned sharply with the facts. Robin knew he was looking at Miss Pratt, his daughter's nanny.

Lady Margaret's cheerful voice cut through the pinging in his head as he absorbed the shock. He felt Caroline slip her arm under his in an affectionate gesture. She hadn't spotted it yet.

"You can see he even invented a religious order's crest for her ring," Lady Margaret was saying. "She's rather plain but we love her anyway. Ronald says the artist couldn't bear a pretty girl being that devoted to God."

"She does look pious," replied Caroline diplomatically. "Don't you think so, Robin?"

Robin turned to stare down at his wife. His mind was spinning with noise and notions as if all his various streams of consciousness were bleeding together. London. He had to get back to London.

"You have been very kind, Lady Margaret," Robin sputtered, earning a surprised look from Caroline. "I must apologize -- I have just gotten a … an urgent text from home. I'm afraid we have to go immediately."

If Lady Margaret was fazed by his sudden urgency, she didn't show it. "Of course! I shall inform Buckle to stand by to assist," she said as Robin spun on his heel and propelled Caroline towards the door.

"You've uncovered something – what is it?" Caroline whispered once they were over the threshold and into the hallway. "Will it help bring an end to …"

"Caro, I need you to take charge of your father and return to Hawkesmoor Castle."

"Don't be silly, I have to get back to Ari," she shook her head. "I've been gone too long as it is."

Robin's head ached from all the white noise jamming his mind. He stopped and grabbed her shoulders, hating the Caroline's surprise at his sudden roughness. "I will bring her to you! Promise me that you'll go straight to Hawkesmoor."

"Listen, Your Serene Highness," Caroline's hazel eyes flashed with annoyance, "I'm not doing a bloody thing until you tell me what's going on."

He pulled her further down the hallway, away from the second reception room and the possibility of Lady Margaret or Buckle overhearing their conversation. Throwing open a Victorian beveled door, Robin directed her into small sitting room that had been pressed into service as an estate office for Sir Ronald.

"Well?" asked Caroline, crossing her arms.

Robin rubbed his temples. His nerve endings felt electric and hot.

"You mustn't worry," he began with uncharacteristic enervation.

"For god's sake, Robin – this is the 21st century. I'm not a hothouse flower."

"Sybil Bannatyre and Miss Pratt," Robin said in a flat voice, "are one and the same."

Caroline's face drained to an ashen color. "I beg … beg your pardon?"

"The portrait – it's Miss Pratt."

Caroline lurched for the door. "Ari!"

Robin caught her by the arm and pulled her to a standstill. He could feel Caroline trembling. "I am going to London where Ari is safe -- protected by the guard. I will bring her to you at Hawkesmoor."

"But I have to," Caroline was breathing too quickly with tears springing to her eyes, "see that she's all right. Robin – what have we done?"

He pulled her into his arms. "Ari's fine. I will see to it."

"What could Sybil Bannatyre want with us?" Caroline's voice broke and a sob shook her frame. "Arianrhod -- she's only six. She's only six!"

Robin felt the roar in his head rise up a notch. Every alert in his preternatural hybrid neural net was firing and demanding his attention. Something was seriously wrong. Something was desperate for his attention.

"Darling," he said quietly, "I need you to take your father to Hawkesmoor. Can you do that?"

Caroline nodded, stepping away from him. She took in a deep breath, sniffling slightly. "Please go now – don't wait. I'll handle Dad."

"I love you," Robin said, producing a white handkerchief and handing it to her.

He smiled, hoping it would be reassuring, and dismantled his outer form, vanishing from Galetaer Castle's estate office like one of its reputed ghosts.

Chapter Forty-four

"I think Bucky and Margaret are just a little baffled by the sudden and complete disappearance of your husband," said the Earl as they both waved one last time at the Bannatyres who stood politely on Galetaer Castle's steps to see them off.

She edged the Range Rover away from the castle. "We'll send them a fruit basket."

Her father looked unimpressed. "Well, that ought to allay their confusion."

Caroline increased pressure on the accelerator and headed down the long winding gravel road towards the public roads. She had brought her father partially up to date, letting him know that an emergency had taken him back to London and that it was best to get an early start on the Christmas holiday at Hawkesmoor. She omitted the detail that the crisis involved Arianrhod because he'd gallantly insist on returning to London to help. It did mean that she felt very alone in her worry.

As soon as the Range Rover cleared a few hundred yards, Culpeper and Tinley shimmered into the back seat. Both Caroline and her father gave a start at the sudden appearance of Robin's guardsmen.

"Apologies," said Tinley, giving them a small bow of the head, "Your Serene Highness."

Culpeper also bobbed his head. "Your Serene Highness."

The Earl turned in the passenger seat, frowning. "You both look cold."

"We've been on watch, Your Lordship," replied Culpeper, rubbing his hands together briskly.

"Turn up the heat, Caro," said the Earl as if vampire guardsmen materializing in front of him was a perfectly normal part of his day.

Robin reassembled in Number 7 Audley Square's expansive foyer near its main staircase. It had been a difficult crossing over an unadvised long distance. He was followed almost immediately by Cyril who had been given an assist by Gabriel. The equerry was shaking slightly, unnerved by the fierce buffeting of the turbulent atmosphere that had made holding molecular structures together almost impossible.

"Your Serene Highness!" One of the guardsmen left behind at Audley Square ran towards them.

"Where is my daughter?" Robin demanded, "And Miss Pratt?"

Hirst came to a stop and snapped a short bow. "Sir! They are taking the usual walk after the princess' breakfast. Bennett is shadowing as usual. Sir, we have a …"

"Sir Geoffrey, sir" said Cyril, still trembling but back at his electronic tablet, "is insisting on talking to you."

"Hirst – take this lot with you and find them. I want them both back without delay." Robin ignored Cyril. "Take Miss Pratt into custody but don't frighten my daughter."

Hirst – another very young-looking revenant who had seen gallant action as a WW1 officer and was officially listed as killed in the Somme Offensive – tried to hide a look of bafflement. "Yes, sir but …"

"But?" Robin raised an eyebrow in annoyance.

"Sir, we had a small situation last night, but we couldn't contact you."

"The storm," murmured Cyril Goforth. "Knocked out everything human and vampire."

Robin turned to his guard. "Go – get my daughter!"

"I'm on it as well," said Gabriel, following Brown and Bramwell.

Robin pivoted back to Hirst. "Explain small situation."

"That Scotsman …"

"Cam Drummond was here?"

Hirst nodded. "Well, sir, he really just knocked on the front door and demanded to see you. Said it was urgent. We didn't know what you would prefer so we …"

Robin tightened his jaw. "Let him take the high road, I expect."

"No, sir – we put him immediately under arrest."

"No, no," gasped Della as he confronted the old vampires. She darted forward to take hold of his arm "Please, this is what your father asked Alin to handle. We were just supposed to …"

"Della," Simon's voice was low but severe, "stay back!"

She released him. "Ten cuidado."

As he returned his focus to the vampires, a sound rose from the Loch's tumbling water – voices. At first, they were as ephemeral as the cascading brook but then took shape. The Tylwyth Teg were warning him. He listened for a moment, trying to decipher their strange metaphorical poetry. While some of the voices sung of Annwfn, the Celtic Otherworld, other voices wove through with tales of the Sluagh – dead sinners who had become vile creatures seeking fresh souls. They sang of darkness and despair.

"You wanted to parley?" he said with no time left to ponder the Tylwyth Teg's beautiful but labyrinthine communications.

The two medieval vampires exchanged a glance, red dots from the Dragos tactical arms shifting uneasily on their heads. The slightly shorter vampire let out a coarse laugh that seemed both a bark and a growl.

"We came a long way to face you." The vampire looked amused. "Mighty effort for a mere stripling such as you, boy."

"You have a point?" Simon asked. "Butcher of defenseless women."

His second spat at the ground in disgust. "Let's be on with it. We are pledgers and must pay our liege debt."

At his words, the atmosphere at the bridge began to grow heavier as if they all had suddenly been transported to the bottom of the sea. Air currents rolled above them, disturbed by something. Simon thought of the Sluagh. Dark and predatory.

Before he confronted the faux Scot, Robin made a detour to his daughter's room with its adjoining governess suite. He wanted to find the sketch of the yellow and black medieval shield that Miss Pratt/Sybil had drawn in her teaching workbook.

The pretty blue room with its pale pink rose accents had an abandoned feel that Robin found very disquieting. Ari's bed was neatly made and her school table beside the fireplace had been recently tidied with all textbooks returned to the bookcase. Miss Pratt's workbook was conspicuously missing from the wooden tabletop and from the schoolwork neatly stacked on a bookshelf.

"Julian?" he called out softly, hoping that the little silver tabby might have some insights into Ari's teacher.

Julian failed to slink out from underneath Ari's bed or trot in from the hallway. Imagining that the cat was taking a gambol about the house or visiting his non-self-cleaning litter pan, Robin moved to the governess quarters. Located just beyond Ari's door, Caroline had combined two former sitting rooms into a very comfortable staff accommodation that featured two handsome windows overlooking the back garden and an especially nice bathroom.

Miss Pratt/Sybil's belongings were all perfectly in place. Although she seemed to possess no personal effects such as her own books or objet d'art, the armoire revealed an array of her plain, almost drab wardrobe. The bathroom held her various soaps and combs exactly where one might expect to find them.

Robin felt his teeth grinding. It almost came across as a set in a play or a hotel room with only a weekend occupant.

There was also no sign of her teaching workbooks. He dropped down to his knees and peered under the furniture in case she had hidden them.

Just as Robin was making sure that nothing untoward was tucked under the bed, Cyril Goforth made a polite coughing noise.

"I apologize for the intrusion, Your Serene Highness," said the equerry "Sir Geoffrey is demanding you speak with him."

"You inform Sir Geoffrey that he can …"

Robin was interrupted by tapping sound. Loud and persistent, it came from one of the large windows. He jumped to his feet and spun in the direction of the windows.

"A raven, sir," breathed Cyril, pointing to an ebony bird that was both striking the window glass with its beak and beating against it with powerful wings. "You're not going to let a bird inside?"

Robin ignored Cyril and unlatched the Georgian window. The raven flew backwards until the window was thrown open and then swooped into land in his forearm.

"Robin! Robin!" cawed Egbert-One-With-The-Apple-Trees. "Mount Street Gardens! Danger! Blood! Danger!"

Chapter Forty-five

Robin was on the run. He had materialized just inside the South Audley Street entrance to Mount Street Gardens and taken off for the center of the small urban park. It was a place popular with locals who, in good weather, enjoyed the peaceful sliver of green, finding spots on benches to read and think.

Fortunately for a panicked vampire, the gardens held a somewhat lesser allure in the middle of winter on a rainy day. It was deserted as he ran down one of the arteries that led to the central point. Egbert flew overhead, leading the way.

"Robin!" shouted Gabriel, stepping free of a heavy collection of holly and laurel shrubs. "Over here!"

The raven circled and dropped down to perch on tree branch as Robin dashed towards the vampire librarian. His revenant heart was pounding. He had rarely known fear since becoming a vampire but the idea of either Ari or Simon in terrible danger filled him with an implacable, cold terror.

Gabriel stepped back and allowed him to access the space between laurel shrubs. There, being tended to by Bramwell was the guardsman, Bennett. He was covered in blood from wounds to his chest, throat and scalp.

"He's been stabbed," said Bramwell as Robin knelt beside the injured vampire. "I think she tried to take out his brain. Be all right in a bit, sir."

"My daughter?" Robin almost didn't trust his voice to speak.

Bennett gurgled as he tried to talk. His throat wound leaked crimson. "I ... I don't know, sir," he whispered through the blood. "Save the c… cat. She'd have done me if … if not for that cat. It ... it went for her. B…Brave."

Robin looked up at Bramwell. "Cat?"

The guardsman pointed away from Bennett. Under the closet bush was the form of a little silver tabby. Julian was still alive – barely – breathing fast and shallow.

"Brown?" asked Robin sharply.

"Trying to track them, sir, in case Pratt's still in the area."

"Join him. Take Gabriel. I'll get Bennett home. Don't come back until you've got my daughter or … something we can use."

"Run, Della!" shouted Simon as a sharp wind picked up and autumn leaves riven from swaying trees spiraled around the old bridge. "Run!"

The two vampires were reciting something together. "To Him, I am both stay and sword. I swear to this until death does take me or the world does end." Then again in unison they surged forward despite the Dragos and their fire power. "Tell Robin DuPlessis we will see him in hell!"

Alin's snipers immediately fired – strangely silent except for a fierce zipping sound and Simon had a second to realize that the ingenious Dragos had modified their weapons. Then he heard Della cry out as both vampires were hit simultaneously from three directions – their powerful frames juddering violently under the assault. A vampire could be destroyed with brain death so the Dragos focused almost exclusively achieving solid headshots. The old vampires fell, their heads exploding in a flurry of well-placed hits. Red mist pulsed up into the atmosphere, momentarily shimmering in the tactical lights before being swept away by the night wind.

Alin pivoted away from the sight, his aquiline face twisting in disbelief. "Suicide! Suicide for god's sake. What could have made …"

"Sacrifice not suicide," replied Simon, looking for Della. "Something else is here – something worse."

Alin registered Simon's words with widening eyes. He shouted urgently in Romani and immediately all the tactical lights began blinking out in the woods surrounding the Loch's bridge. The sudden darkness added to the unusually heavy weight of the atmosphere.

"They're moving out – like us!" said Alin, dropping a hand on Simon's shoulder and pushing him forward. "I have to clear the area. Head for lights and people."

Simon needed no encouragement. He broke into a run, heading for Della who was turning in an agitated circle, unsure of exactly what to do.

"Come on, love! Time to go." He snaked an arm around her narrow waist and pulled her towards the nearest path, hoping it would lead to an urban byway and not deeper into the North Woods.

"Oh, my god," she whispered as they ran. "Oh, my god. What was that?"

"We're not out of it yet," Simon said quietly. The atmospheric heaviness was still with them – as if a huge predator prowled charged, electric air.

A scream knifed through the park's trees. Simon wasn't sure if it was even human. It could be a shrill shriek of frustration as much as terror. A moment passed and more screams ripped through the strange, fractious air. These were dying cries of panic and pain.

Della stumbled in the dark and fell to her knees. "What the hell is that?" she asked breathlessly as Simon helped her to stand. "You think Alin's okay?"

"He's good," Simon said, praying he was right. "More importantly – you okay to keep running?"

She nodded, a gesture barely visible in the gloom. "This is crazy. Your Dad must be James Bond."

"Something like that," sighed Simon.

Chapter Forty-six

Robin cradled Julian's fragile body as he recombined into his three-dimensional form. The brave little cat had managed to avoid being stabbed by Pratt/Sybil, but she had hurled him away and he had violently struck the thick trunk of one of the gardens' many Plane Trees. Julian was pretty sure some bones had been broken.

"Stouthearted fellow," Robin murmured as Number 7's Georgian foyer reassembled in a shimmer of electro-magnetic energy. "You'll be all right."

Once fully returned, he was chagrined to find Sir Geoffrey Constable standing next to Cyril. The civil servant wore a sour expression that was both harried and gloomy. An expression that refused to be dislodged even by the sight of a vampire materializing from the ethers.

"Mystified that you required PM's Gulfstream. Speaking of the PM …"

"I don't have time," Robin announced, sprinting for his office, "just now, Sir Geoffrey."

"You haven't any time left," snapped Sir Geoffrey, following him.

"Cyril – Bennett?" Robin kept up his pace, surprised that the middle-aged civil servant was staying with him. Sir Geoffrey probably hadn't lumbered into a jog since his cricket days at Eton.

"In considerable pain but healing, sir!" Cyril was running too.

"Nothing from Bramwell or Brown? Simon?"

"Not yet, sir! But His Highness will be in the air soon, sir. Landing Durham Tees Valley by tonight. The Dragos are cleaning up."

"Good. Did they find Simon's medievals?"

Cyril checked his tablet on the fly. "Yes, but they were destroyed before anything useful could be gleamed. A couple of low-level mercenaries had been brought along in the assumption that it would be a cakewalk getting to your son. The Dragos wildly underestimated as usual."

Robin was disappointed but unsurprised. Medieval revenants took their bonds very seriously. Even if the Gypsy clan had managed to corral them, they'd have destroyed themselves rather than surrender.

"Lord and Lady Tiffin have returned from Australia," huffed Sir Geoffrey, irritated by the lack of attention to his agenda. "The Prime Minister has felt the weight of their devastation and has begun to radically reassess his position."

"You promised me a week." Robin said over his shoulder. "Children are now involved."

Robin stopped and spun on the civil servant. "My child too!"

Sir Geoffrey caught off balance by the sudden change in velocity, staggered and nearly fell. He flung out a hand and braced himself against an early Georgian oak lowboy. "You have my sympathies, believe me. But this abduction by one of your own does rather seems to confirm vampire involvement."

"There may be no connection," Robin hedged, motioning for Cyril to open the door to his office. "If there is, I will uncover it."

Sir Geoffrey considered the statement. "Three days then. PM has a crucial infrastructure bill in the Commons. It will distract him, but the Tiffin children must be found if you hope to protect your … species."

"Three days," said Robin, his tone icy. He carried Julian into his office without looking back at the Prime Minister's right hand. "Now I have to save a cat."

Simon wanted to look back but he couldn't force himself to do it. He had the sensation that they were being followed. Imagined he could hear an ominous roll of thump, thump, thump on the well-tended park path as if a hideously huge leopard or one of those velociraptors from the films had targeted them as the next meal.

The path – cleverly designed to allow park visitors to feel as if they were truly out, away from the city – seemed endless. They ran around a bend, a cold wind sending an eddy of autumn leaves all around them. In the dark, the leaves took on a life of their own – tumbling creatures. Simon thought again of the Sluagh.

"What's that sound?" Della breathed. "Behind us. Is it Alin?"

Thump, thump, thump. Footfalls on the earth or heavy, leathery wings like a bat? But not his imagination and whatever it was, it was gaining.

Julian was very frail as Robin laid him gently on his desktop. The little cat's breathing was shallow and hoarse, lacking the strength to even mewl in pain. It was clear from his limp, soft extremities that Pratt/Sybil had broken the cat's spine and ribs when she hurled him against the tree. It was remarkable that Julian had survived the trip back to Audley Square.

His Tylwyth Teg bloodline had made him a physical empath who could heal human injury. He had never attempted the same with animals although, in theory, it ought to work.

"Hang on, Julian – just a little longer," Robin sat and closed his eyes, traveling inward to his own cantilevered version of Simonides of Ceos' invention – the memory palace – to find the Tylwyth Teg's thoughts on animal healing.

Modern human psychologists employed the memory palace as useful devices in which a mnemonic image could be stored and then retrieved by its attachment to a specific location. Because he was a revenant-faerie hybrid who had known a human life in the 18th century, his memory palace was vast and constantly evolving with memories and experiences from all of his aspects.

As a human youth, he had spent a glorious month reading in Dublin's Trinity Library. His memory palace had been built with Trinity's spectacular Long Room and its two levels of priceless books – more a cathedral to scholarship than mere library – as the template.

Robin ran down the center of his own version of the Long Room. He nodded at Aristotle who looked up, mildly irritated, from the papers he was perusing at a library table made of gleaming walnut. The memory palace was peopled with personalities Robin had found fascinating throughout his centuries in the human world.

He nipped into the stacks and down an aisle of walnut bookcases looking for a specific volume. Every book shelved in his library was a memory, a thought, an idea or some version of innate knowledge emanating from one of his three bloodlines.

"Bobbity," said a beautifully modulated voice behind him, "we must speak."

Robin turned his head away from the book he had just pulled from the shelf. Striding down the library aisle was an Elizabethan aristocrat in a flawless black leather doublet and velvet cape over his right shoulder. Tall, graceful --

despite a slight limp -- and strikingly handsome with thick blond hair and an immaculately groomed beard, he was the very definition of 16th century masculine beauty.

"I wish I had the time," replied Robin to Edward de Vere, the 17th Earl of Oxford.

De Vere's intelligent blue eyes flashed with impatience and he tapped his cane against the mahogany sapwood floor. "You have forgotten something I've told you. It is the answer you seek."

Sometimes the patrons of his mental library nudged him to remember bits of scholarship or literary allusions. He wished he did have a moment to sit with De Vere and talk about sonnets. The 17th Earl was easily his favorite historical figure – erudite, witty, and a genius who had written the plays and poetry commonly attributed to William Shakespeare.

Robin replaced the book on the shelf. "I'll be back, I promise."

"Bobbity!" Edward was holding up a hand in protest. "There is no moving forward without elucidation."

Robin blinked away from the memory palace and refocused on the mortally wounded silver tabby on his desk. Julian was still breathing rapidly but it was clear he was ebbing. He ran his long hands over Julian's soft fur, drawing out disruption and pain. Unlocking the Tylwyth Teg's ability to spin and weave lines of energy, Robin reworked the toxic line, pulling and shaping a new pattern. There were threads of time and energy coursing through the universe whether ley lines crisscrossing geography or the delicate dosser of one small cat's life force.

Once the septic line had been rewoven, Robin directed it into the tabby's broken body, stitching up shattered bone and muscle.

Julian gave a start on the desktop and shuddered. He let out a meow that translated roughly as I'll be damned! and jumped to his feet.

"Thank you for saving Bennett," Robin said, sitting back in his chair. Unlike the empathetic healing of humans in which he took on the injuries or illness, the repairs to a small animal such as Julian required a slightly different approach and was far less invasive to his strange neural net. But it still took something from him, and he would need a few minutes to recover.

"Thank you for saving me," replied Julian in a series of meows. "I should visit the litter pan though. What of her?"

Robin shook his head. "Anything you could tell me would help."

The little cat sprung onto his lap and rubbed his head against Robin's chest. "I was having my kibble while Ari ate her kibble. That one was …"

"That one – Miss Pratt?"

"Yes," Julian curled up on Robin's legs. "That one told of a friend in a special place. Would Ari like to meet him? Did not like it. I follow."

Robin tensed his jaw, thinking of Sir Neville's bitterness about the fancy man who had beguiled his knights. Anger and panic threatened to cripple his ability to think rationally. "Did you see this friend?"

The silver tabby flicked its tail. "No. That one attacked your guardian without warning."

"Ari saw this?" He would exact a terrible price from Miss Pratt/Sybil when they finally met again. She would regret crossing his path.

Julian sat up. "No. My girl was sent ahead to look at something pretty. Your guardian tried to follow. I tried to follow. That one attacked."

"We're all in your debt," Robin patted the cat's head.

"Now, I must find my daughter."

The silver tabby obligingly leapt to the floor as Robin got to his feet. He felt a little unsteady – his system still somewhat overtaxed from repairing Julian's dire injuries. When blood dripped onto the desk blotter, he realized with trepidation that his nose was bleeding again. The etheric protections he held on Audley, Hawkesmoor and the Bailey seemed be under constant stress either by something determined to get in or something more interested in compromising his ability to act. Neither prospect was encouraging.

Chapter Forty-seven

Caroline and her father walked near a Scottish service station while the guardsmen refilled the Range Rover's tank and discreetly partook of some blood supplies stored in an ice chest.

"I hope Buckle didn't look in one of those fortified picnic hampers," sighed the Earl of Hawkesmoor. "Although he probably served tea at the Battle of Harlow."

Caroline lowered the cell phone from her ear and stared at the screen. "Still no service."

"Can you imagine that medieval clan axe battle?" Her father gestured grandly to the tidy modern filling station with its bright Welcome Break logos. "They call the ground Red Harlow for all the blood that flowed. And not too far from this mecca of petrol and plastic-wrapped sandwiches either."

She pocketed her phone. "I wonder if Culpeper has any news."

The Earl reached out and awkwardly patted her shoulder. British aristocrats of his generation often found expressing personal sentiment very onerous. In his cluttered study at the castle was a framed black and white photograph of a painfully stiff handshake between him and his father, then the Earl of Hawkesmoor. The picture had been taken just after he'd rescued his father from being mortally wounded by a charging bull.

"Your husband is an ingenious and competent fellow. He'll sort things."

This was rare approbation from her father and Caroline was genuinely moved. She turned and hugged him, wishing she could tell him the extent of her worries.

"There, there, old girl," he murmured. "No need to go all to pieces."

"Sorry." She pulled away, half laughing. "I could do with one of those plastic wrapped sandwiches."

"No," said the Earl severely. "I can see now that you have lost your mind."

They rounded a turn in the path and ahead, streetlights glowed above the tree line. In a couple of hundred feet, urban Manhattan could offer safety from whatever had come to Central Park.

"Almost there, Della!" Simon was grateful that the dancer was such an athlete. She fairly flew along the dirt path, barely breathing hard. On his side, he was fit from riding and walking the Yorkshire byways but not like Della. His lungs were burning with the exertion.

"Son – son of DuPlessis." Hoarse and guttural -- a dark inhuman voice of desiccated flesh and metal. It seems to radiate around them like Chinese gong. "You are for me." Della let out a sharp cry of panic. She began to shift around to see just what was behind them in the woods. "What the hell …"

"Don't look back!" Simon threw arm and pulled her close to him. "We're almost to the lights."

Another curve and Central Park West glimmered in the December drizzle. The hum and clatter of traffic proved that New York never slept. Thump, thump, thump – the thing behind them seemed almost at their shoulders.

"Son of DuPlessis – you are for me." The voice was now a brutal whisper with the raking slide of a blacksmith's rasp. Della seemed to bite back another outcry and put on another burst towards the lights. He kept up with her despite the ache in his lungs. They bounded forward towards the urban

286

trailhead and the comforting city street just beyond. Thirty feet to concrete. Thirty feet from the darkness.

At the sound of wings striking his window glass, Robin was surprised to find a Peregrine Falcon alighting on the ledge. He unlatched the window and the sleek raptor slipped in, shaking rainwater off its wings.

"As directed by the Tower Raven, we have fanned out over the city, Your Serene Highness," said the falcon in its language of rolled and slurred chwirks.

"Who do I have the honor of addressing?"

"Lord Redvers of Regents Park, sire." The Peregrine Falcon bobbed forward in reverence. "We spotted your targets heading in the direction of Bond Street but lost them near the tube station."

The news that Ari had been seen wove threads of hope through his worry. It wasn't much but just the thought that Miss Pratt/Sybil might not be strong enough as a vampire to move Ari through molecular transfer was invigorating.

"In your debt, Lord Redvers," Robin bowed as the raptor took to wing, gliding out the office window and into the December rain.

"The honor has been mine," called the falcon, soaring up and away from Number 7.

He sprinted around his desk to the door and flung it open. "Cyril!"

The equerry was waiting patiently in hallway. Next to him was an unamused Sir Geoffrey who raised an eyebrow.

"You're bleeding," he said. "Oh, the irony."

"And you're still here," Robin flicked his eyes from the civil servant to his own secretary. "Ari and Miss Pratt have been sighted heading for the Bond Street tube. Send me Hirst but the guard must deploy now to all the possible exit points and transfer routes. She is extremely dangerous – no doubt now that she murdered Pryce-Atwater and set up that poor, benighted Fletcher Greenwood."

Sir Geoffrey had his cell phone out and was barking similar orders into it. Cyril bowed slightly and darted away to alert the guardsmen to new information.

"Excuse me, Sir Geoffrey," said Robin. He moved away from the civil servant who was still issuing commands over the phone and started to make his way towards the guards' garrison located in the north wing of the Georgian house.

"MI5 operatives are now involved." The civil servant hurried to catch up with Robin's long strides. "We should have CCTV footage soon too."

"Why are you still here?" Robin asked, wiping away blood from his face with a handkerchief.

"Alas, I will be with you until this vampire-created disaster is dealt with. The PM is adamant."

Before Robin could fully express his displeasure, Hirst ran up and stood at quiet attention.

"Your Serene Highness."

"Where is he?" Robin growled, fighting to tamp down his temper. "In the old cells?"

Hirst looked apologetic. "Sir -- you did say you wanted the old cells made redundant. We didn't want to …"

"Where is he?" Robin repeated with bite in his voice.

"Well, we put him up in the attic – with a guard, of course."

The old cells, as they were called by the guard, had been created by the Marquess of Southbrook, Britain's vampire king before a violent coup d'etat staged by Garnet Petherbridge had overthrown him. Southbrook – a lover of the mystical arts – had managed to create a power vacuum in the cells that disabled a revenant's ability to access special traits. These cells had gone on to become a brutal symbol of Garnet Petherbridge's bloody reign as sovereign. He used them extensively to cage enemies both real and imagined, refining the torture of vampires to a science in the process. Robin was determined to render them useless but wasn't quite sure, yet, how Southbrook had done it.

"He hasn't tried to escape?"

"Hasn't wanted to, sir. Quite content to wait for you."

Robin moved off again, annoyed that Sir Geoffrey was on his heels. He would have to sort a way to send the civil servant packing. All that mattered now was recovering Ari safely. The Prime Minister and his radical reassessments could go to hell.

He was almost to the main staircase when – to his very great surprise – Edward De Vere, the 17th Earl of Oxford began descending from the first landing. He was a striking figure on the stair in his black leather doublet and tall Elizabethan riding boots.

Robin froze and Sir Geoffrey nearly ploughed into him. It was impossible that a personage from his mind's memory palace could have escaped to the human plane of existence. Yet, he was striding down the sweeping Georgian staircase as if Number 7 belonged rightly to him.

Robin remained frozen, wondering if something had gone terribly wrong with his aberrant hybrid nervous system. The stress and the bleeding – perhaps his mind was shattering into a million pieces.

"Bobbity, we must speak," Edward De Vere said in his lovely, rich voice. The voice of an aristocrat and an actor just as Robin always imagined the 17th Earl would speak.

"Are you quite all right?" asked Sir Geoffrey, seemingly unmoved by the sight of one of the most famous men of the 16th century. Clearly, he didn't see or hear the genuine author of Hamlet.

"Hirst, could you take Sir Geoffrey up to the attic?" Robin murmured, watching De Vere reach the bottom step. "I'll join you momentarily."

The civil servant was highly intelligent and had made a career out of reading the subtle body language of others. He studied Robin in interest, aware that something unique was occurring but allowed Hirst to direct him towards the more convenient elevator.

Once they had left the immediate area, Robin met Edward De Vere at the base of the staircase. The playwright leaned slightly against the newel post, taking weight off his injured leg.

"My heart is bruised, Bobbity," he said. "And I thought you listened to me in authentic interest."

"I just haven't the time for such wishful …"

"You will manufacture time if you wish to understand."

Robin took in a long breath to steady his nerves and turned away from the vision of Edward De Vere. His mind might be unraveling; he had no choice but to focus on finding Ari. Nothing else mattered.

"A swan above a yellow shield crossed with black bars, surrounded by azure marked with the royal fleur de lis," came Edward's voice.

Robin spun around. "Medieval shield – Norman probably. You know it?"

The Earl of Oxford sighed. "Not Norman. Brittany, Anjou and Poitou."

"Please – I must have a name. She's only six!"

"You recall I told you about a play I'd once had hoped to write? But it was too dark, too terrible a tale for even stout denizens of the Globe. Think, Bobbity, think."

"Brittany, Anjou and Poitou," Robin murmured trying to remember why those three regions seemed relevant.

Edward De Vere tapped his walking stick again the step. "A swan above a yellow shield crossed with black bars, surrounded by azure marked with the royal fleur de lis." He tapped the stick again with more force. "15th century. Brittany, Anjou and Poitou. Baron."

Edward De Vere looked at him with pity, fading away. It was then Robin saw the connection. It struck him like an axe blow. As if he'd pushed aside a heavy velvet curtain to a thousand suns, searing the world. He staggered back and sank to his knees in despair. The identity and history of Sir Neville Ponsonby's visitor with the seductive words rushed around him like a flash fire.

Chapter Forty-eight

Caroline shivered despite the Range Rover's efficient heater. Her father looked over in concern from the passenger seat.

"All right?"

She shivered again. "Just one of those strange someone walked over my grave feelings. It's nothing."

But it didn't feel like nothing. She wished Robin would let her know what was going on -- that Miss Pratt had been successfully dealt with and Ari was fine. Currently they were driving through another storm. More rain than snow, it had blown up as they dropped through the Highlands. Even though the motorway was well maintained, it was heavy going and cell phone reception was poor. Caroline's hopes were all pinned on the notion that failed communication from London explained Robin's silence.

Simon and Della practically leapt from the path to the Manhattan sidewalk. It felt like an explosion to the senses – lights, traffic, rain and the brittle, frustrated keening shriek of whatever had hunted them in the dark.

"That wasn't some mafia guy," panted Della as they jogged raggedly away from the park entrance.

Simon stumbled to halt. He bent over, hands on his knees, breathing hard.

"I don't know what that was," he said truthfully between breaths.

Before Della could pursue why a mysterious monster would single him out specifically, a massive SUV roared up to the curb beside them.

"The cavalry." Simon blew out another breath and pointed at the SUV.

But it wasn't the Dragos who emerged from the plush leather interior. It was a someone who looked as if he ticked every box in the Mafia guidebook. He had a face straight out of a Correggio and was attired in a bespoke Italian suit with a flashy tie.

"You're safe now," he said with a smile and an expansive gesture. "I'm an old friend of your father's – Max Aosta."

"Asher Grey," said Robin, striding into the attic room where Sir Neville's former knight sat miserably on one of Garnet Petherbridge's ornate Louis IV chairs. Sir Geoffrey perched on another one, his expression flat and inscrutable.

The vampire he'd known as Cam Drummond sat back, dumbfounded. Dressed in a kilt in the classic Drummond red and green tartan and a heavy fisherman's sweater, he looked every inch a rugged Highlander.

"How could you possibly know that?" he asked in a voice no longer imbued with a Scottish burr.

"Sir Neville," Robin jerked a chair from the unwanted collection of Petherbridge's furniture and sat down in front of the knight. "I went to Galetaer Castle."

"He no longer exists …"

"You were the only knight to remain loyal," Robin saw Sir Geoffrey's eyes widen in some interest and the civil servant leaned forward slightly. "Loyal for centuries – remaining in Scotland to keep a weather eye out for his keep and the other one. Am I right?"

Asher Grey swallowed roughly. "How could you know about that?"

"I need to find the other one, "said Robin, not wanting to speak the cursed name. His stomach burned as if it were riddled with ulcers.

"I don't …"

Robin fought to keep his churning panic under control.

"You did come here to warn me about Sybil?"

Sir Neville's loyal knight dropped his face into his hands. He took a long, unsteady breath. It almost seemed possible that he would burst into tears.

"Asher!" Robin snapped. He had no quarter for self-indulgent emotions.

Asher Grey pulled his hands away, revealing a face flushed with grief and shock. "That night, I wanted a look at the art on your walls – especially the Tintoretto. She passed me by, on her way somewhere, still hiding as a servant. Five hundred years and I'd know that bitch anywhere."

"So, you left London immediately for Scotland?"

Asher nodded, miserable. "I didn't think Sybil recognized me. Why would she? I just wanted to get back home to …"

"Elsie?" Robin's voice softened a little.

"I loved her." Asher Grey slumped under a mantle of guilt. "It had been so long, I let myself believe that they no longer existed."

Robin watched Sir Geoffrey shift into intense interest. Even Cyril who had been hovering and taking notes in the background, moved closer.

"They -- the other knights?"

Asher straightened in the gilded chair. "I wanted to tell you about Sybil. After … after Elsie, I thought you should know about Sybil."

Robin thought it highly likely Asher Grey had hoped to plead his case and have Sybil punished in the old school Garnet Petherbridge fashion. If so, Sir Neville's most loyal

294

knight was on fortune's watch fob. He had every intention of levelling all the former denizens of Galetaer Castle into dust.

"Where are they? Where is he?" Robin still couldn't force the name from his throat. How it all dovetailed into an English Wendigo that voraciously ate human prey was still unfathomable. It had devoured Elsie – no coincidence.

Sir Geoffrey rose to his feet. He had revised his intense interest into a combination of revulsion and anger. "Well, I think I fully understand. This is a vampire situation after all."

Robin stood as well -- emanating so much authority that the two guardsmen by the attic door, snapped to attention. "Do not presume to comprehend, Sir Geoffrey," he growled. "You will give me my three days."

The aristocratic civil servant looked from Robin to the rigid guards, then back to Robin. "And if I don't – I suppose you'll have my middle-aged A positive for dinner?"

"If I have to go through you for my daughter – I will."

Sir Geoffrey considered Robin's words. "Do you actually have any sort of plan or are you just flailing in the dark?"

"Three days," Robin said icily and swung back round to Asher Grey. "He has my daughter. My six-year-old daughter. You, of all of us, knows what that means."

Asher looked haunted. "Yes. The very Devil himself."

"Sir?" breathed Cyril, clearly surprised that Robin had kept vital information from him.

"Sybil's ring – the yellow shield with crossed black bars and fleur de lis on azure," Robin's voice was hollow – gutted by fear. "It belongs to the French barony of Brittany, Anjou and Poitou. In particular, the Baron Gilles de Rais -- the most prolific child murderer the world has ever known."

Chapter Forty-nine

Since her father had vetoed a plastic wrapped sandwich at the transport café, they stopped at a favorite place of the Earl's just off the A9 in Foulis Ferry. A handsome pale stone building, The Ferry House was a both restaurant and food hall catering to motorway travelers and tourists. During the Earl's beloved sheep trial season, a bucolic setting overlooking Cromarty Firth and the Black Isle with the picturesque Fyrish Hill to the rear was a major part of the restaurant's draw. In the middle of a significant winter storm in which nothing was visible beyond the immediate, they were glad to survive an icy wet and wind-whipped dash into the building.

Unlike the storied historical appeal of the Carberry Hotel, The Ferry House paid tribute to its agrarian past with lots of simple oak farm tables but all was new, bright and modern. Caroline found the gleam of 21st century conveniences strangely comforting. No secret rooms holding the trapped soul of a medieval knight or unhappy ladies in green wandering ancient hallways.

Caroline and her father settled at a corner table while Tinley and Culpeper did a discreet sweep of the area. A Ferry House waitress handed them each a menu and stood by for instructions.

"A vast cauldron of hot tea," said the Earl, pulling off his leather gloves, "will do for a start. Would you care for something more energetic, Caroline?"

She nodded. "I would like a glass of red wine – any kind will do."

The waitress smiled and said in a rolling regional burr, "That'll warm you up. Back in a tick."

"Any luck with the phone?" her father asked as the girl nipped away to collect their drinks.

"No – can't get a signal in the storm." Caroline wished again she could confide in him about how bad it really could be back in London. But there was nothing to be gained in having the two of them on the verge of panic. The Earl studied the menu. "I suspect it's one of those, no news is good news occasions. Zounds – the roast duck with potato dauphinoise is just the thing for this weather."

"Order me something, Dad," Caroline said, rising. "I forgot my phone in the Rover. Be right back." In reality, she just wanted to return to the car and try London again. With the fierce storm, neither Tinley or Culpeper could travel quickly to Number 7 in the revenant way and get an update. They were stuck with human technology.

She yanked on her heavy, fleece lined anorak and zipped it up. Outside the restaurant's windows, snow was blowing around in fierce gusts of wind. It was a brutal storm even for Scotland.

The Ferry House was crowded – they weren't the only travelers taking a break from hazardous road conditions. Caroline skirted around packed tables of chattering diners and through a new group hurrying in from the maelstrom. She didn't spot either Tinley or Culpeper in the restaurant. Presumably they were still assessing the exterior of the building.

Stepping around shivering newcomers, Caroline slipped outside the main doors and walked down the long, narrow stone pathway to the car park, fighting the wind.

Snow was accumulating as the wind drove it into small drifts against the building, fence posts and car tires. The cold stung Caroline's face and bit at her hands, reminding her of many hard rides over a cross-country course during inclement weather. A frigid day competing at the Pan-European finals outside of Dublin flashed through her mind – she and her grey Thoroughbred gelding, Dragon, had jumped the last half of the course in sleeting sheets of rain. They had gone clear but placed eighth with time faults. Getting Dragon safely home was more important that any medal.

Overhead lights created a golden halo over the parking lot, giving the impression of a bubble in the storm. The Range Rover sat under a dusting of snow. She unlocked it with the key fob and nipped inside to get the heater going. As the Rover idled, Caroline tried to send a text to Robin and Cyril, hoping that it might get through cyberspace when a direct phone call might not. No such luck – a red Failed sign flagged her text.

"Bugger!" she swore. Robin must know how worried she was. Even a message wrapped around the leg of one of his raven friends would suffice.

Caroline looked up from the cell phone. In the rear-view mirror, someone was standing behind the Range Rover. Just outside the puddle of light from the light pole, a figure stood, staring fixedly at the vehicle. She squinted, peering into the rear-view. Tall, almost shrouded in shadows as if light particles were sucked in like a swirling black hole. Although the figure was motionless, energy seemed to warp and weave around it – wings of smoke and menace. Instinctively, Caroline knew it wasn't safe in the Rover. She had the distinct impression that her personal safety depended on getting back to the lights and people of The Ferry House. Throwing open the car door, she scrambled out and ran towards the front of the Rover. Momentarily blindsided by the bitter Scottish wind, she slipped on the wet asphalt and fell to the icy macadam.

Caroline scrambled up, using the Rover's bonnet to steady her rise and allow her feet to find some grip on the slick surface. The thing had moved with the quiet precision of a Rook sliding across a chessboard. It now stood roughly twenty feet from her – a black column of swirling oily smoke stabbed with flaring and disintegrating electrical impulses. Eyes – cold and dead like raw diamonds – lit up from within the warp. The intensity emanating from them threatened to snake out and physically strike her. A charged moment passed.

It was then that Caroline saw that she had been mistaken. Everything was fine. Ari was fine. All danger had been vanquished. A lovely Christmas season awaited them. Everything was the best it could and would ever be. No longer feeling the wind or the cold, she stepped forward to greet the new friend when someone roughly tackled her. She again hit the wet asphalt hard. Suddenly the parking lot came back into sharp focus. Her right shoulder stung from hitting the pavement and jerking her head up in panic, she saw Culpeper fly at the thing, fully revenant and battle ready.

Tinley's voice was in her ear. "Run, Your Highness!"

As Tinley hauled her up, Culpeper was thrown violently against the Range Rover. Caroline saw that the undulating inky column had morphed into something far recognizable as a monster. Nearly ten foot tall, the powerful entity was skeletal with grey desiccated flesh stretched over raw bone. It swung around to stare at her, clacking its frightful claws with dirty talons together as if pondering the kill.

Caroline froze in the hardness of its eyes. The cadaverous face was split with a huge lip-less mouth lined with long shards of yellow teeth and surrounded by greasy black hair that fell in matted hanks to its gaunt waist. Her stomach lurched at the sweet and sour smell of death.

"Run!" Tinley repeated as he launched himself at the advancing creature.

She scrambled backwards, unable to look away from the awful thing as it continued to shamble towards her. Tinley pushed the entity back, but it recovered and slammed him into the ground with the swipe of an anhydrous arm.

Culpeper had managed to recover and took over, snapping open a butterfly knife. He charged in low, hoping to throw the creature off balance. Tinley rebounded and went high. They succeeded in driving it back several steps.

Caroline heard it gnashing the jagged teeth together – a hideous scraping, clicking sound. Then it hurled Tinley to one side and Culpeper to the other. Both vampires hit the snow dusted pavement with bone-jarring force. A human would have been broken in two.

Oozing a foul bloody pus from where Culpeper had landed several knife cuts to its chest and thigh, the entity refocused on Caroline. It started towards her, talons clacking with a kind of awful excitement.

A shot rang out and the creature jerked violently as a bullet tore into its shoulder. It shook its cadaver's head as if trying to throw off the effects of the wound and then vanished.

Caroline spun in the direction of the gunshot and saw her father lowering a revolver.

"Damn!" he said, walking towards the recovering guardsmen. "Hoped for a head shot – bloody wind."

Tinley got to his feet with a groan. "Thank you for doing our job for us, Your Lordship."

"I think my leg is broken," said Culpeper, still on the ground. "What the bloody hell was that thing?"

The Earl of Hawkesmoor replaced the gun in his coat pocket. "You mean you don't know?"

Caroline ran to her father – both profoundly relieved and perplexed. She kissed him on the cheek. "Thanks, Dad," she said, knowing it was wildly inadequate for what had just transpired. If there was ever a moment for the legendary British stiff upper lip, it was now. If she didn't rein in her shock at what she'd just seen, she might shatter into pieces and be of no use to Ari or anyone else.

"You should thank your husband. He gave me his Les Baer 1911 just in case," The Earl patted his pocket. "Beautiful weapon. Frightfully illegal, I suspect. You in one piece?"

She let out a ragged breath and nodded. "Still shaking in my boots but all right."

"Let's get Culpeper into the heated car. He looks all in." Tinley already had his flagging partner up on one leg. The Earl stepped in and shouldered Culpeper's other arm. The guardsman looked embarrassed, almost blushing in the snow-dappled wind. Both Tinley and Culpeper seemed acutely aware that they had failed to protect their king's consort.

"You were both incredibly brave,' Caroline said, hoping to assuage their collective guilt. "Thank you. I will be sure to tell my husband how grateful I am."

"We're five hours from Hawkesmoor if the weather doesn't bog us down." The Earl helped Culpeper hobble towards the Range Rover. "We'll be safer there. I'll have them pack our duck to go."

Chapter Fifty

"We passed the years in prayer and farming –
helping to feed the locals," said Asher Grey. "Then Sybil
arrived, the beginning of our order's end. She brought him
to the castle – a fancy man who told us we were weak, that
strength and power could be bought with human blood."
Robin watched Sir Geoffrey's face harden. The case for
vampire responsibility in the English Wendigo murders was
fast becoming a fact for the Prime Minister's right hand.
"What did Gilles de Rais want?" Robin asked, sounding
harsher than he wanted. It was crucial to remain calm and
focused.
"He wanted knights. His own followers. Sir Neville sent me
away – on the excuse that I was to purchase some new cattle
but really a fact-finding mission. I went to France." Asher
Grey almost shuddered. "I thought it would be difficult to
learn anything about a long-gone baron, but Gilles de Rais
was a legend. He had ritualistically tortured, then murdered
two hundred – maybe as many as six hundred – children
before they caught on to him. The French thought he had
been executed at Nantes in 1440 but he had escaped their
justice."
"And when you returned to Galetaer?" He paced the attic
floor. Time was slipping away from him.
"Sir Neville was gone. The other knights were gone – with
him and Sybil. Some distant cousins of hers were busy
setting themselves up as kings of the castle. They told me a
tale of Sir Neville and the Devil. I knew then that Gilles de
Rais had destroyed my liege."

Robin stopped in his tracks and turned squarely to Sir Neville's knight. "Do you know where they went? Where is Gilles de Rais?"

"Do not rightly know," Asher Grey replied, his face a study in dejection. "Stayed in Scotland to keep an eye on the castle. I had failed him."

"Sir Neville is free."

Asher Grey looked up at him, hope rising in his eyes. "Free?"

"He was trapped in the ethers of this plane. I released him. Sir Neville is at peace." Robin saw Sir Geoffrey raise a quizzical eyebrow.

The knight sprang up from the Louis IV chair, startling the guardsmen who immediately went on alert. He took to a knee, bowing his head in profound reverence. "From this day forward, I pledge to you as my liege lord. Where you lead, I will follow."

"Just give me a place to start," Robin breathed, his voice a hoarse whisper that belied his growing desperation. "There must be somewhere I can start looking for my daughter."

Asher Grey remained on one knee but lifted his head, thinking. "I have a theory … You know, in my centuries as a fisherman, I heard many stories of sea monsters, Kelpies, Finfolk."

"I don't give a damn about wretched Kelpies!"

"There's an island to west of the Orkneys – formally Viking, now uninhabited." The knight rose from the floor. "Very mysterious and Scots are afraid of it. They call it Drole Island."

"Goblin Island." Robin frowned.

"Drole is fog bound most of the year. Too small and too far out for habitation. Sailors talk of mysterious lights on the island and ghost ships," Asher continued. "In our village, the old ones say bad things happen on Drole, that it steals the souls of anyone unfortunate enough to lay to in its waters. My friend, Rory, swears one day, coming in with a big catch of mackerel, he saw a line of hooded figures walking on Drole – medieval monks, he thought."

Robin glanced at Cyril who was tapping notes into his tablet. His equerry gave him a grim nod, confirming that he was already gathering information. "You thought it could be your brother knights?"

"Well, I have wondered," he admitted. "Drole Island would be the perfect place to hide from the world and if they are now devoted to human blood …"

"Thousands of people go missing in the UK every year, sir" said Cyril Goforth, studying his screen. "A formidable number of them in Scotland."

Sir Geoffrey's bland face darkened. "Aren't you just flat out admitting that there is some sort of vampire cult in this country, abducting and murdering British subjects?

Robin turned sharply on the civil servant. "If there is, I will destroy it!" Then he rounded hotly on Asher Grey. "Despite all those years in Scotland, you failed to investigate?"

Asher slumped – guilt flashing across his rugged face. "I did not."

"A pity – your Elsie paid the price, did she not?"

"'Tis true," he said, his shoulders bowed by remorse, "she did."

"Well, you shall have your chance to rectify the situation." Robin's voice was icy. He finally had a place to start and if Sybil was reduced to traveling without revenant abilities, it might be possible to overtake her. "Sir Geoffrey, I will need another one of Mr. Hope's jets. We're going to Goblin Island."

Chapter Fifty-one

"We're here to take you to my building – The Cathedral," said Max Aosta, referencing an insanely expensive and gaudy skyscraper on the upper East side. Billionaires, both foreign and domestic, competed to pay obscene prices for one of its overly designed apartments. "You'll be completely safe. I owe your father … so much."

Simon straightened to his full height as a couple of Max's revenants made a show of flanking the flamboyant Vampire King of New York. One of the many pieces of NYC advice his father had doled out when he'd left for Juilliard was to lie low and pointedly avoid any vampires.

"Thanks. I think we'll be okay." Simon found Della's hand. It was shaking a little as she stared apprehensively at the sleek revenants who looked like extras in a Martin Scorsese film.

Max's eyes flashed in annoyance. "You don't get it, do you?"

"Oh, I think I do," Simon said.

"Get in the car," growled the Vampire King of New York. His foot soldiers immediately moved forward with fluid teamwork that spoke of many such confrontations.

"Uh, uh, uh," came a calm voice. Mid-Estuary and clipped. Simon backed up, catching sight of Edmund, one of his father's most trusted men. The guardsman had a Glock up and trained on Max Aosta whose face was turning dark with rage.

"You were given a warning," said Edmund coolly.

Max's hard mouth twisted. "Just you? One against my …"

Like quicksilver – economic and deadly – Edmund shifted slightly and fired off two shots. Both of Max's revenants dropped to the sidewalk, hit in the chest. Pointedly not vampire kill shots. Then he returned his weapon sights to Aosta.

"Now you have none." Edmund's attention never flicked away from Max Aosta even as another SUV careened up. Alin Dragos and some of his cousins sprung out of the vehicle. They moved in to surround Simon and Della.

Max looked from Edmund to the Dragos and then back to Edmund. He sighed, holding up his hands in submission. "Only trying to assist the son of an old …"

"No worries," Edmund interrupted through clenched teeth. "I will give a full report. Now take your crew and go."

Max looked as though he might say something more but again lifted his hands in a faux show of fraternity. He turned on the heel of his Testoni alligator shoes as his vampires began to stagger up.

"You ready to go home?" Edmund kept his Glock trained on the retreating revenants.

"And how," said Simon, letting out a long breath. "Dad sent you?"

"And how." Edmund looked slightly sour.

Doors to Max Aosta's SUV slammed shut, announcing his imminent departure. The massive vehicle's tires squealed as it lurched into reverse and then gunned forward into a now quiet Central Park West.

Edmund lowered his weapon and the Dragos visibly relaxed their stance as Max hurtled into the distance. Alin Dragos gave Simon a slap on the back.

"You see, my friend? The Dragos get the job done." Alin's smile seemed forced.

Della collapsed against Simon, slipping her arm about his waist. "What happened back there?" she asked. "We heard terrible screams."

The tired smile fled Alin's hawkish face. He looked grim. "We lost Mihai. Still don't know what the hell … our cleaning crew is scouring the area now. We will take care of him. The Dragos take care of their own."

"Thank you, Alin," said Simon sincerely. "Thanks to all the Dragos."

Alin nodded, his face still haunted by the death of Mihai Dragos. "We can never repay our debt to your noble father. Now you must go home, my friend and we will bury our dead."

"I could put you on a plane to London at Inverness," said the Earl as he piloted the Range Rover through the rain. "You would find out exactly what's going on in person."

Caroline sipped coffee from a Ferry House paper cup. "Robin was very insistent that we needed to go to Hawkesmoor. I trust him to know his world."

"Oh, your husband's been tangling with a cadaverous monster with yellow teeth and cloven hooves too, has he?"

"I wish I knew."

Her father changed lanes to overtake a slow lorry and then called out, "How are you doing, Culpeper?"

"Fine, sir," came Culpeper's tired voice from the back seat. "My leg should be repaired in another hour or so."

"You, Tinley?"

"Just a bruised ego, Your Lordship," replied Tinley.

"Either of you lads ever see that thing before?" The Earl asked, changing back to the prior lane.

"No, sir," said Tinley. "That was a new one on us as well."

"Clearly your fancy, dance-y martial arts are of no use. At Hawkesmoor, we will have some excellent shotguns to fit you out."

Caroline had the notion that her father was actually enjoying himself. Never one to shirk a battle, he had waded into many dicey sheep breeder disputes and had played a large role in defending Hawkesmoor Castle against Garnet Petherbridge's mercenary army some six years earlier. The idea that a terrifying, unknown monster could appear at any moment hadn't fazed him one bit.

"Thank you, sir," sighed Tinley.

"You don't think that monster will follow us to Hawkesmoor?" Caroline shivered despite the Range Rover's excellent heating system. "It has some kind of hypnotic effect."

The Earl threw her a surprised glance. "A what?"

"When I looked at it, really looked at it" she said, "I felt as if I was, well – almost anesthetized. I think it can throw some sort of paralyzing net over its victims."

"Her Serene Highness seemed frozen in place," Culpeper piped up from the back seat. "Whatever the thing is, it was completely focused on her."

"I'll have to add it to my report," said Tinley. "Mr. Goforth always insists on every detail."

The mention of Tinley's report to Cyril Goforth reminded Caroline to check her cell phone again for a signal. Again, the connection bars were too low in the winter storm to indicate enough of a signal to send or receive. She almost re-pocketed the phone before noticing that her "messages" icon had a red number 1 in its orbit. There must have been a moment of better reception and a message had managed to slip through.

"A text from Robin!" she cried, almost dropping the phone in her rush to bring it up on the screen. "Darling – Ari is absolutely fine and happy. Taking care of the situation with Miss Pratt now. Will bring her home to Hawkesmoor for

Christmas as soon as that's been done. We both send love. PS: Follow Tinley and Culpeper's directions to the letter and be careful – not out of the woods completely yet."

"You see? All is well," said her father, nodding his head. "Now, get some rest, Caro. You look very peaky."

Caroline exhaled slowly and laid her head back against the car seat, closing her eyes. Ari was okay and all was well. All is well. What was it that Robin once said about the All is well moment?

Robin hated lying to Caroline. But how could he begin to tell her that Miss Pratt/Sybil had abducted their daughter and the kidnapping was probably connected to history's most infamous child murderer? Part of what he texted was correct – he would sort out the Miss Pratt situation and bring Ari home to Hawkesmoor. He just didn't know quite how to accomplish it as yet.

"Fascinating," said Gabriel from his seat in the Rolls Phantom. They were headed to London City Airport and a private jet secured by Sir Geoffrey Constable.

"Unless it involves Drole Island," Robin didn't turn his head away from the car window and gazing out at the wet streets of London, "I am not interested."

"It does, in a way. When Gilles de Rais was hung for his crimes and the French authorities believed him dead, they released his body to four women of high rank who had appeared at the execution. Want to bet one of them was Sybil?"

"Hard to imagine her as appearing as high rank."

"De Rais did have a reputation for showering his favorites with rich clothes and pretties."

Robin tightened his jaw. He'd give just about anything to be able to risk a molecular transfer to the northern coast of

Scotland. Always fraught with potential danger, molecular travel over vast distances was particularly treacherous and filthy weather made it virtually impossible. He'd be of no help to Ari at all if the storm pulled him apart and sent his shards irreparably spinning across the universe.

"I can just about make sense of Gilles de Rais as a vampire with vile habits," he said, wishing his revenant system would start healing the stabbing pain in his stomach and chest. "How does our English Wendigo fit in? We know it must because of Elsie's murder."

"Do you remember the tales about Gilles de Rais and his cleric Francois Prelati?"

"That they devised fruitless occult rituals in a quest for more wealth and power -- rituals that required the corpses of children?" Robin winced slightly as pain shot through his body.

Gabriel threw Robin a sympathetic glance. "De Rais was trying to conjure a specific demon – one with the name Barron."

"And you think he's been keeping Barron in a kennel on Goblin Island?"

"Call it a half-baked theory." The vampire librarian leaned forward. "Robin --you're bleeding again."

Chapter Fifty-two

Hawkesmoor Castle had been described as the fairy castle by Queen Victoria in 1850 when she deigned to spend night in it on her way to official engagements in Newcastle-upon-Tyne. Constructed of a pewter grey stone, the 14th century castle's curvilinear elegance came from several towers, a barbican and battlements that surrounded a large courtyard. Once Hawkesmoor had been decommissioned as a military fortress, lavish inner additions were designed by the notable Tudor architect, Sir John Thynne and completed in 1567. It had then been transformed into a very handsome and gracious seat for the Earls of Hawkesmoor. In the rapidly changing world of the 21st century, Hawkesmoor was one of the few castles left in private hands.

Lady Caroline had never been so grateful to see the castle. She gazed out the rain-streaked car window at her childhood home as her father piloted the Range Rover up the estate's long drive. The extensive security lighting illuminated its formal outline – the winter night dusting it with a pearly glow that gave the old castle an otherworldly countenance. She had the quick thought that Queen Victoria probably had no idea how right she was about the fairy castle – Robin's family, the DuPlessis, carried the Tylwyth Teg bloodline in varying degrees since the Bronze Age. The preternatural DNA had culminated in its most powerful hybrid exponents – Robin and their daughter, Arianrhod. At least, Arianrhod had been demonstrating the potential until her powers abruptly ceased.

"Peter is not up from Oxford yet," said her father, interrupting her train of thought. He was referring to her brother, the current Viscount Merritt, who was currently a lecturer in history at Christ Church specializing in the intellectual and political history of the Victorians. "Something about a Lloyd-George conference – the old goat."

"Hannah sticking about for the hols?" she asked. Her sister had elected to forego university in favor of helping to run the castle and had recently become engaged to the Duke of Portland's second son, Lord Fitzduncan.

"Yes – she's home and been mucking about in my tack room again!" he announced sourly. "Apparently, this time, our bridle hooks are inadequate or some such pretentious piffle. I regret to say she has become an insufferable know-it-all."

"Home," Caroline murmured. She hoped she had enough time to ready the castle for Christmas. She wanted everything to be cheering and comforting when Robin brought Ari home to Hawkesmoor.

"I'm looking forward to seeing your castle, Your Highness," murmured Edmund as they disembarked from a borrowed Gulfstream. He and Simon clattered down the gangway steps to the wet tarmac.

Simon breathed in the cold English air. It was an enormous relief to be on home soil.

"You haven't been up?"

"Haven't had a rotation at the castle yet, sir," the guardsman replied, referring to the rota of guardsmen who protected the Sovereign. "Wife's a teacher – Holland Park School – and I try to stay in town as much as possible."

It was easy to forget that vampires – other than his strange family – had private lives as well, Simon thought, pausing on the tarmac, unsure quite what to do next. His father had instructed him to always listen to the protection officers and follow their lead. Durham Tees Valley Airport had a hanger set aside for private aircraft and it was fairly busy with holiday travel. Light aircraft – Cessnas and de Havillands – were parked near the sleek Gulfstream with passengers either disembarking like themselves or preparing for take-off. The flight office was brightly lit with both crew and clients in various stages of business despite a steady rain.

Della stepped out of the Gulfstream's cabin and descended the steps with quick steps. She looked around with bright but tired eyes. "I've never been to England. Of course, I've never been in the middle of international espionage either. Vaya, que dia!"

"Are you sure?" asked Simon as he had back in New York when she elected to come with him to Britain for the Christmas holidays.

The ballet dancer took his hand, nodding. "I've come this far. Got to see how it ends."

"Hired car," said Edmund cocking his head toward a black SUV that was slowly approaching. "Courtesy of our Prime Minister's office. We should go."

PM Alastair Hope was lending them private jets and cars? Just what was his father in the middle of? It was clear to him that the two vampires in Manhattan had been part of some fraction with a score to settle with Robin DuPlessis, the Vampire King of the British Isles. Perhaps their medieval attire had been a political statement stating that their fraction held to the old ways and were violently opposed to the changes the new king was bringing to British vampire life. Whether statement or fashion choice, nabbing the king's son would be a powerful card to play and he understood why his father had been so keen for him to very wary. But had an internecine conflict grown so dangerous that the U.K. prime minister had gotten involved?

"My parents are fine?" he asked suddenly, the faces of his 21st century family flooding his mind. "My sisters and brother – my … you know, my grandfather?"

Edmund offered him a pleasant smile. "All is well."

They reconnoitered on the Scottish coast at its most northeastern point – just outside the village of John O'Groats. It had been decided that Sir Geoffrey would divert to Hawkesmoor Castle to ostensibly man the operation from there and Cyril Goforth would assist him. Neither were happy about it, but Sir Geoffrey was made to understand that if things went south, as Hollywood westerns often put it, as a human, he was unlikely to survive. Cyril was supposedly assisting but actually acting as the civil servant's governess – making sure he didn't make the situation worse and more importantly, didn't irritate the Earl of Hawkesmoor.

At midnight in a particularly frigid December, the most northeastern point in Great Britain was one of the coldest places on the planet. The full moon was an icy silver blue, showering the black sea with enough light to see white caps rolling across the vast undulating waterway. Drizzle alternated with snow flurries – snowflakes seeming to flare like fireflies in the beams of electric torches.

"Asher Grey, Hirst, Bramwell and Brown with me," said Robin, glad the winter storms had weakened at last. It would make what they had to do a little easier. "Gabriel and Bennett – you're to the inn at John O'Groats. Sir Geoffrey made the arrangements so apparently, you are operatives from the Home Office doing some sort of report."

Gabriel looked displeased. "I think you need us on the island."

"Understood," said Robin, blowing out a breath that condensed into a stream of fog. "But if we fail over there, someone has to report back to Sir Geoffrey and our loved ones. Who better than our historian? Then I need you to take the reins ..."

"Oh, no, no," the vampire librarian protested. "I'm a former monk – never a king."

"Bennett – you are the witness to my wishes," Robin turned to the guardsman who had almost recovered from Sybil's attack. "I need you to keep alert. We may need a rescue over there."

The guardsman straightened his spine with just a fraction less speed than he would have before the stabbing. "Yes, Your Serene Highness."

Robin reached out and squeezed Bennett's shoulder. "And try to get a little rest too."

Bennett almost smiled. "Yes, sir. Thank you."

"Asher," Robin turned away from the injured guardsman and looked out at an age-y thirty-three-foot fishing boat – a seiner that the former knight had "liberated" from a nearby boat storage. "Any chance we can land that vessel at Drole this time of the year at night?"

"I could do it, sir," Asher Grey replied without boasting. "If this lull in the weather holds but there's no natural harbor and a very strong tide. It's a long trip – nine hours minimum."

"South Ronaldsay?" asked Robin, his mind turning to the southern-most Orkney island.

"Roughly an hour, sir."

"Could you – and I need a very honest answer – could you get us to Drole through molecular transfer?"

Asher Grey winced slightly. "You mean a link up?"

Robin nodded. "Can you get us there?"

315

"If I go wrong, we end up in the North Sea …"

"Can you do it?"

Sir Neville's knight let out a short breath that hung in the frigid air. "Yes, sir. I'll get you there."

"There we have it, gentlemen. The way forward." Robin regarded them all with approbation – a handful of vampires shivering on wintery beach. "Just in case things don't … well, thank you for helping me find my daughter. You're a grand group."

Instead of paying traditional obeisance to a vampire king, the guardsmen grinned and looked a little embarrassed at the tribute. Gabriel nodded, more somber – clearly still unhappy about staying behind in a comfortable inn while the rest went forward into the unknown.

"Cheer up," said Robin, taking the librarian aside for a moment. "Once we clear the island, you can be in charge of cataloguing its history."

Gabriel shook his head. "You're not yourself. The nosebleeds … you need me …"

"I need you," Robin lowered his voice to a murmur, "to be my voice. Caroline, Simon – you will have to relay the story from Drole Island if it all goes wrong."

"We're not even sure Sybil is headed to this wretched island. We're just guessing based on some flimsy story from Asher Grey's fisherman friend who could have been drinking."

Robin shifted his feet on the sand as the pain level in his body shot up again. The assault on his etheric self was increasing and led him to believe that Goblin Island was exactly where the heart of the mystery was located.

"If I fail," he said, ignoring Gabriel's protest, "the Prime Minister will immediately move against British vampires. You know what that will mean for my family."

The vampire librarian exhaled slowly, his breath rising in a stream up into the December night. "Right then," he replied finally. "Mind how you go, Your Serene Highness."

"Oh, to be serene again." Robin gave Gabriel a tired smile and turned back to his guard. "Gentleman! Goblin Island beckons."

Chapter Fifty-three

Ari picked herself off the floor and looked around the filthy room in which Miss Pratt had shoved her. She might only be six, but it occurred to her that – despite Miss Pratt's assurances – her father did not want her thrown roughly into such a place and that the nanny's entire story about needing to go into hiding was probably false.

She wished her Tylwyth Teg abilities hadn't vanished. It would be nice to see how they could help her contact her parents. At the thought of her mother and father, tears welled up in her eyes. They would hate that she was so far from home and lost in a dirty, frightful room. She wanted desperately to be back in her pink and blue bedroom, curled up with Julian, reading a Famous Five adventure story.

The Famous Five! They wouldn't just mope around. They would investigate and figure a way out. She could do that too.

Ari brushed away a few tears and straightened her back, examining the room in more detail. Cold, damp, windowless and closed in with grey stone walls, it looked like an ancient cell in one of her fairytale books. The floor was dirt, packed hard and the ceiling was vaulted, climbing high above her. There were odd pieces of wooden furniture, barrels and old boxes tossed in what seemed to be an immense space that stretched out forever in the dark.

Miss Pratt had left her a thick white candle. Ari picked it up carefully and walked slowly further into the room. It seemed to be a castle store like the ones underneath Hawkesmoor but not nearly as well cared for and organized. In fact, there seemed to be all sorts of things scattered around – shoes, bits of clothes, even jewelry. Some of the debris looked old and other bits quite modern. Victorian ankle boots thrown against the kind of handbag the Queen might carry.

She paused by a barrel with a pile of old jewelry on it. Earrings, rings, watches and necklaces just piled in a thoughtless heap. Her mother always said jewelry was easily damaged and should be looked after respectfully. Whoever dumped the jewelry on the barrel top hadn't cared whether it tangled or was scratched.

Ari touched a tarnished silver locket. It was large oval one with some fancy engraving still visible through the dirt. Unable to resist, she pried it open. Inside were two black and white pictures of a young couple – both young and handsome with hairstyles that reminded Ari of a movie she had seen about Beatrix Potter.

She felt sick. Something was very very wrong. Tears welled up again. If only her father could find out where she was. A clattering sound in the distance seized her attention. It was followed by someone shushing someone else. Ari dropped the locket and held out her hand with the candle. The candle glow revealed that the room was L-shaped and that there was a turn to the left. She proceeded forward gingerly.

"Hello?" Her voice sounded thin and frightened in the cavernous space. She was sure George from The Famous Five would never sound as scared. "Is there somebody there?"

As Ari rounded the bend into another segment of the storage room, she saw a boy holding out a candle just like hers – and stout stick. He looked tense as if expecting to defend himself.

"I'm Arianrhod," she said softly. "Do you know how to get out?"

The handsome boy – ten or twelve – slowly lowered the stick. "I wish I did," he admitted in a crisp upper-class accent. "Who the blazes are you?'

"Arianrhod," she repeated, coming closer. "Arianrhod Dashwood."

"I'm Jasper Tiffin," he said and held out an arm to indicate a small girl a little younger than Ari who was hesitantly emerging from behind a stack of boxes. "This is my sister, Lucy."

Lucy was pale with fright, her oval face stained with dirt and tears. "I want to go home."

"Me, too," said Ari.

"We've been here for a couple of days." Jasper Tiffin laid his stick on top of another collection of rotting boxes. "Can't remember how – just woke up in this place. You?"

"Miss Pratt brought me. She's my nanny but I'm not so sure she's a good nanny anymore."

"Did you see where we are?" Jasper put an arm around Lucy's small shoulders. The little girl was dazed and exhausted, dressed in a white flannel nightgown and a light blue sweater.

Ari shook her head, unsure of how to explain her arrival. Her parents had warned her that some of the things that were normal occurrences in their world were frightening to outsiders. She didn't want to frighten Jasper and Lucy with Miss Pratt's different ways. "It was too dark to see much but sort of a castle, I think."

Jasper's blue eyes flashed with keen disappointment. "We need to find a way out – get to a phone or a policeman."

"My father is coming to get us," said Ari with a certainty she didn't fully understand. Somehow, instinctively, she knew her father was already on his way.

"Right then." Jasper ran his fingers through his longish dark hair. He didn't look as convinced as Ari about her father swooping in to save the day. "We ought to get to where he – or a policeman -- can see us."

"I want to go home," Lucy cried plaintively.

"There's a door," Ari pointed at the direction in which she had come, "that way. Maybe it isn't locked."

"Worth a try," said Jasper, taking Lucy's shivering hand. "Thanks, Arianrhod. Hope you're not offended but that's an awfully strange name."

"I'm rather a strange girl," she replied truthfully. "Call me Ari."

Drole Island was wrapped in a damp and cold fog when they reassembled on its narrow rocky beach. Even the full moon was unable to penetrate the dense swirls of moisture that had settled over the island.

Robin flicked on his torch, scanning the fog for his guard. One by one they emerged into the circle of electric light. Hirst, Brown, Bramwell and Asher Grey who looked particularly grim.

"Seen it in daylight," he said, tightening the closures on his winter gloves. "Roughly kidney-shaped with sharp cliffs above. Ruins of a fortress or a failed religious order in the center."

"How strikingly appropriate." Robin raised an eyebrow. "Remind me again how many of your former brethren we can expect to encounter – minus the two destroyed in New York."

"Eliminating me and Sir Neville, there would be twelve left, sir."

"And what did they promise you," asked Robin, "to feed us information about Drole Island – to lure us here?"

Asher Grey's eyes widened, and he involuntarily stepped back in shock. "I did no such thing."

Hirst, Bramwell and Brown had immediately shifted into full alert, hemming in the former knight who jerked from side to side, trying to find an escape.

"I believe you to be a true knight of Sir Neville's, but they got to you somehow – Elsie?"

Asher Grey turned back to Robin, despair in the slump of his shoulders and bowed head. "How could you know?" he asked hollowly.

"Because I'm guessing when Elsie was murdered, you took your boat here to Drole."

"But how …"

"You know far too much about bringing a vessel into the island's waters," Robin said, wishing that the pain in his stomach and chest would abate so he would be better able to deal with whatever was coming their way. "You came here to get revenge for Elsie?"

Asher Grey dropped to his knees in the sand. "I knew Sybil must have spotted me at your house that night. Like I told you, I figured Drole was where they had gone after Galetaer Castle. I wanted to get some kind of justice for Elsie."

"Instead, you became one of them – again."

"They promised me that Elsie could come back." Asher Grey's voice broke and he slumped even lower. "Very soon they were going to be able to restore the dead. All I had to do …"

"We know what you had to do," Robin cut in sharply. "Set the stage for an ambush and doom my daughter."

"Permission to end him, sir," said Bramwell, unable to conceal his disgust.

Robin stepped forward and kicked the former knight in the side. "Get up, you bastard."

"I'm sorry …"

Robin kicked him again, harder. Asher Grey groaned and spat up blood. Hirst and Brown hauled the knight to his feet. Bramwell prepared to finish him off at Robin's command. "We've wasted enough time," Robin snapped. "Let him go – he's coming with me."

"Sir?" said all three guardsmen in an almost unison cry of astonishment.

"Whatever's up there knows we're here or soon will be. I want you three to spread out around the island and find the most strategic points you can in this bloody fog. Come in when I call." Robin reached out, grabbing Asher Grey by the front of his padded coat and yanking him close. "You are going to get me in so I can save my daughter – yes?" Asher nodded, blood still dripping from his mouth. "Yes."

"Cross me -- I'll rip your throat out."

Chapter Fifty-four

Ari watched as Jasper pulled one of the endless wooden boxes away from what they thought might be a door. She was in charge of holding up their candles so he could see properly. Lucy sat on a barrel top, softly singing a Raffi song about biscuits and baking.

"Two more," he gasped, turning to deposit box with the others, "and I think we can get to it."

But as he attempted to shift the box onto the pile, it knocked against Lucy's barrel and fell from his grasp. The old wood shattered upon contact with the packed dirt of the floor, revealing its contents – hundreds of small white objects spilled around the rotted wood.

"Pearls!" breathed Lucy, forgetting Raffi and biscuits. "Mummy has pearls!"

Jasper knelt and picked up a handful for a better look. Then he let out a strangled cry, hurled Lucy's pearls back to the floor as if they had burned his fingers. Ari took her candle down so she could see what had upset Jasper Tiffin who seemed steady and not easily frightened.

"Don't touch them!" Jasper whispered, glancing up at Lucy who had gone back to singing about biscuits and was swinging her feet along in time. "They're human teeth!"

Ari recoiled, almost dropping the candle. In its soft glow, she could just make out that most of the ivory-colored teeth had gold embedded in them. Why would Miss Pratt bring her to a place where gold teeth had been collected like pearls?

She stood up and moved to the boxes Jasper had already moved away from the door. Using her free hand, she pushed open the lid of the top crate. Jasper joined her and they

stood together, peering down at the box's contents –
hundreds of gold rings. Fancy rings with jewels, rings with
pearls, simple gold bands, ancient rings, new rings.
"We have to get out of here," Jasper murmured.

Robin nimbly ascended the trail up the cliffside
from the fogbound beach. He followed Asher Grey who was
trudging his way up like a man heading to the gallows. The
island felt heavy and strange – almost claustrophobic in the
closeness of the fog that hugged the pathway. It wasn't
difficult to imagine that phantoms lurked in the mist,
spinning into half-formed apparitions and then unraveling
again to nothing. Drole had seen a lot of death. He could
sense it like an electric hum emanating from the ground
under his feet.
When they reached the summit – the veil of sea mist lifted
to reveal a rolling expanse of scrub grass stabbed with
brutal rock protrusions. Asher lifted an arm to indicate a
northwesterly direction.
"The old monastery is built over a Norse settlement,' he
said. "Huge underground spaces."
"You know, I expected to see a few of your brother knights
by now." Robin scanned silvery fields illuminated by a cold
moon. The island seemed as deserted as the locals claimed.
"Any thoughts, Mr. Grey?"
The knight turned back to look at Robin. His face, in
Robin's torch beam, was a study in grim defeat. "I know
nothing," he said in a hollow voice. "Just wanted Elsie
back."
"It never occurred to you that they lied about resurrecting
Elsie?" Robin continued to walk in the direction that Asher
had indicated. The energy from Drole's ground vibrated
through his nervous system. Death. Death everywhere.

Asher waited for Robin and then fell into step with him. They headed across the field of wild grass for several minutes before he spoke. When he did, it was with palpable regret.

"I was out of my mind. No genius at the best of times."

"Evidently," said Robin, remembering Asher's outburst as Cam Drummond at the Hong Kong performance. "And a hot head too."

"I'm a great stupid man."

"Well, at last, something we can agree on." Robin shivered as the strange vibrations from Drole ran up and down his system. It almost felt as if he were walking through heavy mud – as if hands were reaching up through the earth, clutching at his legs and trying to pull him under. He had the impression of a restless, predatory energies rolling under the surface like sharks. "Asher, we're walking on graves. All of this – it's a feral necropolis."

Asher glanced at him, baffled. "Vampires have a lot of remains to dispose of."

"This is different. Wild, searching," Robin tried to make sense of what his Tylwyth Teg attributes were trying to tell him. "Hungry – sentient but not thinking."

"You have a bloody nose," said Asher Grey, clearly believing Robin's impressions were the result of some kind of medical episode.

Robin pulled a handkerchief from a pocket. He wasn't sure getting across Drole on foot was do-able for his beleaguered nervous system. "We're going to have get to your monastery our way."

"It's not my monastery!"

"Go on – pull my other leg." Robin said sourly. "You must lead, Mr. Grey. Is there a covert way into this bastion of brotherhood?"

Asher Grey shrugged miserably. "I don't know."

"Right then. We'll roll the dice."

Edmund had taken the A67 from Darlington and then left the major motorway for the eccentric jumble of country roads that wove across Yorkshire. He was a confident driver, handling the twisting roads and blind turn lanes cautiously in the light drizzle.

"What does your wife teach at Holland Park?" asked Simon, watching the windshield wipers brush aside raindrops. Della was sleeping on the rear seat, under the Prime Minister's tartan blanket.

"Latin. She's much brighter than this old plod."

Simon sucked in a sharp breath and sat up – someone, something had just materialized on the wet country road, staring into the beams of their headlamps. It was tall and gaunt but strangely powerful.

"Jesus Ffffing Christ!" Edmund swore, swinging the hired car hard to the left to avoid hitting whatever it was obstructing the road. The car swerved past the creature, hit a slick spot on the asphalt and into a slide that sent it spinning off to the side of the road, only a hair away from fully crashing into a ditch.

Della let out a choked cry as Simon slammed forward, only his seatbelt preventing him from serious injury against the dashboard. His father's guardsman wasn't so lucky. The airbag failed to deploy, and Edmund struck the steering wheel on impact. He slumped over it, his face bleeding heavily.

"Get the girl and run, boy!" Edmund groaned before collapsing completely.

Simon unlocked his seatbelt and turned violently in his seat to see where the mysterious entity had gone. Through the rain glazed rear view window, he saw it lurch around to stare back at him. Skeletal with rotting, grey skin stretched over mottled brown bones, it didn't seem possible that such a monster could even stand up, let alone move. It gazed at him with large black empty orbs instead of eyes and then started deliberately towards the disabled car – a kind of twisted pleasure erupting from a lip-less mouth filled with craggy yellow teeth worthy of a Megalodon.

"In one piece, Della?" Simon knew Edmund kept a handgun. A Glock 18C – highly illegal in Britain but none of the guardsmen paid any attention to the UK's stringent gun laws. He yanked open the center console where he'd seen Edmund stow it at the airport. "Hey – Della?"

She popped up, looking through the space between the headrests. "I'm okay, querido. Should we call an ambulance for … what the actual hell? What is that?"

Glancing up, he saw the entity had almost reached the rear of the car. It would be on them in a matter of seconds. For a paranormal creature of such ghastly proportions, it moved with a smooth predatory purpose – no hulking or shambling – with long, claws with filthy talons that it clacked together as if hungrily anticipating their use.

"Stay down, behind the seats!" he said with more authority than he felt.

"You're not going out there?"

"If I can lead it away – run." Simon retrieved the Glock and kicked open the passenger door. He rolled out of the car down into the muddy ditch, conscious of having twisted his left ankle upon landing. With a short cry of pain, he pulled himself up and lifted the weapon, hoping he could manage to do some damage.

Easily eight feet tall, the monster clacked its nails and advanced, hideous torn mouth widening to show its jagged teeth. The nauseating smell of death that emanated from it was overpowering, shedding off the decayed grey skin and brown gelatinous muscle in waves. Simon fired. The Glock had a fierce and unexpected recoil that knocked Simon back, affecting his aim. The bullet was flung wildly off course, shattering the rear side window of the hired car. Simon dropped the gun as he staggered to regain his balance. Looking up in panic, he saw that the entity had morphed into something else entirely.

A tall, pulsating column of black energy – somehow possessing more depth and danger than the skeletal monster. Eyes like ice shards locked on his. He was suddenly filled with an implacable sense of well-being that flooded every nerve ending, eliminating any other distraction. He was all right. He was going home.

A shot rang out. The column of energy wavered and morphed. The grotesque monster stood in its place, clacking cruel claws. Another sharp retort fired off, hitting the creature in the neck. The tall cadaver staggered, lurching back from the ditch and clutching at its neck which was pumping out a foul greasy pus. Then it evaporated into the drizzle.

Simon felt any remnant of well-being yanked away and his ankle started to throb. He turned his head to see from where the shots had come and saw Edmund leaning heavily against the driver's door frame, another gun in his hand. He must have had a second one tucked away for back up as they liked to say in law enforcement.

"Fetch my Glock from the mud puddle," he said, his voice tired. "You're going to have to drive."

Della jumped out from the back seat, looking pale but otherwise unhurt. "Simon – you okay?" She darted across to offer him a hand out of the ditch. "You're soaking wet, mi amigo. Are you freezing?"

"We have to get to your castle. I think they may be needing us." Edmund gestured loosely at Simon. "Well, not you. You couldn't shoot the broad side of a barn."

Simon picked up the soaked Glock and threw Edmund a rueful glance. "I wasn't expecting so much recoil."

"Just get in the car," the guardsman said with a sour face. "Unexpected recoil, my plebian ass."

Chapter Fifty-five

Drole Island, according to Asher Grey, was approximately four miles long and a mile across. It consisted of rocky scrub only suitable for seabirds. Only inhabited once by humans -- sometime around 600 A.D. -- when St. Machar was said to have established a leper colony. A noble effort reputedly destroyed by raiding Norsemen who massacred every monk and every one of the lepers under their care.

All that was left of St. Machar's colony was their keep – a moldering mountain of raw grey stone that gave the impression of being both cruciform church and Norse watchtower. It sat on the highest rise on the small island, crouching like a gargoyle on the wind-creased terrain. Robin and Asher Grey recombined next to what might have once been a colony outbuilding. In the cold silvery blue of the moon, the main structure looked abandoned and lonely with no phalanx of brother knights at the ready.

"The top of the iceberg?" asked Robin, gazing at the window slits that had allowed some natural light into the building but also repelled some of the sub-zero wind.

Asher Grey continued to look glum. He nodded.

"Everything underground."

Then, golden light flickered from within the main ruin, illuminating the narrow window slits. Robin could well imagine the glow would translate as eerie Will O' The Wisps to passing sailors and fishermen.

"The proverbial welcome mat." Robin winced slightly as pain stabbed at his chest.

"What to do now?"

Robin didn't look away from his examination of the old colony's stone face. "Well, I am going to walk in what's left of the front door."

Ari and Jasper were able to pry open the heavy wooden door that had been hidden behind debris. They secured Lucy and both candles, cautiously emerging into a catacomb of tunnels and stone steps that seemed to stretch onwards and upwards forever.

"There are so many different ways," whispered Jasper, holding his candle out at the confluence of pathways. Far in the distance there was a banging sound as if a door had been slammed or something heavy had fallen.

"Up," said Ari, jumping at the sound. "We want to go up."

"Home?" asked Lucy, tugging on Jasper's hand.

"Well, I don't …"

"Up," Ari repeated. Up was where there was fresh air and light. Up was the way home.

Jasper crept forward, towing Lucy behind him. "Might as well try these," he said, referring to the first set of roughly hewn steps. "Okay, Ari?"

She nodded and regretted again that her strange abilities had deserted her. Jasper and Lucy Tiffin were good and kind. She had been a reasonably good girl too. The incident with the glue pot didn't really count – her father's hair had grown back. They were good children. They deserved to escape, to go home.

There was another clattering sound down one of the cold passages. A little closer than the one before. The three of them gasped at the sharp sound that seemed shriek down the dark, heavy vacuum of the corridor. The cavernous space was vast but not empty.

"Up!" Jasper whispered and they scrambled onto the crude, uneven steps.

Robin paused at the archway that had once supported a massive wooden door. He let out a long breath, studying the entrance to the ruins. Pain was wrapping around his spine, seeming to crush his heart and lungs. The relentless assault on his etheric self was escalating. He'd have to master it if he was to be any use to Ari, wherever she was on Drole Island.

"In for a penny, in for a pound," he murmured and stepped through the crumbling arch.

Not much was left of the central monastic structure other than the exterior walls with the roof and oak support beams long gone. Scrub grass and mud had reclaimed the fieldstone floor and seabirds nested on broken ledges, sheltering from a constant marine wind. It was desolate and lonely – a place where many had died. Death. Death everywhere.

Yet, storm lanterns had been lit. They were scattered along the edge of an internal wall, throwing dappled gold light against the ancient stonework. It was an invitation.

"I am here," he called, "for my daughter."

Robin was conscious again of something moving under the surface – wild, unthinking malevolence. An island of graves.

There was movement to the rear of the ruins. Robin pivoted to confront Asher Grey's former brother knights. Instead, two women stepped into the pale light of moon and candle. Dressed in black leather versions of 15th century gowns, they were both tall, stately, virtually albino and almost identical. One lady had thick bone-white hair coiled into an elaborate chignon pinned with jewels while the other creature had hair that was waist-length, loose and silver.

"Your Serene Highness," said the lady with the alabaster hair. She spoke in medieval French. "We have been waiting for you."

"My daughter. I want her now," he snapped, responding in the same ancient French.

The lady of the silver locks looked bored. "You are in no position to dictate terms to us, Englishman."

"Garcelle." The other vampire threw a warning glance to her virtual twin and then returned her focus to Robin. "Welcome, King of the British Vampires. A king who has established his own bloodline."

"Children," added the one named Garcelle, running a long languid hand over the bodice of her gown, "make the softest, prettiest leather."

Robin clenched his jaw. He remembered Gabriel's mention of four finely dressed women who claimed Gilles de Rais' body after his supposed execution for the torture and mass murder of children.

"My daughter," he said, ignoring the pain in his chest, "now."

"Your Serene Highness," the alabaster vampire widened her blue eyes in a pastiche of unctuousness, "we invited you here to broker a deal – a treaty."

Robin lifted a hand and directed a shot of energy at the one called Garcelle. She rose off the ground as if he had seized her by the throat. Clearly surprised, Garcelle's smug expression was lost to gurgling and choking. She grasped desperately at her neck as if she could rip away the energy particles. He hurled her against one of the rough walls. There was a cracking sound as Garcelle's spine snapped. Her arms and limbs slumped, falling useless. Her face twisted in agony, blood spraying from her mouth -- glossy and crimson against her pale skin.

With a flick of his wrist, he pulled her away from the wall and twisted her head brutally to the side. The force of it splintered her neck, tearing her head from the spine in a cascade of blood that splattered the ancient walls and frightened the seabirds. Then he sent what was left of Garcelle -- in her human-skin leather dress – crashing into the ground. Her head rolled into a mud puddle with its eyes dull and sightless.

Robin returned his attention to the white-haired vampire. She looked genuinely taken aback and impressed.

"My daughter -- now."

"Such undiluted power," she murmured in her ancient French, gazing at him with canny covetousness replacing her initial astonishment. "You are the future of us all."

He raised his hand.

"No, no, no," the vampire said, dropping to one knee in reverence. "I am Mazelina. Your daughter has not been harmed – you will see, you will see."

Chapter Fifty-six

"I think someone is coming," whispered Jasper as he, Ari and Lucy paused at the top of the long staircase they had climbed. He quickly blew out his candle. Ari did the same.

There was some light at the terminus of the steps suggesting that the passageways here saw more use and therefore needed to be lit. The children crept down a couple of the stone steps, retracting into the shadows. They pressed back against the stairwell and Jasper covered Lucy's mouth as something heavy rolled along the hallway above them. It rumbled on the floor and squeaked.

"The boy should have been brought to me by now," said a masculine voice – deep, labored and heavily accented. "He will want the boy. It will want the boy."

"Understood. All will be ready."

Ari recognized the second voice as belonging to Miss Pratt. The thing that rumbled and squeaked came closer.

"Once I am, he," said the man, wheezing, "even time will be my slave."

The thing that rumbled and squeaked came even nearer. Shadows began to flutter across the passageway light. Ari began to make sense of it as a wheeled chair – a very old one in need of oil. She and Jasper caught their breath, shoving back against the stone as Miss Pratt came across the stairwell entrance, pushing along a skeletal figure wrapped in velvet robes. The man in the chair reminded Ari of an unwrapped Egyptian mummy. He was gaunt, brown with age with alert, acquisitive eyes and a kind of imperial presence.

There was something else too about the skeleton man. Ari realized her special abilities had disappeared, but her instincts remained intact and they informed her that the man in the chair was ferociously dangerous. Evil floated around him like a dark net fishing for souls. The Skeleton Man would hurt them if he could – and he would take pleasure in it.

Miss Pratt and the Skeleton Man rumbled past the stairwell without pausing to capture escaped children. The old-fashioned push chair squeaked into the distance and out of earshot.

Jasper lowered his hand from Lucy's squirming face. "Do you reckon I'm the boy?"

"I'm hungry," said Lucy, trying to talk softly as they'd asked.

Ari ascended the steps again to the entrance and peered out, looking from side to side. The corridor was empty and was, indeed, lit by candles on ledges. As with the lower level, there was a confluence of differing passages and doors. Finding the way to the outside was going to be a puzzle.

"Whatever direction leads away from them." Jasper joined her at the entrance.

"He's very bad," Ari said.

"My feeling too." Jasper picked up Lucy and sat her on his hip. "On three?"

Ari nodded. "One, two … three!" she whispered.

They stepped out into the passage together – than ran to their left, away from the Skeleton Man and whatever plans he had made for them.

Caroline, unable to sleep, sat with a cup of tea in the Hawkesmoor kitchen. She stroked the head of the family's yellow Lab, Molly and worried about what was

happening in London. Robin still wasn't reach-able –
neither he nor Cyril had deigned to contact her with any
further information about Ari or the dangerous situation in
which they were all embroiled. Not only flustered by worry,
she was angry too. Furious was a better word. She was
furious that Robin had left her out of the loop.

Still, common sense tried to make a case for calm. What she
had told her father was true. She trusted Robin. He
understood his cantilevered universe and if Robin had
chosen a certain path to pursue, perhaps she ought to just sit
tight in the saddle and allow him to work.

With an un-butler-like bang of the swinging kitchen door,
Potterswood – who had relocated to the castle with Cyril, a
disgruntled Sir Geoffrey Constable and a small domestic
staff – clattered into the kitchen. He was ruffled – rather
more than was indicated for the sin of brewing her own pot
of tea in her own family's kitchen.

"I … I just know where everything is," she began, "I …"

"Highness," Potterswood breathed, strangely uninterested in
the teapot, "your stepson has arrived with Edmund. I think
you'd better come."

      "There were four of you," said Robin. "Surely Sybil
is about somewhere."

If alabaster Mazelina was surprised that he knew anything
about their history or Miss Pratt's true name, she was able
to conceal it. Instead, she raised an annoyed eyebrow.

"There were three of us. Sybil has always been a servant."
Mazelina had led him below. There seemed to be a number
of chambers and passages – some dug out and constructed,
others part of a vast natural underground cave system that
probably encompassed the island. The perfect geography for
a hidden community.

He allowed himself to be led down into their stronghold where clearly there would be some kind of ambush either literal or threatened. Their caverns were where Ari would be found, and her recovery was the only thing that mattered in the end.

Mazelina's destination was essentially a medieval chapter house. Circular with a vaulted ceiling, with archways in four directions suggesting that every underground road led to it, the room was simple and seemingly unaltered from the time it was originally occupied. Dun-colored walls bare of decoration encircled spartan wooden benches, tables and chairs. Banks of candles – very much like a Catholic church -- were arranged against the round walls. The burning tapers themselves had a peculiar odor that persuaded Robin that the tallow had been rendered from human victims.

A slightly elevated stone dais was the focal point of the space and on its ancient, pitted surface sat a man in one of three high-backed wooden chairs. Wrapped in a red velvet cote-hardie, the wizened figure gazed at Robin imperiously. He was more cadaver than breathing humanoid – ancient brown skin stretched tightly over bone. Wealth was displayed in the jeweled rings on his long, grasping fingers and the heavy gold torque at his throat. The skull-like head was covered in an improbable shoulder length mop of glossy black hair. Robin guessed it was a wig and wondered at the vanity of such a repulsive creature.

Mazelina left Robin's side and stepped up onto the platform, taking her place on one of the empty chairs. She arranged the skirt of her human leather dress fastidiously and then sat quietly, waiting for her companion to speak. "We welcome you, King of English Vampires," said the repulsive creature in old French. The voice was hoarse and labored. "It is high time that a new treaty was struck between England and Drole Island."

Robin had the immediate sense that he was lying, perhaps using the concept of diplomacy as a delaying tactic. There was something else too. Something that didn't fit the narrative – a vampire wasting away on an island of successful hunters.

"I am here only for my daughter," Robin said, crossing his arms and regarding them both with distaste. "Return her to me, unharmed. Now."

Mazelina's eyes narrowed. "This is a sacred space …"

"It's an abattoir," he cut in, his tone both icy and dismissive. "I don't recognize Drole Island or the scum of the earth who pretend to rule it -- Gilles de Rais or his doxies."

Mazelina jumped to her feet, seething – but either remembering the vampire Garcelle's fate or reluctant to act without permission, failed to act on her fury.

The skeletal creature's black eyes widened and the thin, ugly mouth twisted with distemper. He lifted one of his emaciated arms and pointed at Robin. "You presume to know me? You know nothing, vampire."

It was then Robin understood what didn't fit – why Gilles de Rais seemed to be a decaying wreck despite an operation devoted to the predation of humans.

"Gilles de Rais," he frowned, tilting his head in thought, "you're really not a vampire at all, are you?"

"I'll be all right, Your Serene Highness," murmured Edmund as Caroline daubed his blood-stained face with a warm cloth. "Won't even know it happened in an hour."

"You took a big knock," Caroline replied, returning the cloth to the bowl of hot water for another rinse. "And please, no Serene Highness titles here at Hawkesmoor."

A large group had congregated in the kitchen, gathered around the long wooden table that the 18th century Countess of Hawkesmoor, Augusta had procured for her kitchen staff. Simon was wolfing down hot tea and a sandwich, his injured ankle elevated on the chair next to him. Della had been welcomed warmly. Hannah had taken her upstairs to a guest room to decompress a bit and change into dry clothes. The Earl leaned against one of the counters. He sipped from a cup of tea from a pot that Potterswood had quickly brewed and cleared his throat. "The creature you dealt with sounds remarkably like the one we ran off in Scotland."

Sir Geoffrey rubbed his forehead as if all the new information was hurting his brain. "Not a vampire?"

Edmund tried to nod while Caroline attended to his bruised face. "Never seen anything like it. Maybe 8 – 10 feet tall, all bones and rotted flesh like a corpse. Clearly targeting young Simon here."

"That's the scary thing," Simon added. "It found me on a road in Yorkshire. We think it might be headed here next."

"Makes sense," said Tinley, grim-faced. He and Culpeper had immediately deferred to Edmund upon his arrival as he was the senior officer on duty.

"We'll need to be ready," agreed Edmund, wincing as Caroline wiped at a deep wound in his scalp.

"I thought Robin had created some sort of forcefield around Hawkesmoor and the London house," she said. Her worries about Ari and her husband jumped yet another queasy notch.

"The Bailey in New York as well," said Cyril with a nod. "It's the first time we've had such protections and they've been very successful from what I can make out."

"Yes," interjected Simon. "I think it tried to get into The Bailey."

"Better to be part of the safer rather than sorry group, I feel," said Edmund, wincing again. "Tinley – you join Culpeper on watch. Potterswood – you been trained in basic security measures, right?"

The butler nodded from his spot near the tea things. "I have three staff members here too. All of them can do their bit."

"I can attest that reasonably placed gunshots seem to be effective. We have a pretty extensive shotgun collection here." The Earl had another sip of tea. "My daughter, Hannah, is an excellent shot."

"Right," said Edmund. "Let's weaponize and be ready."

"Not a vampire?" Sir Geoffrey repeated, shaking his head. "PM will need to be updated on this development. I shall …"

Culpeper suddenly materialized in the center of the kitchen floor. He looked out of breath and agitated. "Never seen the like! Come quick before they move!"

Chapter Fifty-seven

"Why in blue blazes are they just standing there?" asked the Earl.

The entire kitchen party was up on the east edge of the Great Walk, staring down. Just beyond castle walls, standing in pools of light thrown by the security system were twelve tall and gaunt figures – seemingly medieval knights dressed in tattered leather surcoats and broken bits of chain mail. They stood with grey, desiccated skin barely stretched over exposed bone stood in a row like grotesque statues. Silent and motionless, they gazed fixedly at the castle. A moor wind wove through their long, greasy hair, blowing shards of it around cadaver faces. Waiting for a signal, some sign to start forward.

"Blimey" breathed Tinley.

"Are those vampires?" Sir Geoffrey peered down at the line of nightmarish figures, his face wrinkling as the sickly-sweet odor of death rose up with the breeze. "The more traditional type?"

"Sir Geoffrey," said Cyril with slight tightening of his normally implacable voice, "I've never seen vampires such as these."

"But they might be our fancy killers," Edmund threw Sir Geoffrey a pointed look and turned away from the castle ledge. "Your Lordship, time to raid your gun cabinets."

"Good man," said the Earl with a nod.

"You can't be serious?" The civil servant was aghast. He pointed in the direction of the eerie figures. "Go to battle with them? Just the handful of inhabitants of this castle against them?"

Caroline linked arms with her father and Simon. "We have done it before, Sir Geoffrey."

"English dog," wheezed Gilles de Rais.
Mazelina moved next to his chair and laid a hand on de Rais' velvet shoulder. "Highness," she said to Robin, transitioning from fury to sycophantic purr, "ask your questions but allow us to answer. Then we will talk of treaties and your daughter will be returned."
Robin again had the impression that they were stretching time. He clenched his jaw and decided to proceed in cautious hopes of learning something that might reveal their weaknesses. It would be a singular pleasure to dispatch them both as he had the smug Garcelle but until he had some idea of where and in what conditions Ari was being held, he did not yet dare destroy them.
"What precisely is this thing?" Robin asked, pointing at Gilles de Rais' ruined frame.
He watched Mazelina's eyes narrow behind the obsequious mask she now wore. "A great general – the leader of hunters." Her voice rose with the kind of fanatical reverence he associated with religious zealots. "A general – an emperor -- who will restore the old ways and remake the world as he desires."
"The old ways?"
"Revenants were designed to hunt, to kill without pity. Here, we follow the old ways. We hunt humans. We do not sip faux blood in crystal glasses and take our prey as mates." Mazelina delivered the last line pointedly.
"Your grasp of history is poor." Robin dismissed her with a loose, uninterested gesture he hoped would unsettle her.
"We have always had a complex relationship with humans

and the way forward is consentient not adversarial. Sybil was your envoy to the outside world?"

Gilles de Rais jerked his head to look at Mazelina. His death-mask face twisted with something that almost appeared to be anxiety. "The boy. Barron requires the boy." Mazelina half-smiled and murmured. "Sybil has gone to secure the boy. Soon."

"Barron will be pleased with such a beautiful boy. As will I." Gilles de Rais' black eyes lit up with avarice and a hideous pleasure. "The neck curving into the blade. The blood as it begins to seep …"

"Sybil is your envoy?" Robin repeated, his stomach flaring with pain. He had no intention of listening to a recitation of Gilles de Rais' vile desires although it was interesting to learn that the French child murderer did indeed interact with an entity called Barron. Keeping Barron in a kennel on Drole Island …

"Sybil serves us in many ways. She has even gone to university on our behalf to learn what the new thinking is," the alabaster vampire said with some pride. "A spy for the ages."

Robin returned his focus to Gilles de Rais and pointed again at the ancient creature in the chair. "What is he and why did you rescue him at Nantes?"

"So much exquisite death – imaginative, cruel and productive," Mazelina's voice took on a rough warmth at the words. Her memories of Gilles de Rais' notorious child murders appeared to be sexually arousing, and she unconsciously ran a hand over the bodice of her leather dress. "There were three of us then – Theodora, Garcelle and I. We had heard of children disappearing in France and assumed a vampire was fulfilling its purpose. We sought out this vampire but instead, came to know Gilles de Rais – a human. He offered us pleasure beyond our revenant capacities to comprehend. Pain and panic – an elixir that we drank as deeply as we did their blood."

Robin's chest throbbed. He straightened his spine, not wanting either of them to take note of his growing infirmity. "A human – yet here he is. Alive in the 21st century after being executed in 1440."

Mazelina stepped down from the platform, now serpentine and erotic. "Kiss me," she said, "and I will explain the magic of Gilles de Rais."

He suddenly thought of Asher Grey's explanation for why he betrayed them. A chance to resurrect Elsie – Very soon they were going be able to restore the dead. Before he could get any further with the concept, Mazelina threw her long, sinewy arms around his neck.

"Kiss me," the vampire breathed and then pressed her lips against his for a moment, "because you want to know about magic, and I won't tell until you do."

Mazelina did possess a raw kind of sexual chemistry. Exuding it as if she produced pheromones through her pores – a poison flower releasing spores. He bent in and kissed her hungry mouth. She was powerful – he was sexual prey. Her arms pulled him closer and her tongue probed his with the relentless constriction of an Anaconda. He found no pleasure in it.

Finally, Robin pushed Mazelina back so he could breathe. She smiled at him, almost dreamy with satisfaction. Ripping her bodice open with a short, brutal gesture, she reached for his hand and laid it across her bare left breast.

"You could have me now – right now in front of Gilles de Rais. He likes such spectacles. You will too. I promise." Robin pulled his fingers from her erect nipple and clasped his hands behind his back. "The magic?"

Mazelina dropped to her knees. "Will it be sodomy then? De Rais calls it the English Way."

"The English are conquered by sex," Gilles de Rais said in hoarse disdain. His voice was a little stronger as if the potential to watch Mazelina in a sexual interlude had awoken his spirit. "Women, boys, little girls – it's of little matter to them. They speak of lofty things like honor and discipline but in the end, so easily seduced by anything laying on its back or on its knees."

Robin had the notion that he now understood de Rais' insidious campaign to wreck Sir Neville's order and steal his knights. After an eon of celibate religious life, good works to ungrateful local Scots and the bland blood of domesticated farm animals, Gilles de Rais had promised them thrilling hunts for human blood and endless sex with anything that moved -- both consensual and forced. To a group of deeply bored, battle-hardened former soldiers, de Rais' pitch must have been irresistible. Little wonder they helped dump Sir Neville off in the hidden chapter house on their way to Drole Island without a backward glance. Gilles de Rais and his vampire lovers gained the powerful, committed but not particularly bright force they required to rebuild a hidden empire of kidnappings and death. He had a brief moment to admire Sir Neville and even his most loyal knight, Asher Grey, for living up to the civilized ideals they had sworn to abide.

"Time for you to produce my daughter," he said. "Then I will decide what to do about Drole Island."

"Big English words," sneered Gilles de Rais, making an airy gesture with his skeletal hands. "Our murders ruined your way forward, did they not? Your feeble and vainglorious campaign to fuse together a society of hunters and their prey? Now the humans led by their prime minister will want to contain you – a war that I will win."

"You are not a vampire," Robin's voice was sharp. "You are nothing to us."

The gaunt face broke into a snide smile. "English dog – you know nothing of me and what I will offer British vampires." Then he swung his head to the other. "Mazelina – is he ready?"

She leapt to her feet and refastened her leather bodice. "From what I have tasted, his defenses are very low – weakened by our constant intrusions on his etheric protections. We can begin."

Gilles de Rais closed his black eyes for a long moment. "I have sent them forward," he said finally.

Robin was suddenly aware that his mouth was bleeding. Blood spilled over his bottom lip indicating a severe rupture somewhere in his system. He pulled a handkerchief from a pocket and pressed it against his mouth. Pain ricocheted through his body – severe and debilitating. He staggered. Tried to summon the energy needed to attack Gilles de Rais – nothing. All revenant and Tylwyth Teg abilities offline. Ari, he thought desperately, wherever you are – run, hide, survive.

"You will have noticed that our knights are no longer on the island," purred Mazelina as he stumbled backwards, falling against one of the heavy wooden chairs. "Gilles de Rais has ordered them to Hawkesmoor Castle where they will sweep over your puny defenses and murder everything that moves."

Robin stared up at her from the floor. "Apparently you don't know my wife."

Chapter Fifty-eight

Ari, Jasper and Lucy crept along a shadowy passage. It was lit sporadically with candles, allowing them to see without needing to carry their own.

Jasper paused, breathing deeply. "Do you feel it?" he whispered.

"A breeze," said Ari, shivering as the cold air brushed over her skin.

"We must be near a way out."

"Does out mean food?" asked Lucy in the whisper that she had been reminded to use. "Extra, extra hungry now."

The sound of a door banging shut somewhere in the distance sent them into a deep doorway where they huddled in its shadow. A figure, carrying a light, moved up the same corridor. Ari thought it looked to be Miss Pratt. For a moment, it seemed her dangerous nanny would continue walking towards them. Without a real hiding place, they would easily be discovered. Then Miss Pratt turned to her left into another passageway – one that would lead her to the staircase they had just scaled.

"We're going to run," murmured Jasper. "Run towards the breeze. All right?"

Ari nodded, liking Jasper all the more. He was bright, brave and nice. A nice boy. She hated where they were but glad, too, that they had met. Lucy and Jasper were her first real friends.

"Ready?"

They sprung from the doorway and ran through the shadows of the corridor, seeking the cold wind that managed to find a way into the endless tunnels. Ari led the chase with Jasper close behind with an exhausted Lucy on his back. The corridor narrowed and turned slightly to the right, plunging into darkness with no more candles providing light.

The dark forced them to move a little more slowly to avoid falling. Eventually, conditions seemed to improve. An icy, grey light settled into the tunnel, allowing them to make sense of the rough stone walls and dirt floor as more cave than corridor.

"An opening!" whispered Ari, pointing at what looked like a window in the rock wall.

"Awfully high up," replied Jasper with a sigh. "I was kind of hoping for a nice wide door."

They bolted the last stretch to the hole. Ari saw immediately that it wasn't a large opening but children such as themselves could probably slip through if the hole could be reached at all. Cold air rushing in from the outside brought the comforting odors of sea and grass.

"I might be able to lift you and Lucy up," said Jasper, staring up at the square opening in the rock. "You could go for help."

"No." Ari shook her head. After all, The Famous Five wouldn't leave a team member behind. "We are not going to go without you."

Jasper shrugged and was about to speak when a strange, ruddy face appeared in the center of the opening. In fright, they fell back against the opposite wall. They had been discovered after all. There would be no going home. No escaping the dark and damp tunnels.

"No, no – no worries," said the face at the opening. The voice was both apologetic and comfortingly English. "I am here by command of His Serene Highness. One of you – the Princess Arianrhod?"

Jasper glanced at Ari. "He's a real nutter. Just our luck."

"I am Arianrhod," she said, earning an astonished look from her new friend as she stepped out of the shadows. "Are you one of my father's men?"

"Asher Grey, Your Highness," he replied, pushing an arm through the opening. "Let's get you out of there."

"Lucy first!" Ari said, taking the little girl's hand and leading her forward.

With Jasper's help, they lifted Lucy up to Asher Grey who pulled her through the child-sized opening. Then it was Ari's turn to be hauled up into the cold night air and finally Jasper who had a little more trouble with the small opening.

"Crikey, I'm glad you found your way here. I was having a devil of a time trying to get in. Now to get you down to the beach," Asher Grey told them – an imposing figure in a heavy sweater, navy peacoat and genuine kilt. "When he can, your father will join us there."

"We're on an island," breathed Jasper, gob-smacked as he scanned the wild, wind-whipped expanse above the sea. "Hebrides?"

Asher threw him an approving look. "Bright lad. North of the Orkneys."

"Gosh," the boy said and turned to Ari. "And you're a real princess?"

She shrugged. "Well, sort of."

"Gosh," he repeated.

Asher Grey gazed out at the silver sea. "Fog coming in again. Will Lucy let me carry her?"

"Yes, please," piped up the little girl, walking towards Asher Grey with her arms reaching for his assistance. "I'm tired and hungry and I would like some food -- also a drink."

He picked Lucy up and set her upon his broad shoulders. "We've got to move fast and quiet. This is a strange island."

"Mr. Grey, my father is here too?"

"Your Highness," Asher Grey tossed Jasper a flashlight, "he'll meet us on the beach."

There was something in the way he said it that felt uncertain to Ari. As if Asher Grey wasn't fully convinced her father would turn up as promised. Maybe once Jasper and Lucy were safe on the beach, she could come back to look for him. He might need some help.

A plain, hand-beaten copper cauldron sat on an equally simple table that seemed to have been pressed into service as a kind of altar. Mazelina had brought the copper cauldron into Drole Island's quasi-temple with great reverence, practically genuflecting to the thing when she placed it on the makeshift altar.

"In 1432, I very nearly bankrupted my family's vast fortune to acquire this," said Gilles de Rais, indicating the cauldron. "Originally made and destroyed by the Celts. Restored for my personal use at great cost."

Robin had retreated to the back of the meeting room, collapsing onto an oak bench that had been attached to the wall. He was breathing with difficulty. His lungs felt crushed as if they were taking on internal bleeding. The only plan he currently had up and running was to hope Asher Grey had gotten to Ari. If his daughter was safe, then, perhaps, the others could move in from their island positions to assist in eradicating Gilles de Rais and whatever was happening at Hawkesmoor. Until then, he would have to wait and try to assess the level of Gilles de Rais' power.

Celts – Robin thought of the Welsh and their cauldron tales. There was one – sometimes called Pair Dadeni – that purported to resurrect the dead but had been ultimately destroyed by Efnysien during a great battle against the Irish. Had Gilles de Rais convinced himself that, somehow, he possessed the legendary Pair Dadeni? It might explain the boasts to Asher Grey about bringing the dead back to life. With effort, he propped himself up against the wall.

"History tells us your pathetic attempts at black magic yielded nothing," Robin said, hoping to goad de Rais into divulging something – anything – that might help in bringing an end to the occupation of Goblin Island. "Gilles de Rais – the failure. Gilles de Rais – the joke."

"Human history rarely records the truth. You --King of English Vampires – ought to know that much at least." Gilles de Rais' eyes narrowed with enmity. "In 1432, I tortured and murdered two children, cut them into pieces and placed some of the parts into specially prepared glass vessels. That night, I made a first contact with the demonic entity, Barron."

Keeping Barron in a kennel on Drole Island. Robin let out a long, erratic breath. Was it possible that some day-tripping interdimensional had allowed Gilles de Rais to imagine he had summoned one of Satan's cohort? Stringing along the psychopath until the moment arrived in which the fortified human could be of real use? After all, Morvidus – the Shadow Being – had run just such an insidious shell game and unintentionally, created the vampire bloodline.

Robin wheezed, his lungs in agony. If true, a larger plot was unspooling in front of him and the hidden emperor of Drole Island would also have to be destroyed or banished. He didn't dare think about Caroline and Hawkesmoor yet. The idea that she could be in immediate peril had the power to render him utterly paralyzed with panic.

"The magic of Gilles de Rais," said Mazelina in her irritating croon. "You will see – you will see."

"Isn't this all a bit Halloween-y even for old timers like you? A magic cauldron?"

"In exchange for the blood and bodies of children," Gilles de Rais focused his black, merciless eyes on Robin who gazed back, coolly, without flinching, "very much like your little daughter, Barron has renewed my life over and over again. Blood and viscera of children poured into this cauldron as payment and tribute. But, finally, even that is not enough. Barron has told me that my human form cannot absorb another rebirth."

"Sybil told us a new vampire had emerged – a vampire not only of enormous and strange power but with the ability to produce a living bloodline. A vampire who had also made it his destiny to change our ways – to modernize and eradicate the cult of the hunter." Mazelina again stepped off the platform and walked across the stone floor towards Robin. "We knew two things immediately. One – this vampire was a heretic and had to be stopped. Two – we had to have it." Robin forced down a wave of electric pain that radiated throughout his nervous system and made himself stand to confront the alabaster vampire.

"Sybil suggested that a few well-placed murders and violent incidents would dismantle the delicate rapprochement you had built with the human government. There would have been more, but you moved faster than we anticipated."

"But why Lev Black? Why Oliver D'Aubigny?" He straightened his spine despite the white-hot pain irradiating his bones. The Hong Kong delegation incident suddenly made a certain sense. Emperor Ai Di was making huge strides with synthetic blood production. Creating an instability with a nervous Asian kingdom could derail the whole process. Sybil/Miss Pratt was no slouch. She was way ahead of the ones in front of him.

354

"Sybil enjoys research," replied Mazelina with a smug smile that rivalled anything Garcelle had been pleased to put on display. "She tracked down descendants of the Ponsonby family and picked the most successful ones. A little joke. An amusement."

"The Tiffin children?"

She smiled again, disinterested in the children. "They are meat for Barron. And more reason for the humans to despise you."

At the mention of Barron, Gilles de Rais was unsettled enough to half-stand from his chair. "Where is the boy? Barron desires the boy."

Mazelina paused her supremely confident saunter. Momentarily, she was anxious as her repulsive emperor. Clearly, neither of them wished to frustrate the thing known as Barron.

Robin took in a shaky breath. If his thoughts about Barron were correct, he knew exactly how to send the entity into whole new realms of vexation and disappointment. But, before he could act, he had to know Ari was safe.

Chapter Fifty-nine

"Zombies?" Della asked Simon as she peered down from the Hawkesmoor battlement. "Are those real-life zombies?"

Simon slipped an arm about her waist. "You're being awfully good about everything. Don't you want to run screaming back to New York?"

She sighed a little. "This is way more than crime cartels. If it's just a crazy dream – hey, I'm still in love with you and happy."

Simon kissed her forehead and said nothing.

"Right then," barked Edmund, "Time to get down below. If they get in, they'll have to find us and if they do, we can do some damage in close."

In response, humans and vampires began to pull off the old battlements. Down below, as if sensing the tactic, all twelve decaying relics – as if of one mind – looked up. Despite their gaunt frames and rotting flesh, they gave every indication of strength and agility. Then they began to move forward.

"We have learned that the cauldron is more than just a vessel for exchanging blood for life," said Mazelina who had returned to her former state of bravado. "Much more."

Robin almost smiled at her naivete. The interdimensional being they knew as the demon, Barron, had certainly dangled rewards in front of them in hopes of the big score. Rather like a New Age prosperity huckster with a pyramid scheme to flog. Sadly, this one had cost the lives of many humans. It was also disquieting to know that other interdimensional beings found their way onto the human plane through doorways the Tylwyth Teg did not recognize. The universe was vastly more complex than any human, revenant or entity could ever hope to comprehend.

"Come -- you will see."

He shook his head. "I have no interest in your old cooking pot."

"A pity," rasped Gilles de Rais, walking stiffly and with great difficulty to the table that held his infamous copper cauldron. "Sybil anticipated you would send your court to Hawkesmoor Castle after she brought us your daughter. You imagine that your knights will be able to protect your castle against my knights. But you know nothing of my knights and the obeisance they pay me."

Robin inhaled another erratic breath, trying to press down the surging pain ripping through his nerves. "Illuminate me," he said, at last.

"The Cauldron of Rebirth." The cadaverous thing who had once been the handsome, strapping Baron Gilles de Rais, former Marshal of France, ran his thin hands around the rim of the copper vessel. "Fourteen knights – two to America to find your bastard. Twelve left to die for me."

Robin ignored the crippling pain and walked forward, past a gloating Mazelina, towards Gilles de Rais and the cauldron. "Vampires destroyed for you?"

"Have you ever seen a braquemard?"

"Short, double-edged sword – yes." Robin continued forward. Maybe if he could get to the cauldron, he'd be able to use it to control de Rais.

"Twelve knights knelt before us – twelve throats offered up for the cut. The supreme sacrifice to preserve the old ways and the cult of the hunter." Gilles de Rais stroked the ancient copper with reverence. "The braquemard did its work. Twelve heads, twelve good, strong bodies for the Cauldron of Rebirth."

"The magic," said Mazelina.

"Twelve were returned – superior, stranger, stronger. Knights for the demon's use. You've seen Barron's work, have you not, King of English Vampires?"

Robin was unsurprised to learn that the entity, Barron, was responsible for devouring the tragic victims of de Rais' vendetta. It could both satisfy ghastly urges and encourage machinations that would eventually benefit some glittering goal on the human plane.

"Imagine what they are now doing to your court at Hawkesmoor," Gilles de Rais drew up his mummified facial muscles into a crooked smile. "Your knights unable to contain them. Your wife consumed. Family estate destroyed."

Without uttering a word, Robin broke into a run. He flung himself at the copper cauldron with the intent of wrenching it from the table and de Rais' grasping fingers. He figured Mazelina would be on him like a light but if the copper vessel was in his hands, she might be tractable.

A blow struck him from the side, and he staggered violently to his right. Attempting to recover his balance, Robin saw Sybil wielding a short, double-edged sword – the braquemard Gilles de Rais preferred to use as the ideal decapitating tool. She, too, was now dressed in a simple leather tunic. No dress of ornate design such as the ones Mazelina and Garcelle chose to wear for the humble servant. Still colorless and wan but infinitely cleverer than either Gilles de Rais or his fancy vampires, she advanced on him.

He managed to regain his equilibrium. Her initial blow had added to the deterioration of his physical self. "Sybil," he said, wheezing, "whatever do you see in these fundamentalist morons?"

She said nothing and continued to move towards him, the short sword at the ready.

"Do not take his head yet," warned Mazelina. "Gilles de Rais is not ready."

Robin had nowhere to go and no power left to alter the situation. He stood quietly, waiting for Sybil to act. As he took his next breath, she did act – darting forward, seizing his right shoulder with her left hand and plunging the Braquemard into his torso.

An atomic fission rippled through his nervous system – pain so intense it threatened to short out every nerve ending. With everything collapsing, it seemed as if the only thing keeping him on his feet was the blade itself. He choked on blood and acid as it surged up through his throat.

Sybil stepped in closer, whispering in his ear as she jerked the blade up to penetrate his lungs. "I allowed the children to escape. Help you die only once – yes?"

He stared at her, blood dripping from his mouth and off his chin. Already in shock, Robin nodded. All he could hear through the nuclear blast in his brain and body was that the children – Ari – were out and presumably safe.

Sybil jerked out the braquemard and pushed him away. Robin pressed his arms against the gaping wound. It did little good. Blood, stomach acids and viscera washed from the sword strike. He sank onto one of the wooden benches, wondering what Sybil had up her duplicitous leather sleeve.

"The cauldron is safe," Sybil said, tossed the bloody sword to Mazelina who had returned to the stone platform. "His revenant system will heal him up enough for what you require."

Robin had realized early on that Gilles de Rais had chosen him as his new receptacle. De Rais' human body was failing after countless regenerations; he needed a new one and who better than Britain's King of the Vampires? He could assume power and return vampires to the old way, satisfying his nightmarish desires with unparalleled access to human children in the bargain. Building an army of demon replicants, he would eventually take on the human government. That was the aspect of genuine interest to the entity called Barron – the potential to infect the entire world.

With Ari out, he could now concentrate on deciding how best to destroy himself. He had to die before Gilles de Rais was ready for the exchange. He also had to be extinguished in such a way that he could never again be resurrected through the copper cauldron. What Sybil meant by Help you die only once – yes? She needed his death too – for her own plans, whatever that might mean.

Chapter Sixty

"This is it!" shouted Edmund. "Move!"
They abandoned the battlements and ran to Edmund's
muster stations. Revenants linked with the humans for
molecular transfer. It had been decided that long distance
transfer to Audley Square was too dangerous and
transporting somewhere outside the castle might meant
innocent humans could be killed if the twelve medievals
pursued. They were fortunate, as it was, that the castle was
both set into its vast acreage and adjoined a national park.
Locals, too, were used hearing the occasional shooting party
so the authorities wouldn't feel it necessary to swing by for
a look.

Using a map Caroline had drawn for them on a kitchen
napkin, the vampires managed to transport everyone down
into the ancient stores under the castle without embedding
someone in the stonework. The room Caroline had chosen
as a retreat was the laundry room from Victorian times until
the 1970s when a modern laundry area was installed up
above in the old wet room near the kitchen.

The old laundry room still had its massive wooden baths
and hanging wires overhead. Metal washing tubs and
mangles from various 20th century eras were scattered
about as well, lurking in the shadows like domestic ghosts.
Caroline had chosen it for stout doors that still closed
properly despite time and the damp. Edmund and the other
vampires moved two of the heavy wooden and porcelain
baths against the laundry door in hopes of slowing down the
intruders once their hiding spot was found.

Then they were quiet. Against the furthest wall from the
door, behind a bank of linen racks and a couple of mangles,

revenants and humans huddled together around a set of electric lanterns, waiting.

Up above, there were stretches of deathly silence punctuated shrilly by bangs and the occasional crash. The twelve entities were in the castle proper and hunting.

"Thank you," said Jasper to Ari.

"What for?" asked Ari. They were sitting on the sand in a little cut away in the rocks that formed the base of cliffside. Asher Grey had built a fire and the three children sat around it, eager to feel some warmth again. With Asher and three guardsmen keeping watch over them, for the first time in a long while they almost felt safe.

"I'd never have gotten Lucy out of there without your help," he said. "You're all right … you know, for a girl."

Ari laughed. It felt good to laugh. In the underground place, she wondered if she'd ever laugh again,

"Let's always be friends," she said, including Lucy in her smile. "Best friends."

"Friends," yawned Lucy, her head using Jasper's leg for a pillow. "Can you eat sand?"

"No!" Ari and Jasper said together.

He laughed and held out a fist for Ari to bump. "Best friends until the end of time."

"When my father gets here, we can go home." Ari bumped his fist. "What's the first thing you're going to eat?"

Jasper thought for a moment. "Sausage rolls, I think. At least ten. You?"

"An American hamburger with lots and lots of French fries – and a chocolate milkshake."

"That does sound good," he conceded, with a grin. "I may change my mind."

A golden haze drifted into the little inlet. It shimmered, floating over the makeshift campsite like a warm and comforting fog. Jasper and Lucy vanished into the burnished light.

Ari stood up in the glittering gold. She felt no danger. Her father had explained how ribbons of time and place existed on many levels and wove through the reality she recognized as the world.

"Arianrhod," said a voice in old Welsh.

Gilles de Rais was livid. Mazelina slapped Sybil and the servant accepted the rebuke without protest, clearly accustomed to punishment. She simply retreated to the side of the room to await further instructions.

"They cannot have gotten far," said Mazelina. "It's an island. Go get them."

Sybil bowed from her place on the sidelines. "The children are lost to us – the cliffs. It's dark and the ground is very unstable." Her bland tone indicated that other Drole Island victims may be died in abortive escape attempts and the fate of these humans carried about as much weight as factory farmed chickens.

Robin's revenant healing process was as compromised as was every other system in his strange hybrid frame. He propped himself up on the bench, trying to calm his nervous system so that it might accomplish some repairs –just enough to manage a molecular shift that could pull him apart at the seams. Scattered across the island -- embedded in rock and lost to the wind – he could never be resurrected by Gilles de Rais' demon and used to create destruction to humans and vampires alike.

"The boy would have ensured every success," said the ancient cadaver that had once been the strapping, infamous

Baron Gilles de Rais. "Young blood, young body parts to wax and wane the cauldron."

Mazelina offered him the handle of the still bloody braquemard. Gilles de Rais held the sword over the maw of the cauldron and allowed Robin's blood to drip from the blade. Where the drops struck the metal, the cauldron began to glow and hum.

The sight of his blood igniting the demon's lantern was intensely unsettling. Robin tried to sit up as much as the brutal sword wound would allow. Was he now connected to the cauldron once his plasma with all of its encoded DNA touched its surface? Would it invalidate his plan to scatter his sub-atomic structure to the winds before he could be used?

The copper cauldron turned white-hot, losing itself in a blinding strobe of energy that screamed with voices who had known terror and torture. Robin looked away from the light, feeling its cold fission bite his skin like a million shards of glass.

Then the electric white of the awakened cauldron was gone. Barron – Gilles de Rais' demon familiar from 1432 – had arrived.

Barron was everything expected of a member of Satan's cohort. Tall, powerful with a shaggy pelt, blood-stained claws, cloven hooves and a huge head reminiscent of a wild goat complete with curved horns. Its eyes were devoid of humanizing expression – just empty black ovals. The sour stench of death that its matted fur threw up was almost unbearable.

Mazelina and a far cagier Sybil dropped to their knees in reverence while Gilles de Rais who considered the entity to be his supernatural servant, remained standing, holding on to the back of his wooden chair.

"He is the one," said Gilles de Rais, pointing at Robin with one of his withered hands. "I would take his body. If you make it so, I can promise you rivers -- oceans of blood. I can promise you the bodies of countless women, men and children to do your bidding or to fulfill any desire."

It growled and displayed a wide mouth of serrated teeth that belonged to carnivore not a grass eating member of the Capra Aegagrus species.

Robin pushed himself up to his feet. Some healing had begun, and he just might be able to ignite a self-destruct mode. But first, he wanted to see if it would be possible to discover just what Barron was and how the cauldron – his gateway to the human world – might be destroyed as well. The notion struck him as he gazed at the hulking creature in the center of the space that Barron was almost too perfect. Barron was exactly what a medieval man -- anxious to strike a bargain with the devil -- imagined he would conjure up during a ritual. The carnivorous goat's head, the cloven hoofs and foul-smelling viscera-soaked pelt – Barron could have stepped out from a drawing in a medieval alchemist's notebook.

"Why don't you show us your true self?" said Robin, pressing an arm against the sword wound, hoping to hold himself together for a little longer. Whatever was happening at Hawkesmoor, he prayed his family was managing to back off Gilles de Rais' horde. He loved them more than could ever be expressed in human terms and Caroline most of all. He loved her desperately – had since their first night in Manhattan. Any sacrifice he made was worth it if she was all right.

"You do not speak!" hissed Gilles de Rais, rocking unsteadily on his pins. "Barron – let it begin. I long for my new body."

Barron growled again and then spoke Latin in a voice of broken glass. "Quoniam litare fas & coeant faciam. Non prius. A puero erat promissa: Gilles de Rais!"

Robin translated it in his head as the entity spoke: When I deem it right and meet, I will act. Not before. A child was promised, Gilles de Rais. He watched as the arrogant Frenchman seemed taken aback at his demon's words.

"I have provided you with perfect children, women and men for centuries," Gilles de Rais sputtered. "You have gorged yourself on their bodies and blood. I have done my part."

"Est nihil tempus tuam ad me. Nunquam satis dolor metus carnis."

Your time means nothing to me. There is never enough pain, fear and flesh. Robin saw that Gilles de Rais moved to sit on his chair, rattled by the demon's displeasure. He was pretty sure the repulsive de Rais was more used to Barron happily raping and devouring his tribute to the general delight of all present.

"Nunc se incredibili creatura negarit?" Barron turned to gaze with its dead eyes at Robin who fought to stand straight.

Now you would deny me this extraordinary creature? Such a pronouncement did not sound positive for either himself or Gilles de Rais. The moment had arrived to challenge and hope that he learned something useful.

"Please drop the schoolboy's Latin," said Robin with disdain. "You don't even particularly speak it well. While you're at it, why not lose the cloven hooves and horns? It might fool these morons, but it doesn't work on me. What do you really look like?"

Gilles de Rais pounded the armrests of his chair with clenched fists. "You will be silent!"

Barron's outer form began to warp and weave, turning it on itself and then out again over and over. Mazelina rose, clearly unnerved by the swirling form in front of her. She stepped back, off the platform and out of immediate range. The wiser Sybil had already backed off to watch warily as the demon began to reconstitute into a single form.

The medieval demon had been replaced by something quite different but no less ghastly. Barron was now angular and alabaster – almost a Greek statue if the Greeks had immortalized distorted, crooked monsters and used an ugly heavily veined marble mottled with brown rot to do it. Its overly large chevron-shaped face resembled an ancient mask with eyes that were still onyx but now glittered with a kind of liquid malevolence.

Barron smiled. The hideous mask cracked open, revealing a huge mouth with three rows of blade-like teeth. When he spoke, the basso growl of the demon had been replaced by thin, high-pitched warble that sounded like the wind coursing over and through broken pipes.

"What are you?" Barron asked in singsong English. It focused its attention on Robin.

"I could ask the same of you, Barron."

"What do you think I am? They call me demon."

Robin glanced at the seething Gilles de Rais and then back at Barron. "I'd call you a bottom feeder interdimensional sustained by negative energy and flesh."

"Panic and pain sustain my species." Barron said, seemingly unoffended by Robin's insult. "We hunt in many realities. This one has been very profitable."

"Enough," blasted Gilles de Rais. "Give me his body."

Barron smiled again, staring at Robin with its inky eyes. "Take his head and I will do your bidding. But I will have bodies. Blood must flow."

"Sybil – the braquemard," the Frenchman gestured sharply at the bloody short sword. "Take the head. He's too weak to fight."

Chapter Sixty-one

Caroline held her breath at shuffling sounds outside the old laundry's double doors. She watched as Edmund and Simon slowly lowered the level of the electric lanterns until they barely emanated light. The guard had their service revolvers at the ready as did Cyril and her father with Robin's Les Bauer. Potterswood and his three staff members were armed with Hawkesmoor's long guns. Even Simon's friend, Della was equipped with a stout kitchen knife. The American girl had quietly pitched in without showing any signs of going to pieces. Caroline had been impressed.

The double doors – bolted shut – were being tested, creaking under pressure. The sliding bolts jangled and squeaked. Dry clacking noises came from the hall beyond the old laundry. Caroline recognized it from her work as a large animal vet – grinding teeth. Outside the laundry, gnashing teeth came in fits and starts from several beings – clicking and clacking as a form of communication.

Then there was silence. A silence that lengthened into a full minute, then two. Caroline let out a long, trembling breath. She squeezed the hand of her younger sister, Hannah, who gave her a relieved smile in return.

"Do you think Robin will be here soon to save the day?" asked Hannah in a barely audible whisper, referring to the events at Hawkesmoor Castle six years previously in which Robin had dealt with a malevolent invasion of shadow beings.

Caroline's throat tightened, thinking of her husband and daughter out somewhere, conditions unknown. She only hoped to be able to see them both again.

"I can only imagine he will," she whispered back, with another squeeze to Hannah's cold hand. "We just have to hang on …"

A violent cracking sound obliterated the rest of her sentence. The old laundry doors shuddered ominously under the attack, but the bolts held.

"They'll be through in another couple of go-rounds," whispered Edmund hoarsely under the thundering noise of another assault. "Be ready, lads. Potterswood – you and your lot ready to transfer the family and Sir Geoffrey outside the castle when I say?"

"Yes, sir," said Potterswood with a serious nod.

Such a transfer was a last resort. Dangerous at the best of times with vampires uncertain of the castle's geography, it was a virtual suicide run with twelve entities scattered throughout. The things might well have anticipated such a maneuver and left their own guard in place to deal with it. Out in the open, with vampires now unable to manage another energy transfer so quickly, they'd be easy prey.

"I shan't be going," said Sir Geoffrey, armed with Culpeper's spare service revolver. "You'll need an extra hand."

The doors were slammed again. This time the top bolt ripped from its moorings. Both vampire and human tensed, ready to spring to the end-game tasks Edmund had assigned. Caroline saw the beautiful American dancer move closer to Simon. They instinctively clasped hands. She prayed the young couple would have a chance together and that their story wouldn't come to a horrible end in Hawkesmoor's old laundry.

"Damnation," said the Earl, "Fine old bolts and hinges – at least three hundred years old."

Edmund raised his Glock. "Next one is it, lads. Been an honor serving with you all."

Sybil took the short sword and approached Robin with confident, relaxed steps. He could see that she had taken the heads of many and thought of his excellent guardsman, Pryce-Atwater. The poor sod would never have seen it coming. Miss Pratt was just a milquetoast nanny who taught maths and saw to it that Arianrhod had her tea on time.

"On your knees, Your Serene Highness," she said.

Robin eyed her warily. He pressed his forearm against his earlier wound – although beginning to heal – was still leaking. His trousers and shirt were soaked with blood, stomach acids and viscera.

"On your knees," Sybil repeated, lifting her eyebrows to emphasize her next statement. "I will help you die."

I will help you die – only once. Robin nodded at her, defeated. All that was left to him was self-immolation. His only option in preventing Gilles de Rais from starting a human and revenant holocaust. He'd break apart his atomic structure and send his pieces into the rock, the wind and the sea. His consciousness, in an eerie echo of Sir Neville's fate, left to go mad on Goblin Island.

He awkwardly dropped to his knees, wincing as pain warped through his system.

Sybil bent over him, pushing his long red-gold hair to the side, off his neck. "When you feel the blade bite," she whispered in his left ear, "do as you will."

That said, she grabbed a handful of hair and jerked his head up, exposing his throat.

Robin caught a glimpse of Gilles de Rais rising to his feet for a better view as Mazelina did the same. Barron cocked

371

its strange overlarge head to the side, liquid onyx eyes glimmering with a dreadful excitement.

"I love you, Caroline DeBarry," he said.

Sybil swung the braquemard down in front of Robin's exposed throat. He rallied what was left of his energy in preparation for one final effort. His nervous system answered with the subtle vibration that always rippled across his senses before an energy transfer. She cut into his neck with the blade. The white-hot agony almost derailing his focus. As promised, Sybil paused to allow him to regroup.

Through blinding pain, he heard Gilles de Rais shout at Sybil to finish the job. Just enough time to command his neural net to begin dismantling …

"I am here," said a young girl's voice.

Ari's voice! Robin shut down the directive to his nervous system. "No, no, no, Ari! Run!" he cried hoarsely, the braquemard still biting into his neck.

Sybil dropped the short sword. It clattered the stone floor in front of him. He felt her presence leave the space behind him, but it mattered little to him as he desperately looked for his daughter.

Ari walked across the room, a preternaturally beautiful child in a sensible British jumper and pleated skirt. Robin wasn't sure if it was the odd lighting in the meeting room, but she seemed to walk with a golden aura.

"Ari – run!" he croaked again, holding a hand to his bleeding throat.

"Come, child," cooed Gilles de Rais in his old French. "We welcome you."

Barron swiveled the mask-like face to gaze at Arianrhod as she approached. It opened its hideous mouth – all three rows of dagger teeth flashing in the candlelight – like a dog sensing its next meal, as if it was powerless to stop the prey instinct.

"Ari!" Robin staggered to his feet, preparing to shield his daughter.

"What a lovely child," said Gilles de Rais. "Come and allow us to worship you."

Arianrhod didn't acknowledge her father in any way. She was completely focused on the interdimensional being known as Barron and kept walking towards it. Barron was mesmerized. A long, dripping tongue was expelled from the grisly mouth and stretched towards her – a snake's sensing device that relayed prey information back to its brain. The entity crouched slightly, preparing to spring at the little girl. Robin struggled to his feet and threw himself at Barron, managing to send the creature sideways. Barron struck him with one of the heavy alabaster arms, flinging Robin against one of the rounded walls. Before he could recover, Barron returned to Ari and leapt towards her.

Tears filled his eyes. He had failed his daughter.

"Banished from this place," he heard her say in her clear, confident voice.

His vision began to clear. Moving with a shimmering gold light – a gold energy that rippled with vibrancy – Ari twisted Barron up into the air with a wave of her small hands. Gilles de Rais' demon flailed in panic like a cobra battling a tenacious mongoose. Sounding like fractured calliope, it screamed – not in rage or frustration but in genuine fear. She turned him around and around in the air above her, faster and faster, until Barron became a marbled blur with flashes of teeth. With a simple, compact gesture, Ari sheathed Gilles de Rais' creature in the legendary cauldron of copper and then crushed it in mid-air. Barron and its gateway winked out of the human world with a whoosh and pop.

Gilles de Rais' meeting room lapsed into shocked silence. Mazelina and the repulsive de Rais stared at Arianrhod, stunned.

"What have you done?" he cried in shrill hysteria and rose unsteadily to his feet. "You will regret this, I promise. Mazelina …"

"This is for all of them," said Ari.

She raised her arms again. Gilles de Rais lifted off and rose into the air, his blood red velvet robes billowing like a medieval banner. His black wig shifted and fell, revealing a completely bald, skeletal head covered in festering sores.

"Stop!" he shrieked in a quavering voice. "I will give you riches – jewels!"

"No, thank you," said Arianrhod. "It's time for you to be gone."

She waved her hand and Gilles de Rais snapped back – breaking in half. He mewled in agony as his spine shattered with a loud crack. Then the little girl folded him over and over until he had been reduced to a red velvet square box with a hideous face. Ari hurled the box down into the ground where it tumbled off to the side, inert.

She looked up from her appraisal of where the box had fallen. Mazelina had used the instant to hurl herself at Arianrhod, the discarded braquemard now in her hand. Ari stepped back, momentarily unsure.

Robin intercepted with what was left of his energy. He grabbed Mazelina in mid-leap and threw her into a wall. The vampire cried out, dazed from the force of the blow. As he had done with Gilles de Rais' other doxy, he pulled her up and snapped her neck with a twist so brutal it removed her head. The vampire fell to the meeting room floor with a dull thud.

"Dad!" Ari cried, running towards him. She looked horrified at the blood on his clothes as if noticing it for the very first time.

"Darling girl," Robin whispered, falling himself to the floor.

The Earl fired, winging one of the desiccated knights as it pushed aside one of the Victorian baths and came through the door. The creature – a nightmare soldier in a tattered leather surcoat fell to the side, momentarily offline. Edmund, Cyril Goforth and the guard were up on their feet, moving forward to intercept other skeletal entities as they began to lurch through the destroyed doorway.

Sir Geoffrey aimed his borrowed service revolver and pulled the trigger. A skull shattered as the bullet struck, dousing a preternatural glow – blue eyeshine from presumably empty sockets. "By god," he breathed, "I got one!"

Simon wrapped an arm about Della and led her behind huge Victorian drying racks where Potterswood and his staff were ready to transport them to the outside at Edmund's command.

"When we get to the grounds, you're all going to have to move very quickly," Caroline told them as she and Hannah also joined Potterswood. She flinched at the gunshots. "Think you can manage?"

"Just watch me," Della replied, her dark eyes wide and anxious.

Simon squeezed her shoulders. "She's a gazelle."

Another volley of gunfire obliterated any response from Caroline. The massive drying rack next to Potterswood's circle of vampire staff suddenly rocked violently. Then it crashed into a splintering heap and two skeletal knights surged through the debris. Caroline pushed Hannah down into the cobwebs behind an old mangle. Potterswood's staff members immediately encircled them, intent on protecting their queen first and foremost. Della screamed, finally cracking as one of the creatures – a hulking blur of mottled brown bones, ruined flesh and one working eye – seized her by the hair, pulling her away from the circle. Simon snatched up the kitchen knife she dropped in the attack. He lurched forward, ignoring his injured ankle as he slashed at the entity who dragged Della back with the single-minded focus of a lion with a zebra in its jaws.

Potterswood slid the bolt on one of the Earl's Purdeys as the second monster knight suddenly turned away from the vampires surrounding Caroline, training its attention on an oblivious Simon. He fired, striking the skeletal creature in the back. It staggered, momentarily stunned.

"Hold fire!" shouted Edmund. He sounded strangely perplexed.

Edmund, Tinley, Culpeper and Cyril had stepped back, weapons up but no longer firing. The entities had frozen – much as they had been before when discovered outside the castle walls. The ones that hadn't been destroyed with headshots, stood, weaving slightly on their feet and staring up at the ceiling as if listening to a subsonic call. Then they began to disintegrate like mummies exposed to fresh air. Grey, rotting skin and bone turned to powder. They fell where they stood and vanished, leaving no trace.

"Good bloody riddance," said the Earl of Hawkesmoor, breaking the tense silence. "Potterswood – we could all use a stiff whisky and some of that synthetic blood falderol."

Potterswood, staring at where the monsters had been, gave a little start at the Earl's words and then recovered himself. "Very good, Your Lordship."

Chapter Sixty-two

Dawn brought a cold winter light to the castle and the moors beyond. Caroline sipped a cup of tea out on the Great Walk. She took a moment to stop and lean against one of the embrasures, gazing out at bucolic, snow-dusted pastures. Although she had yet to hear from Robin, she felt a peace slipping over her tired frame.

"Where's Dad?" asked Hannah, falling in next to her. "He's got the keys to the gun cabinet."

"He's letting the dogs out of the stable and checking on the two quarantined ewes."

"Crikey." Hannah let out a long breath. It hung in the air as wispy steam and then evaporated. "Do you think Fitz could ever fit in here? You know, with vampires hanging around and the odd unknown monster attack?"

Caroline laughed and slung a comforting arm around her sister's shoulders. "If our father can make sense of it all, Fitz is going to be fine."

"Dad did look pretty cool – very James Bond with that gun."

"Lady Caroline, "came Sir Geoffrey's precise Oxbridge voice.

They both turned away from the view of Hawkesmoor's pastures to find the civil servant approaching. It was clear he had made sartorial repairs and was now dressed in a fresh suit.

"A car is coming to fetch me. I will be returning to London this morning to brief PM."

Caroline sighed. Things would be a lot more difficult once Alastair Hope decided the revenants were an enemy he could do without.

"You've been a good sport, Sir Geoffrey," she said, too tired to care much what he did. "Thank you."

"When your husband turns up, be kind enough to tell him that we will be in touch to debrief. It is clear to us that there are more things in heaven and earth, than dreamt of in your philosophy and all that. Better to have vampires with us than against us."

"Happy Christmas, Sir Geoffrey," she said, reaching out to shake his hand.

"Feeling better, Dad?" asked Ari, as they emerged from the Norse underground tunnels into the harsh morning light of Drole Island.

"Completely," Robin said with a smile. Ari had used some of her energy to restore his. He felt much the old self. "You were very brave, my girl."

"Oh, that was all Ceridwen. I just took her there." She reached for his hand as they walked from the monastic ruins. Ceridwen was a powerful member of the Tylwyth Teg who had been instrumental in helping Robin defeat Morvidus at Hawkesmoor six years previously. "She told me I won't have my abilities for a while – probably five years or so."

"Will you miss them?"

Ari shook her head, her long, amber-colored hair spiraling out in the sea breeze. "I just want to be … me – a girl – and have friends. Can Jasper and Lucy come to stay at Hawkesmoor? Please?"

"First, let's take them home to their parents who are very worried. After Christmas, we'll invite the Tiffins for a long weekend." He turned and picked her up so she could ride piggyback. "Speaking of panicked parents, your mother is due for update."

Robin paused for a moment. He could still sense something under the surface of the island. Sentient but unthinking. Hungry. Wild. There was more to Drole Island than Gilles de Rais and his vampire knights. It would bear watching.

"Let's pop down the fancy way," he said, not wanting Ari anywhere near whatever lurked below.

A moment later, they reappeared on Goblin Island's rocky shore.

"It's Ari!" shouted Jasper from some distance away. "Ari!" He started running towards them, followed by Asher Grey, kilt flying in the breeze and carrying a dozing Lucy.

By the time Jasper and Asher had reached them, the guardsmen had appeared as well.

"It's a long story," Robin told his anxious guard. "Later."

"But, Your Serene Highness," began Bramwell, earning an impressed look from Jasper, "we ought to clear …"

"Drole Island's not going anywhere," he murmured, taking a real look at Jasper who was an extraordinarily handsome boy of nine or ten. Tall for his age with a thick, wavy nearly black hair and bright blue eyes. The beautiful boy Gilles de Rais had promised to Barron. It was good that Jasper would never comprehend how close he'd come to a kind of horror few would ever know.

"We have three very brave young friends who need a hot meal," Robin added, reaching up to pat Ari's knee, "and to get to their families for Christmas."

"Christmas!" both Ari and Jasper cried in near unison.

"Asher Grey," Robin turned to regard Sir Neville's loyal knight who stood shielding Lucy from the wind, "We're down a man. I hope you will join us."

Asher's face flushed with emotion. "I'm a great stupid man, Your Highness."

"We've established that," Robin smiled. "Are you in?"

"Yes, sir. It would be my honor to serve." The knight looked down, embarrassed by a break in his voice.

"Gentlemen – Asher Grey will lead us back to something like civilization."

Bleary-eyed Lucy lifted her head from the knight's shoulder. "Food?"

"American hamburger and French fries," said Jasper, grinning up at Ari.

She laughed. Robin loved the sound – something he thought he'd not hear again.

"Sausage rolls," Ari sang out. "Lots and lots."

Epilogue

Since the mid-19th century, it had been the custom of the Earls of Hawkesmoor to lay on a festal lunch for local farmers and villagers on Christmas Eve. As it was a highly anticipated jolly for many good-hearted people and featured a hotly contested cake auction that benefited St. Michael's, Caroline had – with Cyril Goforth's able assistance – pushed forward despite their recent fright at the castle. Following the return of Robin and Arianrhod, Hawkesmoor's 14th century Great Hall was rapidly transformed into a festive banqueting space. Cyril and the on-duty guardsmen had helped to erect an enormous Victorian Christmas tree and had strung the rafters with thousands of fairy lights. Hannah whimsically decorated scores of holiday dining tables while Simon and Della hand-lettered place settings and seating charts. Outside the castle would be the Earl's domain with his annual livestock show in which local youth were encouraged to bring their prize animals for gentle judging and ribbons.

Christmas Eve found Hawkesmoor alive with happy locals walking the snow-dappled grounds, watching livestock judging or exploring its public staterooms. In the Great Hall, Potterswood and his staff had established a monumental buffet worthy of Henry VIII who would have approved of its hearty roasted meats, Yorkshire puddings and traditional trimmings. The atmosphere throughout the castle was joyous. Strains of Baroque music and Christmas carols floated through the air, underscoring convivial conversations as guests sipped hot beverages before lunch was served.

The day had also seen the weather delayed arrival of Garnet Petherbridge's personal effects from Number 7 Audley Square. Robin had decided to exile the material to the castle's vast attics where it could molder away forever, unseen and untouchable by any embittered revenants eager to pay tribute to the former king. It was now abundantly clear to Robin that not all vampires wished to modernize revenant society. They were out there lurking -- the vampires who wanted the old dangerous ways. Sybil was out there somewhere with her intelligence and Machiavellian plans. It would all bear watching.

"Well, it would just turn up today, wouldn't it? Brilliant," sighed Robin as both he and Hirst stared at a large muddy van that was pulling in next to the fleet of village shuttle buses and private cars. "We'll have to stage it all in the west hallway. Pretty much out of the way there."

"Right, sir." Hirst nodded. "Shall I get on the delivery men?"

"I'd be grateful to you. I'm supposed to be helping Lady Caroline greet people."

The former WWI officer grinned at him. "Happy Christmas, Your Serene Highness."

Robin put his finger to his lips. "Keep the royal titles on the down low. It might confuse the locals."

"Right you are, sir."

"And Happy Christmas, Hirst," he said, turning to head back inside.

Nipping through a side entrance, he strode up the main hallway, hoping to find Caroline unannoyed by his failure to be on time. With luck on the morrow, his Christmas present to her – a 1938 George VI silver café au lait set he'd found at the inestimable Bassetlaw Silver and Antiques in London – would bring him out of the doghouse. But she wouldn't be annoyed anyway. It was his great fortune to be married to a thoroughly extraordinary human. Was there another woman in the world who could defend her castle against supernatural knights, then catch her breath and organize the annual fete? He rather thought not.

"Hey Dad," came Simon's voice behind him. "Mum's looking for you everywhere."

Robin flinched in mock fright and turned to see his son limping to catch up. "Annoyed?"

"Seeth-y," Simon threw him a grin. "Just joshing – you know, she's never really mad at us."

Robin felt another wave of admiration for his wife who had woven a silver thread around them all and created a strange but wonderful family. He took a step forward and hugged his son.

"Proud of you and love you to bits, Simon," he said, his voice cracking a little with emotion. "But I am sorry about your life in …"

"New York?" Simon pulled away from the hug. "It's all right, Dad. A leave of absence isn't the end of the world."

"I like your Della." Robin squeezed Simon's shoulder. "Glad she could stay for Christmas."

"Me, too. Thanks for squaring it with the ballet company and everything."

"Mrs. Dragos and I worked together. Apparently, she sits on the board," Robin shrugged. "You know, never …"

"Underestimate the Dragos, my friend" Simon said, copying Alin's Eastern European accent. Then he took a moment and a breath. His voice grew serious. "Hey Dad, our life here … you know, real monsters and everything."

"Not for the faint of heart."

Simon took another moment and then brightened. "I think Della is okay with all of it. I think we're going to be okay."

"I like her," Robin reaffirmed, throwing an arm around his son's shoulders. "If she decides to join up, I've no worries."

"Speaking of joining up, you should have seen Granddad with your Les Bauer.

Are we really sure he wasn't an MI6 operative in the old days?"

Robin laughed as they pushed off to find Caroline in the Great Hall. "Tracking international sheep rustlers for Queen and country."

The Great Hall was filled with chattering locals, enjoying drinks served by hired staff on silver trays. Robin scanned the ancient room he had loved for nearly three hundred years. Caroline's brother, Peter stood on the massive staircase, deep in conversation with Edward de Vere, the 17th Earl of Oxford. The Elizabethan character – now dressed in one of his better tweed suits --had inexplicably come fully into the human plane, joyfully joining the family. As with many things of late, it would bear watching. He shifted his gaze and spotted Arianrhod chasing the castle dogs around the base of the Christmas tree, giggling – enjoying being a little girl at Christmas. As a laughing Della darted up to take Simon away to the upcoming livestock awards, Robin saw Caroline moving through the throng of proud Yorkshire men and women, having a word and making them feel welcome at the castle. She was stunning. Perfectly dressed in a long, pleated red tartan skirt and black cashmere sweater, Caroline was understated and elegant. She caught sight of him and her face lit up. Excusing herself from the current conversation, Caroline joined him in his spot by the Great Hall's fireplace.

"There you are, at last," Caroline said, her eyes growing worried. "Feeling all right?"

"Darling, I am tiptop." Robin caught up one of her hands and kissed it. He had not fully explained the horrors of Drole Island and Gilles de Rais to Caroline – only giving her the broad story and what she needed to know to help Ari bounce back. He doubted he ever would. Some ugliness was best forgotten.

"Let's not say all is well," said Caroline with a faux shudder. She slid an arm around his waist. "I do have something important to tell you … about me."

"You're finally leaving me for Lord Kenworthy's second son, Archie?"

"Oh, stop," she laughed good-naturedly. "He collects Victorian railroad pamphlets."

"Then – I'm all yours." He bent and kissed her quickly. "Spill the proverbial beans."

Caroline took in a breath and straightened her spine. "Well, here goes – I'm going to have another baby …"

A clanging sound interrupted her. Robin looked away from Caroline quickly. Two of the delivery men had made a mistake and wandered through the wrong door, dropping the heavy load they had been carrying.

"Uh oh," Robin murmured. He made for the two discombobulated workers, pulling Caroline along with him by the hand.

The narrow wood crate they had been bringing in, had cracked upon hitting the flagstones of the Great Hall. A heavy gold gilt-framed portrait had slipped from the casing and lay on the floor surrounded by dumbstruck locals.

"Cor blimey!" exclaimed one of the movers to Robin once he and Caroline pushed through the crowd. "Sorry! Sorry! We'll make it right!"

"I tripped," explained the other, mortified.

"Happy Christmas, gentlemen," said Robin trying not to sound urgent. "No worries. Could you …"

"Good lord! Is that a Munnings?" The village priest, Father Hazelton, knelt by the large portrait and gently pulled it fully free of the crate. "Forgive me for being so forward but it's just such a treat to see a real Munnings."

There were gasps and appreciative murmurs as Garnet Petherbridge's superlative portrait was revealed. Painted in his riding habit, he was imperially handsome with burnished blond hair and large, captivating blue eyes – a hint of triumph or perhaps, cruelty in the set of his perfect mouth.

"What an unusual ring!" said Mrs. Teasdale – a farmer's wife. "Very unusual."

Robin exchanged a glance with Caroline and they both gazed down at the painted Garnet Petherbridge. On the former vampire king's left hand was a signet ring – a black barred yellow shield bearing a swan and marked with the royal fleur de lis.

ABOUT THE AUTHOR

Anne Merino, devoted to her horses, hounds and books, was raised in the UK and then in Arizona; hers was a very British childhood, filled with history, country life and eerie tales of
ghosts, elementals and haunted byways. It is perhaps unsurprising that storytelling and the theatre became her passions: Anne went on to become a professional ballerina and writer. Now happily retired, she is married to a filmmaker and has two fascinating sons.

www.ingramcontent.com/pod-product-compliance
Lightning Source LLC
Chambersburg PA
CBHW072022020726
47501CB00006B/1906